DEVIL'S
DILEMMA

#4

SATAN'S DEVILS
COLORADO
CHAPTER

MANDA MELLETT

COPYRIGHT

Disclaimer

This is a work of fiction. Names, characters, businesses, places, events and incidents are either the products of the author's imagination or used in a fictitious manner. Any resemblance to actual persons, living or dead, or actual events is purely coincidental.

Warning

This book is dark in places and contains content of a sexual, abusive and violent nature. It may not be suitable for persons under the age of 18.

CAST OF CHARACTERS - COLORADO

Officers

Demon – President - Old Lady - Violet
Children: Theo
Beef - Vice President - Old Lady - Steph
Buzzard – Secretary / Treasurer - Old Lady - Sindy
Thunder – Sergeant-At-Arms
Mace – Enforcer
Sparky – Road Captain

Patched Members

Hellfire - Old Lady – Moira
Children – Demon, Kennedy, Samuel
Bomber - Old Lady – Jeannie
Cad
Ink
Lizard
Pyro
Paladin - Old Lady - Jayden
Rusty
Skull
Judge

Wills

Prospects
Karl
Beaver
Smithy – Failed Prospect

Sweet Butts
Bella
Breezy
Sheila
Titsy
Tulia

Deceased Members
Blackie – Previous President
Furnace – Previous VP
Ingot – Previous Enforcer
Taser

CAST OF CHARACTERS - LAS VEGAS

Officers
Red – President
Crash – Vice President
Fox – Secretary/Treasurer
Indian – Sergeant-At-Arms
Twister – Enforcer
Shadow – Road Captain
Keys – Computer Guy

Patched Members
Titch
Rope
Cuff
Cobra
Sarge
Hammer
Petty
Roller

Prospects
Scrapper

Owl
Meat

Old Ladies
Rosa - was married to old president who died –
children – Twins Tristan & Tom
Tiffany - Fox's Old Lady

Sweet Butts
Pixie
Jinx
Angel

CHAPTER ONE

Melissa

I t's Friday evening. I'm sitting giggling, or at least making a show of pretending to understand what's so funny, with my group of fellow co-workers at a bar. They're all younger than me and it shows. They seem to be more in tune with life while I, at thirty-four, seem old among the group of early twenty-somethings.

Even the music they talk about I've never heard of, though they're not exactly a different generation. Some even live at home, while I've managed to get to the place where I can support myself and have a small house I managed to buy, with an eye-watering mortgage of course. That's the reason I've been sipping my one drink all evening, while others seem to throw cash around without a care.

"Didn't you watch it?" one of the younger office workers asks. When I shake my head, she continues, "I can't believe you don't watch that talent show. I find it hilarious."

I prefer spending my free time cooking, producing meals for the week that I can freeze and just heat up when I'm tired, or the confectionary concoctions I love conjuring up. It's my form of relaxation. Along with reading, those two hobbies take up most of my time. The TV in the corner of my living room is rarely turned on.

Beth, my exceptionally tall and model slim friend, is animatedly telling the others about her preparation for a marathon, something else I tune out. Me and exercise long parted company. I like to relax when I get home. I'm perfectly happy with myself and my life and don't feel the need to have an exercise regime or try the latest fad diet to influence how I appear in anyone else's eyes. Not that I didn't spend my late teens and a few of the following years trying to become what nature never intended me to be, but I could never match the image of the ideal woman who I saw in magazines. I've always stood back and watched men home in on my slender and ideally endowed friends while the years have passed, and I've ended up alone. I don't resent it. When I look in the mirror I know what a man sees, and that's not a future with a curvy woman like me.

I'd been fourteen when I first became aware I was different, and because of it was subjected to the cruelty common in kids of that age. I was the fat girl, the girl never chosen to be on a sports' team, the girl no one wanted to be friends with, as though my size might have been infectious. Fat, the boys called me, baby fat reassured my mom, and that I'd grow out of it. But neither more years nor diet had worked and I remained as I am today, stout and rounded, but luckily, no longer bullied because of it.

While the conversation about running leaves me once again out in the cold, I amuse myself, looking around, people watching. The bar we've come to is one I haven't been to before. It's pleasant enough, with the strong enticing aroma of food that's making my stomach rumble. Good choice of drinks and cocktails too, I muse, watching the bartender expertly mix one, shaking a shaker vigorously then twisting it behind his back and tossing it into the air. As I look on, amused and entranced while he goes through his routine for a couple of giggling girls who can't take their gaze off him, I suddenly notice eyes staring at me.

I look away fast, already feeling my face burning, but not

before I've seen enough to be able to recreate his image in my mind's eye.

He's younger than me, much younger. There's a cocky tilt to his head, dark hair flopping around his face in no particular style, and a worn leather cut that warns me to stay far away from him. *He's a biker, from one of those biker clubs that articles in the news often warn us about.* But my eyes had remained on him long enough for me to wonder what I'd have done had I been a few years younger. My brief glimpse had shown me he was handsome and muscular, tall but not overly so, shorter than Beth but still much taller than me. About five foot nine or ten I'd estimate. I'm just five foot three.

Why the hell am I estimating our height difference?

Of course he wasn't looking at me, or only critically. I've been a victim of his sort before.

"Yeah, Beth. This weekend." I force myself to concentrate on the conversation going on around me. "What do you want me to make? Cupcakes? Muffins? Both?"

Beth's tongue actually licks her lips in anticipation. "Both? Of course, you're coming, aren't you, Melissa?"

I shake my head. "You don't want me around."

They do try to include me in their activities, but the thing is, I'm not comfortable mixing with them outside of work. It's not that I don't get on with them, I do. We're just interested in different things. Clothes, fashion and young men are not my scene. I'm sure one day they'll realise I'm boring.

"Have you got anything better to do?" Her eyes narrow.

"Oh, don't worry about me." I wave my hand dismissively. "I'll be busy." I decide to keep quiet that I'll be trying out a new recipe and looking at getting some wool for a knitting pattern I found online.

Used to me turning down any and all invitations, Beth just shakes her head, then grins. "One of these days we'll drag you out into the land of the living, Melissa."

I smile back, offering only a tentative, "Maybe."

I may have only had one drink, but my bladder signals it needs emptying. Pushing back my chair, I stand, and make my way to the restrooms which are over in the direction of the bar. As I enter the small hallway, the door to the Men's opens, and the biker I'd been admiring earlier steps out. Up close, he looks even younger than the age I had first pegged him.

We do that sort of awkward dance, him stepping to his left and me to the right at the same time, then laugh in embarrassment, and repeat it to the other side. He quickly tires of the game, putting his strong calloused hands against my biceps, and moving me to one side so he can get around me.

A zing of electricity goes through me at the touch of his warm hands, but it's all too fast, and job done, he moves them away. Then, with a wink, he walks off.

I stay, for a moment needing the wall to support me, and my hand covers my heart which seems to be fluttering. Half of me wishes I was ten years younger, the other half acknowledges he wouldn't have looked twice at me then, either. But, the demon sitting on my shoulder whispers into my ear, no one will know if I use him to fuel some fantasies when I'm using my vibrator later, and in my dreams, I can be any age, and any shape or size that I want. I could even be a woman who'd tempt a handsome biker.

I only take a few seconds to recover my equilibrium, then step into the Ladies and do what I came here for. After washing my hands and drying them, I prepare to reverse my steps through the crowded bar and return to my friends once again.

"Hey," a voice interrupts as I exit the hallway. "After dancing together, I think we should at least exchange names."

For the second time this evening, my face turns bright red, and I'm tempted to check behind me that there's no one else there.

"I'm Skull." His mouth turns up either side, and I'm subjected to the full force of his attractiveness, noticing the gleam of sin and temptation in his eyes.

"I'm too old to play games." I come straight out with it. I'm not easy, and so far away from the type of person this man should hook up with, it's too much of a joke to even consider. If he's got mommy issues or fantasies, he can keep them.

"Whoa." He holds up his hands. "Who said we were playing a game?"

"I do," I say, firmly. "When a man speaks to a strange woman in a bar, it's not to exchange views on the weather." I might be a homebody, but I'm not naïve. "An approach out of the blue is usually taking the opportunity to flirt."

His grin widens, and he shrugs. "What's wrong with flirting?"

"Nothing. As long as it's with someone the same age and in the same ballgame."

"You saying you're out of my league?" A frown appears.

"No," I deny hastily, "I'm saying you're out of mine. Why on earth would a handsome young man want to talk to an older woman like me?" I haven't missed that we're surrounded by many, more-suitable girls with a lot less years under their belt, pretty and airless, and who would probably love to take a ride on his bike.

"Handsome?" As he cocks an eyebrow, the grin comes back. "You think I'm handsome?"

"Whether I do or not isn't the point. Now if you'll excuse me, I'd like to go back to my friends."

He stares at me, his eyes softening slightly. Then his gaze goes toward our table, and his lips turn up in that devastating smile once again. "Okay, you do that. Nice to meet you, er…?"

"Melissa." For the life of me, I don't know why I told him.

"Melissa." He tries it out.

Heaven help me, but my name falling from the lips of this sexy biker, almost in a reverent tone, does something to me. That session with my vibrator is definitely on the horizon when I'm by myself later, along with that fantasy that I'm twenty and nothing more than a size 0.

5

Knowing I need to get away before I make a fool of myself by grabbing hold of his leather vest and insisting he eases the arousal inside me by taking me outside, I stumble in the direction of where my friends are sitting.

"What was that all about?" Beth's the one to ask, but not the only one staring wide-eyed between me and the man at the bar. "He a friend of yours?"

"I don't know him from Adam," I admit, my lips thinning, unable to stop my eyes returning to the man with the peculiar name. He appears to have lost all interest in me and is now deep in conversation with the bartender. Hmm. Probably ordering his next beer. Could well be a drunk as well as a biker, an overindulgence in alcohol would certainly offer an explanation for his strange behaviour. I frown, though I hadn't noticed him unsteady in any way, it could be that I'd had a conversation with a drink and not a man. Only one inebriated would show the slightest interest in a woman like myself.

Beth grins. "I think he is now."

"What?" I've lost the thread, obviously.

"A friend." She nods at a heavily laden tray that's being carried our way. From the concoctions upon it I can see it's meant to be ours. Up to now we've all been buying our drinks on separate tabs.

"I can't afford…" I start, as a fresh margarita is slid over the table toward me.

"Is it on the house?" Carter asks, optimistically.

I wait, hopefully for a positive but inexplicable answer, but my spirits fall when the waitress replies, "Nah, Skull sent them over." She turns to nod at the man now watching from the bar so there can be no misunderstanding.

Beth nudges me. "Told you it was him, and he's paid out for a full round. That doesn't come cheap, girly. Think you must have made an impression."

I glance around the table at the other workers from the government offices in town. Sian, she's got Irish heritage and

Celtic looks, and tonight is totally stunning wearing tight leggings and a latest fashion top. Her hair is cropped. Holly, sitting next to her, is her opposite in every way, fair complexion and blond hair which seems to glimmer in the overhead lights. Her brilliant blue eyes are sparkling as she sips her free Sex on the Beach. I remember wondering whether she really likes it when she placed her order, or just wanted to try and make the bartender blush. Beth, striking, over six-foot-tall, is still in her twenties and lacks for nothing in the looks department. Then there's Macey and Shayla, both pretty girls.

My lips press together as I wonder whether one of them had caught his attention. That seems more fitting. Try and befriend me to get an invite to the table, yes, that would make sense. The ones I doubt he's got much interest in are Carter and Brice—the only men here—but then, nowadays you can never be certain.

Having decided he's got his eye firmly fixed on one of the others, I'm not that concerned when Beth turns around and beckons him over to the table.

God, even the way he walks is sexy, his swaggering gait making his slim hips move side to side. His form fitting jeans and tight tee leave little about him to the imagination and make me suspect he's got one of those delicious Vs leading down to his forbidden parts, the type in the pictures I sometimes swoon over when they're posted in the online groups I frequent. As he draws closer, I see he's got a small scar, a tiny white line parting his left eyebrow, intriguing rather than ugly.

"Ladies." He raises his glass in salute, then, lifts his chin in acknowledgement of the two men for whom he's also purchased drinks.

Carter imperceptibly stiffens and gives him a manly chin lift back. Brice, too, does likewise while pulling his shoulders straight. It's as though they sense they're in the presence of a superior masculine specimen.

Holly preens, her lips forming a pout, Sian's eyes sharpen with interest.

Beth's also gushing when she's the one to use her voice. "Thank you." Her hand points quickly to the drinks, some on the table, some already in hands. "This was very generous, er...?"

I glance up quickly, peering through my eyelashes, interested to see which of the women his eyes will zoom in on. I see his lips move, hear his voice, and it takes a moment for his words to filter through the jealousy that seems to have taken over my brain.

"Skull," he offers, adding, "wasn't anything at all. You're Melissa's friends."

CHAPTER TWO

Melissa

*H*e said my name.

While I'm trying to process what he meant by his statement, taking care not to read more into it than it merits, Beth scoots her chair over, and the biker pulls up another and places it in the gap that's appeared between hers and mine. As he sits, I glare at her, and receive an unapologetic shrug in return.

Skull takes a moment to look around the table, then grins. "You work together?"

"You can tell?" Macey queries, her eyebrow arched.

He chuckles. "It's Friday night, the end of the work week. Six women and two men who don't look to be in relationships with each other. Yeah, I deduced you share the same place of employment and are out to celebrate."

Holly nods. "You're right, and observant."

"So, where do you work?" Skull's words are spoken with a lazy confidence, showing no nervousness at having intruded in on a group of strangers, already sure of his welcome. But then he has just paid for an expensive round of drinks. Of course, everyone is going to be friendly.

"At the Clerk and Recorders office for Pueblo County."

"Yeah? What do *you* do?" The first word was for Holly, but he even sounds interested as he pointedly directs the second question at me.

It would be rude to evade answering it. "I record land deeds. Nothing interesting."

"Motor vehicle licenses," Holly half raises her hand. It looks like she's trying to regain his attention.

"Marriages, births and deaths," Macey and Sian say together.

Beth chuckles. "I work with Melissa."

Not to be left out, Carter indicates Brice and himself. "We clean up after everyone."

"Yeah?" asks Skull. Then he adds with a chuckle, "I know a bit about clean up, myself."

"What do you do?" Beth asks him, with a pointed look my way, clearly annoyed that I'm staying quiet.

"I work at our auto-shop and also turn my hand to a bit of this and that."

It's an odd answer, but I zip my mouth shut not wanting to show any interest or encourage him.

Brice finds his voice and starts asking about the type of bike Skull rides, and whether his club's like *Sons of Anarchy*. I half-listen to the answers, and half ask myself why he's sitting next to me. I keep sneaking sideways glances, but his attention doesn't settle for long on anyone else, just briefly on the person who's asked a question. Currently it's Brice who's querying the cc of his bike.

"Was an eight-eight-three, but I got it bored out to twelve hundred." Skull pauses and shoots me a quick look. "I suppose I shouldn't admit that to you lot."

I raise and lower my shoulders. "It's Friday night, we're not at work." And with the amount of alcohol the others have consumed, by Monday they'll have forgotten.

"So, Melissa, do you like your job?"

Another shrug. "It's a job. Boring like any other."

"What do you like to do in your spare time?" He seems intent on dragging responses out of me.

I don't even have to open my mouth to answer.

"She cooks," informs Beth.

"Yeah?"

"Her cupcakes and muffins are to die for." Brice smacks his lips. "Love Mondays after Melissa's been cooking up a storm over the weekend."

Now that's going to put him off. Inwardly I roll my eyes.

I'm a thirty-four-year-old woman who tries everything that I bake. Well, someone's got to taste test. I suppose eating nearly a whole tin full of muffins is a bit over the top, but it's hard to stop. I know it's turning my body into something resembling the things that I bake. When I wear anything with a waist, my stomach rolls out over the top.

I can't complain about my life. I'm an only child with good parents who live up in Denver, and I try to visit when I can. I have my own small house, with dreams of eventually having a larger one with a big yard. Then I'll get a dog, maybe a cat. They'd be good company.

Men? I've never had much luck with them and have decided I'm happy by myself. If I ever step into the relationship game, I want a man who wants me for my personality, not because I'd make a good unpaid housekeeper. Yes, I may have been there and done that with my one and only foray into living with a man, and it turned out a disaster. I'd gotten out fast, deciding I'd rather clean and cook for one. I don't need a man to complete me, something I've learned over the years. My thoughts make me glance at Holly and Macey, seeing the hungry look in their eyes as they watch Skull speak. If their tongues start hanging out, I wouldn't be surprised. One day, they'll get taught that lesson too, I suspect.

Or maybe not. At least they've got something going for them which I haven't. They've got the figures and looks that certainly broaden the pool they can fish in.

"Melissa, Skull asked you a question," Beth chides.

"Oh? Sorry." My face reddens again. It's not like me to be so impolite.

"I asked if you'd like to go for a ride tomorrow?"

"A ride?" My voice squawks.

"Yeah, on my bike," he explains as if I could misinterpret it in some way. *Yeah, right, I was only just fantasising about another ride later on tonight.*

But, me...on a motorcycle? My head automatically starts to shake. *Impossible.* "I'm sorry, I've got plans this weekend. Tomorrow I need to bake for Beth's party on Sunday, and that day I'll be tied up, as I'm going to the party myself."

A snort comes from the other side of him, and Beth leans forward and twists her head so I can see the expression on her face, her wide eyes clearly signalling, *what the fuck?*

She's quiet for just one moment, then she pipes up, her mouth forming a cocky grin. "Why don't you come too, Skull? You've bought us drinks, it's the least we can do to pay you back."

Please be busy. Please.

Skull purses his lips, then pinches the brow of his nose. "Sunday, huh? Haven't anything planned, so yes, that would be good Beth."

"Chuck me your phone and I'll put my number in it, then I can text you the address."

My mind eases a little, and a small smile curves my lips at her audacity. She's tricked him into giving her his number. I watch undisturbed as phones come out and ping as messages go between them. For a second I'm wistful, wishing it was my number he'd wanted instead, but knowing that would only lead to disappointment. Whatever reason he has for offering to take me for a ride on his bike was probably that he'd lost a bet. Someone like this biker could never be interested in an older woman, carrying too much weight.

My purse is lying on the table. It suddenly vibrates. Curious,

I reach for it, and slide my phone out. My brow creases and I narrow my eyes and look to my side.

"I gave him yours too, just in case." Beth sounds unrepentant.

Right now, I hate my co-worker.

Then I look down and read the text.

Skull: One day you'll be riding behind me. That's a promise.

I quickly shoot back.

Melissa: In your dreams.

Skull leans in. "I like women who play hard to get."

Another phone pings the other side of the table, making me wonder if Beth had given him everyone's number.

Holly starts getting her things together, stands and slips into her coat. "Right, that's me. My brother's waiting. You want a lift, Macey?"

The other girl nods and hurriedly gets up.

It signals the end of our evening. People start getting out phones, or Brice, who hasn't had much to drink, gets out his car key. My phone's still in my hand, so I call up the Uber app.

Skull notices. "I'll give you a ride home if you want."

My sharp eyes land on him. I don't know this man at all, and he rides with a motorcycle club that he's just told my co-workers is yes, a lot like *Sons of Anarchy*. I'm someone who's watched the whole series twice, well okay, three times. Like so many women, I'm secretly in love with Jax. But know I wouldn't be able to handle a real-life biker.

"I'm okay, thanks." I tap on the screen. "There, done. My Uber's only a couple of minutes away, so I'll wait out front."

I pick up my purse, pull on my jacket and stand.

"See you Sunday," Beth shouts out.

"Yeah, see you Sunday, Melissa." Skull winks.

To my relief, he doesn't try to follow me out.

When I get home, I don't go anywhere near the drawer which holds my vibrator. Skull's got me riled and uncomfortable, but no longer in an arousing way. I'm not old enough to be his mother, but I am older and by a lot.

Questions keep running around my head. *What does he want with me? Was he serious when he suggested I go out on his bike with him? If so, why? I wasn't dressed in a 'I might meet someone I desire so might as well get dolled up to attract them' way. There was nothing to suggest I was on the prowl for a man—unlike some of the other women I'd been out with. Why did he focus on me?*

I end up convincing myself I'm being used in some way. Maybe he was attracted to Sian, for example, and is going to use a friendship with me to get close to her.

After a restless night—the few bouts of sleep I did drift into being haunted by dreams of scenes from the *Sons of Anarchy* series, but instead of it being Jax's face, it was Skull's instead—I wake tired and irritable.

My solution? Obviously, to bake. An activity which calms and soothes me.

I've just finished icing the final batch of cupcakes when my phone rings. I jump for a moment, then sigh with relief, seeing Beth's name on the screen.

"Hey, Beth. Got cupcakes, chocolate chip muffins, those cheesy biscuits you like, cookies, a carrot cake, oh, and a pecan pie."

"My God, woman! You opening a shop or cooking for my get-together?"

I look around at all the Tupperware filled to the top. Maybe I have overdone it. "If there are any left over, people can take it home." I consider the arrangements. "I'll bring it in my car tomorrow and drop it off. What time do you need it?"

"You're thinking you'll leave it and go, aren't you?" Her tone warns me to be careful.

"Look, Beth, we both know me saying I was going to your party was just an excuse I concocted to appear to be busy. You know I don't like to socialise. Did enough of that yesterday."

"Skull said he'd come."

I huff a laugh. "Like he's actually going to." And if he does turn up, that's a very good reason for me not to be there.

"Oh well, if he's here, and you're not, I'll give him your address." She says it so breezily it takes a moment for the implication to sink in.

When it does, I hiss. "Don't you dare. He's a biker, Beth. Who knows what he wants to do with me? Don't you find it suspicious it was me he approached?"

"No, I don't. Melissa—"

But I'm in full flow. "The reason's simple. He thinks I'm easy. Thinks I'll be flattered. Thinks a fat old woman like me would just be grateful for the attention. I don't know exactly why, but there has to be a reason. I won't be made a laughingstock."

"Have you quite finished?" She can't see my nod, but from my silence assumes it. "I don't know where you get these stupid ideas from. You're gorgeous Melissa. Okay, you might carry more weight than Sian or Holly, but you're the only one who worries about it. You've got amazing eyes, your hair is beautiful, and your face is so expressive. I don't know who you think you see when you look in the mirror, but you're clearly not seeing the same things I am. *I* don't find it odd that Skull targeted you."

"He's young," I cut across her objections. "I must be ten years older. What would we have in common, Beth?"

"That, you'll never know unless you give him a chance to find out."

"*He's a biker!*" I snarl, as though that makes all the difference.

At least it gives her pause for thought. "Okay," she begins again, slowly. "I'll give you that. Haven't heard much about the Satan's Devils he rides with, I just know they run a strip club, but they also have an auto-shop *and* a family orientated bowling alley. Those things don't give much away about what they really get up to. Look, maybe I wouldn't be happy with you going off with him alone, but tomorrow you'll be in company. If he comes, spend some time talking to him. At least you can let the poor boy down gently, but you might surprise yourself."

I'm quiet. Thinking.

"Wouldn't it be nice to come eat things you haven't baked yourself? Sian's bringing some steaks, Holly's making salad. Mom's inside right now conjuring up all manner of dressings."

She seems to have got everyone bringing stuff. "What are you doing, Beth?" I chuckle.

"Oh," she replies airily, "I might risk straining myself and open a few bags of chips."

I laugh, dutifully, knowing my friend will be doing a lot more than that. She's probably already running around making sure she's got tables and chairs set up and has plans in place in case it rains.

"Say you'll come, and stay."

Another moment to think. She's right. At least there will be people all around, and all I need to do is to tell him firmly I'm not interested.

Shouldn't be difficult. It's not as if he knows enough about me to be serious.

CHAPTER THREE

Melissa

S unday dawns. I won't say I'm not a bag of nerves, I am. I'm usually quite balanced and sure of myself in any situation. But the thought of meeting the biker again does make me uneasy. If he turns up, I don't know what to expect, or, more accurately, what he expects from me.

I certainly don't want him to use me to get to one of my friends. Uh uh, no way. That would make me feel dreadful, and I'd have to warn whichever of them he's targeting. A man who plays such games is not one to be trusted. But why else would he pretend to be interested in me?

He won't turn up.

He was probably drunk on Friday night, seeing me through the bottom of his beer bottle rather than over the top. When he sees me again, he'll realise he's woken up in a bad dream. Even if he comes to Beth's party, he won't stay long. He'll soon go once he realises I'm not who he thought I'd be.

To that end, I choose my clothes carefully. I'm for whatever makes me comfortable. I no longer feel I need to dress for anyone else, and today I'm looking for something that makes me clean and presentable, but not sexy. No, definitely not that. *Huh,* I laugh to myself, *as if I could look sexy if I tried.*

I choose a long gypsy skirt and team it with a flowing blouse, nothing figure hugging at all. I leave my long wavy hair loose, and put on minimal makeup, just a little foundation and powder to keep the sun off my face. No lipstick to draw attention to my lips, and nothing to enlarge my eyes.

When I'm ready, I pack up the car with the results of yesterday's efforts and leave.

Beth has the door open and is already walking toward me before I put the car in park. Without being asked, with just a quick 'hi' my way, she's filling her arms with my baked offerings.

"Mmm! These smell and look so good. You've outdone yourself, Melissa."

It's always nice to be appreciated. I glow with pride.

"And you're looking gorgeous."

Oh. Am I? Glancing down at the clothes that I'm wearing, I assume she's just being polite.

Taking a few of the Tupperware tubs she hadn't managed to carry and balancing the plate holding the pecan pie, I follow her inside.

Beth lives with her mom, and Patsy greets me. "Hey Melissa. You look lovely."

Politeness runs in the family. "So do you, Pats." She does. She looks rocking for a woman approaching her sixties. I can't wear shorts like the ones she's wearing even now, my thighs are far too large. I sigh. Even if I could resist sampling the goods that I bake, nature would still work against me.

I help setting up what I'd brought and then lend a hand getting everything else set up. The table looks amazing, and I tell Beth and Patsy so, while my hand finds my stomach, realising I've little chance of doing more than adding to my weight today. Everything looks so tempting.

I mingle with my friends and soon find myself laughing and starting to relax. As expected, the biker hadn't turned up, and I tell myself the only disappointment I feel is in men who say they'll do something, and then don't.

I've been here an hour before the sound of a motorcycle reaches my ears. While it's strange to hear one so loud in this residential neighbourhood, I don't think too much of it, expecting it to pass right on by.

My breathing speeds up when the engine cuts out in close proximity to Beth and Patsy's house.

Oh shit. Is it Skull?

I'm a thirty-four-year-old woman who's never had a prime and doesn't expect to have one. He must be a twenty-year-old with his whole life in front of him. My mind wanders back to the thoughts I'd had when I met him before; any attempt to get close to me is more likely to be the result of a bet rather than any desire to bed the curvy older woman that I am.

He's used me to get to know one of the other girls.

Idly I wonder, which one?

Beth herself? Could be. A lot of men don't mind a girl being taller than them.

I can't help my eyes going to the entrance to the backyard, and my heart flutters—or part of me does anyway—as the man clad in leather despite the heat of the day comes into sight.

Oh, my God. If anything, in daylight he looks even more attractive.

He saunters in without a care, even though everyone here are virtual strangers. He pauses to survey the crowd, seeming to look for someone. As his eyes come my way, I turn my head, but not before I see a smile cross his face.

"Did you get that report finished in the end?" Ian, one of my co-workers asks me.

"What? Oh, yeah. Eventually. Getting figures out of the other departments was like getting blood out of a stone, but I got it done in the end."

"You know," he remarks, conversationally, "you'll have a ton of questions to answer."

I purse my lips looking glum. Yeah, any report prepared for the lawmakers results in hours of digging for information you know they don't really want. But it's the result of any committee meeting, asking for detailed follow-up data is just a way to prove they've read the report, and me, as the author, will be expected to provide it.

"Par for the course," I begin to tell him, as I become aware of a large shadow falling over me.

It's Skull. He's made his way across to where I'm standing, having taken the chance to fill himself a plate while passing the food-laden table. It could be coincidence or deliberate, but he's managed to snag a few of the items I brought.

"These muffins are great. Beth said you made them. Mmm mmm. Very good." The last is barely distinguishable as he speaks through a mouthful of crumbs, then wipes the back of his hand over his lips.

Ian has exchanged a nod with Skull, and with an interested look back my way, has walked off to talk to someone else, leaving me alone with the biker.

"So, how have you been since I last saw you?" Skull is now attacking one of the pastries I made.

"Busy." I point to his plate with a sardonic grin.

A quick grin comes to his face. "There's a mountain of food in there. Any left over, I'll offer to take back to the clubhouse."

My food ending up feeding the Satan's Devils? My eyes widen in surprise.

"What about you?" I ask, slightly sarcastically. "Been scaring kids? Robbing banks?"

He throws back his head and laughs loudly. "Yeah, some-thing like that." Then his face grows serious. "Seems you need some educating in what my club stands for."

"I need no education," I snap. "I know as much as I need to."

His face hardens slightly, and he looks around. Beth and Patsy have a beautiful backyard. While people are milling around, most of the guests are keeping closer to the grills and the tables laden with food and drinks. There's empty space down at the rear of the yard, including, a secluded gazebo. Skull nods that way now.

"We need to talk," he tells me.

"I have no idea what about," I say back, my teeth worrying my lip, uncertain whether I should give him the opportunity. But to do what? I too survey the gathering. My co-workers are here with their families, the yard is crowded with my friends. Nothing can happen to me, even if we'll be tucked away in a corner. A shout would bring people running.

I have no idea why this young man has become focused on me, but perhaps this is the chance to find out and knock any unsavoury ideas on the head.

"Okay." But I flinch and shake off the hand that lands on my arm possessively and take the lead instead.

At the gazebo I sit on a comfortable chair, moving the cushion slightly so it better supports my back. Instead of taking the other chair, Skull leans against one of the upright supports, one knee bent and the flat of his sole against the wood.

He grins, easily. "You don't like me, do you?"

"I like you fine," I counter. "I don't *know* you, is all. And I don't know what you are after."

"Melissa, you seem to have some doubts about me. Let's get a few things straight. I saw you at the bar and was immediately interested in you, not anyone else."

"I'm almost old enough to be—"

"Stop it." It's nearly a snarl. "How old do you think I am, Melissa?"

"Twenty?" I hazard.

He barks a laugh. "I'm twenty-five, almost twenty-six, and you're what…"

"Thirty-four," I admit, grumpily. "Just." I add, accusingly, "You look younger."

"I don't know whether that's good, or whether it's the bane of my life. It earned me the handle of Runt when I was a prospect, hated that fuckin' name. Thank fuck they changed it to Skull when I was patched in."

Runt I might be able to understand, he's skinny and probably not the tallest biker I've seen, but, "Why are you called Skull?"

His lips narrow and his eyes flicker with something which looks like a bad memory. "Because I've got a hard head." He taps his forehead. "Can take the knocks well."

I lose interest in his monikers. "Skull, okay, you're older than I thought. But look at you." I wave my hand toward him, wanting to get all this out in the open now. "You don't have an ounce of fat on you, you're good looking and could probably have any girl you want…"

"Good looking?" His eyes crease, then instead his brow becomes etched with lines. "And I can have any woman I want? What if I want you, Melissa?"

He's actually said it. His question makes me fidget. I decide to point out a few things. "Are you blind? Look at me. You look like you keep fit, while I'm allergic to exercise. I bake and sample my products. I have a sedentary job while you… you… you probably ride around on your bike all day. I know just what I look like, I'm homely and curvy…"

"And you're just my type."

Suddenly he moves. Instead of standing, he's now sitting beside me. I'm relieved he's keeping a respectful distance, but his hand covers mine. "Melissa, I'm not proposing or anything, but from the moment I saw you, you intrigued me. What's the harm in us getting to know each other a little more? Go out on a date or two…"

"Bikers date?" I huff incredulously, not able to imagine it.

Another laugh. "Bikers are people, Melissa. We eat, drink, and do what anyone else does. Oh, and we fuck." He winks.

It shouldn't, but his easy reference to sexual pleasure starts a tingling in my body that it shouldn't have. The gleam in his eyes makes me doubt it's an empty promise.

"I don't," I say, sharply. "If all you want is to get in my panties, I'm not the woman for that."

"Melissa, Melissa, babe. I want the whole package. Yeah, I want sex. I want to feel those magnificent tits in my hands, I want to see you come on my fingers and on my tongue. I want to know if you're a screamer, and if you're not, what I need to do to hear you scream out. You made my cock rock hard the first time I saw you..." He breaks off, and grins again. "But I also want to take you out, show you off. Date you like you deserve to be dated. Spoil you and have you on the back of my bike. Yeah, Melissa, I want everything. When you're ready, I want you riding my cock, but not until that's what you want too."

Jesus H Christ. My eyes widen at his declaration. I've never heard anything of the like. I'm the woman men want to cosy up to as I remind them of their mother and they think I'll provide the comforts of home. Or, they want to bed a curvy woman just to see what it's like. I'm not the woman men fantasise about, and I certainly don't get offered the whole world, which, in my eyes, is what Skull's offering.

I object once more. "You want to show me off? Are you listening to yourself? What kind of couple do you think we'd make?"

"A great one," he replies without missing a beat. "You're gorgeous, Melissa. You're just the woman I want."

CHAPTER FOUR

Melissa

God help me, but I had agreed.

As Skull continued to promise the world to me, my doubts began to slide away. He seemed so adamant, so sure of himself, and, that it was me he was determined to win. While doubting I was the prize he really wanted—was it because I was playing hard to get, that made him so sure? I found a hesitant yes coming out of my mouth. Sometimes in life you have to take a gamble, and if I expected the worst, what did I have to lose?

It was too soon to worry about my heart being broken. Skull intrigued me, but he wasn't the man I could see as my life partner, so the organ that pumped blood around my body wasn't involved. My lady parts though, well they were something else altogether.

I've read books, sure, but have never experienced the intensity of orgasms that were usually described within their pages. No, mine were polite little ripples and not particularly explosive. Already the thought of sex with Skull was turning me on like never before. Sex was something expected after you'd been dating a while, a culmination of a man and woman giving each other time. A few minutes of activity, a cuddle after, and then back to watching the game or, in my case, cooking to satisfy another appetite.

Skull though, there was heat in his eyes. Along with a promise he wouldn't rush me, his whole being signified that when the time came and I was ready, I wouldn't be left wanting or disappointed.

What harm would there be in having a date with the man?

Which brings me to today, and why my stomach is full of butterflies. Yes, I'd agreed after he'd worn all my objections down. Me, Melissa, had caved and accepted to go out on a date with a biker.

All week I've had doubts about my decision, my hand going to the phone several times to cancel it, but a little voice at the back of my head constantly asked, why should I be the one always missing out? It could be something wonderful would come of the date and we'd have many more, however much I thought one night in my company would end it.

How our conversation had finished on Sunday kept echoing around my head.

"Melissa, I must warn you. I'll take you out Friday. We'll have a meal, conversation, and then I'll drop you back at your door. However much you beg me, I don't put out on a first date."

"Skull!" I batted his arm with my hand.

"What, babe? You disappointed?"

A loud laugh escaped me. "No. I…"

"Tut, tut. You thought you were going to corrupt me?"

I bristled. "It's the other way around, surely?"

His face filled with cockiness. "You know you want to, Melissa. Say you'll come on a date with me. Friday."

I wasn't agreeing to an abstract concept, by adding on a day he was making a concrete proposition. And heaven help me, I was interested enough to agree.

It seemed easy on Sunday. Something to look forward to Monday and Tuesday. On Wednesday the worries began to creep in. By Thursday I had serious misgivings—which made me bake three trays of cookies which were received gratefully at work the next day, well, what was left after I'd tested them. When I woke today, I seriously doubted I could go through with this.

Wear jeans, he'd said. Does that mean he expects to take me on the back of his motorcycle?

No, of course he wouldn't. Just look at him, then me. I must weigh much more than he does. I'd unbalance his bike for certain. *Do curvy women like me even ride?* I've never been on a bike or taken much notice of them.

I'd rather wear a dress that would hide my large hips, I muse, as I struggle with the zipper on my jeans. I turn and look over my shoulder critically in the mirror. *Yes, just as I thought, they show off my fat ass.*

My top, though, he didn't issue any instructions for. I go with a flowing shirt that disguises the size of my tits. Why on earth people get enlargements I'll never know. Who would willingly put themselves through the back ache that comes with carrying these bazookas around? And the boob sweat… *Perhaps I should consider a reduction?*

The top also hides the roll of my muffin top.

It has to be a joke. What would a man like Skull see in me?

I should cancel. Yes, I should. But there's a part of me that is curious how this evening will go. I've a broad enough back that if I find out I'm the butt of a joke, it wouldn't overly bother me. And, there's a chance, albeit a very slight one, that this strange relationship might actually work.

Fat chance.

A ring on my doorbell signifies it's now too late. I've lost my chance to back out.

Picking up my purse, I check I have my phone and my wallet, then open the door to find Skull waiting there, and behind him like a lurking beast waiting, his motorbike.

"Looking good, woman."

I stare but can't see anything other than appreciation in his expression. He seems to be genuinely pleased by the way that I'm dressed, and the light makeup I'm wearing.

He's wearing a button-down shirt under his leather vest, the contrast with the black leather and his tanned skin is striking, making him look... edible in a word. My tongue licks my lips automatically.

As he smirks, I step around him and point my finger. "You parking that here?"

"What?" He turns in the direction I'm indicating. "No, that's our transportation."

I stare at the motorcycle as though I'm looking at a hang-man's noose, and before I'm aware of what I'm doing, take a step back. I would have taken another, had his hand not landed on my arm with just enough pressure to prevent me.

"Look," he starts earnestly. "You give it a try. All you need to do is to put your arms around my waist, and lean as I do at the corners. You don't like it? We'll come straight back. Don't care if we've only gone a few hundred yards, but please, for me, give it a chance."

I hang onto him?

My glance meets his eyes. "Lean with you? What if I lean too far and over balance us? I'm no lightweight you know."

He leans back his head and laughs. "You'll be fine. I know what I'm doing."

It's his confidence that gets me moving forward, then turning and locking my door and sliding my keys into my purse which he eyes carefully, before taking it off me, and slinging it over my neck so it hangs slanted over my body.

"Safer like that."

He leads me over to the chrome and black beast, then dips into a saddlebag and takes out a helmet which he's soon fastening on me.

"Stop shakin'. You'll be fine."

"At least *you* will be. You'll have a cushion to land on."

Another hearty laugh, but offered with a shake of his head,

and his hands touch my arms gently as he looks into my face. "Sweetheart, you think there's too much of you, I happen to love it myself. And I won't need a cushion, I don't intend to drop the bike, with you on it or not."

Well, okay then. Guess I'm going motorcycle riding, or at least as far as the end of the road. "You will turn back?" I ask, biting my lip.

Skull might look young, but now I'm up close to him, there's an ageless depth to his eyes, and an earnestness in his voice that persuades me. "Melissa, I'd love you to enjoy this, but if you hate it, you just tell me. I promise I'll bring you right back, and we'll get an Uber or taxi instead. Now, you gonna give this a try?"

Taking a deep breath, I give a little nod. I notice he must've backed his bike onto the driveway as he's parked facing out.

He gets on, then takes the stand up. "Okay, slide yourself on behind me."

I do. The seat is slightly higher than his, and when I take the leap of faith, I find I'm on the cushioned leather with my feet dangling off the ground. *Yikes.*

"Put your hands around my waist darlin', then put your feet on the pegs to keep them clear of the pipes." He glances down, left side then right, to make sure I've done as he's asked. Then throws a look over his shoulder. "Keep your hands where they are. No sneaking them down to feel the size of my cock. I'll show you it later if you're that impatient, but don't want anything distracting my riding."

As I breathe in a gasp of disbelief at his audacity to even suggest I'd do such a thing, I realise he's started the engine and is already pulling off my driveway. As I cling on for dear life, it dawns on me his comment had been made to distract me from any last-minute doubts I may have had.

It worked.

At the end of the road he stops and again turns his head. "You okay?" he shouts over the rumbling thunder of the engine.

Suddenly it hits me that I am, very much, okay. Even though I'm out of my element, having to trust a man I really don't know, I already feel a thrill that I don't want to end. "I'm fine. Why have we stopped?"

The revving of the engine almost drowns out the sound of his laughter, but I feel his body shake as he gives a carefree chuckle. Then he lets out the clutch, and the bike moves slowly forward, gradually picking up speed as he kicks through the gear changes.

I have fresh air cooling my face, an exhilaration like the one you get when riding a roller coaster, the feeling that you're perfectly safe, yet absolutely not as the pavement rushes by beneath us. At the corners I lean with him, making sure my body moves with his, scared in case the bike continues to tilt right over, but the rider I'm holding onto for dear life feels totally relaxed with no tension or worries.

After a moment, I too allow the tension to seep out of my muscles. *I'm enjoying this.*

All too soon he pulls into the parking lot of a restaurant just outside of town. It's not fancy, so jeans will be perfect, but not a dive either. I've been here before, and the food is amazing.

A very good choice for a first date.

I belatedly realise that I should have found out about our destination before and told someone who I was going out with tonight. Truth is, I expected my co-workers and friends to find it amusing, so had kept the details of my date quiet.

But hey, we're here. I'm safe.

He taps my leg and I interpret it as a sign that I should get off the bike. I do, balancing my hand on his shoulder, then stand back as he walks the bike back into a parking spot. The ground feels firm and stable under legs which are still trembling from the vibration of the engine.

After taking my helmet and securing it in the saddlebag, he holds out his hand for me to take, his expression suddenly nervous. "I didn't check, should have. This going to be okay for you, babe?"

I smile, possibly the most genuine I've yet summoned for him. "Perfect."

"Come on then. Let's get you fed."

The next few minutes are taken up with being shown to a table he'd already had the foresight to book, then perusing the menus. Strangely I quickly become relaxed in his company and feel no need to make any pretence. I've been on dates before when I've eyed all the delicious sounding dishes, only to restrict myself to a salad as I think it's expected, but with Skull I have no qualms in ordering the same as him, a steak with loaded pota-toes. He nods approvingly as I do.

It's while I'm sipping my wine and him slaking his thirst with a beer, that he reaches over the table and takes my hand.

"Tell me about yourself, Melissa."

Another good sign. Some men I've been with make the evening all about them.

"I work for the city, but you already know that. I've got good folks up in Denver, no siblings, I was an only child. I love cooking and reading. See, I'm quite boring."

"You're not boring, Melissa. I reckon there's a lot you're not saying."

I shrug. With me, what you see is about what you get. "How about you, Skull? Tell me about the MC and what you actually do for them."

"Yeah." His mouth twists. "The MC. Okay, you deserve to know what you might be getting into." He takes another mouthful of beer. "The Satan's Devils MC is like one big family. We've got a few chapters around—our mother chapter is in Tucson, Arizona—but I ride with the Pueblo crew."

"The mother chapter. Do you have to do what they tell you?"

"Nah and yes." He gives a quick grin. "The by-laws and regulations are the same all over, but the local prez runs things how he wants. We choose what businesses we want to get into."

My heart stops. *Is this where he's going to tell me he's a criminal?* It's easy sitting here with him, more natural than I would have thought. If he's now going to list the reasons why he's not right for me, I already know I'll be upset. But I can't tie my flag to the mast of a man who walks on the wrong side of life.

"Your face is very expressive." He takes back my hand that I hadn't realised I'd moved away. "Our businesses won't cause you worry. We run a strip club, yes. Let's get that out of the way. All the dancers work for us voluntarily, none of them are forced, and we don't allow drugs on the premises. We also run a bowling alley that's very family-orientated, a tattoo parlour and an auto-shop. Recently we've started up a new security business."

I'd stiffened at strip club, but slowly became more relaxed as he listed the rest. "What do you do for them?"

"I started off at the auto-shop, but also work with Cad—he's our computer expert—and one of my other biker brothers, Pal in SD security."

My teeth worry my lip. "That's not code for protection rackets, is it?"

Again, he tosses back his head and gives a hearty laugh. "Nah. We install state-of-the-art security systems."

I'm thoughtful for a moment. "Sounds like any other company with diverse interests. How did the MC decide to get into those businesses, and how long have you ridden with the Satan's Devils? Oh, and why?"

CHAPTER FIVE

Melissa

"That's a lot of questions," he observes. But he doesn't seem at all upset I've asked him. "What do you know about motorcycle clubs?"

"I've heard of the big ones which have quite a reputation." Mostly I've just watched *Sons of Anarchy* three times, but I keep that to myself.

"Yeah, I suspect you're referring to the Wretched Soulz?"

I nod, I am. Though there are others, Wretched Soulz make the headlines quite a lot. They're known throughout the southern states, all over North America really.

"We do have an affiliation with them, as we're set up in their territory, but all that means is that they approve of how we run the club." A strange look comes into his eyes. "We stay out of drugs and gun running."

I tilt my head at his expression, though quickly it's replaced by the more familiar smile once again. "Some clubs are set up by vets when they return from overseas. They're looking for something they find is missing when they come back to civilian life. The Pueblo club started in the early eighties when the steel industry crashed. In fact, our clubhouse is in an old steel mill.

Our barbeque pit is a furnace where they could melt half a train at a time."

My eyes grow wide. "It must be huge."

"It is," he agrees, with a quick grin. "Well, getting back on topic. The ex-steelworkers who started the club wanted something to belong to, a place to call home, a family and an income. Back in those days the club wasn't as clean as it is now. When Hellfire, that's our current prez's Demon's father, took over from his dad, Blackie, he joined forces with the Satan's Devils and got the club out of the worst of the shit."

"Hold on. You're saying Demon is the grandson of the founder?" I shake my head. "Sounds like nepotism is alive and well." I soften my statement with a smile.

"Well that's their familial relationship, but anything else isn't how it sounds." He frowns. "No one got their position because of who they are. We were all happy to vote Demon in. Fuckin' good man to lead us."

Message to me, stay out of things I don't know about. "You say it's like a family?" I ask, wanting to get onto a safer topic.

"Yes. Take me, I've got no one of my own. Now, I've got more than a dozen brothers who'd give their lives for me. A few have ol' ladies, and there's even a kid."

"Old ladies? *Grandmothers*?"

Another bark of laughter. "Nah, that's what we call the wives or significant others."

Sounds derogatory to me. Suddenly I realise bikers are a breed I know nothing about. "You don't have an old lady?"

His eyes grow wide, then he snarls, "Wouldn't be here with you if I had. Don't roll that way. One woman at a time is all I can handle."

Well alright then. I seem to have touched another nerve. "So, tell me more about this family."

Our steaks arrive. For a moment, conversation stops as we apply our fixings to our meals and begin to eat.

"I like that," Skull points his fork at me.

"Mmm?" With a mouthful of delicious steak, I can't respond.

"Your expression. You enjoying your food." His face becomes heated. "Can't help wondering if you wear that look when something else is in your mouth."

A glass of water is hastily pushed in my direction as I choke on my food.

Recovered, I rasp, "I cannot believe you said that." An unrepentant grin encourages me to have the courage to add, "That's for me to know and you, if you get lucky, to find out."

"Oh, I fully intend to get lucky at some point." Skull catches me off guard once again. "Those lips and that sinful mouth, and your…" His hands wave down my body, and his eyes land on my breasts. "Mmm mmm. Bet you taste better than any steak."

Flustered, I reach for my wine.

He's not leering or making me uncomfortable. There's something about the way he's speaking that shows his appreciation of liberties he eventually anticipates, but there's no pressure either. Despite him being so forward, instead of making me uneasy, he's making me feel things that no one else ever has. He's making me think of myself as a desirable woman. Suddenly it doesn't matter that I'm larger than most, curvier than models in magazines and on billboards. Skull's completely focused attention is making me feel feminine and wanted.

"If you could do anything, or go anywhere, what would it be and where?"

His question makes me do a one-eighty, but as though he realises he's skating too close to the edge, Skull reels the conversation back in.

The rest of the evening continues in the same vein. Mostly spent getting to know each other, with occasional inappropriate comments from him, and heaven help me, a bit of flirting from my side too.

At one point I feel bold enough to ask, "How did you get that scar?"

He looks puzzled.

"Over your eye." I tap my brow to show him.

"Oh, that. Long, long time ago." He leans in. "I could make up some story about single-handedly disarming an armed robber, fighting pirates or something. Sure, I could come up with something that sounds sexy, but I'll start as I mean to go on. Total honesty. I was a four-year-old-kid, I got it by falling out of bed and smashing my head on my bedside table. Bled like a bitch."

Honesty. I like the sound of that.

I like everything about this evening. It's easy, companionable, with a promise of sexuality. As the end of our meal and our date approaches, it hits me with a start that I can't remember having enjoyed myself so much with a man before. We might not have known each other long, but now I'm already counting him as a friend, and someone who could possibly become more.

We've laughed, been serious, commiserated. Shared jokes and anecdotes in my case about co-workers, in his, his brothers. I've heard about Bitch, the cat who appears to be the boss of the compound, and even about the sweet butts who live there as well. I'd frowned when he'd mentioned them, but while he admitted he'd gone with them when he first patched in, having a woman to himself was more to his taste, and not one who'd been shared by all the men of the club.

Skull had apparently spent nearly a year as a probationer, or prospect as he referred to himself, and has only become a patched member for the last couple of months. Another tell, a twitch of his cheek, and I gather there's a story there he hasn't yet told. But hey, this is our first date, and we've already talked about more coming after. I don't need to learn everything tonight.

I'd forgotten our age difference and why it had ever bothered me. And who gave a damn I was big and him slender? Now I'm getting to know him, if he finds my curves sexy, I'm certainly not going to argue. I'm not trying to hide so he'll know what to expect when he eventually ends up in my bed.

My bed. Where I'm currently lying. Alone.

True to his word, Skull had dropped me home, not wanting to come in. He couldn't trust me to keep my hands to myself, he'd said, while wearing a big wide grin and winking.

Tomorrow night he's providing security for one of their contracts, but on Sunday he's going to take me out again.

I can't freaking wait.

Totally unexpected, having predicted tonight would be a one and only, thinking either him or I, or both, would be bored, I'm already looking forward to the next time I see him. Skull seems far more mature for his years than his looks would have led me to believe.

I really like him.

I hadn't anticipated doing so.

I thought I'd have found his company tedious.

I did not.

His leaving me on the doorstep with just a peck on the cheek? *I'd wanted more.*

Saturday passes far too slowly, and I try to occupy myself doing chores. I bake, of course, then notice the state of my oven and clean it. Anything to keep busy.

When Skull pulls up on Sunday, I'm already at the door, having grabbed my purse when I heard his motorcycle's engine roar. My eagerness is greeted with one of his cocky grins.

As I'm unused to riding, he doesn't want to take me too far. His choice of destination is again perfect, as we ride up into the forest where it's cool. Once the bike is parked, we walk hand in hand along a shaded path with the sweet smell of a soft carpet of pine needles underneath, conversation flowing easily, never stopping.

Suddenly Skull comes to a halt, his pause in steps ceasing my forward momentum. As I turn, it's to see a gleam in his eyes.

"Want to kiss you, Mel. That okay?"

More than okay. The warning, though, has me swallowing nervously. First kisses can be awkward, not knowing what to expect. Where should I put my hands, for example? Does he expect tongues, or just a brush of our lips?

To give myself a moment, I query the shortening of my name. "Mel?"

His eyes darken, then he places his hands on my biceps and he pushes me until I'm pressed up against a tree. "Everyone else calls you by your full name. Want to have something for me."

Wow. Romantic or what?

He pauses just a second longer, and then, his lips lower.

I shouldn't have worried, as he takes complete control. My hands naturally go to his shoulders and just hold on for the ride. His tongue invades, his taste immediately mingling with mine, our mouths meld together as though we've done this dance many times and this isn't the first.

The aroma of pine mingles with the leather of his cut as I now know his vest is called, and birdsong, which a moment ago sounded loud, now only just reaches my ears above my murmurs of appreciation, and his growls of encouragement.

Time stops, my brain quiets, and all I can think of is how we are joined, mouth to mouth, his hands holding me close, mine grabbing onto his arms.

I can feel his hard cock pressing into me, but he doesn't grab my breasts or touch inappropriately.

At last he pulls his head away, leaning down to place his forehead against mine. "When I get you in bed, you're not coming up for air for a very long time," he rasps against my skin. "Be warned, darlin'. Once you let me in, that's where I'm stayin'."

There's nothing about that statement of intent that concerns me at all.

In fact, the words spill out of my mouth in a breathless gasp, "Your place or mine?"

He chuckles, softly. "Yours, babe. I live at the club at the moment. But for now, how about another taste?"

After that second kiss, and a few more as we make our way

down the mountain, we arrive back at the bike. As he fastens the strap of the helmet under my chin, I find myself trying to picture how I left my place. *Is there underwear strewn across my bedroom floor? I shaved my legs, are there hairs still in the shower tray? Is there makeup left around? That box of tampons isn't still left out from last week is it?*

He stares into my eyes. "Doesn't have to happen today, Mel. Not if it's too soon."

The fact I'm worrying about all the insignificant things perhaps means that it is.

The fact he doesn't mind, shows me Skull is a good man.

When he drops me off, Skull smooths his hand down the side of my face. "Can't make it tomorrow or Tuesday, I've got work." His grimace shows he'd prefer to spend time with me instead. "Wednesday we've got church, that's our club meeting. But Thursday I can be all yours if you want."

I want. "How about I cook?"

"Yeah?" he grins.

I nod vigorously. "Any requests?"

"Anything you come up with, I suspect will be great." He leans in, adding, suggestively, "I'm particularly looking forward to dessert."

I turn bright red.

The days pass oh so slowly. I can't wait to see Skull again. Eventually it's Thursday, and I leave work right on time.

In preparation I cook something that is simple but tasty, that I can turn down and leave in the oven if necessary, and doesn't take a lot of fluffing around getting up and down and taking stuff in and out of the oven. I make an apple pie and have whipped cream on standby, hoping that the dessert he's thinking of means the pie goes uneaten.

My house is spotless, everything in its place, and nothing left out that could cause me embarrassment. I'm excited as I wait for him to arrive.

I'm wearing a knee-length floral dress that's as flattering as anything I own.

A knock on the door.

When he steps inside, it seems symbolic.

He sniffs the air. "Smells good." Then he turns his heated eyes on me, looking from my head to my feet, his gaze lingering on my breasts for a moment. He swallows. "You look amazing. Tell me, are you wearing panties?"

My brow scrunches, and I shrug.

"Go take them off. I want to eat dinner knowing I've got dessert ready and waiting for me."

No man ever has asked me to do something so risqué. Oh, I've read such things in books, but the men I've been with have had their meal, and only then started their version of foreplay which may or may not have been successful in getting me aroused. That Skull's kicking off this night, making our dinner something that whets our carnal appetites as well as filling our stomachs makes me feel immediately aroused.

And, playful.

Instead of retreating to my room, I keep my eyes on his, bend, and sliding my hands under my dress, discreetly remove my panties right there in the hallway. When he holds his hand out, I place them in it.

Then gasp, as he sniffs them, breathing in deeply. "Oh yes, I'm looking forward to what I'll be tasting later. Mmm mmm."

Did he just do that? Did he really just sniff my underwear?

I stand gawking a little too long, as he chuckles. "Is that your oven beeping?"

Shit it is! I turn and run into the kitchen, turning the heat right down. "Want to..." I start calling out, only to find he's come in behind me.

"What do you need me to do, darlin'?"

A man offering to help in the kitchen? Skull's already getting straight As tonight.

"Nothing, really. I've got the table set. Want to eat now, or..."

"Now," he decides. "Then you, we, can relax."

We eat, talk, laugh. All the time he's fixing me with those dark eyes full of promise. Cool air from the air conditioner seems to flow under my skirt each time I get up or down to fix the food, reminding me I'm wearing no panties. Just his stare is enough to make me grow wet, and I squirm, feeling my own moisture on my thighs.

"Fuck, woman, you make it difficult."

I tilt my head to one side.

"I'm rock hard, thinking about you all but naked under that dress." His eyes meet mine once again. "Take off your bra."

"What?"

He waves his hand. "Bet you can do that thing all women do. Remove it without getting undressed."

Well, of course I can. I shoot him a look of disdain and proceed to prove it. It's front fastening, so I manage to put my hands demurely down the front of my dress, and undo the clasp, then slip the straps down my arms and slide it out through one arm hole.

"Give." He holds out his hand, and I pass it across the table, a slight wave of discomfort going through me as it's not dainty and small.

His eyes lock on mine, and then, suddenly, his vest is slipping down his arms and he's half turned to place it over the back of his chair. Then, one hand goes to the back of his neck and *oh sweet Jesus*, his tee comes off and he's sitting at my table, completely naked from the waist up. I'd already felt the hardness of his torso, but now I see his amazing six pack, confirming this is a man who works out.

As if nothing's happened he asks, "Pass me the salad?"

I think he has had to voice his request a couple of times before I can bring myself to move and do as he's asked.

Suddenly replete with sufficient food, I place my fork down.

His gaze meets mine and slowly, he nods.

CHAPTER SIX

Melissa

I've become comfortable with Skull, used to his company, but I still expected to feel gauche the first time we went to bed. I mean, what's a man like this going to expect? I'm no siren, my experience has been of a very vanilla variety, and with not too many men. Skull has got an assurance and confidence that I've not come across with anyone else. I think he's cocky, but I also believe he's probably entitled to be and will know what to do with his equipment and won't disappoint.

When he gets up and stalks to the end of the table, I can't help but lick my lips. His jeans are low-slung and as I had expected, there's the outline of a delicious V leading downwards.

"My eyes are up here," he smirks, while holding out his hand. "Where's your bedroom, sweetheart? First time I think we'll use your bed. We'll try out the table, counter, and other possibilities later."

Later as in another day? Or, later tonight? My gut clenches in anticipation.

Automatically I place my hand in his, then lead him into my bedroom. He stares at my bed, then smiles.

I suddenly suck in a breath. He's got my bra and panties, and the only thing I'm now wearing is my dress and a smile. If it's a choice between losing one or the other, well, my lips immediately turn down into a frown.

He walks me backward until my legs hit the foot of the bed.

"Lie down." His voice seems to have dropped an octave.

I obey, first sitting, then lying back, expecting him to follow me down, but no. In one smooth action he's pulled up my dress, baring my lower half to him. I suck in air, feeling tears prick at the backs of my eyes knowing he's seeing thick tree trunk thighs and a roll of fat over my stomach.

"Fuckin' beautiful, Mel," he says fast, getting in before I can apologise.

Squeezing my eyes shut, I try to stop my brain from forcing a catalogue of what's wrong with me out of my mouth.

"I've waited far too fuckin' long for this, not waiting any longer now."

Jesus. His mouth is there. His fingers too. His tongue circles my clit, then licks me. I already knew I was wet, now he's making me voice appreciative sounds as more cream comes from me, summoned forth by his expert touch. His voice vibrates against me as he tells me again how beautiful I am, how my skin is soft, just how he likes it and that he's a man who doesn't like angular bodies with bones sticking out, adding how much he likes my curves.

His words thrill me, nothing there to suggest I'm any kind of disappointment at all.

Part of my brain wonders where and how he's learned the tricks he's bringing into play. It's as if he knows precisely what a woman wants. Fingers and tongue work in unison and very soon I'm nearing the edge. My last thought before giving in entirely to sensation is if they could make a vibrator as talented as his touch, there'd be no need for men at all.

"Oh God, Skull. Skull, yes, there, Skull." I cry out, words escaping with no conscious thought. "Skull, oh Skull. *Skull.*"

I hover for a second just nearing my peak, stay there until the right pressure on my clit sends me completely over.

I see stars and my lungs heave.

Before I've recovered, he's lifted my hips, then pulls my upper torso off the bed, and before I can stop him has completely removed my dress. Somewhere along the way his jeans have come off, and I now have a very naked man straddling my thighs, wearing nothing but the smile on his face, and that glowing look which darkens, dilating his pupils as he feasts his eyes on my chest. My very, ample, chest.

His hands almost shake as they reach out to touch, pillowing my breasts, one in each hand. He flicks his thumbs across my nipples, his smile becoming a knowing grin at my sharp intake of breath.

"Fuckin' gorgeous. Real woman's breasts."

"Too big," I counter.

"Not a thing, babe. Not as far as I'm concerned."

I'm not going to protest. If having to carry these motherfuckers around gives him this much pleasure, I'll stop complaining about them. As he continues to play with my chest, I lie back and enjoy it.

Honestly, I think I'm close to coming again when he sucks first one nipple then the other between his teeth.

"Skull, Skull." I arch my back, pressing more of me into his mouth.

"Uh uh. My turn now."

His warmth moves away, and I hear the crackle of plastic, and then raise my head to see him slide a condom down a slightly longer than average, though not too thick dick.

Perfect.

Then he's lining himself up and sliding home.

I'm wet, he pushes in easily.

At first languid strokes, then he speeds up, then he's hammering as he chases his release and I'm crying out, so, so close.

43

I need more, so I take it, reaching down myself.

"That's it, babe. Fuckin' love you playing with yourself. That's it,"

Then his voice changes to grunts, and I'm almost there myself.

His body presses in hard, he groans and stops, one more rub and my muscles are clutching at his cock.

"Fuck, babe, fuck, that's good."

We stay like that for a moment, both trying to regain our breath. When he gets up and goes to dispose of the condom, I'm glad he's the one who's had to leave the bed. Me? I can't move.

Skull ends up spending the night. We have sex again later, then I wake to an early morning booty call which I certainly don't object to.

Then he leaves to do whatever his club wants of him, with a promise to come back the next evening.

The thought did cross my mind that now that he's got what he wanted, he'll give up the chase and I won't see him again. But I'm proved wrong. Over the next couple of weeks, we see each other almost every day. He takes me out as much as we stay in. When it's the latter, I cook for him, for once happy to prepare meals for a man. He pays me back handsomely with orgasms, so I have no complaints.

Sex stays great, if anything it gets better as we get to know what each other likes. I give head as it's expected, and Skull doesn't hide his obvious enjoyment even if he knows I prefer him to pull away before he comes.

We go out with Beth and her friend. Skull doesn't seem to object at all at being subjected to girly talk. He's come along and met my co-workers again a couple of times. The one thing which bothers me is while I'm letting him into my world, he's not reciprocating. I've yet to meet any of his club brothers.

One day, I overhear his side of a phone call.

"Yeah, I've found someone." His eyes catch mine. I get up to leave, but he shakes his head.

"Not yet. But soon I hope."

"Yeah, I think she'll fit. Hopefully Demon's woman will take to her. Yeah, we'll speak later."

He replaces his phone in his cut and raises his eyebrow at the curious look on my face.

It prompts me to start a long overdue conversation. "Why don't you introduce me to the other bikers, Skull?" The words I've overheard make me nervous. "Why is there a chance your prez's woman won't like me? Are you ashamed of me, Skull?"

I'm not certain I want to get involved in his world, still nervous of what it represents, but if we're getting deeper into a relationship, surely I should go into it with my eyes open, and know all there is to know about the man I'm with. And that means getting to know the people he spends most of his time with. On my part I'm an open book, while he keeps his cover firmly closed.

"Babe," he starts to reply, going serious. "You may not like the sound of it, but in my biker life, there are two types of women. Ones you fuck, and ones you make your old lady."

I bristle. "And I'm one you fuck." Clearly not one worth introducing to his brothers.

"Nah, I didn't fuckin' say that." He wipes his hands down his face. "Look, Mel. We've got a good thing going, and I don't want to fuck it up."

"You met my friends." I round on him, realising I'm waving a wooden spoon in the air, so lower my hand. "Why would meeting yours fuck us up?"

He stands and comes over, curling his hand around the back of my neck, taking the utensil out of my hand and placing it down on the side. "Mel. These last few weeks have been amazing. When I first saw you, I knew you were going to be something special to me. That's only become truer the longer we are together. Before we go on with this conversation, there's something I need you to know. I've fallen for you, hard, Mel. I love you, babe."

It's lucky his hand is holding me up or else I might have fallen. I've been trying to ignore my growing feelings for him, telling myself, it's too soon, and he's not the kind of man for a forever.

"Nah, you don't need to say anything back." He's misunderstood my hesitation. "Mel, in my club, well, not sure how you're going to take this, but when a man takes an old lady, the words are, he's claimed her."

I'm listening to his words very carefully, nervous of any misinterpretation. Is he saying he wants to claim me, and if he is, do I want to be claimed?

As if I'd spoken aloud, he puts his finger to my lips. "Not quite there yet, Mel. Just, listen up." He takes my hand and tugs it, leading me to the couch in the living room and pulling me down to sit beside him. "Remember I told you, the club is a family?"

I nod.

"Well, it's family we've chosen, not one we are born into. We've spoken about prospects, how they, and recently I, do all the shit jobs for a year or so, or long enough to prove not only that they're trustworthy but that they're a good fit to the club. Anyone joining has to find their place there, we don't accept anyone in off the street."

Where is he going with this?

"You expect me to prospect? Or whatever the appropriate term is for an old lady?" I don't like the thought of that.

He laughs softly. "No, but no one can take an old lady unless she's voted on and accepted by the club."

My eyes narrow. "So, we're dead in the water if your club doesn't like me?"

He shrugs. "I can't see any reason they wouldn't like you, Mel. But if for some unknown reason they won't accept you, our options are, either we part, or I'll rethink my commitment to the club."

Now I'm staring at him, my eyes open wide. Club's everything to him. I may not have known him that long, but know he lives for his brothers and the life the MC offers. He worked hard for a year just to earn his place. What would he be without it? "I couldn't ask you to do that."

His hand grasps my hair, and he pulls my head back, leaning in for a kiss. When he's finished, and I'm released, he tells me softly, "I know you wouldn't. I'm just trying to explain. And it's not just my brothers. We've talked about the club, haven't we? How we still wear the one-percenter patch, not because we're into the shady business of the past, but because we live outside citizen's laws. You become my old lady? Well, you've got to be happy with that."

That makes sense. It was one of the reasons I played hard to get in the first place. While my unease about what Skull is has settled as I've learned more of the man under the leather, if I'm honest, I try not to think about what he might get up to when he's out of my sight.

I haven't been around Skull as much as I have not to be able to read he's leading up to something. "What are you proposing?"

He stares at a point beyond me. "I'm going to tell my brothers I'm seeing someone special. Then, if you're willing, I recommend you start coming around the clubhouse." He breaks off and grins. "Bake 'em some muffins. Quickest fuckin' way to their hearts. Worked with me, didn't it?"

I laugh. Well, he's got a point there.

"You can see if you like them. Get to know the other women and decide if you can live with them."

"You want me to move to the club?" I've got my own place. I don't want to give that up.

"Not saying we have to. But I've got a room there. You can keep this as your home, we'll split our time between both. I claim you, woman, that means you're mine. And that means we're together. Every fuckin' night, not three or four times a week. We can work out the living arrangements later. But you must understand, being my old lady is like being my wife."

Wife? It suddenly dawns on me how serious he is about our relationship. Am I as into this as he is? I hadn't been looking for a life partner. Looks like I might have found one. But isn't that often the way, I think to myself. Something appears when you least expect it. Shouldn't I at least give whatever this is between us a chance?

"So," I begin, slowly, "this is sort of a trial. Seeing if your brothers like me, seeing if I like them. Experiencing your way of life."

"Exactly." He pats my hand and smiles triumphantly.

"Hmm." I think for a minute. Can't see anything wrong with that. I get a glimpse of the life my man lives when he's not by my side and have a chance to walk away if I don't like it. Worst thing that can happen, I find I'm not going to fit in, but better to find that out sooner rather than later.

"Not ruling out, me leaving the club."

I nod to acknowledge the comment but at the back of my mind know, if I can't make it in his world, he probably won't be able to make it in mine.

Which could mean we'll part sooner rather than later.

Surely it's best to find out before we get in any deeper.

"Okay," I say quickly, then soften my features. "Just tell me when to bake muffins."

CHAPTER SEVEN

Melissa

S kull tried to prepare me as much as he could. I'd asked him endless questions about the men in the club, and the women. In my experience, the former aren't as difficult to get on with as the latter.

Of the women, he warned me, three names I really need to know. Violet, who's the current president's old lady, Moira, the mother of the president, Demon, and wife of the former prez, Hellfire. The third name was Jeannie who's the mother hen and ruled the roost until Violet came on the scene. There's also Sindy, another woman with a long-standing relationship with one of the brothers, and Jayden, far younger, who transferred with a member from Tucson.

I've learned their names by heart and have pulled as much information as I can out of Skull about them.

Then there's Bella, Titsy, Sheila, Breezy and Tulia, the club girls or sweet butts as the Satan's Devils call them. I do find it distasteful that they are there to be at the men's beck and call for absolutely anything that's asked of them, but I suppose to each their own. As long as Skull doesn't go with them, and they don't make a play for my man, I'll just have to put up with their presence and try my hardest not to appear judgmental.

As suggested, I've come armed with Tupperware tubs full of muffins and other offerings to tempt sweet and savoury appetites alike. But when I drive up to the gates to find a man wearing a vest with the word prospect on it, I find I'm shaking when I drive around to where he's directed I should park.

There's no way to disguise this building from what it is, an old steel mill. I can only hope it looks more inviting on the inside.

Where's Skull? He said he'd be here to meet me.

I delay getting out, thinking I need his strength to help carry everything in, as well as to be moral support. I don't think I've felt this nervous since my first day at high school.

A noise catches my attention, and I raise my eyes. In front of me there are a group of leather clad men walking to the back of the yard with rifles slung over their shoulders. I'm staring at them so avidly, worrying about the sight, that I don't see a man approaching, and jump as he raps on my window.

My heart races wildly until I see it's Skull with a welcoming grin on his face which slides away when he sees my horrified expression and follows the direction of my eyes.

He opens my door. "They're going for target practice. There's a range up in the woods. You didn't think we had our own army, did you?"

"Something of the sort," I admit.

He laughs. "Nah, don't let it worry you. A lot of them are ex-services and like to keep their skills sharp. Need help?" But one look in the back seat shows him I do, so he opens the rear door, and starts loading up his arms.

I take a couple of tubs. Even with what he's managing to carry there's still more left. I do get carried away when I'm nervous, and nervous is an understatement for how I'm feeling today.

"Wow." He studies the amount I've brought. "You cooked for an army, anyway."

"Too much? We can leave some…"

"Never too much, darlin'. These will all be gone in a flash. Come on in. I'll take you via the kitchen entrance so we can drop these off and I'll find a prospect to bring the rest. Then I'll introduce you to whoever's around. After which," he waggles his eyebrows, "I've got some etchings to show you, up in my room."

I'd rather skip straight to the part where I'm showing off my own artistic skills to him, I tell him as we walk, making him laugh.

"Hey, like that look on you Skull. I suppose this is your Melissa who's responsible for that?"

"Jeannie." Skull raises his chin. "Yeah, meet Melissa. Melissa, Jeannie. She's Bomber's."

"Bomber's mine," Jeannie corrects with a growl. "Pleased to meetcha, Melissa. What have you got there?"

"Muffins, cupcakes, some cheesy biscuits, er…"

Jeannie peers in for a closer look. "Christ, woman. You make all these?"

"She cooks when she gets anxious," Skull replies observantly, making me realise he hadn't been fooled at all.

As I'm about to protest that I may have been a little apprehensive about meeting these women today, Jeannie winks at me.

"Don't blame you at all for feeling a little on edge. Bit daunting meeting all of us. Hey, Vi, meet Melissa, and look what she's brought."

Violet, Demon, the prez's wife, I remind myself, my teeth worrying my lips. *Got to stay on the right side of her.* "Have a muffin," I suggest. "Or a chocolate chip cookie." Then want to slap myself around the head at my display of the limit of my conversation.

"I don't mind if I do," Violet smiles as she replies easily, opening up a tub. "Ooh. These look good."

Another woman, well, teenage girl by the looks of her, walks in carrying a baby. "Theo's good, Vi. I just changed him."

"And this is how the club works." Vi winks at me. "Someone's always around to help with the messy jobs."

"Messy it certainly was." The girl twitches her nose, but she's smiling. "I'm Jayden, Jay," she introduces herself, still holding the youngster in her arms as though reluctant to relinquish him. "I love babies and I really don't mind helping out."

"When are you and Pal going to have one of your own?" Jeannie presses her.

"Got plenty of time to start a family." Her eyes light on what's on the table, and once again her lips curve. "I enjoy giving them back." To make her point, she passes Theo to his mother, then starts opening containers and looking at the goodies I've brought.

Skull tugs my hand. "Want to meet Prez?"

No, but I suppose I have to.

"It's alright. He doesn't bite," Vi tells me with a smile. "Well, not too hard, anyway."

"I don't think I want to know," murmurs Skull, pulling me out of the room.

"They seemed nice," I remark as he leads me across a room I view with interest. A couple of men are playing pool, completely engaged in their game, and not watching us. The whole of one wall is taken up by a bar, and there are matching sofas, chairs and tables. It's better furnished than I expected a biker's club-house would be. Strangely it smells of fresh paint and can only recently have had a makeover.

Skull knocks at an office door, waits until a voice calls out permission, then pushes it open. "Prez, this is Melissa. Melissa, Demon. My prez."

The women were welcoming. The prez though, his glance is assessing, as if I'm yet to prove myself. His eyes look me over, then meet Skull's. "All good?"

"Yeah, she's met Vi, Jeannie and Jay. Oh, and she brought cookies and shit."

He grins, his face transforming. "Trying to bribe us, Melissa?"

"I, er..." That's exactly what I'm doing. So, I shrug. "I like cooking."

He comes around and perches on his desk. I notice there's a huge flag behind it carrying the same insignia as Skull wears on his cut, Lucifer with a scythe hovering over three little devils.

"Now Jeannie can cook and get the sweet butts churning out good grub, but they don't bother with the fancy stuff. Reckon we can find a place for your talents."

"I do work," I tell him, defending myself.

"She's got a good job in the government offices, land registry or some such shit." Skull sounds proud.

Prez nods and grins, "So you said, but if Melissa has got any spare time…"

"I'll keep you in muffins," I laugh.

"Good enough. Skull, you've got that job on later…?"

"Yeah, I'll be there, Prez. It shouldn't take long."

"While Skull's working, Melissa, you're welcome to hang around and get to know us."

As Skull had explained, if I'm going to be accepted here, I'll have to show my face. "I'd like that. Thank you, Prez."

"Nah, Demon to you. Only these fuckers have got to jump to my word and give me my title." He laughs, jerking his head toward my man.

"I like him," I tell Skull as we walk out. "I wasn't sure I was going to, not with a name like his. But he reminds me a bit of my Chief Exec."

Skull chuckles. "Probably describes him well. Though I'd say he was a CEO with an edge." His face tautens momentarily, then is masked quickly by a smile. "Want to see my room now?"

I nudge him. "Your etchings?"

A chuckle. "Yeah, right." He winks.

He leads me up an industrial looking staircase with doors off to the left and the right. Halfway down he places a key in a lock and turns it. The room he reveals is pleasant enough, larger than I expected.

Walking in I look around, knowing you can tell a lot from a person from the way he lives.

"Tidy," I comment, noticing there are no dirty clothes on the floor, and through the open door to the small adjacent bathroom, I see towels hanging neatly on the rail.

"Um, yeah. Might have cleaned up."

"Well at least you know how to." He should see the state of my house before he comes over.

He clearly doesn't want to waste time as he demands, "Want you naked."

"You do, do you?" I grin.

"Well someone's got to take care of this." He rubs his hand over the bulge in his jeans, drawing my attention to it. "You being here in my club? Fuckin' sexy as hell."

"Me being here with my man turns me on too," I respond in a hoarse voice. Not that it takes much with Skull. One of those looks full of promise and I get a tingling inside.

He goes over and lies on his bed. "Now show me what you've got, babe." He's been controlling before. Here, in his element, there's even more of an edge to his voice.

For some reason Skull thinks I'm beautiful, he's told me so often I've started to believe it. To him my tits are just the right size, my thighs meaty enough to hold on to, and my cushioning around my waist a softness he admires. With him I've become far more confident, knowing baring my body will turn him on rather than off. Now I've no hesitation stripping for him, putting on a show which makes him groan.

As I divest myself of my tee and jeans, he removes his cut and his shirt.

"Get over here, woman." Impatient, he moves forward, takes my hand and yanks me down onto the bed. "Need your lips."

We kiss, then he strips naked and gets to work. An orgasm on his tongue, followed by one with his fingers. I'm completely sated and languid when he enters me in one thrust. Momentarily unable to be an active participant, all I can do is give in to the sensation.

Part of me retains enough sanity to stuff my hand in my

mouth, but he pulls it away. "Don't care who hears you screaming, Mel."

Soon, neither do I. Christ he feels good. He's long enough to touch my cervix, not too thick to cause a burn, but he knows what he's doing with what God endowed him with. As normal, I use my hand to make sure I'm there with him at the end, and yes, I do scream. It feels so good, I can't hold back.

He grunts and groans, and then it's all over.

He pulls out. And swears. Instead of leaving for the bathroom, he sinks back on his haunches and drops his head into his hands.

"Skull?"

"Didn't use a fuckin' condom."

I go cold as I feel our combined juices leaking out of me. "I'll go clean up." I get up jerkily as my brain tries to process what we've just done.

"Yeah."

I leave him sitting on the bed as I go into the bathroom, washing myself with a cloth, knowing there's no chance in hell I could remove all the sperm left inside me. I take a second, silently questioning the mirror in front of me.

I always saw a kid in my future, probably more than one. Not as a single mother, though, I wouldn't want that. But would I be single? Skull's brought me here to the club to meet his brothers as he said he's serious about me. We'd never spoken about kids, but Demon and Violet have Theo, and downstairs young Jay talked about having a family in time. It's not as though there's a law against members procreating here.

If Skull wants me as his old lady, and if in his world that's as good as taking a wife, then a family must eventually figure into the equation. If we've made a mistake, maybe all we've done is moved it up the agenda.

How would I feel to have Skull's child? I place my hand on my stomach. *I'd feel good.*

The face reflected in the glass frowns. *Skull didn't look happy.*

I'll just have to convince him this could work. I'm not getting any younger, and my biological clock is ticking faster than his.

Breathing a deep breath, I return to the bedroom to see Skull exactly where I left him, with the same angry expression on his face.

He looks up as I enter. "Fuckin' sorry, babe. I totally forgot."

His ire is directed at himself, not at me. "I should have reminded you." I take some of the blame, to which he just nods. *I'm not totally exonerated.* Moving closer, I take his hand. "What will be, will be, Skull. You and me, we're together aren't we? If there's a result of the carelessness today, we'll cope."

"There's the mornin'-after pill," he offers, suggesting he's been doing some thinking.

"You'd want me to take that?"

"You wouldn't?" He seems surprised I haven't jumped at the chance. "Ain't a thing at all at the moment, babe. That shit would just make sure it stayed that way."

"You don't want a baby with me?" I go still.

"Not what I'm saying. All I think is that now is not a good time." His hands swipe at his hair, pushing it back from his face.

"When is?" I ask, pragmatically. "I love you, Skull. I'd love our baby. In nine months, in a year, two years from now. I'm not getting any younger, I'm not some flighty young girl." Then I remember he isn't as old as me, most times now that's something I forget. "Are you saying it's too soon for you to be tied down?" Suddenly I'm the one who's angry, thinking he might have been leading me on. "Are you saying you don't want me to be your old lady? Because, if you are, I'd rather know now. Before I get involved any deeper."

I start putting on my clothes.

"What are you doing?" he asks, sharply.

"Getting dressed and going home." I choke back the sob that arises.

"No! You can't do that!" He's off the bed, and soon we're having a tug of war with my jeans. "Mel, I need time to get my head around this. Didn't see myself as a dad, or not so soon, anyway. But if you don't want to take precautions, we'll let the cards fall where they will. I'll deal, okay?"

Do I want him to deal? The expression on my face must be a window to my thoughts.

"Fuck, I'm saying everything wrong, aren't I?" Allowing me custody of my jeans, he again rubs his hands through his hair. "It's a shock, that's all. Never thought I'd be careless like that. You want the pill? We'll get it. You want to take the chance? I'll be behind you all the way. Whatever you want, Mel."

"What do *you* want, Skull? Do you really want a relationship and all that entails?"

"I want to claim you. Told you that, so yeah, I want it all. A relationship, which would probably include a kid or two further down the line. Just a shock that it may be sooner rather than later."

I feel relieved that he does see us together. "It's highly unlikely that I'm pregnant, Skull. But if I am, I don't want to do anything about it." I don't know why. I've no real feelings one way or another, always thought the woman should have the choice. But if fate has stepped in and decided now is my time, I don't want to do anything to prevent it.

I wouldn't even have predicted my reaction had anyone asked me.

Children are a blessing in any relationship, doesn't matter how they are conceived. Out of one? A totally different picture. But I've a man who's promised he's going to be there for me.

Again, his head bows into his hands, but when he looks up, he's smiling. "Okay. Let's let things ride. You're pregnant? That would be amazing. Yeah, this would have happened at some point. Just a bit earlier than I expected."

"And from now on, you'll be careful?" I'd rather a pregnancy was planned. I suspect the chances that one mistake would bear fruit are highly unlikely.

"You don't need to ask."

CHAPTER EIGHT

Melissa

That first evening, while Skull was at work, I am thrown right into the thick of things with the other old ladies. The whores, I notice, keep their distance.

I'm entranced by the kitchen which, it appears, has for many years been Jeannie's domain. I'm informed that even while Hellfire was the prez, his old lady, Moira, rarely came to the club, so Jeannie had become the de facto head old lady. Not that there were so many of them then, just her, Moira and Sindy. Jay and Vi have only joined the club recently.

Jeannie's had the kitchen fitted out so she can cook easily for all the members, and there's an industrial-sized oven the size of which I hadn't seen before. My eyes gleam as I look at it.

"Anytime you want, hon, feel free to use it. I suck at desserts and cakes, and many here have a sweet tooth. You want to cook that shit? You're welcome to do it." Seeing my interest, she opens cupboards and drawers, showing me that the place is well stocked with every item of equipment I could wish for.

At home I've got most of the items I need but have to cook for events like Beth's party in batches. Here, I could get more done at once.

"I sound boring, don't I? Saying my hobby's cooking?"

"Not boring at all, doll face," a rough voice sounds, "I ate one of your cookies earlier."

"What Pyro means," Jeannie glares at him, "is that he ate one tub. One fucking tub. All to himself."

Pyro, a tall, muscular and heavily tattooed biker is uncontrite and just shrugs. "You handed it to me."

"For you to take one."

He winks at me. "Not what you said…"

"Get out of here, Pyro. Haven't you got some fires to put out?"

"Got to start them first." His shoulders shake as he laughs. But he moves off quickly when Jeannie bats him with a cloth.

She smiles fondly at his retreating back, then turns to me. "They're a good bunch. A bit rough around the edges, but fairly easy to keep in their place. Which is outside of this kitchen unless they're being fed."

"A women's domain?" It sounds a bit sexist.

"We need somewhere to ourselves." Vi's gentle voice sounds from behind me. She's carrying Theo in her arms. Suddenly I remember how indiscreet Skull and I had been, and that might be me in another year.

"Can I hold him?"

"Help yourself. He's getting really heavy. If Skull had brought you around earlier, maybe you could have baked his birthday cake. He turned one last week."

Taking Theo, I realise why Violet was so keen to hand him over. He's a solid baby, much heavier than he looks. Spying a chair, I go sit down and hold him on my lap. He's a lovely boy, all smiles and chuckles as I bounce him on my leg. Within moments though, he wants to get down.

Vi nods, I place him on the floor where he holds onto the chair leg, then takes a couple of steps, weaving like a drunk. It's not long before he collapses.

"He took his first step last week. I'm going to need eyes in the back of my head soon," his mother says proudly.

Jeannie puts her arm around her. "He won't be allowed to get into trouble. You know everyone will be watching out for him."

"Especially Jay." She turns to me. "Jay's training to be a nanny, she's always loved kids. And she's really taken to Theo."

"That's because the Tucson club is overrun with children. She misses them," Jeannie explains. "She misses her niece, Faith. Such a shame she can't be with her sister."

I wonder why she can't, but don't want to pry.

There could be worse places to have a baby than in this club, I realise. I suspect the same support Vi's getting will be offered to me. I file what they've told me about Jayden away. If I'm pregnant, I'll need some childcare while I'm working.

When Skull returns from whatever he's been doing, he takes me up to his room, and this time, remembers the condom.

"Mel," he starts, when afterwards I'm lying cuddled in his arms, "how did you get on while I was gone?"

"It was good," I reply, truthfully. "I met some of your brothers who all treated me with respect."

"As they should," he butts in. "May not have voted on you, but they know that you're mine. How did you get on with the old ladies?"

I roll my eyes. "I was getting to that. Very well. Seem to have some common ground with Jeannie as I admired her kitchen, and Vi's easy to get along with. Didn't see much of Jay."

"Nah, you wouldn't. I passed her and Pal's room earlier, seemed they had an early night." He winks, suggestively, making me laugh.

"Sindy came in. She's quiet but friendly enough."

"What did you discuss?"

"Cooking and babies." Women shit in other words. But I'd enjoyed it well enough. I'd shared a few recipes.

He frowns for a moment. "Can you make sure you get on with Violet, Mel? Do me a favour and become her friend, will you?"

I glance at him strangely. "I'm hoping to get on with every-one. Why are you singling her out?"

"Oh come on, Mel. She's the prez's old lady. You get close to her, and you'll be a shoe-in with the club. She's the one you should keep on the right side of. Can't tell you much, but before she came here, she had it rough. Reckon she could use a sympa-thetic ear from time to time."

Oh. He's starting to make sense.

"She's our queen, Mel. Upset her, and it wouldn't be good."

I start to tell him I don't intend to upset anyone, that I go out of my way to avoid things like that. At work, I'm usually the peacemaker. But I don't get a chance, as Skull hasn't finished.

"Making yourself indispensable, giving her a shoulder to lean on, well, that would probably count for a lot."

Over the next couple of weeks, I try to do just that.

Remembering this is my opportunity to see if I could live his life, I spend most weekends at the clubhouse, but return to my own home during the week. With working, I like to follow the routine I've fallen into. Skull pops around between Monday and Friday and always ends up staying the night, but we don't offi-cially move in together, even though he alludes to us doing so in the near future.

Skull and I don't refer to our accident again. As time goes on, I feel no different, and after a couple of weeks, nature runs its normal course, letting me know I'm not pregnant. I feel slightly disappointed. Skull, when I tell him, just nods. Whatever he feels he keeps hidden.

What seemed to have gotten to Skull most, however, hadn't been the fact we might have started a family, but that his reaction had given me cause to question his commitment. Since that day he's been going out of his way to make sure I feel loved and wanted.

Sometimes I'm embarrassed by his show of affection in front of the other members and women, but secretly I'm pleased that he's not trying to hide our relationship. It amuses me that this strong biker isn't ashamed to declare his love for me publicly, if not with words, then by the kisses and caresses.

I suppose it was a little test for him when I asked if he'd like to meet my parents. Like any man, it didn't seem a suggestion he found thrilling, but he had the right answer. "*Anything for you, babe,*" he'd replied.

So we drove one Friday to Denver and spent the night there, my mom putting us in separate bedrooms which Skull accepted without complaint. He acted politely enough, refrained from overt PDAs, and chatted to my father. Before we'd left, Mom pulled me to one side.

"Not thrilled about what he does, Melissa, but he's pleasant enough. Seems to hold you in high regard and is respectful. We won't stand in your way if you've found what you're looking for."

"I think I have Mom."

"Then you have our blessing."

After hugs and goodbyes, Skull and I make our return trip to Pueblo and resume our routine.

Friday nights I drive to the club with a weekend bag beside me, nowadays arriving feeling pleasure at being here instead of afraid, occasionally remembering the first time I was let in the gate and had parked my car at the rear of the compound. Now I'm more likely to greet the prospect with a friendly wave and join in the ribbing when someone gets out shot when they go target shooting. It doesn't bother me at all when they come in putting rifles I've not once seen used in anger away.

Club members and women have all been so welcoming, genuinely pleased to see me each time I've arrived. More often than not they show they've adopted Skull's shortening of my name, and I feel it's like they're accepting me. The only females I don't have much time for are the sweet butts, but they stay out of my way, and I out of theirs.

This evening, like so many others, I spend time helping in the kitchen alongside the other women. We're all good at multitasking when it comes to cooking a meal and talking. My contribution tonight are apple pies, and knowing how much the men like them, I make extra.

Skull snatches me away after we've eaten, and we make love, tonight so tenderly. It's after, when we're snuggled up together that he asks a question.

"Saw you talking with Vi, earlier. What did you discuss?"

"Theo's new tooth," I say fast, smiling as I remember the way he'd toddled over to me and proudly showed me his mouth, his chubby finger pointing to the new addition.

Skull stiffens. "Nothing else?"

"What do you mean?" I'm confused. I recall he'd asked me to get close to the president's wife, but what better way could there be than to show an interest in her son? It's not contrived, either, I'm growing to love that sassy little boy. I'd even offered to babysit for her if she ever needed someone. Not that she has a shortage of volunteers, but she'd accepted with genuine pleasure. I feel I'm doing exactly what he wanted.

"You're missing your chance, Mel. Look, I want us to be together. Permanently. Which means you need to understand the club from a woman's point of view. It's not all rainbows and unicorns. You have a laugh with the women? Cook in the kitchen? Play with the kid? That's fine as far as it goes. But there's a darker side to an MC, and you've got to know you can live with it. If you can't accept everything, the good, the bad and the downright ugly, well, you're not going to make a good old lady."

I hadn't thought about that. I know the Satan's Devils have a reputation, but from what I've seen, they're about nothing more than their legitimate businesses. Sure, they play hard too, sometimes, in my view, too much out in the open in the clubroom with the sweet butts, but that's just their way of life. I, as a newcomer, have no say in it.

Now Skull's suggesting that there is a side to the club I haven't yet seen and that might not settle so well with me.

Inside, I feel a trickle of fear. What is it he's alluding to, and should I try to find out? Before I get in any deeper. Who am I kidding?

"Skull. I don't know if I want to know. What if there's something I don't think I can accept?" I sit up, looking down at him. "What if I discover something I can't live with? Would I lose you?"

He pushes himself up, and his hands hold my upper arms, stopping just short of giving me a shake. "Told you before, Mel. It's you I want. You can't take the club, then I'll leave it. I can get another job working security or some shit like that. It's you and me. For life." He stares at me, intently. "Sure, I worked hard to get my patch, and I'd love to hold on to it, but now I've found you, I don't want to lose you. I'll leave if I have to. Do me a favour, Mel. Ask Vi what really goes on. Then we can make our decisions. Do it, for me, babe? Look, I've claimed you, okay?"

How can I refuse? The way he's putting it, I can't. Every word out of his mouth makes sense. If Vi, the wife of the president, can't give me the lowdown on what goes on behind the scenes, and what really will be asked of me as an old lady, who else could?

The next afternoon I offer to bake. As normal, bikers start hovering before the muffins are even made. A tray of chocolate chip cookies disappears as soon as it comes out of the oven. When Jeannie finally has enough and chases them out, I get my chance.

"So, what's it really like to be an old lady?"

The kitchen door opens. In walks a biker I haven't met, and he's got a woman with him who he introduces as Stevie. It's immediately apparent she's blind and is accompanied by her service dog. She seems to have been here before and knows everyone, as she addresses Violet by name. She hasn't met me though, so I introduce myself.

"I'm Melissa. I'm with Skull."

Beef, as it appears his name is, asks whether Skull's at last claimed me, and Jeannie replies, putting her arm around me, yes. Which seems strange, but I don't question it. If he has, that wasn't what he told me, or not that it was official. *Maybe he'll tell me tonight.* He might be waiting until I report back I can take whatever happens in the club.

"Melissa likes cooking," Violet explains. "Especially baking. Get ready to put on some weight when you taste her muffins."

Max, the newcomer's dog is introduced. He's a big Labrador retriever who I fall in love with on sight, though he seems to be injured. Within a few moments there's an altercation between Bitch—the huge cat who's put in an appearance to put the canine interloper in his place—and Max. The dog gets a scratch on his nose, and cuddles from Jeannie.

When Beef is satisfied the dog is okay, he leaves Stevie with us, telling her he's got to talk to the prez.

"So, Melissa. You wanted to know more about the club." I notice that the blind woman cocks her head toward us as though to hear better. I take it she's new to all this too.

For the next hour or so, the women let me in on the workings of the Satan's Devils, and the dreaded term, club business. I come away with the view that yes, the club may very well get involved in some shady stuff, but only occasionally, and only when one of theirs is at risk. Old ladies are never involved, and actively kept away and, or, protected. Such as the protection they're extending to Stevie right now. Far and away from worrying me, it makes me look more favourably on the club. Who wouldn't want to align their stars with a group of men who'd do everything they can to keep you safe?

"Max is adorable," I tell Skull, later that night.

"Did you find anything out?" he asks, tersely.

"That I think the club is amazing. The way they're rallying around Stevie." Of course, I don't know what's going on, but surmised from all the activity that something was. And that it revolved around her.

"Keep your ear to the ground."

A strange request from my lover. But I agree.

Soon after I make the decision I'm all in with the club, Stevie goes missing. Beef is distraught, but it appears her handler has taken her somewhere safe, or that's all us women can surmise. Max, the dog, has been left behind.

It's a worrying time, but, life, as it does, goes on. I find myself involved more and more in the activities of the old ladies. I'm dragged into cooking when a barbeque is arranged to celebrate the rough ground out back having been transformed into a beautiful yard. I'm even persuaded to drag out a lounger and relax along with Violet and Jay on the newly laid lawn. I don a two piece, well, Vi was very persuasive and, compared to the sweet butts, I'm overdressed. The light in Skull's eyes is worth it, as well as the reward he gives me that night.

Sheepishly Skull has admitted he had indeed officially claimed me. As I'd already felt like I was his, and he mine, it had made no difference to me.

Stevie, no, Steph now, returns permanently to the clubhouse, after she's testified against the bad guys and is accepted into our old lady clan.

I happily cook for the celebration when Beef's made VP.

It's an enjoyable afternoon and evening. As I watch Theo stumble around, the men and women all keeping an eye on him, then watching everyone having fun and laughing, I find it hard to remember how I ever felt satisfied spending every weekend alone.

"Do you think Beef will make a good VP?" I ask Skull later that night when we return to our room.

"Of course. He'll be good. Now come here and love on your man."

Skull's slightly tipsy, the bikers had partied hard to celebrate Beef's permanent transfer to the club. He's slightly clumsy when he rips off my dress, but I giggle, liking the feel of my man.

He might be drunk, but he still makes me come before taking his pleasure himself.

When he's finished, he pulls out. And roars, "Motherfucker! Not a fuckin' gain."

No condom. Again.

"It's okay, Skull. We got away with it before." I sit up, putting my arms around him. "And you've claimed me now, it's official. This shit flies? Well, it was going to happen sooner or later."

"Not the fuckin' point, Mel. Timing is fuckin' off." He looks at me out of the corner of his eye. "Will you take the fuckin' pill this time?"

"Nothing's changed, Skull, except our commitment is deeper. So, no." I'm being stubborn. But to me, it may only have brought forward something that's been increasingly on my mind.

"Fuck," he roars again.

I hope it's the drink driving him, but Skull abruptly stands and throws on some clothes. He walks to the dresser, fumbles in a drawer, then leaves the room carrying a phone which isn't the one he normally uses. He doesn't come back that night.

The next morning I'm awakened by the sound of the door banging open.

"Babe, I'm so fuckin' sorry."

It's Skull.

Sitting up, I rub my raw red eyes.

"It was the drink talkin', not me." He looks so contrite, it makes me want to take him into my arms.

But then I remember the restless night he'd put me through. When he walked out without a word, I feared he wouldn't come back. Thoughts had gone around and around my head. If I agree to take the morning-after pill, would he come back to me? That warred with did I really want a man who'd control me like that? Then it would circle to, decisions about kids should be made jointly, so maybe I should do what he wanted me to.

He approaches, sits on the bed, and takes my hand. "You're right. We're a couple. You do whatever you want to do. If it happens? I'll love him or her. If not? We'll revisit this discussion. Okay?"

I honestly don't know what to think. "What's on your mind, Skull? You said now wasn't the right time."

He reaches across and taps the tip of my nose. "Club business."

I only wish I knew so I could help, but those two words are final. As an old lady, I'll never know. It's the one thing he can say that stops any further discussion.

"You going to do laundry at home? Got some shit I need to take with us."

"Yeah, Skull." We've been living together for weeks, half at the club, half at my house. I can't remember the last time I've slept alone. And yes, I've gotten pretty used to throwing his dirty clothes in with my wash. I don't mind. It's what couples do.

CHAPTER NINE

Pyro

"Hey, boy. Come to see your Uncle Ro?"

"If you sneak him another cookie, Steph's going to be mad," Beef, our new VP, warns me.

"They're not the chocolate ones," I reassure him.

He shakes his head. "You're trying to buy his affection."

I'm unrepentant. "It's working."

Beef snorts. "Fuckin' right. But he still prefers me. Max, down."

Max turns away from me with one last tail wag, takes a step toward Beef, and dutifully collapses at his feet, letting out a sound that suspiciously sounds like a humph. His master must think so too, as he grunts, "Fuckin' dog."

I stare at the English lab for a moment, then pick up the pool cue again as Beef racks the balls. "Steph enjoying her job?"

Beef breaks, then, after he's sunk far too many balls for my liking, answers the question when the cue ball topples down a hole.

"She loves it. She needs to feel useful, you know?"

His face is interesting to watch. One moment he's smiling, next, concerned, now he's cautiously optimistic again, then his brow creases when I successfully sink a ball. I hear a sigh of relief when I eventually miss my shot.

I've a sneaking suspicion that this time he's going to clear the table. *Damn. That will be a few dollars gone.* Should have stayed at work rather than skip out to play pool.

"You know," Beef says thoughtfully, as the last ball disappears down the hole, "I think I'll teach Max to play. He'll probably be better at it than you."

On today's showing, I don't doubt it.

"Rematch?"

"Huh," I splutter. "Not until I find my form."

Beef grins, stacks his pool cue away, then slaps my back. "Beer?" After I nod, and we turn in that direction, he says, "I thought Cad might find it distracting being in the same room as Steph, but he seems to love it."

I soon learned once the VP has decided on something, he doesn't wait for grass to grow under his feet. Cad, he had seen, needed an office as his computers were multiplying and spilling out, threatening to overtake the clubroom. What helped was that his wife, Steph, wanted one too. Though they are looking for a house together to put down roots in Pueblo, she enjoys being in the thick of things, and Beef saw a way to do that by having her work here too. Well, all it takes is a computer and she's set.

The old storeroom was cleared out in a couple of days, wasn't difficult, most of the shit was old junk that could just be trashed. We got Beaver and Karl on painting it, and Sparky and Cad put new wiring and outlets in. A week after the idea was first agreed at church, Cad and Steph had moved in.

"Cad's used to the hustle and bustle of the clubroom around him. Steph's talking computer is probably welcome background noise to him. And he doesn't mind her being there, she can't exactly look across to his screen and see what he's up to." Beef's old lady is blind. But when she's in a room she knows, you'd hardly be able to tell. Her eyes look just the same as anyone else's, she can't see out of them is all. I don't feel sorry for her, though. Having been around her a while, I know pity is the last thing she wants or deserves.

She always has to use a stick or rely on Max in the clubroom though. Brothers try hard, but we're always leaving some shit lying around.

Beef grabs two beers then points to a table.

"Steph's it for you, isn't she, man?"

"Fuckin' right." Beef picks up his bottle and drains half the contents in one go. "Never expected to find her, not how I did anyway."

I spare a glance for Max, now stretched out on his side where we'd left him. Uncaring that people need to step around him if they want to play pool. He'll be off duty until Steph needs him. "That was bad," I tell Beef, remembering Max lying still and bleeding on the pavement. "I thought that dog was a goner for sure."

"Me too, Ro. Me too."

We're quiet for a moment, thinking back. Then I'm driven to ask, "Did you know, Beef?"

"What?" His brow furrows.

"Did you feel something for Steph—Stevie as she was then—at that point?"

He chuckles. "Yeah, some part of me knew. But I didn't want to get into another relationship, so I convinced myself I'd just be a friend. Had gotten out of the clutches of one needy bitch, didn't want another to weigh me down."

"Steph wouldn't do that."

"Didn't know that then, did I? Tell you the truth, Brother. All I saw was a blind girl who'd always need a helping hand. Didn't know how fuckin' wrong I was." His head tilts questioningly as he regards me. "Why the questions, Pyro? You getting fed up being a single man?"

"Whoa. What? No way. Why would I want to settle down, Beef? I've got everything I could want. Pussy in the clubhouse, and with this cut and this face?" Putting my elbow on the table, I cup my chin with my hand. "One look at me, and a glance at my cut, any bitch would drop her panties. I don't need a bitch to be blind." I only just manage to rear out of the way of his punch, but Beef is laughing as well.

Then he grows serious. "Used to be like you. Used to think I could get by on casual pussy. Then I saw my brothers settling down. There's a lot to be said for a woman who's yours and yours alone."

"Used to laugh at you lot in Tucson, most brothers hooking up with their women. But now it seems it's happening here too." I grin at him. "Think Pal must have brought something with him."

"Infected your water?" Beef laughs. "Well count me out, unless it's in the air. I met Steph before I'd set foot in the club-house." His head moves in a negative gesture. "From what I heard, Demon couldn't resist when he found Violet again. Pal was always certain he'd end up with Jay. I reckon you're safe if you're getting worried about it. It's only Skull's relationship that happened out of the blue."

"Yeah, and well, there's a woman. I'm not surprised Skull couldn't resist. You see the tits on her, man?"

Beef chuckles. "Can't really miss them."

"And she can cook too."

Beef cocks his head. "That do it for you? Big tits and culinary skills?"

He's joking, but I give an honest reply. "Don't know what would catch my eye. Certainly not Mel, she's Skull's. Would never step on another man's toes."

He nods. None of us would. Apart from the normal rights and wrongs of it, the man would lose his patch and receive a beatdown too. Particularly in this club. Man doesn't go near a woman who's claimed. Hellfire's father, Blackie, had put his hands on Hellfire's woman and was dispatched to Satan for it.

"Hey, speak of the devil..." Beef nudges my arm.

I swing around to see which one he's referring to, then offer a smile of welcome. "Hey, Mel. Don't normally see you here during the week. You gonna cook for us? Skull with you?" It's unusual, but not uncommon for her to be here on her own.

She walks toward us, and it's then I notice the worried expression on her face. She nods toward the VP. "Beef, I was hoping to speak to you or to the prez."

"Yeah? Well I'm here. What can I do for you, sweetheart?"

She flicks her eyes toward me, then back to the VP, then, adorably bites her lip.

"Want to speak in private?" Beef offers.

She shakes her head. "No, it's okay. Look, I know about club business, alright? I know you won't tell me what he's doing, I just, I just want to know if Skull's okay? He's been gone since Sunday morning, and normally he'd contact me, but I haven't heard anything from him. Can you just tell me if he's alright, and when he'll be back from whatever he's doing?"

My brow creases as I look at Beef. I can almost see the wheels working in his head too. Fact is, I haven't seen Skull around. Not that that's unusual during the week, as nights he spends with Mel, and days he's working with Cad and Pal. But then he does normally come into the clubhouse a time or two.

"You had an argument, Mel?"

Her eyes sharpen. "He's *here?*"

"Answer the question, sweetheart."

"No, Beef." She looks suspicious. "Look, if he's here, it looks like we've got some talking to do. I'll go to his room."

"Yeah," Beef says, his gaze finding mine. "Go see if he's there."

We watch until she's halfway up the stairs, then I say out of the side of my mouth. "She's not going to find him, is she?"

"Nope." Beef pulls out his phone. He taps on a number and holds the device up to his ear. After a moment he shakes his head. "No reply." He then selects a different contact. "Pal, is Skull with you?" I watch his face. It darkens. "And you didn't think that was odd? Yeah, okay. I got you."

"Well?" I question when he ends the call.

"Hasn't seen Skull all week. Apparently, that's not unusual. If they hadn't got a job on, he works at the shop, so Pal thought he was with you."

"Nope," I repeat the word Beef had used. "He's not been at the shop. Think we might have problems?"

"If he doesn't turn up at church tonight, yes."

I press my lips together. "Not happy waiting to find out. Need to know what she knows. Might be nothing at all…"

"Or we might have a brother in the wind," Beef finishes for me. "When I tried his number, I just got the message the call couldn't be taken. No option to leave a voicemail."

Melissa chooses that moment to walk back down the stairs, a dejected look on her face. "He's not there," she tells us, unnecessarily.

"Mel," Beef says, patiently. "Tell us what happened, and where he said he was going."

He's said nothing at all, but far too much. Mel is not stupid. "You don't know where he is, do you?" She looks completely aghast.

Beef's calm, patient. "Not right now, no," he admits. "Tell us what he said, and when he left."

"It was Sunday morning. He said he had some shit to do, club business. Not to worry if he didn't come back that night. But it's Wednesday now. Since he made me his old lady, he's never stayed away for the night, except… But, anyway. Is this how it's supposed to work?" Her face tightens. "If you know anything Beef, please, tell me."

The VP stays in inquisition mode instead. "Did you have an argument, Mel? A falling out?"

"No, not since… Well, after your patching in party, Beef, the week before last, he'd stayed out all night, but we made up. Things have been going great since then. But now I need him, I need to speak to him. I can't contact him; I don't know what to do."

"Hey, hon. It will be alright. Perhaps your argument's been playing on his mind and he's taken off to clear his head. He'll be back. Probably walk in the door any minute." Over the top of her head, my eyes meet Beef's. We both know I'm giving her assurances I can't make.

"But it was sorted," she whispers. "We've been getting on well. He kissed me when he left, told me he'd see me again soon."

Beef seems to come to a decision. "Look, Mel. Either stay here or go home. Skull may walk in the door any moment. It's church tonight. In the meantime, I'll check with Prez and see what I can find out. It's possible he sent him somewhere without telling me."

I hold back my snort. Yeah, like the Prez would go behind his VP's back. But then, Beef is fairly new to the role, and maybe he hasn't cottoned onto that yet. Or, more likely, Beef's just giving Mel something to hang onto.

Mel looks from him to me, then back again. Then, for a second, finds the floor fascinating. Then she straightens her back. "Not much else I can do. I'll hang about here while you speak to Demon, Beef. I'd like to hear as soon as possible if there is any news."

"I may not be able to tell you, sweetheart, if it's club business."

Which means Beef's buying us time.

"But at least you'll be able to contact him, tell me he's okay. He won't answer when I try to call."

If he's not answering her calls, it suggests he's taken off to clear his head after the argument she'd thought he'd recovered from. But that doesn't sound like the Skull I know or fit with the way I've witnessed him treating his woman. My gut feel is that there's something wrong.

"Hey, Steph," Beef calls to his woman who's emerged from the office she shares with Cad. She changes course heading for his voice. Beef takes a second to get the harness on Max, then places the handle in her hands. "Will you keep Mel company for a few? She's lost track of her man."

"Of course, I will."

"You want to come?" Beef jerks his head toward Demon's office door.

I might as well. I've got nothing better to do.

"I'd sure as fuck like to know what's going on," I agree, keeping my voice low so Melissa doesn't hear.

CHAPTER TEN

Melissa

Max leads Steph into the kitchen, I follow along.
"You okay, Mel?"

I shake my head, then realise she can't see me. "No, I'm not, Steph. I don't know what to do."

She places her hand on a chair, pulls it out, and sits down. "Want to tell me about it?"

I take a seat opposite her and pull my thoughts together. I thought I'd turn up, find out at least when he'd be back, then return home and get on with my day. Now it seems it's not going to be that simple. "Skull and I have been getting on really well. We're together most of the time if I'm not at work, or he's not doing something for the club. It came as a bit of a surprise on Sunday morning when he said he had club business, and could be away for the night."

"Okay. That's something I could see Beef doing. Would hate him to be gone, but sometimes they go to other chapters to do stuff. That's how Beef ended up here."

Yes, I can see that. "But if Beef was gone, don't you think he'd contact you? Or answer the phone if you called?"

She shrugs. "I suppose so. But if he is doing something where he doesn't want to be distracted, maybe he can't spare the time to talk to you." She pauses and thinks. "Though that sounds pretty lame, doesn't it? What did Beef say?"

"That's the point. I need to contact Skull, so I came here to see if they had a way of getting a message through, or, at least, tell me when he'd be back. But," my voice sinks lower, "Beef didn't seem to know anything about it. He's gone in to check with Demon in case he sent Skull off on some business that Beef doesn't know about."

She's quiet. I try to read her face.

"I'm clutching at straws thinking that's the answer, aren't I?"

"Beef and his prez are pretty tight," she agrees. "If you'd asked another member, maybe that could be the case, but Demon? Can't think what he would want to keep from Beef."

"Could, could he have had an accident?" I breathe out. I'd had no thought in my head other than anger at the club taking Skull away from me, I hadn't dreamed for a moment that no one here knew he was missing. I hadn't considered he went out on his bike and never came back.

But he'd told me he'd be gone a day or two.

Where else would he have gone, except on club business?

Why hasn't he come home?

"Oh Steph, what's happened to him?" My mind pictures him dead or dying by the side of the road. Tears prick at the corner of my eyes, and I wipe them away. *Focus, Mel. I won't help my man if I can't stay strong, at least until I know whether I'm right to worry or not.*

I realise the time. I'd only skipped out on my lunch break with every intention of going back, now it's early afternoon. At least I have the presence of mind to text Beth and ask her to say I'm ill and to make my excuses. Returning to the office right now is not what I want to do.

I've just finished my reply reassuring my friend that every-thing's fine, glad I texted and hadn't placed a call, easier to prevent her guessing I'm lying, when I hear bikes in the distance. *Maybe it's Skull?* I get to my feet to go check, when Pyro appears in the doorway.

"Could you come see Prez, Mel?"

I wave in the direction of the front of the club. "That could be him arriving back now."

Pyro shakes his head sadly. "Prez is rallying the troops, Mel. That's unlikely to be him. But I'll make sure. Prospect?" He turns and yells the last word. When Beaver appears at a run, he addresses him, "Check whether Skull's come back. If you see him at all, come to Prez's office immediately, okay?" Then he turns back to me. "Come, Mel."

The last time I'd been in Demon's office was the first day I'd come to the club and Skull had introduced me. This time, I'm just as nervous, albeit for different reasons.

Demon looks up from his desk and doesn't even bother with a smile. "Come in and sit, Melissa."

I do so, noticing Beef is in the other chair. Pyro stays too, standing, leaning his back against the wall.

"First, I'm sorry, but Skull wasn't doing anything for the club."

I suppose if that's so, it's best I hear it straight away. But the alternative is that my man had lied to me. What a stupid woman I'd been. All he had to say was 'club business', and I'd known I couldn't pry.

But is there a chance Demon's got it wrong? "Could he have been doing something for you on his own? Found a new business lead to follow?"

"Possible," Demon confirms, "but unlikely." He leans forward, placing his elbows on the desk, and resting his chin on his clasped hands. His dark eyes focus on me. "Tell me everything, Melissa, what he said, the exact words he used, what happened between the two of you before he left, and the mood he was in. Anything and everything could be significant."

I wring my hands together, biting my lip and wondering where to start.

Beef prompts me. "Start with the argument you had after my patching over party. What started that?"

I look to my side. I really don't know what to say. "It's private," I settle for, at last.

Demon pinches the bridge of his nose. "We've got a brother missin', Melissa. I understand you want to keep some shit between you and your old man, but anything that gives us a bearing on where he might have been headed, or why, could help us find him. What I want to assess is whether something between you upset him enough that he's gone somewhere to cool his heels."

"I can see your point, but when he left, he was upbeat. Kissed me as normal. Didn't give me any clue that he was upset, or that he hadn't come to terms with our situation."

"Situation?" Demon's quick to catch on. "What situation?"

"Do you want your man back, darlin'?" Pyro's voice rumbles from behind me. "'Cause we can only help if we know what we're dealing with."

"No judgement," says Beef. "If you stepped out on him, another man looked at you twice, then we won't say a thing."

"It's nothing like that," I gasp, indignantly, then realise the truth may be less embarrassing than any conclusion they might dream up themselves. "That night, after Beef's party, he forgot to use a condom again."

"Again?" Once more, it's Pyro's voice, and he doesn't seem happy.

"It happened once before. But we got away with it then."

"This time?"

I shake my head. "I don't know," I say quietly. "But it was two weeks ago, and I want to take the test. I just wanted him with me when I did it."

"What was his reaction?" Demon doesn't look pleased.

I sigh deeply. "The first time, he tried to get me to take the morning-after pill. I can't really explain why, but I didn't want to. I wanted to leave it to fate, and I wasn't unhappy either way. We had words, I told him I thought his reaction showed he wasn't serious about our relationship and that pulled him up and made him think. We worked it out. He assured me he was all in with me, wanted a forever and eventually, he wanted kids. He'd just wanted to wait for a while until we started a family. Like I said, we got away with it that time."

Beef sits forward, his hands clasped between his legs. "Let me get this straight. Skull knows nothing more than he's fucked up again, and you may or may not be pregnant. Neither he nor you actually know."

I nod. That's right.

"Don't see this has anything to do with Skull going, Prez," Pyro states. "If he'd known, maybe, but he doesn't. Surely he'd have hung around to find out?"

"It was worse this time though. His reaction, I mean." I might as well tell them everything now. "He asked me again to take the morning-after pill and again said it wasn't the right time. It sounded like it was even less so than the time before."

Demon's eyes sharpen. "He tell you why?"

"Club business," I snarl the word. The excuse that works for these men every time. "He let me believe it was something to do with the club. That was all I could understand, that something external was putting pressure on him. I thought we were in a good place. He'd claimed me, we're in a stable relationship. We both agreed we wanted kids. Okay, so maybe it's still early for us, but at least on my part, I'm all in."

Beef nods, I catch the movement out of the side of my eye. "I'd have said that too. He seems to care a lot for you, Mel."

"After... it... happened that night, he'd walked out. Took a phone, presumably to make a call. Stayed out until the morning. But that was two weeks ago. Since then we've been fine. I'm sure that's got nothing to do with this." *Could he have left because he was scared I was pregnant?* I really don't believe so. Maybe if we knew for certain, but even then, the man I know and love would have stayed.

"He took a phone." Demon's brow creases. "Right. I can get Cad to look at his phone records and see who he spoke to then. Might be a friend we don't know about who he's reconnected with."

"Someone he stayed with when he left for that month?" Pyro suggests.

"Could be, Ro. Could be."

Their comments mystify me. I hadn't known he'd left the club at all, must have been well before I met him. "Why are you talking about a call he may or may not have made two weeks ago? That's got nothing to do with his disappearance now."

Demon stares at me for a second, then sighs. "Mel, look, we don't know what's relevant or what's not. There's a man who isn't where he should be, so we've got to figure out where he may have gone. You might not have expected the man you know to walk out on you, pretty damn sure I speak for everyone here to say they'd feel the same. Sure, we may be grasping at straws, but let's think this through. Maybe he went to stay with someone. Maybe he bumped into an old friend and has gone on a bender. You ever meet with or hear him mention being close to anyone outside the club?"

Shaking my head, I tell him, "No. If I did, I'd be contacting them myself. He said he had no family at all."

There's a knock at the door. Demon calls out, and Cad steps in. For a second, I wonder whether he's summoned him by some kind of power of thought, but it seems Demon's already got him on the case.

"I've checked police reports and hospitals in the area. No mention of him or his bike. Not saying he didn't have an accident, but if he did, it was out of town. I can widen the search but would be useful to know where I'm looking."

"Cad, Skull called someone. Early hours of the fourteenth.

Can you check who? It's possible it could be his go-to for advice."

"Will do, Prez."

Cad steps back out, closing the door behind him.

"That's the place to start," Beef comments. "Friend you call in the dead of the night is probably someone you make a beeline for when you want to get your head on straight."

"Melissa, you're looking concerned."

I am. Nothing makes sense. "I'd say you were right, Demon, if he'd been upset when he left. But he wasn't. It was just like he was setting off for a normal day at work. There was nothing unusual in either what he did or said."

Pyro chuckles behind me. "Men are strange beasts, Mel. Sometimes we don't let the wounds show in case they're seen as a sign of weakness. We just retreat and lick 'em in private."

Could it be as easy as that?

The door opens again, and once more Cad pokes his head around it. "Skull made or received no calls at all between six pm on the thirteenth and noon on the fourteenth."

"Sorry," I admit, having led them on a wild goose chase. The fact that he left with a phone didn't mean he'd used it. Just took it in case.

"Okay, Melissa," starts Demon, "I've brought church forward by a few hours so I can get the boys together. We'll thrash things out and take it from there. You're welcome to stay here at the club or go home. If you want company, I'm sure Vi will be happy to stay with you until we've got word."

If something's happened to Skull, something bad, the time I'll need support is when we know. For now, I'd rather be at home where he'll expect to find me if he comes back.

"I'll go to my place, Demon. I'll be fine. I might have worried you for nothing, and he'll turn up tonight."

"Tell him to get his ass here if he does," Demon, no, *the president*, snarls. "No member walks off and disappears without explanation."

Oh no. Because I've opened my mouth, Skull could very well get into trouble. But what else could I do? My man's missing and has been for four days.

"Mel," Pyro stops me as I'm about to walk out the door. "You take care of you. If you..." he doesn't have to say it, a glance down at my stomach is enough. "Well, look after yourself."

CHAPTER ELEVEN

Pyro

"Hey, Ro. What's all this about?" Ink heads straight for me as I'm at the bar getting a beer. "I had shit planned before church. Why call us in early?"

"Skull's missing."

"What?"

I nod. "Melissa called it in. Well, brought it. Got worried when he hadn't come home."

Ink shrugs, unconcerned. "Well it's their business. Bet he'll be in later for church."

"Pal's not seen him, and he's not been at the shop." I focus my eyes on him. "He's not been near the club. No one's set sight on him since he left his ol' lady on Sunday morning. I say we're right to be concerned and hash it out sooner rather than later."

He looks around. "Christ." He sweeps his hands through his hair. "And she's only started worrying now?"

I raise my brow. "He told her he was off on club business." I need say nothing more.

"Melissa still here?"

"Nah. Gone home in case he turns up. Way Prez is feeling now though, he'd do better to keep clear."

"Demon won't be happy that a brother's done a disappearing

trick," Hellfire, having overheard, confirms. "If it was personal shit he could have had time off, but to go without telling anyone? Kid's gonna have to have a fuckin' good excuse."

We tend to refer to Skull as a kid as he barely looks old enough to shave. He's supposed to be in his mid-twenties though he doesn't look it.

A loud whistle gets our attention. Keeping hold of my bottle of beer, I turn and make my way into the meeting room and take my seat at church. As people are getting themselves settled, I take the opportunity to look around. It's good to see Thunder back in his rightful place. As sergeant-at-arms he's seated to Demon's right and appears more relaxed than I've seen him in months. Beef already looks comfortable to Demon's left. It's my estimation that the man didn't know his own strengths until the rest of us pointed them out. Whatever he thought, he is VP material, and a man we all respect.

The gavel comes down.

Conversations cease. We don't often have an emergency church so everyone's taking this seriously. Some brothers know why they've been called in, others who have yet to hear are wearing expressions which combine mystification and concern.

After only taking a second to confirm he's got all our attention, Demon wastes no time summing up. "Skull's disappeared. May or may not have to do with a disagreement between him and his old lady. Fact is, there was one, but in her view, they made up before he left. So that could be a red herring."

Hell clears his throat. "Let's say Skull headed out after an argument with his ol' lady. Heard he hasn't turned up for work, which is a fuckin' disrespect on the club, but we can address that. Fact is, it's Wednesday. In a couple of hours he may well turn up for church, and all this worry will be for nothing."

Demon gives a slow nod. "While I hear what you say, Hell, fact is, neither his ol' lady nor any of us can contact him. I, for one, hope bringing church forward was unnecessary, and Skull will walk in, hopefully with an explanation. If he is indeed missing, I don't want to waste a moment when we could be searching. First off, if anyone around this table knows anything about why Skull left or where, speak the fuck up now."

Brothers look at each other, brows are raised questioningly, heads are shaken, but no one says a word.

The VP raises his hand slightly. "Could he have been lured off? Someone getting back at the club? What about the mafia family, the Silvestri, that you were up against a few months back?"

"No," Demon says firmly. "I doubt it. It's not their style. If they've got Skull, we'd have heard about it before now."

"Surely that would be the case with anyone else? They take one of ours, they'd want us to know they've got him, and tell us what they want in return," Hellfire observes.

"Not if they came across him and killed him. We might never find the body." Lizard sounds and looks sombre.

It's not as if that possibility hadn't crossed my mind as well. My concern is how Mel would be able to cope if that was the case.

Demon taps the table. "Melissa says he was going off for a couple of days. His going was planned, as presumably was his coming back."

"He in touch with anyone?" asks Pal. "Could he have thought he was doing something for the club? What exactly did he tell his old lady?"

Beef responds, his voice dry, "Only that it was club business."

Pal nods. "So maybe it was. Or, he thought it was."

Or, I think to myself, *it was a sure-fire way to stop her from asking questions.*

"What else we got, Brothers?"

I waggle my hand causing Demon to focus his eyes on me. "The night of your patch over party, Beef, Mel thought he'd placed a call. Turns out he hadn't, but that doesn't mean he hasn't got someone he could hole up with. He may simply have gone to get a break from his ol' lady, get his head on straight without her nagging in his ear." I frown. Can't see Mel's a nagger, but hey, what do I know what she's like at home? "What about whoever he ran to when he spent that month away from the club? He ever tell anyone where he went?"

All I get back are shakes of heads.

"Don't know and never asked." Mace sums up our response.

"He might not have made a call that night. Did he make one later?"

Cad nods at Ink. "Like all of us, he made a few. I'm going through his phone record checking for any out of state numbers, or ones I don't recognise. Haven't found anything suspicious as yet." He breaks off, and glances at the head of the table. Leaning forward, he clasps his hands and informs us in an even voice, "Before you ask, first thing I did was check. Skull has made or received no calls from his club phone since the morning he parted company with his old lady. Well, since the night before to be precise. The last one was to you, Pal, Saturday evening."

Pal's brow creases. "He asked me if I needed him Monday, and I said we," he nods at Cad, "had it sorted."

I widen my eyes. "Sound like he thought he'd be back by the next day if that was all he mentioned."

"Can you trace his phone?" Thunder asks, his jaw tight.

Cad throws him a look that screams *what the fuck do you think I've been doing?* but his reply is polite. "Nah. Not in itself a worry. Could be it's run out of battery, or he's turned the phone or just the Wi-Fi off, or hell, the sim card might have gotten damaged."

Beef and Demon exchange glances.

"He had words with Melissa, you say?" Bomber asks. When Demon nods, he continues, "Then I say that it's likely he wanted a break. Sometimes it's best to just head out on a long run, we all know that. Could have turned off his phone as he didn't want to hear from her."

Buzzard, our treasurer, who's married to Sindy, nods in agreement. "Saying 'club business' means nothing if he wanted to clear his head. This argument his ol' lady dismissed as nothing and resolved, might be anything but to Skull. That he headed off and wanted no distractions could make sense. The fact that he hasn't come back could mean he's met an accident and can't."

I wonder whether Buzz has a point. Demon's quite rightly kept Mel and Skull's personal details private, but I know the truth. It's possible Skull could have made a baby. That's sufficient to make some men run, or at least, take a moment to get his head on straight and decide how he feels about it. As the treasurer said, their argument, as Demon had put it, is far from reaching a conclusion. Not until Mel takes that test. I begin leaning toward the explanation that Skull's not returned through no fault of his own.

"Okay," starts Demon, "we're coming up with options. One, he wanted space from his old lady. He's either taking longer about it than he first thought, or has had an accident and can't get back, or maybe he's been arrested. The other, he's been lured away and is being held, or has been killed, by unknown enemies of the club."

"There's a third option, Prez." Beef's eyes meet Demon's. They seem to have a silent conversation.

Demon growls. "Don't want to go there, Brother. Man's proved himself."

"Or," contradicts his VP, "he was just waiting. Biding his time, getting something set up."

"You're talking about him betraying the club because of how we treated him?" Mace's eyes open wide. "Hell of an accusation there, VP."

Beef shrugs. "Wasn't here then, only heard what happened. He went through hell and back."

"And was patched in for it," Hellfire reminds him. Well, being prez at the time, it had been down to him.

Beef's not going to give up, and in my view, he's right. It's an explanation which needs some exploring and not dismissed out of hand. "He might have needed time to set something up. Then he fucked off when he knew it was going to go down."

"He's been gone four days," Hellfire states. "You weren't here, Beef. I was. I concurred that Skull bore us no ill will for what we had done. Yeah, sure I may have been mistaken, but it's the least likely explanation that I've heard."

"We'll probably find he fucked off, then found someone to shack up with instead of his ol' lady," Lizard grumbles. "All this fuckin' worry for nothing."

"If that's the case," Demon's eyes gleam with that unnatural flare that led to him getting his handle, "he's due a beatdown worse than he had before."

Murmurs of agreement go around. I nod my head. I'd make my punch count just for the worry he's causing his old lady.

Demon's pinching the bridge of his nose, a sign he's thinking. I'd hate to sit in his chair. Something blows up? Everyone looks to the prez for an answer. I think everyone's conscious of the weight on his shoulders and gives him the space to come up with his views. Or we're silent because, none of the rest of us have any ideas.

Cad's staring at his tablet in front of him. "Six pm," he suddenly announces.

Time church is scheduled. We all look at the door expectantly, but it doesn't open. I glance at Ink and raise my eyebrow. He shakes his head back. Other brothers around the table are making similar gestures.

"Fuck," breathes out Hell.

"Okay," Demon says after one more moment. "That's our confirmation. Cad, widen your search, perhaps get Mouse, Token and Keys on it to help." He lists the computer experts in the other chapters. "What are we thinking, a two-hundred-mile radius?"

"Make it three," suggests Beef. "Does he have any contact with the other chapters?"

"Not that I know," Pal states. "We did talk about him going

to Vegas to look at the way they run their security business, but he hasn't been yet."

"Okay. We'll focus on the hospitals and police reports looking for accidents or arrests. Three hundred miles in any direction." He waits for Cad's nod. "Next, though I think it unlikely, I'll talk to the Silvestris. Beef, this would be a good chance for you to meet them. We'll also talk to RIP, see if he knows anyone who's gunning for us."

Again, I raise and dip my chin along with my brothers. Yeah, the prez of the local Wretched Soulz might have heard something.

Demon hasn't finished. "Lastly, we go on lockdown."

"What?"

"The fuck? Prez?"

"Hell no."

Demon's hand slams down on the table. "Hear me out." He waits for silence. "We've got a brother missing. Could be nothing at all, in which case I'll tear him apart myself as soon as he shows his face. Could be accidentally dead or injured. Could be deliberate. Could have been captured or lured away. Not risking anyone else and not risking any of our women or my kid being taken. Until we know what's happened to Skull, I want everyone, and I mean *everyone*, Hellfire, here." He has an extra glare for his father. Moira, his mother, hates being at the compound.

As I've had the thought which no one else seems to have, I suppose it's down to me to suggest it. "I know this is unthinkable, Prez, but your reaction, quite sensibly, is a lockdown. No," I say hurriedly holding up my hand, "not protesting or saying that's wrong, but it's the predictable response. Skull's been missing four days, so why hasn't something hit us sooner?"

"Because they were waiting for everyone to be called in," breathes Beef catching onto my meaning fast, "and then launch an attack."

"Yes," but I haven't finished, "or something's already here on the compound."

"Explosives?" Lizard suggests.

I nod at him. "It's the way I'd do it, yes."

Demon doesn't waste a second. "First off, we search the fuckin' clubhouse. Top to fuckin' bottom. Ro, need your expertise. If you were Skull, if you knew every inch of the compound, where would you hide that shit?"

I rapidly work to get my mind in gear. "Fuck, Prez. Depends if we're looking at a man who hid something in a hurry, or whether this has been planned for some time." My hands massage my forehead. "He's been gone a few days, if it was the former, what was hidden could already have been found. I'd go for long-term planning, so could be fuckin' anywhere we wouldn't normally stumble across. Loose floorboard? We'd better check under it. Backs of cupboards, anywhere he could have hidden shit."

Demon stares, then nods. "You heard Pyro. We fuckin' tear everywhere apart. Then, when we know it's clear, or," a glance of pain goes over his eyes as he knows, in that case he'd have to admit we'd all been betrayed, "we've cleared it, we go on lockdown."

Serious looking men start getting to their feet. When Liz and Ink hang back, the others take their cue from them, and suddenly, everyone's looking at me.

"Where first, Ro?" Bomber throws out.

I roll my head back, close my eyes, and visualise the compound. "It would either have to be in the clubhouse, or in one of the outbuildings close enough to cause damage. We'll start in the basement and work our way up."

"The businesses?"

"Yeah." I seem to have been put in charge of the search, but hey, I know fire and its behaviour. "Liz, get the tattoo parlour checked out." We've just opened a new one. Fucking bad time if that was taken out. "Rusty, check the bowling alley." Christ, we have families and kids going there.

"I'll take Tits Up," Mace offers, as we've yet to put in a permanent manager.

"Sparky," I ask, "can you check the auto-shop?"

"I'm with you," Bomber offers.

"Me too," says Ink.

"We..." Pal nods at Wills and Judge, the newly made up members, "we'll check the furnace."

"Everyone else fan out. Every inch, every bike, every fuckin' car, needs checking. We'll each do our rooms and I mean look in the closets, under beds, any loose floorboards. Oh, and Cad, do a sweep..."

"Did one earlier, Pyro. We're clean."

"Thank fuck for that." Demon sighs loudly. "Meet back here in an hour or call Pyro if you find something."

I nod but close my eyes briefly. I'm known for starting fires, putting them out, and am the closest thing the club's got to a bomb disposal expert. I sincerely hope no one finds anything.

Men disperse. As I go out into the clubroom, I see them all rushing past Mel who's standing with her mouth open. Brushing a hand over my face, I know she's here for an explanation, what I don't want to do is tell her the situation could have gotten a whole lot worse. Demon's worried about a fuck load more than just her, but who else is going to take a moment to talk to her?

Obviously, no one. I approach her. "I thought you went home."

Her face turns slightly. There's no way she can miss the clubhouse has suddenly become a hive of activity. "I came back. I couldn't settle. What's going on, Pyro? I heard you coming out— have you any news? Where's everyone going?"

Her questions are valid as she can hear a number of bikes starting.

"Whoa, darlin'. No, no news. We're just checking some shit out." I eye her, she looks tired. And in her possible condition, with the worry, it's understandable. "Look, Mel, why don't you go back home? You can't do anything here. I promise, as soon as we know anything, I'll come update you. We may know more in another couple of hours." Or, so I hope.

"Home feels so empty. If I'm here and you get news…"

She'll be safer at home if I end up having to play with explosives. "Nah, Mel. As you said, Skull will expect to find you there. You go home and see if there's been any sign of him. If he comes back, tell him to get in touch with us at once."

A little frown plays at her lips. Christ, I hope she's not going to argue. I want to get on with what I need to do.

She'll need to come in on lockdown once the place has been cleared. Will need someone to encourage her, and that can't be left to a prospect. Might as well be me as anyone else, she seems to trust me. And, as so far, Demon, Beef and I have kept her secret, doesn't seem any point bringing anyone else into it right now. Women like to keep that sort of shit under wraps, at least until it's confirmed.

"Look, Mel. I'll come around to your house later, make sure you're updated, okay?"

"You promise? Any news or not?"

"Yeah, I promise, Mel. I'll be there as soon as I can. Can't say what time it will be, but I promise I'll come." Unless I'm blown into smithereens before then, but that I keep to myself.

I didn't realise Demon's come up behind me. "Scat, Melissa. You're more use to Skull at home for the moment. Pyro *will* come see you later. *I* guarantee that."

She glances at Demon, must see by his set expression she won't be able to budge him from his instruction, then gives me a look. I respond with a sharp nod. At last, she collects her purse and leaves.

"Now what?" Demon asks, his eyebrow raised.

"Now we start tearing this fuckin' place apart."

There are three false alarms. Twice my heart is in my mouth as I'm faced with unfamiliar objects, and a third not so strange, though why a prospect would think a butt plug could conceal an explosive I've no idea, but I check them all out. I even have to race to the bowling alley to investigate some piping. But, thank fuck, at the end of it all, we're as certain as we can be that there's no explosive hidden on the compound.

One by one brothers report in that apart from the items I've already examined, they've found nothing suspicious.

I'm tired, mentally drained. It's not fun staring death in the face as I examine something that could be booby trapped or have a hair-trigger on it. So, at the end, when Demon reminds me of my promise to go see Mel, I wish I hadn't rashly taken that on myself.

Around us men and women are coming in carrying bags. Some looking happy, some resigned, and some complaining.

Demon watches them for a moment. Then, to me, instructs, "Bring her in, Ro."

"Tonight?"

He thinks for a moment. "Either that or stay over at her place and bring her in in the morning. I'd send someone else, but…"

"But I know she could be pregnant so will handle her with kid gloves."

"Exactly."

CHAPTER TWELVE

Melissa

S omething *was up*. Something they didn't want me to know about. Do they have any idea why Skull disappeared?

If they do, they're doing better than I.

My period should have arrived yesterday, it didn't. I've had no tell-tale cramps, cravings or water retention that I've come to expect in the days before I'm due. On the way to work today, I headed down to the pharmacy and bought a pregnancy test. I'd wanted to use it with Skull beside me. If we were starting out on this new journey, I wanted it to be together. As I'm normally regular as clockwork, I'm starting to think that test will be redundant, just confirmation of something deep down inside I already know.

I'm pregnant.

Or, maybe I'm not? Maybe not knowing where Skull could have gone has mucked up my cycle. But it was only today I'd started to worry, and even then, had been more annoyed at his club for keeping him away when I'd expected him home. It was only when I found out they knew nothing about his disappearance that I became distressed.

Where is he?

I love him. I'd know deep down inside if he was dead, wouldn't I? My own heart would stop beating.

His club doesn't know where he is. Could he have lied? Could he have shut me up with those words, *club business,* knowing it was the one thing he could have said which would stop further questions?

The test on the counter taunts me. *Should I find out for certain?* If I'm not, that would be one less worry on my mind. Conversely, a positive result could be a comfort, if Skull has really gone, he may have left part of himself behind.

He can't be dead. But what other explanation is there for him staying away from me, and from his club?

I stuff my hand into my mouth and bite down hard with my teeth in an effort not to cry. Even if it's just me, I've got to be strong. Can't break down.

My phone rings. I pick it up fast. It's Beth.

"Hey, Melissa. You okay? Why did you need the afternoon off? I told them you'd been sick."

I could tell Beth. She's my friend, she'd be around like a shot to comfort me.

But what could I tell her? My man, my biker, the person I expected to spend the rest of my life with has done exactly what had held me back at the start. He's gotten fed up with an over-weight, older woman, found a newer model, and had moved out.

Okay, so that's just supposition. Is it easier to think I've been abandoned than to imagine Skull losing his life? Neither thought brings any relief.

In the end, I tell her nothing. "Beth, it's actually the truth. I was sick, didn't explain earlier as I couldn't stay out of the bath-room long enough."

"Oh, Melissa. Do you need anything? Shall I come around? Is it something you've eaten?"

"No, and no, Beth. I think I've caught a tummy bug or some-thing. Don't want you to catch it. But can you tell them at work?

I don't think I'll be in tomorrow, and maybe not Friday." But I hope to be. I hope I'll get news, an explanation. Or, best of all, see Skull walking through the doorway. "I've got to go, Beth. Nature's calling... again."

My excuse has her ending the call quickly, with just a few words, "Feel better soon."

Light dims, evening arrives. I flick on the light automatically but see nothing it illuminates. Instead my mind goes over and over the words Skull spoke on Sunday morning. But no matter how I try to analyse his final phrases, there was nothing, no warning, no indication he wouldn't return.

He'd expected to come back, hadn't he?

Of course I was concerned when he hadn't, but I hadn't allowed myself to really worry until I'd gone to the club for the explanation. Instead, I found what Skull had told me had been a lie.

Where is he? What is he doing?

He said he loved me. Only death would keep him from coming home.

No, no, no, no, no. I can't afford to think like that. I can't imagine I'll be bringing up a fatherless baby. Can't, just, can't.

I honestly couldn't tell how long I've been just sitting, with thoughts going around and around my brain. I'm startled when at last I hear a motorcycle engine.

Skull?

No. However much I want it to be, it doesn't sound like his bike.

But it does stop outside. Realising it's probably Pyro and he may have news, I rush to the door and open it before he knocks.

"Shouldn't do that, Mel," are his first words out of his mouth, then he explains, "it might not have been me."

I go to tell him that it had been the logical, and as it turned out, correct assumption, but the expression on his face shows he's completely serious. For some reason he's annoyed that I've thrown open the door without checking.

Because of something they've found out about Skull?

It's my turn to speak. When I do, the floodgates open.

"Have you found anything out? Do you know where Skull is? Have you found him?"

Instead of answering, his hands come to my arms and apply pressure, so I move back out of the doorway. Turning, he closes the door behind him, shooting across the bolt.

He shrugs when my eyes question him. "Can't be too careful."

"What is it, Pyro? Please, tell me whatever you know."

"Can we sit?" He sends a pointed glance toward the sofa.

I don't answer with words, just step over to my comfortable three-seater, taking a place at one end. He sits at the other, and for a moment, holds his head in his hands. There's something about his posture that shouts out this man is exhausted.

"Can I get you anything?"

"What?" He glances across the space between us. "Nah, thanks Mel. But I'm okay. Just been a stressful day."

"Because of Skull?" I make the assumption. "What is it you know?"

He takes a deep breath, then sighs. "Easier to tell you what we don't know. We don't know where he is. We're trying to find leads of where he might have been going or gone. He may have gotten to his destination and stayed. With fuck all to go on, we're checking in every direction. All I can tell you is that so far we've found no body in a morgue, no injured biker in any hospital, and no police reports which could show he's been arrested."

"That's good news, isn't it?" I'm clutching at straws.

"Could be worse," he agrees.

"Can you really be sure of your information? What have you been doing? Making calls?" Even if someone had been on the phone ever since I left them, they couldn't have contacted every organisation he's named.

He gives a half-smile. "Nah, we've got other ways. Got the computer experts in all our chapters searching."

"Oh." I didn't realise they could do that. Computer hacking probably comes under their one-percenter ways which Skull had alluded to, but never told me about. "You are searching under his real name, aren't you?"

He rolls his eyes. "Kris Cox, yeah."

Of course they are.

"So, he's not dead, dying or arrested," I surmise.

"So far we can't say that. Not locally that's for certain. We're casting our net wider and wider, Mel. We'll keep trying."

"What..." I struggle to get out my thought, "what if he crashed, and his body's not yet been found?" I sob. "What if we never find out what happened to him?"

"Darlin', don't be defeatist," he says sharply. "We'll find him. It's just a matter of time."

But even if they discover his whereabouts, there's no guarantee he intends to come home. If he did, he'd have contacted me. Skull had never proved to be anything but dependable and he cared for me. But perhaps that too, had been a lie. Maybe disappearing had been his intention. If he left of his own volition, if nothing's preventing him returning...

"Maybe he left me. Just didn't want to tell me."

"Then he's a fuckin' fool." Pyro's eyes blaze. "Skull's got everything going for him. A good woman, a *beautiful woman*," he corrects, and now it's time for my eyes to roll. "The possibility of a family and his club. Man doesn't walk out on that unless he's crazy. There are ways of leaving the Satan's Devils if that's what he wanted. Bikers do not simply walk out on family."

The notion I'd been selfish hits me. I hadn't considered it wasn't just me he'd abandoned. He must have work commitments for the club. Is it really possible he just walked out and left them?

"Something's happened to him. We just don't know what yet."

Pyro doesn't contradict that statement. "You got beer, darlin'?"

"Yeah, sure."

"Nah," he holds out his hand, palm facing me, "I'll go get it. In the fridge?"

"Yes, through there in the kitchen."

He stands, walks the few steps to where I'd indicated, and I hear a door opening and closing. It's a few more seconds before he returns. As well as a beer, he's holding the pregnancy test kit.

Pressing my lips together, I throw a horrified look at him and shake my head.

"Mel, you probably could do with a drink yourself. But until you know for certain, you can't have one."

"I was waiting for Skull," I respond in a whisper.

He shuffles, looks uncertain, then says, "Let me be here for you instead."

I close my eyes, thinking. Pyro's right. I'd kill for a glass of wine or something stronger at the moment. If I'm wrong and I'm not incubating a child, I could have one. How long will I be waiting for a man who may not return? Nine months? Huh, I'll know for certain long before then, but not for weeks yet. Unless... I take that test.

"I'm scared."

His eyes soften. "Of course you are. But you're not alone. You're club."

"Not without Skull."

Suddenly he's no longer standing, nor seated at the far end of the couch. He's sitting up close beside me. "You are club," he repeats. "Skull claimed you, which makes you a Satan's Devil's ol' lady. If Skull's not here to take care of you, everyone else will step up. You're part of our family, darlin'."

My eyes widen. I'd assumed they'd want nothing to do with me.

"You hardly know me," I object.

"Don't need to know you, Mel, though I think we probably know more than you're thinking. But you're one of us now. Sure, you've got the choice. Skull doesn't reappear? You don't need to have anything to do with us, but we're here if you want."

I like the club, the atmosphere, the men and the old ladies. May be able to do without the whores, but that's another matter. I've enjoyed all the time I've spent at the compound. But to go there without Skull? To take from his friends when he's not there to support me?

Eventually I shake my head. "I don't know, Pyro. I can't take advantage…"

"Take advantage?" he rears back. "Mel, whether or not you take us up on the offer, you'll find we're there for you. We owe it to Skull. Wherever he is, whatever he's doing, he's still a member of this club. If he's got himself locked up, we'll look after his woman for him until he's able to do it himself. That's the way it works, Mel. You're still his old lady."

"I'm still his old lady?" I gaze at him incredulously. "He walked out on me…"

"Nah. You don't know that. Want my view? That's the last fuckin' thing he'd do. Something's stopping him coming back."

"Something made him leave in the first place," I counter.

Pyro's eyes fall to the packet he's still holding. *Could Skull have left because he was scared I was pregnant? Didn't want to step up and do the right thing?* Before I can have second thoughts, I stand, snatch the test out of Pyro's hands and head off to the bathroom.

I need to know.

If I'm not, perhaps somehow he'll find out, perhaps someone would get the message through and he'll come back.

Although if that's the reason he did, would I really want him? A man who left because he was too scared to have a baby.

I read the instructions, do the necessary, then walk back out to where Pyro's still sitting. I leave the test on the side, suddenly changing my mind. *I don't want to know.*

If it's positive, life as I know it changes.

If it's not, I'm still on my own.

Minutes tick by.

"Want me to look?"

I haven't got the nerve to do it myself. I give a small nod. Then watch, trying to read the expression on his face, but his features give away nothing as he stares at the result.

Then he comes back. Dropping to his knees he takes hold of both my hands, and gazes into my eyes intensely. "You are *not* doing this alone. You've got me and the club behind and beside you. This baby will have all the love it could have, whether or not Skull's here to take up his responsibility. Think I told you before, you're club, and so is your baby."

Baby?

I'm pregnant.

Even though I had suspected it, the result comes as a shock.

"Skull couldn't have known," I explain, trying to justify my man's actions more to myself than to Pyro. "It wouldn't be the reason he's gone." Though it could be the reason he won't come back. "We talked about having a family, Pyro. The first time it happened…"

"Man's a fuckin' idiot," Pyro snarls. "Forgetting once is one thing. A second time? Sheer fuckin' carelessness. If he likes it bare so much he should be prepared to deal with the consequences."

"He was drunk, Pyro. I didn't think to remind him."

"This is not on you, Mel."

I glare. "I think it is. I was the one in bed with him. I was fully into it when we made love." And Skull had gotten me so aroused and in such an orgasmic haze, I didn't know which way was up, and certainly not capable of realising he'd forgotten the condom. But I was a fully active participant, and to be truthful, had I realised, I might not have minded. My body clock is marching on, if I'm going to have a baby I want to be in my prime. I want to see my child grow while I can be active along with it.

My child.

Oh my freaking God. *I'm pregnant.*

Pyro's face has gone tight, then it relaxes. "When we find Skull, he might be over the moon. You've got enough on your plate without second guessing his reaction."

One thing is for certain. *However much I feel I need it, I can't have that drink now.*

He understands. And, as the tears start rolling down my cheek, looks around and takes some tissues from the box I keep handy, passing them to me.

Then, he hesitantly puts his arms around me, pulling me in close. I rest my chin on the leather cut which smells slightly different to that of my man. But, I take comfort from the warmth he's emitting and his strong arms, trying to ignore the little voice that reminds me they're not the right ones.

CHAPTER THIRTEEN

Pyro

Today started off as normal. I'd gone to the auto-shop and put some hours in, then, having left my fucking phone of all things back at the compound, took a break to go retrieve it. Got suckered into a game of pool with the VP—well, I manage the shop, who's going to criticise me?

That's why I'd been there when the day took a downturn with Mel's revelation that Skull was missing.

This was news that none of us like hearing. We've heard it too often before, only a year or so ago, Ingot, our old enforcer, had been run off the road and killed. My first thought, and still the favourite, although unthinkable, is that we'll find that's the answer to Skull's disappearance, he hasn't returned as he's not able to. This life we live is not without risk, either death dealt out by our enemies, or from the simple fact that we ride around on motorcycles. The fact that medical staff view us as potential organ donors on wheels isn't too much of an exaggeration.

I've also had to deal with the stress that comes with disarming potential explosive devices. Trying not to shake or cut the wrong wire, dealing with something designed not to be interfered with all carries a strain of its own. While a hundred percent concentration is required, at the back of my mind is always the question, *will I know? Will I feel my body disintegrating? Will it hurt? Or will I simply cease to exist?*

Now, I've got a pregnant weeping woman in my arms. Today seems never-ending.

But she's Skull's. I hadn't misled her. Whatever has happened to him, he claimed her, which makes her the responsibility of the club.

I wasn't particularly close to Skull. Would give my life for him as he was one of my brothers, but he hadn't sat around the table long enough for us to become friends. Nevertheless, something drives me to take personal responsibility for his woman.

Doesn't hurt she's exactly the type of woman who'd attract me.

But being Skull's, she's completely out of bounds.

My hand moves up and down her back, rubbing gently. Contradicting what's going through my mind, I repeat in what I hope is a soothing tone, "It will be okay. It will work out. You've got us, you're not alone."

Gradually her sobs start coming less often. She pulls away, sniffing loudly then blowing her nose. She stares at me, then looks horrified.

"Your tee shirt's wet, I'm so sorry."

"No matter." That's the least of my worries.

"I'll be okay. You don't have to stay."

I'm not surprised she's embarrassed. I'm a virtual stranger, I'm here in her home. Yet I was the one to confirm she is indeed pregnant, and now the man whose clothes have been dampened by her tears.

I'm also the man who's got one more blow to deliver.

"I do," I contradict, wiping my hand down my face. "I'm sorry, but I'm not leaving you alone."

Her reddened eyes crease. "What?"

"Until we know what's happened to Skull, we need to take precautions."

"What?" she repeats. "What do you mean, precautions?"

I breathe in deeply. "You know we're a one-percenter club?"

A little nod. "But I thought you weren't into shady stuff."

My mouth quirks at the way she describes it. "We're not, much, nowadays. In fact, we can't name an enemy who'd want to hurt us." Or not until Demon and Beef have their meeting with the Wretched Soulz. "But there's always the chance someone is using Skull to get to us, which means we pull up the drawbridge just in case."

Her head moves side to side. "I don't understand."

"Tonight, I stay here, sleeping on your couch. Tomorrow, you move to the compound."

Her head shakes more emphatically. "I can't. Not without Skull. This is my home. And how long for? I've got work..."

"Tomorrow you call in sick. Fuck, woman. You're in no condition to go to the office."

"I've already told Beth I can't go in tomorrow." Before I can ask, she adds hurriedly, "Not why, not until I know more. I've told her a lie for me, that I'm sick."

"You're worried sick about your man. That's not a lie. No one can blame you. I'd stay off until after the weekend. If you want to go back then, we'll make it happen if we're still on lockdown."

She's quiet for a moment, then, "You're right, Pyro. I'll not be able to concentrate. Hopefully Skull will be back between now and Monday, and if he's not?" She gives a little shake as if she's no idea what she'll do. If he doesn't reappear, she'll have to start to come to terms with a new normal. Fuck, I'm hurting for her now.

"But I'll stay here. I'm not coming to the compound." Her mouth sets in a stubborn line.

How do I make her see sense?

"Mel, look. Skull's missing. You're Skull's woman. May not have had much trouble in the recent past, but if someone does have him, if someone's starting a war with the club, then they'll hit us where it hurts. You know what our weakest spot is? You know what would fuckin' destroy us?"

Again her head moves first to the left, then to the right.

"Our women. Someone wants to hurt us, they'll go after our women first. And you, being close to Skull, would be one of the first targets. Can't leave you unprotected darlin'. Need you on lockdown at the compound."

"Lockdown?"

"We call everyone in and stay for the duration."

"I can't do that. I can't afford to lose my job. I can't let everyone down."

She's feisty, and loyal to Skull and her colleagues. Now all I've got to do is get some of that loyalty the club's way. "Already said, we'll make that happen. You'll just have an escort there and back, got it?"

Her lips press together. "You really think it's necessary for me to move to the compound?"

It seems she's starting to listen to what I'm saying. "I do. If you don't, then either I or a prospect will stay here with you. Look, it's easier if we have everyone under the same roof. The compound can be protected. If we have everyone scattered all around, it spreads us thin and makes it harder to keep everyone safe."

She stands while I move out of her way and she starts to pace the room. It's in the middle of her third back and forth that she stops. Her eyes come to my face. "Do you really think I'm in danger?"

"No," I say fast. "But we don't take risks. Not with something so important. Fact is, we don't know what the fuck's going on, but want to be prepared for anything. Don't want anything to blindside us."

"Sort of like taking out insurance. It's just in case."

"It's exactly that."

She takes a lungful of air, then comes, "Okay," on a long drawn out breath. "But you don't need to sleep on the couch. I've got a spare room."

"Couch is fine." Give me the comfort of a bed and I might fall fast asleep given the stress of the day. A restless night also means I'll have one eye open. Just in case.

As if realising she's got bigger battles ahead which she should save her energy for, she capitulates with a simple, "Goodnight." Then disappears into what I assume is her bedroom.

For a moment I stare down the hallway, my mind once again asking, *where the fuck are you, Skull?* I find it hard to believe he's walked out on a woman like her.

I already know I admire her body and love the food she bakes. While this evening's conversation hasn't been easy, I know now I also respect the way she thinks.

It makes me believe Skull didn't leave because he wanted to, but because he had no choice.

Which begs the question—if he was in trouble, why had he not come to the club?

He didn't just leave her in the dark, that's where he's left us as well.

Why, Skull? Why?

As predicted I have a sleepless night. I jerk awake when I hear footsteps coming back down from where Mel had disappeared to last night. She's wearing sleep shorts and a tee, perfectly respectable and well covered, but I can tell she's not wearing a bra under her clothes. I bite back my desire to cradle those sumptuous breasts with my hands, with a reminder she's not and will never be mine. Her reddened eyes and large yawn that she tries to hide betray she's also had an unsettled night. It comes as no surprise, she's worried about Skull, and her newly discovered condition as well. My personal desire is immediately quashed as a wave of compassion floods through me. *Skull, where the fuck are you? You're needed here.*

She's spoken, lost in my thoughts, it takes me a second to process what she's asked.

"Yeah, coffee would be great."

She looks a bit glum. "I suppose that's something I'll have to give up."

I don't have a clue about pregnancy. I shrug. "You can talk to Violet when you get to the compound. She'll probably know about shit like that. But if you're not having one for yourself, I can wait."

"I've got some muffins…"

I launch myself to my feet. "Ones you've made?" At her nod, I follow her into the kitchen, looking around urgently. "Where, babe?"

My eagerness pulls forth a small smile. Opening a cupboard, she pulls out a tub. Then her face falls. "I made these for Skull. It's the type he likes."

As her bottom lip quivers my hunger rapidly fades. "Oh, hon." I pull her into my arms. "It's going to be okay." I have no fucking idea how, but it's what she needs to hear.

"I'm glad you stayed," she says, quietly, making an effort to hold back her tears. "It was a comfort having you in the next room. I didn't feel quite so alone."

"I was only a call away, hon. Lean on me. While Skull's not here, lean on me."

Her breasts, separated only by the thin material of her tee, are pressed against my chest. My cock thinks it feels wonderful, so with one last hug I step away before there's any physical evidence that my interest in her is more than platonic. Yeah, I can admit that. But I'll never be acting on it. She's not for me, but I can be her friend.

Friends can get hard-ons, can't they?

We forego breakfast in the end. I bring in my empty saddlebags and she stuffs what she can into them. I turn away as I see her come out with an armful of lace, bras and presumably panties. My imagination doesn't need to be fuelled by images of what she wears under her clothes.

She's efficient and is quickly packed.

It's rare I ride with anyone behind me. When she gets on, my bike feels strange, and I take a moment to adjust to the extra weight.

"I'm sorry, I'm too heavy…"

"Stop the fuck right there, woman." I hate it when women disparage themselves. "I'm not used to a passenger, that's all. You've ridden with Skull, just do the same as you'd do with him."

"I put my hands around his waist," she says, hesitantly.

Reaching back, I take hold of her wrists and place her hands firmly around my middle. "Now hang on," I tell her bluntly, pressing start and selecting first gear.

Then, aware of the precious cargo she's carrying, point the bike toward the compound and ride carefully through the streets of Pueblo.

When we arrive at the clubhouse, I place my hand on her arm, making her turn and look up at me questioningly.

"Speak to Vi," I urge. "I know women like to keep shit about being pregnant quiet at the start, so I won't be telling anyone else, except for Prez and VP as they already suspect. But you need support, Mel. Vi's straight, and she'll know what you're going through. Let her help."

She's thoughtful for a moment, then nods. "You're right. I wasn't going to tell anyone. But I don't have a clue about doctors, making appointments, and what I should or shouldn't be doing. It's a good idea to speak to someone who knows." She breaks off and covers the hand which is still on her arm with her own. "Thank you, Pyro. For everything. I'm glad I didn't find out alone."

"You're not alone," I remind her.

But the look she gives me back tells me the one man she wants is still missing.

I enter the clubhouse carrying the saddlebags full of her clothes having told her I'll dump them in Skull's room, where she can sort them out later. I'm heading toward the stairs when a voice bellows out.

"Ro!"

"Prez? Can it wait a moment? Just dropping Mel's shit off in Skull's..."

"That's what I wanted to talk to you about. Can you come in here a moment?"

I change direction and follow him into his office.

He's standing behind his desk, pinching the bridge of his nose. "We got a problem. Well, same one as always. Lack of space."

Okay. I shrug. That's not news.

"Hellfire."

"But he can... oh."

"Yeah."

Hellfire had given up his suite so Demon and Vi had a bigger space. Of course, most of the time they live off compound in Vi's old family home which Demon had purchased as a surprise for her when she thought she had to sell it. But being on lockdown, means her, Demon and their son, Theo, will be staying here now.

"Beef's moved into my old room."

"So where are you putting Hell and Mo?"

He shrugs. "Skull's is the only room available."

Fuck. There's no space for Mel. "Mel needs to be here, Prez. She took a test. Wants it kept quiet, but, yeah, she's expecting. Being Skull's she could have a huge fuckin' target on her back. If she's not here, she'll need brothers protecting her at her..."

His hands slam down on the desk. "I'm all too fuckin' aware she needs to be here, Ro. But things had to be decided fast last night. I had Mo swearing up a storm at having to come in on lockdown, what was I to say? That there wasn't a fuckin' room? Only solution I could come up with fast."

As the ex-prez, if there's anyone out for the club, Hellfire would be in the direct line of fire. No way he or his wife could stay home.

I shake my head, closing my eyes briefly. "Prospects?"

"Already sleeping two to a room. You know this, Ro."

Mel needs somewhere to sleep. The only way she's going to

get one is for someone to give up their room. I can't see anyone offering, Skull being so new, it's not just me he's not particularly close to.

I sigh. "She can have mine."

"And you'll, what? Sleep on the couch? No, Ro, can't ask you to do that."

"Don't think you asked, Prez. I offered." I roll back my head, trying to get the kinks out from last night when I slept, or tried to, on Mel's sofa. Now I'm committing myself to having uncomfortable nights for fuck knows how long.

Sleeping arrangements decided, I move this along. "Any news, Prez?"

"Not one darn thing. Don't even know where Skull went during that month. No one fucking knows."

"Judge? Wills?" They prospected alongside him.

"Nope and fuckin' no. I've pressed them, but they don't know any more than the rest of us. That's the bare facts. He was injured, hurting. Left without a word, and returned just as quietly. Pal was the first to speak to him, but he just welcomed him home. No one thought to ask him where he'd been. Didn't seem important at the fuckin' time."

I knew Demon would have called if there'd been news, so that there wasn't, isn't surprising.

I just wish we knew what we were dealing with. As I'd told Mel, without information, all we could do is prepare for anything.

CHAPTER FOURTEEN

Melissa

"Melissa. Oh, Mel. Come here."

Violet holds out her arms. I step into them, then quickly pull back, rubbing at my eyes, still sore from last night. I hold up my hands. "Don't make me cry again, Vi," I warn. "I take it they're no closer to knowing where Skull is?"

I would have heard, I'm sure. The small shake of her head is just confirmation that my man's still in the wind. Jeannie's paused in her task of chopping up vegetables presumably in preparation for dinner tonight. Mo, who I'd met briefly at the barbeque a few weeks back is working alongside her, banging utensils in a way that shows she's unhappy.

"It's not her fault, Mo," Jeannie hisses.

But Demon's mother doesn't turn or even look in my direction. I know she rarely comes to the compound, so is likely to think even less of being on lockdown than I do. I feel like apologising, but Jeannie's right, it's not down to me, although it is my man who's the cause of the disruption.

"Can I speak to you, Vi?"

She sends a glare toward her mother-in-law's back, then smiles toward me. "Outside?"

That will do.

I follow her out to a picnic table on the lawn Beef had prepared for Steph. When I'd first seen it, this yard looked like a bombsite with rubbish strewn everywhere. Full of hazards for a woman who couldn't see anything. Even though she'd been missing at the time, Beef had planted a garden just for her, everything flattened and perfumed flowers all over. It's now a beautiful space we all enjoy.

Vi barely lets me get my butt on the seat before she starts, "I apologise for Mo, Melissa. It's just a shock to her that lockdown has been imposed so quickly. She's got reasons not to like coming to the club. She'll come around, but right now she's looking for someone to take out her irritation on."

It wasn't what I'd wanted to talk to her about, but now it's out in the open, I'm happy to discuss it. "I wish it wasn't happening myself. I hate that I'm here and Skull's not. Hate that I don't know where he is or what's going on with him." I break off and swallow back down that threatening sob.

"Melissa…"

"But that wasn't what I wanted to talk to you about. Vi, I need your advice. Can you keep a secret?"

She straightens her back and grins. "I'm the prez's old lady."

I nod. "I'm pregnant. Only just. I found out yesterday."

She frowns. "Did Skull know?"

"No. He knew it was a slight possibility, but we'd only been careless a couple of times. Got away with it the first time, thought this would be the same."

She digests that. "What can I do to help? You say it wasn't planned. Do you intend on keeping it?"

"Yes," I say firmly. There isn't one doubt in my mind. "But I don't know anything, like whether I can drink coffee, what I should be doing, what vitamins I should be taking…"

"Whoa, hold up. I can certainly help. You know my story? I didn't have the best pregnancy."

I recall hearing she'd been raped. Theo isn't Demon's son, but he couldn't act more like a father to him.

"Thing is, Mel, we can't always control how or when we get pregnant, but we have to deal with it when it happens. I know you must be missing Skull terribly, but the men and old ladies in the club will step up and help. One thing to remember, you're not on your own."

"That's what Pyro told me. But I can't understand it. Skull was a member, not me."

"While Skull's gone, everyone will step into his shoes to help you. Whatever he'd have done, they'll do for you. You got a doctor's appointment? Someone will be there with you."

But they won't hold me in the night, they won't love on me. And, if Skull, *heaven forbid*, doesn't return, won't be there to be a father to my baby.

"I feel so disorientated, Vi. One moment I thought I was in a relationship with the man I loved. Next it appears he's walked out on me, and now I'm having his child. A child he may never know." I sob out the last word, then fight to regain control of myself.

She frowns. "Let's break this down. First, you don't know what happened. You don't know that he left you. Second, yes, you're pregnant and you want this baby."

"With everything that I am. Might not be good timing, but yes, I want my son or daughter."

She raises her eyebrow. "Even as a single mom?"

Again, I'm positive. "Yes. Vi, you say I've got the club behind me. I've also got parents. If I'm struggling, I know they'd help."

"They in Pueblo?"

"Denver."

"You thinking of going to them?"

Am I? I examine my feelings. Right now, my explanation would indicate I'm a failure, that my man left me pregnant and alone. I'd rather go to them when I can give them some firm information. Like why Skull left, where he's gone, and whether he can, or intends to, return home.

"Not until I know what's happened," I sum up. "I, er, I don't know what to tell them."

Leaning over the table, she pats my arm. "In the meantime, you'll have us. Want me to set up an appointment with my OB/GYN?"

"Is it too early?"

"What are you, four or five weeks?"

"Thereabouts."

She thinks for a moment. "I'll make it for a week or so's time. In the meantime, I can talk you through the basics. No, or very limited, caffeine."

This is going to be a very long nine months. No, not nine, I realise. One has already passed.

"Stress isn't good for the baby, Melissa. I know it's hard but try to think positively. The club is doing everything possible to find your man and get him back where he belongs. There's nothing you can do that they can't. Please, try not to worry."

Good advice, but probably impossible to follow. Not worry about my man? How on earth could I do that?

"You coming back inside? I'll tell Mo her grandma cuddles with Theo will be restricted if she's not nice to you."

I laugh, as I'm meant to.

"You know," she adds, shrewdly, "it's early and people don't normally announce it so soon, but in the circumstances, as you don't have your man to share it with, if I were you, I'd let people know you're expecting. That way, if you start getting irritable, everyone will understand."

I really hope I don't start acting like a prima donna, but who knows what pregnancy hormones will do to me? I'm in uncharted waters from now on.

"And," she continues, "Mo adores babies. If she knows there'll be another on the compound, she'll be over the moon, and might just overlook the reason why she has to be here."

Vi might have a point.

Saying she'll give me some space, she gets up and leaves. My natural impulse is to keep my news to myself, but she's right. I don't have a man to share my excitement and fears with. Perhaps this is a different situation. I could tell my mom, but a long-distance phone call isn't a satisfactory way of doing that, and would leave me open to questions I don't have answers for, like is Skull excited about the news? Coming clean, at least to the club who've apparently adopted me as one of their own, might just make things a little easier.

And, if the worse happens and I lose the baby, which isn't unheard of in the early weeks, I will need support.

"You okay, Mel?"

I glance up at Pyro's deep voice and watch as he takes the place so recently vacated by his prez's wife. "You were right."

"Yeah?" He waggles his eyebrows. "Usually am, darlin'."

I curb the impulse to swat him. "About coming to the club. It's better than being alone with my thoughts."

His chin dips then rises. "That's why I love this life. If I'm angry, I can rant to my brothers. Spar with them to lose the physical rage. Unhappy? There'll be someone with a shoulder to cry on, metaphorically speaking," he adds fast. "I'm a man after all."

Another small smile curves my lips. If I was alone at home, I'd be weeping and bemoaning my fate. While here, Vi's being practical, and Pyro's doing his best to make me laugh.

I can't help getting my own dig in. "And if you're horny, there are the sweet butts."

His eyes widen. "You did not just say that Mel."

Oh, I think I did.

His face is blank for a moment, then he laughs loudly. When he stops, he grows serious again. "Want to go get your bags unpacked and settled?" Without waiting for my answer, he stands and holds out his hand to help me up. Then, when I'm on my feet, abruptly let's go. "Come on, then."

It seems he intends to escort me.

"It's okay, I know where I'm going."

"Er, about that, Mel. You're not staying in Skull's room. As everyone has had to come to the compound, we've been moving people around."

"Oh?" I'd like to protest. I like the thought of staying in my man's bed, even if he's not in it with me. But if he hadn't disappeared, neither I, nor the club, would be in this mess. So I settle for, "Where will I be staying then?"

"In my room," he says, adding fast before I can object, "but not *with* me. I'll be elsewhere."

I glance up at the man so much taller than Skull. He wasn't kidding about people being moved around. It seems lockdown is putting him out, and under the circumstances I can't complain.

The only room I know is Skull's. I've no idea where Pyro's is, so I let him lead me up the industrial metal staircase, taking in the doors along the corridor off to the right and the left. Something looks different. I stop when I see what it is. All the door handles are now upside down.

"Er," I speak, my voice making him stop. "Is this some new club fetish? A charm against evil spirits, perhaps?" It reminds me of stuff I've read about the Winchester House where it was built deliberately to confuse.

"What?" Then he notices where I'm pointing, and again, laughs. "Nah, that's to stop Bitch getting into the rooms. Darn cat can swing on the handles to open them."

I know that. Skull had always locked his door to keep her out. Once when he'd forgotten, he'd asked me to lift her up and carry her out.

"Yeah," Pyro continues with his explanation, "our new VP got them turned around as one of his first jobs."

I spare a longing, lingering glance at Skull's door, as we pass. Pyro notices, for a second his hand squeezes my shoulder. Then, two doors down, he opens another. He's right that the handles have only been changed recently, it seems to take him a moment to work out how the mechanism now works.

"Fuck." He swears as he opens the door. "Sorry, Mel. Give me a sec." He rushes in, picking up bundles of clothes from the floor and moving, well, I don't know what it is, but it looks like part of an engine.

I notice his saddlebags containing my stuff have been placed on his bed. I step toward them.

"Prospect brought them up. I'd have tidied if I'd remembered, well..." his voice trails off. I don't need the explanation he's an untidy man.

But it doesn't take long for him to make the room cleaner, most of the clothes go into a linen basket. He opens the closet and nods. "There's some space to hang your clothes, just push mine aside." Then he moves to the drawers and starts emptying one. "Will this do, for now?"

"Yes, I just need somewhere to put my underwear."

He tenses slightly as men sometimes do when a woman's unmentionables are brought into the conversation.

"The bathroom's through there." I nod. Same layout as Skull's room, perhaps a little larger. The bed, itself, is massive, but then Pyro is a big man.

"Right." He's stopped busying himself. "Okay then. I'll leave you to get settled."

All of a sudden, I don't want him to go. "What happens now, Pyro?"

His hand rakes through his hair. "Jeez, Mel, I wish I could tell you otherwise, but all we can do is wait. Cad and the others are still working their magic. Hopefully they'll turn something up, or not. Once they've searched everywhere, if they don't find him, it's a good sign. Might mean he's holed up with a friend."

"Or someone's holding him." *Or there's a body to find that hasn't been discovered yet.* But I don't voice that fear aloud.

Pyro slowly nods. "If they are, I'll put money on it that it wouldn't be long before they make contact. I mean, without someone stepping up and taking responsibility, it sends no message and makes no sense."

CHAPTER FIFTEEN

Pyro

"It makes no fuckin' sense," I slam my hand down on the table. Sure, I'm feeling irritable. Five nights sleeping on the all too small couch in the clubroom will do that to a man. Now the brothers attending our normal Wednesday church are bearing the brunt of it. "He's been gone over a week, and we've found no fuckin' trace. Neither he, nor anyone else has made contact."

"Hate to say it, but the obvious answer is he's gone dirty side up and is lying in the bottom of a ravine somewhere," Lizard comments, the corners of his mouth turned down.

"Our search parties have found nothing. Skull is a good rider," Thunder observes.

"Could have been oil on the road, an animal run out. Accidents happen, Brother," Mace counters.

"Or it could have been fuckin' deliberate," offers Buzzard.

"That doesn't make sense either." Prez wipes a hand over his tired face. "Someone wants a Devil dead, they'd step up and take responsibility."

Wasn't that what I just said? Truth is, we're going around and around in circles, making no headway at all. I've been out enough times trying to find signs of an incident anywhere an unreported accident might have happened. A damaged guard rail, debris on the road. Anything I've found I've stopped and investigated. Trouble is, there are miles and miles of road where Skull could have upended his bike, we don't know which direction he was headed. There's always the possibility that however eagle-eyed we try to be, we might miss something. At the end of the day there's an empty seat around the table that should be filled. That I find unacceptable.

"It's fuckin' worrying he hasn't used his credit or debit cards at all. Would he have had much cash on him?"

Trust our treasurer to think of the money trail.

"Who the fuck knows?" Thunder leans back and folds his arms. "If he's staying with a friend, maybe he isn't paying for anything."

"Before anyone asks, his phone's not come back to life," Cad puts in.

"How's Melissa coping?" the VP asks, his brow furrowed as he too tries to work through the conundrum of Skull's continued absence.

"She's being brave," I tell him. "I think the fact she's pregnant is helping her through. She's trying to be strong and doing the right things for the baby. She's got an appointment with Vi's OB/GYN arranged." Mel had decided to tell everyone she was pregnant, Vi's advice apparently. It had been good advice too. Everyone would have supported her as I'd already told her, but knowing she was carrying a Devil inside had somehow made all the brothers more protective than they would otherwise have been.

Demon's nodding. "Good. It gives her something to focus on. I've asked Violet to get her involved with Theo, talk about baby shit. Anything to keep her mind off where Skull could be."

"How long are we going to be on lockdown, Prez?" I glance at the person who asked the question. I swear Hellfire gets a glint in his eye when he refers to his son with that title. As if he's pleased he's no longer got the responsibility of sitting at the head of the table, and proud he raised a son good enough to be voted in in his place.

Demon glares, a hidden message of 'ask me something easy, will ya?' then rubs at his beard. "How's everyone managing?" He sees the look on my face, then grimaces.

"Mo's complaining. Wants to get back to her yard. Reckons she's got plants needing watering." Hellfire raises his hands in a *what can you do* gesture when the mention of flowers brings snorts.

"Well send a fuckin' prospect to do it," Prez snarls. Followed up with, "It poured down yesterday, how much water do fuckin' plants need?"

Hellfire shrugs.

"Sindy's fine. Long as she gets out to do her job, she's happy enough." Buzzard's wife is a receptionist at our auto-shop. Prospects are on a rotation taking the old ladies to work. Mel started back a couple of days ago, but I've been following her myself.

"So, apart from Mo, no one's going stir crazy?"

"Not as yet, Prez. But it will come."

Demon acknowledges Mace. Then thinks for a moment. "To sum up, Skull's still missing. Wretched Soulz had nothing, as you know, and the Silvestris are having enough internal problems without trying to start a war with us. If anyone has got Skull and is enjoying making us sweat, they may be holding on before issuing their demand or threat. I appreciate everyone's cooperation, no one likes being cooped up. And agree, this can't go on forever. At some point, we'll let people go home."

"Can you firm up on a date? It might make Mo happy to know there's an end in sight."

Demon gives a slow nod. "We'll reassess at next week's church. If nothing happens by then, we can only assume Skull's dead, or decided to fuckin' walk out on the club without turning in his patch."

"You going to strip him of his membership?" Beef asks.

As growls go around the table, Prez bangs his fist. "If we find him breathing, got to be done, Brothers. We get patched in because of our loyalty to the club and the trust we've earned. Skull left with no word. This time next week he'll have been gone almost three weeks. He won't deserve his patch unless he's got a good fuckin' excuse."

"If he's not breathing?" I ask.

"Then he's still a member, even dead." This time there are murmurs of agreement.

"If he is in the land of the living, or dead by someone else's hands, Prez, we got another problem. We've a cut in the wind."

"Like that about as much as you, Beef. But until the man turns up, got to assume it's lost."

No club likes losing one of their cuts. It's not unknown for someone to impersonate a member of a different club to get them into trouble. As glances are exchanged no words need to be said, but one more possible reason for Skull going missing has to be acknowledged. Someone didn't want *him* but wanted our colours instead.

"Time will tell," Demon says, pragmatically. "All we can do is record its loss. If it ever turns up with the wrong man attached to it, he'll fuckin' wish he'd never been born."

Amen to that.

I remain seated as the others move on out.

Demon starts to move past, and then stops. "You okay, Ro? Apart from having to sleep in the clubroom?"

At the reminder my hand goes up to the back of my neck and I rub it. "I'm just wondering how the fuck I can tell Mel we're giving up."

"Not giving up, Ro."

"Seems like next week we will be. If we call lockdown off, to her it will appear we're assuming Skull's dead."

"You think he's not?"

I shake my head. Can't deny that I do, though of course, I'm keeping that from Mel. "I just expected a body to turn up, you know? Have a funeral, bury him with club honours. Give her and us closure."

Demon's finger and thumb find the brow of his nose. "Melissa's been pretty tied up with all this pregnancy stuff. Worrying whether she was, then, wondering how she'll cope. I reckon early pregnancy under normal circumstances is stressful enough."

"What's on your mind, Prez?" My senses sharpen. Something definitely is.

"I'm wondering whether she's got info she hasn't shared."

I scoff, "You think she's holding out on us? She's not. I can assure you of that. Girl's fuckin' distraught."

"Sometimes people know more than they think they do. Things which seemed insignificant at the time, can add up."

As I stare at him, I realise he may well have a point. "Want to talk to her now?"

"No time like the present, as they say."

Mel's out in the clubroom, she's actually chatting to Mo. That's one person whose attitude toward Skull's woman did a complete turnaround once she knew she had a child on the way. I interrupt, having to say quickly there's no news when her eyes light up briefly, and then ask that she come with me to see Prez.

"Need to pick your brains, Melissa," Prez starts after she sits down opposite him. I stand against the wall behind her. "Sometimes people let things slip when they don't mean to, and we've been wondering if that applies to Skull."

"I've told you everything I know." She looks mystified.

The door opens, I move out of the way.

"Yeah, come in Beef. Thought it would be useful to have the VP in on this. You mind?"

Mel shakes her head. "I just don't know how I can help you. I've told you everything that happened. If I'd have thought of anything else, I'd have let you, or at least Pyro, know."

Beef raises his chin toward Demon and gets a jerk of the prez's head back. He takes a breath. "Something's been playing at the back of my mind like an itch I couldn't scratch. Wasn't able to grab hold of it until Prez mentioned he was going to speak to you just now. Something that Steph said months back. That day when we'd returned from the cabin."

Mel looks confused. As do I. I fold my arms and wait for the VP to elaborate.

"I was going to have 'the chat' with her," he uses air quotes, "about the club. Turned out most of the things I was telling her, she already knew."

None of us are up to speed yet.

"I'd left her with you, Mel, VI, Jeannie, and I think Jay was there too. I asked her outright whether she'd asked about the club, and her reply was no, that was you." Beef pauses and sends an apologetic look toward Demon. "This may be nothing at all, and I'm not accusing you of anything Mel, but it's been bugging me as to why you would have to have asked. Skull must have surely had 'the talk' with you? You'd been together a while by then. I know he wanted you to get comfortable with the club before he claimed you, and us with you. In that case I would have thought he'd have explained what to expect before you set foot on the compound."

"He did." Mel frowns, then puts her hand to her head and rubs at her temple.

Beef opens his mouth, but she holds her palm toward him. "Wait a moment." We give her that minute, then another. Finally, she opens her mouth. "He'd asked me to ask about the club. I'd forgotten about that. Yes, you're right. He'd told me all the stuff about the cut, what it meant, the brotherhood, but... he kept asking what Violet knew."

We look at each other, then back at her. She's shaking her head. "The day before he left, he'd asked me what I'd been talking to Violet about. I told him Theo's new tooth. It wasn't the right answer. Oh, he wasn't angry, he was disappointed. I don't know what he meant. He never told me exactly what to ask, or what he wanted me to find out."

"Did it strike you as odd?" Demon asks in a deceptively quiet tone.

"No. I was more confused."

Her head is bowed, and her eyes are half closed.

"Mel?" Beef asks, like me, wondering if perhaps she's become overwhelmed.

But when she looks up, she gives a quick shake of her head and her eyes contain a spark. "You're right! There's something else. Something I hadn't thought particularly odd at the time, but now you're asking... That night when he walked out of the room and I said it looked like he was going to make a call... I was more shocked that he'd got dressed and I couldn't understand what he was doing."

Demon's already shaking his head. "There was no call. Cad's already found that out."

Mel ignores him and carries on, "He had a phone, but not *his* phone. Not the one he normally used. He fumbled in the back of a drawer and brought it out. I'm sorry, I didn't even register it at the time. I was too shocked at his reaction. Didn't think it was important. It's only when you asked if he'd said or done anything strange."

My jaw drops. He could still have indeed made a call, but from a burner that we didn't know about. The questions are, why, and who to?

Demon stands so fast his chair falls over. "Come." He's looking directly at Mel, but she's not the only one to follow him out of the room. Both Beef and I are hot on his heels as he clangs up the metal stairway and along the hall, pausing only to rap hard against the door before slinging it open. Then closes it fast.

"I did not need to see that," he snarls, then raps the door again. "Get your fuckin' clothes on fast. I need to come in."

The door opens again and Hell's standing there wearing jeans with the button undone and a smirk.

"You've fuckin' scarred me for life, old man," Demon rasps, while behind him, Beef and I are trying our best not to laugh.

I do have some sympathy. Who wants to walk in on their mom and dad having sex?

"Where's Mo?"

"In the bathroom," Hell responds. "What's so fuckin' urgent you stopped me, well…"

"Fuckin' traumatising me."

Yeah, but as he supplied the word fucking, Beef and I lose our battle and crack up.

Hell ignores us. "What do you want?"

In turn, Demon ignores Hell, turning instead to Mel. "Which drawer?"

Stepping gingerly into the room, Mel points it out. Beef goes across, yanks it out, and feels behind it, then shouts in triumph. I go across and look. It would be too much to hope that we'd find the phone, but what we do discover is that the drawer has a fake bottom. All manner of stuff could be hidden in there.

I turn to Mel, but she's looking as confused as us.

Skull, it would appear, has secrets.

Demon glances at Mel then jerks his head toward me. Taking the hint, I take her hand and encourage her out of the room.

"What does it mean, Pyro?"

Opening the door to her… *my* room, I can only shake my head. "I have no fuckin' idea, and that's the honest truth."

"He had a secret drawer where he kept a phone hidden." She proves her eyes work as well as mine. "He wanted to find out information about the club by using me. What on earth could I find out that he didn't already know?"

I suspect the prez and VP are having a very similar discussion now, but I can't leave Mel. She's too worked up.

I have a few ideas of my own. "You know how Skull got patched in?"

"He prospected for eleven months, then got voted in."

I nod. "That's true, but not quite all of it." I point to my own bed, and she nods her permission for me to sit. "Have you spoken much to Jay? About what happened when she first came here?"

"She gave me a summary. Said she was kidnapped by one of the members who's gone now."

"Yeah." I rub my beard. "Someone was causing trouble for the club. Tried to get people arrested for shit they hadn't done. That person caused a drive-by shooting and all signs all pointed to Runt as we called Skull at the time. Changing his name was one of the bargains he made."

"I knew he'd had the name Runt," she corrects. "But what are these bargains? And why did he make them?"

I ignore her question. It will be answered in time. "We thought he was the one responsible. Went after him pretty hard. Hurt him, bad. He wasn't saying anything. We thought he was planning worse. Turned out the culprit was, plans were already in progress to take Jayden, but as Runt didn't know, he couldn't warn us." I glance at her; she rightly looks horrified. "It was fuckin' serious, Mel. Jayden could have died. We knew an asshole was fuckin' with us and it had to stop. Turned out Runt had been set up. He wasn't telling us anything as he didn't have anything to tell. We were so fuckin' sorry when we found out. Made a man hurt when he was innocent."

"What did he do? How could he ever trust you again?"

She's gotten straight to the heart of it. "He left the club. I agree with you, we thought that was the last we'd seen of him. How could he come back when he'd suffered through that?"

Her eyes crease. "But he did return?"

"Yeah, he returned darlin'." At the time I'd respected him for it.

Her head shakes. "Why?"

"Couple of reasons he said. He knew he'd been set up by an expert. He was away for a month licking his wounds, when he came back he said he understood what we had done. Had had time to cool down and a chance to clear his head. He missed the camaraderie and wanted it, knew what we'd done was to keep the club safe, a club he'd worked hard to be part of. We agreed to patch him straight in, named him Skull as he has a hard head, and that, we thought, was the end of it."

She stares at me but doesn't ask more. I leave her to come to her own conclusions, which she does. "You think he's waited all this time for some sort of revenge? No, Pyro. That is not the man I know. Not the man who's the father of my baby. You're crazy if you think that."

"Mel, I haven't told you anymore than everyone here knows. Skull's been a good brother since he was patched in, we all trust him. But he does have reasons to hate the club. Now you're saying he tried to use you to get info and it turns out he may have had a burner which he could have used shortly before he disappeared into the blue. Two and two sometimes does add up to five."

"Or doesn't add up to anything at all. Pyro, he wasn't using me. He loved me. I'm certain that was true. He couldn't fake that. If he was going to leave, why didn't he take me too? Why leave me here?"

"What if he had been going to hurt the club, but couldn't do it in the end?" I'm thinking aloud. "Maybe his leaving was him cancelling his plans, not commencing them."

"But what about me?" she wails. "Where do I fit in? Tell me that, Pyro. What about me?"

CHAPTER SIXTEEN

Melissa

"What about me?" I scream at Pyro.

I'm so angry at the man who I thought was my friend. Perhaps Skull would have told me what happened in time, perhaps I'd have heard…

"That's it!" I exclaim. "Skull was worried one of the women would let drop something about what happened to him, and he was worried it would turn me against the club."

"No, I don't think it's that." Pyro shakes his head sadly. "You said he encouraged you to speak to the women and find out about us. If he was worried, he'd have kept you away, not pushed you in.

I suppose that's true. Anger wells up again. Pyro admits they hurt him, and badly enough he went away for a month. But Skull looking for revenge? That doesn't work. "Skull loves the club, Pyro. He joined for the family he doesn't have and loves all of you." He sold it to me enough in those terms and haven't I seen that for myself? Demonstrated by how everyone's rallied around to make sure I'm alright, and just because, in their eyes, I belong to their lost man.

"What do you expect him to do? Hurt you? Hurt one of the women? Theo? That's not the man I know." Skull might retaliate if he was directly attacked or would step in to save somebody else. I'm certain Skull wouldn't want a dish served cold, which revenge in this case would be. Skull is not a man who'd let ill done to him fester.

Pyro's holding out his hands palms up, as if confirming he hasn't really thought this through.

"You really think he's hung around biding his time to get his own back on you. And he does this how, by disappearing?"

"Mel, I don't have the answers. All I know is that it's raised more questions. You're right. I could more easily believe it if it wasn't for you. You're an amazing woman, Mel. No," he looks cross, "don't dismiss yourself like that. You are, beautiful too. So, Skull lands himself a real winner. Why would he leave *you*? That makes no sense."

A real winner? Amazing. Beautiful? Pyro needs his eyes tested. I shelve that for now. "Because he was worried I was pregnant."

"Nah," he shakes his head. "Even that doesn't ring true. First, he didn't actually know, and second, Skull was, *is*, a good man. I can't believe he'd walk away from his responsibilities. Okay, so there may be some of us who don't like the idea of being tied down with kids, but if it's no longer theoretical, most men change their minds and step up to being a dad. I think that would have been Skull."

I give a small nod. I think that would have been Skull too.

"And you're also right. Skull's not the type to wait for revenge. We were surprised he came back to the club, suspicious of his motives for a while. But to wait this long? To claim an ol' lady, and then fuck off? Doesn't make sense. And don't you fuckin' doubt it, Mel, that man loved you. X-rated demonstrations in the clubhouse proved that."

He winks. They were not X-rated, but perhaps PG.

Skull loved, *loves*, me. Even his brothers could see it. *So why has he gone and left me in the lurch?*

Pyro stands. He walks to the door and drops his forehead

against the wood. "What do we know, Mel? Let's talk it through."

"Skull could have called someone on a phone no one knew he had." Unless my memory is at fault, and he hadn't walked out with a phone at all. *Could it have been something else?* I shake my head, doubting my eyesight now. "Then he came back and acted quite normally for almost two weeks. He left that morning, saying he'd be gone only a couple of days."

"He gave you every indication he'd be returning?"

Now I go through the conversation in my head. "He was definite. Maybe not so much about the timing, but he said it was only one night that he'd be away."

"So, if we take it at face value, Skull had every intention to come back. We're left working on the premise that something or somebody stopped him."

"He didn't tell anyone in the club he was leaving at all."

Pyro continues thinking aloud. "Perhaps he didn't think he had to. He went on a Sunday, intended to be back the next day. The security work was slow, Pal didn't expect him to turn up. Members are trusted to put their hours in, so there was no reason for Pal to think anything other than he'd been working at the auto-shop instead. Likewise, there was no need for Pal to tell me to expect him, so I didn't have cause to miss him when he didn't turn up."

"I don't come to the club during the week when I'm working, so you wouldn't have found out that way."

"You speak to the women. When he'd returned, you could have dropped in conversation he'd been away. We'd have eventually found out."

"So, he'd have had an excuse ready, and it would have to be something the club would accept."

"That's easy, darlin'. He could have said you and he had had words, and he'd taken off to clear his head. But really, he'd have needed no explanation if he'd been back the next day. Brothers don't need permission to do their own personal shit, not unless it impacts the club."

Maybe that is what happened. I frown. "We had had an argument, but it had been a while back. I'm sure that wasn't the reason he left. We'd cleared the air, he'd apologised, and there was nothing in his behaviour leading up to him leaving that would have suggested he was still brooding."

"Us men are funny creatures, Mel. Sometimes we just get the urge to go riding."

"Would you have done it that way, Pyro? Walked out on a woman having told her a lie?"

"We're not talking about me. But, no. I don't think so. Though I don't have an ol' lady, so I can't really say what I'd do. Skull may have wanted to avoid more discussion. If he'd said he needed to feel the wind in his hair, what would you have said?"

I think for a moment. No, I wouldn't have agreed without discussion, not if I'd thought he was brooding about whether or not I was pregnant. "If it was just a ride then I'd have understood, but if he wanted to work out how he felt, I would have tried to persuade him to stay so we could talk through our problems together."

"I think that's enough said. That could have been his reason for telling you it was club business." He turns so he's now facing me. "He might have used the phone to call someone who calmed him down that night. He came back after the call, didn't he? Made it up to you? But maybe in his mind it had festered... Maybe he went to the person he'd called to talk it through. Who knows? But I agree, he had every intention of returning, but didn't, or, he couldn't."

"We're no further forward, are we?" I wipe an errant tear from my eye.

He notices. "Oh darlin'. Don't upset yourself."

I wave him off, not wanting my sorrow to cause this conversation to stop.

He must realise I'm strong enough to continue. "There's just that nagging doubt of why he felt the need to hide shit."

I rest my head in my hands, trying to work it through. "Skull loved the club, loved the life. I've no doubt of that. Whatever you did to him, he'd gotten over it, I'm certain. If he felt the need for secrecy, maybe it's something in his past?"

"If he went to stay with a friend, he could have called them from his club phone." Pyro seems like a dog with a bone. "Why didn't he?"

"Perhaps he, or she," I grimace, "is someone the club wouldn't approve of." Once again wheels turn in my head. "Skull goes to them injured after he was beaten up for something he hadn't done. If they're a good friend, they might not have liked him going back to the club. Maybe he wants to keep that side of his life completely separate."

"Maybe, could be, might." Pyro's head moves side to side, and his jaw tightens. "Too many questions, not enough answers."

What he means is, we're no closer to finding my man.

"I want to know, Pyro," my voice breaks, "if he's dead, I want to know."

"Oh sweetheart." He sees another tear fall and comes over, his strong arms wrapping around me. "Hang on to the hope he's still breathing. You may think you could accept the worst, but if it comes, it will be bad. While we don't know, you can be optimistic, which you need to be right now. Don't give up, not yet. You owe it to you and the baby."

Another tightening of his arms, then he pulls back. "I've got to go see Prez. You going to be okay, or do you want me to find Violet and send her to you?"

My emotions are swinging from one extreme to the other. Probably hormones have something to do with it, but also the situation I'm in. One moment I'm angry at Skull for leaving me, the next grieving his absence. Talking with Pyro has helped, but I feel totally wrung out now.

"I don't want to keep talking about it. I'll be fine on my own. If I need company, I'm a big girl." My mouth twists at my unintended double meaning. "I can go find it." That's one thing about lockdown, there's usually someone around.

Leaning forward, he places a chaste kiss to my forehead, then stands and leaves.

I stare at the door after he closes it. They think there's a possibility Skull might be some kind of traitor, but I know he'd never betray them. That is not the lover I allowed into my bed, and certainly not the man who's captured my heart, or the one who's currently breaking it.

Thursday passes like any other day. I pull myself together, am escorted today by the prospect, Beaver, to work, then, after a tedious day conducting land searches, I'm followed by a different bike on the return journey.

It might be psychological, but already pregnancy seems to be making me tired, and I yawn my way through the dinner Jeannie has prepared.

"It gets you like that," Violet observes. "Tired all the time."

"Even this early?"

"One of the earliest symptoms, yes."

"Second trimester is normally better," Mo puts in. "You get a second wind. I think it's nature's way of giving you energy to get your nest ready."

"And in the third, you're so big you can't do anything," Vi laughs. "Oh, I've spoken to Lizard. He's happy if I take the morning off for your appointment."

I, too, have already booked time off work, but she really doesn't have to. "You don't need to come with me, Violet."

Her look tells me she'll have no argument on this. If I'm honest, I'll appreciate the company. Let's face it, I've not been pregnant before, and I don't know how any of this works. Having her with me when I have my first check-up with the doctor could be good.

"Hey, I found this. You might like to read it. I found it was good and helped me know what to do and what to expect."

This turns out to be a large illustrated book about pregnancy and childbirth. My eyes light up. I'd certainly like to read it. When she passes it over, I start to flick through the pages. Stopping at one, my eyes open in horror.

"Oh, God, no."

Jeannie, who's come up behind me, leans over, takes a look, and snorts. "Your poor pussy," she comments.

"I do not stretch that way." I complain.

"You will," both Vi and Mo speak at the same time. They're laughing. I glare. They've both experienced birth and know what to expect. I've got this to look forward to in less than eight months.

"How the hell did you do this three times, Mo?"

"It's easier with the second," she replies, giving her daughter-in-law a pointed look.

"What?" says Vi, innocently.

"Anything you want to tell me?"

"Mo, stop. You know we want to wait until Theo's a little bit older. I promise, when I am, you'll be the first to know."

Demon's mother pouts, then pulls her chair in a bit closer to mine. "Then I'll just have to be a proxy grandmother to Mel's for now."

I give her a genuine smile. That actually sounds nice.

But it reminds me I haven't told my parents. How can I? How do I explain I might be a single mother? I don't think they'll be judgmental, it's just, I still haven't found the right words to form an explanation, when I don't know what's going on myself. I won't be able to put it off forever, soon I'll have to admit Skull is gone.

Each day I hope for news, but it never comes. Days pass slowly, one after the other, each twenty-four-hour period the same as the last. I go to work and try to concentrate on doing my job. Because of my reddened eyes, my forlorn expression of hope when the phone rings, I've had to tell co-workers that Skull's disappeared, but not that I'm having his baby. Unfortunately, they treat him being missing as an intriguing mystery, and I have to put up with a daily inquisition. Is there news? *No.* Any new ideas why? *Again, no.* They offer up theories and then look at me with that sad look in their eyes. It was Carter who dared to say the words, *Bikes are dangerous, he probably had an accident.*

It's not much better at the weekend when I'm in the club-house. If people talk about Skull I get upset, if they don't, I want to cry. Life goes on and they're moving onto other things now, Skull being gone is yesterday's topic.

Time also rushes by all too fast. Each day gone is another that he's been missing, and they are starting to mount up. Even I know as the period of time lengthens, it's hardly a good sign. If he was able to return or wanted to, he'd have come back by now.

The day of my appointment with the OB/GYN comes around. When I descend the staircase, I don't just find Violet waiting for me, but Pyro as well.

When I cock my eyebrow, he nods to Vi, then takes me to one side.

"Mel, if Skull was here, he'd be going with you. But he can't be, so I'm coming in his place."

"You don't have to do that."

"I know, but I owe it to him as my brother."

"I've got Vi…"

"Let me go with you, instead. Mel. Let me give you the support Skull would have given."

But he's not Skull.

Pyro's been there for me since Skull went missing.

I might not have my man with me, but Pyro seems hellbent on making sure I won't be going through this alone.

"If you're not comfortable with the arrangement, Mel, we can stick to the original plan," Vi offers, anxiously.

I won't have Skull, but Pyro seems intent on being his proxy.

While I'm sure the doctor won't be judgmental, there's something comforting about walking in with a man.

"Okay," I say slowly. "Thank you, Pyro."

Vi leans over to the sofa and picks up a cushion, asking casually, "Did this make a difference Ro?"

Pyro rubs his neck. "Yeah, it did. Thanks Vi."

"Make a difference to what?" I look from one to the other.

"Sleeping on the sofa," Vi informs me.

My eyes crease. "You're sleeping on a sofa? Why?"

Pyro's eyes close briefly, then reopen. "Because you're in my room."

I had no idea. "Why aren't you in another one?"

"We're short of space, Mel. No others were available."

Vi delivers her parting shot, then walks off carrying the cushion, presumably to put it away until tonight, while I'm still trying to process the fact Pyro's been sleeping uncomfortably while I've taken his bed.

"No, Mel. Before you even think it, I'm not going to let you swap places. I'm quite comfortable now I've got myself sorted. You're a pregnant woman and need a bed."

I really don't know what to say.

I'm quiet on the short journey to the doctor's, realising how much the man beside me is doing for my comfort and never complaining. Well, not to me. Vi had known he was suffering from a stiff neck.

As if he knows I'm still worrying, after he parks the car, his hand touches my chin and turns my head. "Darlin', I used to be in the Army. I've had far worse places to lay my head. Believe me, a soft couch and a pillow is a luxury compared to some of the places I've slept. There's nothing you can say which will change the situation."

"Thank you?" I offer, as a question. The words seeming inadequate as they leave my mouth.

"That'll do," he responds, simply. Then, "Ready to do this?"

I nod. "Yes."

CHAPTER SEVENTEEN

Pyro

I hadn't intended to accompany Mel to the OB/GYN today. In my head, it was women's shit, and Violet seemed the obvious choice as her companion. It hadn't been until I'd overheard the women talking after Mel had had an early night and gone to bed the previous evening and heard shit which had changed my mind.

"Poor girl," Mo had said. "Skull should be here with her. Hell was amazing with me. He came to every appointment right from the start."

"I know what she's going through," said Violet. "I had to go by myself. I felt so alone, even though Vicky was with me. Happy expectant couples all around me, and there I was, without a man."

"Pal would want to be with me." Jay laughed. "I wouldn't be able to keep him away."

I'd cursed Skull in my head. What the fuck is the man doing leaving her to cope all alone? Okay, so he doesn't know she's pregnant, but she could be going through anything as far as he knows. Not the least worrying and missing him. Another sign, surely, that the man has to be dead. Why else would he stay away from his woman, let alone his club?

Skull should be there to support her at her appointments, to share every step of the pregnancy with her. If he can't be, then I'll have to step up instead.

Whoa. Hold on there. Why me?

I have no answer for my own question, yet it already seems I'm already invested in Mel having a baby. It was me who was there and who read the positive sign on that pregnancy test. Seems by doing so, I've become unwittingly involved. She might not be having my baby, but I'll give her the support she needs until her man returns. Though that seems to be increasingly unlikely.

I wish she hadn't learned I'd not only given up my bed for her, but that I'd had no place other than the clubroom to sleep instead. I've gotten used to the couch, and that pillow properly positioned does indeed help my neck.

Though Skull will undoubtedly be with us today—he's the baby's father after all and she won't be able to forget—I didn't want to raise his spectre in a negative way. Therefore, I'd refrained from telling her there will probably be more space in the clubhouse after church tonight. As nothing has happened, lockdown is bound to be lifted. Mel's not stupid, she'll realise two options will have been taken off the table. The first being that Skull himself is gunning for the club, which would be good in her eyes, but the other, that an enemy is holding him captive. No longer considering that as a viable possibility is basically admitting he is dead.

I hadn't thought it through, I realise, as we sit in the waiting room along with an assortment of women in various stages of pregnancy, many with their partners beside them. It's not being here that bothers me, but the form I'm asked to fill in. *They think I'm the father and want my medical history.* I put it aside, raging again that there are things we don't know. Has Skull got any genetic issues that might have a bearing on the baby's health? There's no way of knowing.

Mel's biting the tip of the pen as she completes her own information.

Discreetly, while waiting, I study the room's other occupants. Noting one man looks excited, another bored, and the last like they'd rather be elsewhere. The women, though… There's one who seems likely to drop any day now, and I wonder if Mel will have the same glow on her face when she gets to that point. Fuck, but she'll look beautiful when the baby starts growing, I fucking know she will. For a moment I wish her baby was mine, and like the proud excited father, I could take personal pleasure in today. But it's not. I'm not even her partner. *I'm lucky. A woman and baby would tie me down.*

When our time comes, we're shown into a room where we wait for the doctor.

It's not long before she enters. "Right, now, Melissa, isn't it?" When Mel nods, the doctor looks at me and frowns. "You didn't fill in your health information."

"I'm not the father," I say fast. "He's unable to be here, so I've come in his place."

"You okay with that, Melissa?" The doctor's eyebrow is arched.

"Yes," Mel says positively, with a quick grateful glance my way.

"You think you're about six weeks?"

When Mel replies in the affirmative, the doctor commences a complete check-up, sending me out of the room while she performs certain examinations, but I'm there when her blood pressure is taken and a sample of blood. Mel squeezes my hand tightly, and I get the impression she doesn't like needles.

Mel goes through her health, mentioning her concern about her weight and whether it would affect her carrying a healthy baby. The doctor agrees she's got a high BMI score—whatever that fucking is, and that she should watch what she eats. Mel looks beautiful to me. Rounded and shapely, in my eyes exactly how a woman should look. I glare at the doctor.

She then talks to us both about what to expect in pregnancy. I learn her tits are already sore and will increase in size. *Oh baby, I could ease that pain with my hands and lips.* Then mentally slap myself around the head before I get a hard dick in a very inappropriate place.

The doc thinks it's too early for a sonogram, and as Mel's certain of the timing of her last period estimates a delivery date. As she does Mel turns to glance at me, and I can see a mixture of fear and excitement on her face. Being given a date has just made it real for her.

"When can we see it? And when can we learn whether it's a boy or a girl?" It's me that asks that question.

Mel raises her eyebrow, but she grins. I shrug. Can't help but get involved when I'm sitting here with her. Some of her excitement must be contagious.

The doc answers me, "After sixteen weeks we should be able to tell. We can schedule that in. If there are any problems, we might have a look sooner. We'll schedule your next appointment for a month's time. If anything comes back from your blood work that we need to discuss, then I'll be in touch. Oh, and if you can get the health information from the father, that will be useful."

My face tightens as the excitement on Mel's face disappears.

She's still down as we walk back across the parking lot.

"I wish Skull was here. I'm so glad you were, Pyro, but there's so much I don't know about him. I don't know whether there's anything in his medical history I should know about. What if there is, and it harms the baby?"

I know I'm starting to do this more often, but it just seems natural to pull her into my arms and to cradle her head against my chest. "Don't worry about things that might not exist. Just focus on doing the best that you can."

"I hate this," she sobs. "I should be happy I'm having a baby. I am, but I want Skull to be with me."

"I know." It's all that I can offer.

Suddenly she cries out, "He's dead, isn't he, Pyro? I'm never going to see him again."

What do I do? Do I hold out false hope? Do I tell her what my thoughts really are? Can I lie? No, I can't. "Mel, I'm so fuckin' sorry, but I think he is. There's no other explanation why he wouldn't have come back to you. I don't know where it could have happened, I don't know how, who—or even if anyone else was involved—but I'm certain he'd have come back if he could."

People come and go around us, but I ignore the looks. Let them think what they like. If Mel needs to cry out her anguish in a hospital parking lot, she's allowed to.

Eventually her tears dry. On the drive back to the compound the odd sob sounds, but she's slowly pulling herself together. I'm not sure if I handled the situation rightly or wrongly, but Mel's distress was caused by her beginning to accept she'll never again see her man. In my view, to allow her to keep hoping, to give her false platitudes after she'd come to that realisation herself, didn't sit well with me.

Skull's gone. Deep down in my bones, I know it.

Life has to go on. Particularly that special bundle of cells in her stomach on which Mel's currently resting her hands.

Taking my right hand off the steering wheel, I place it on hers. "Skull still lives on, Mel. You're carrying part of him. You can keep him alive in your child and in your mind."

"I know," she replies, her voice quiet and low. "I'd never met a man like Skull before, Pyro. He truly ignored our age difference. It didn't matter to him, and he saw past my exterior to the woman inside. No one's ever loved me for me before."

"You don't want to hear this now darlin', I know. But when you're ready, there'll be someone else for you."

"Will there?" she snaps. "There never was before. No one wants the fat woman, and a fat woman with a child?"

I pull over to the, slam the car into park and turn on her. "Shut that shit up now, woman. You are not fuckin' fat. You've got curves in all the right places. Those men who couldn't see how beautiful you are? Fuckin' blind motherfuckers."

"You heard the doctor…"

"I heard her say you're to eat a healthy diet which she'd say to any fuckin' expectant mother. You are not fat, Mel. You're so fuckin' perfect..." I stop before I tell her she's exactly the kind of woman I want. I stop before I allow myself to even think it. This dilemma is fucking with my head. She's another member's old lady. Whether he's living or no longer breathing, she's his. If I let myself continue to contemplate in the direction I'm going, I'll start doing the unthinkable, wishing a brother was dead.

She's looking at me strangely as I put the car back into drive and pull away.

We say nothing more until we reach the compound, and I tell her I've got to get back to work. It isn't a lie or excuse, but I'm using it as one. I need space, before I say something I might later regret, or, inadvertently, hurt her.

Some hours later I walk into church. Having lost myself in fixing an exhaust on a bike that didn't want to be fixed, having to concentrate on nuts which didn't want to be turned and screws that didn't want to be screwed into the right place, I arrive almost to the dot of when the meeting should start. I'm the last one to take my place.

"Lockdown?" Hell queries before Demon can begin the meeting.

Demon seems to ignore him as he doesn't immediately leap to answer. Instead, in my view, he starts in the right place.

"First item on the agenda, any news about Skull?"

From all around come shakes of heads. No one has seen or heard from him, and none of our searches have borne fruit.

"He's dead." Rusty shakes his head sadly. "No other explanation."

"We've had no word from anyone. No reason for him to have been taken, and no reason for him to have left. Makes sense he was worried about the situation with his ol' lady and wanted to get things straight in his head. He must have known it would be soon she'd take the pregnancy test, maybe he wanted to get himself in a space where he could trust himself to have the right reaction. Whatever the result."

I nod at Thunder, how he's put things together sounds right.

The sergeant-at-arms continues, "He could have been mentally working things through, lost concentration as he rode. That makes more fuckin' sense than anything else. He wanted revenge? We'd have known about it by now, but there's been no threat to the club. Someone else out to get him? Unless it was personal shit from outside the club we'd have heard, and if it was personal, we'd have to suppose the result is the same and he's dead."

"That he hasn't been found yet, doesn't mean he won't be eventually," Beef agrees. "I think we should call off the search parties. We don't know the direction he went. Hate to say this, but even if we're on the right road, we could be passing straight by him. If he came off his bike and was injured, trapped, after two-and-a-half weeks, he has to be dead."

Cad nods slowly. "He's still not accessed his money. Man needs dollars to live. Much as I hate to say it, we won't see Skull again."

Beef takes the floor back. "We don't normally deal with the cops, but in this instance, Prez thought we needed to. We reported him missing."

Much as I don't like involving the authorities, Skull wasn't doing anything for the club, and from what I know of him, wouldn't have been carrying drugs on his own time. Cops find him, at least we'll know. Though they'll probably be looking for a body.

"Doubt they'll do much."

I tilt my head toward Lizard. I, too, don't have much faith in them putting themselves out for a member of a biker club.

"Nah," Thunder clearly agrees.

Prez is taking it all in, you can see by the focused way he watches each speaker. When it seems brothers have said all there is to say, he pinches the bridge of his nose, then says in a tired voice, "I tend to agree with Cad, that we won't see our brother again. I can't see how the club could be in danger, so lockdown is raised." Hell breathes out an audible sigh of relief, but Demon continues, "We still need to be vigilant, but people can go home to their own beds."

"What about Mel?"

"Goes without saying, Ro. She's welcome to stay here or go home. Whatever she feels most comfortable doing. We'd support her in any event, but especially so seeing as she's carrying our lost brother's baby."

"At least you won't be getting any more stiff necks." Mace grins at me.

"Have to say, Ro. I thought you'd be sharing your bed with her by now."

What the fuck? I turn to glare at Ink, who shrugs.

"You are getting pretty close to her," Lizard backs him up. "What's all this about you going to her doctor's appointment with her?"

I bang my hands on the table. "She needs someone. Skull's gone. I'm just stepping up for a brother."

"Are there death benefits like prison ones?" Judge asks.

"You'll get a fuckin' death benefit if you carry on," I warn him. "You'll get dead."

"Nah, I think it's a good question," Hellfire puts in. "If Skull was in prison, someone could step up and see to his woman's needs. And pregnant women can certainly have them, if you know what I mean."

Yeah, yeah. I've heard pregnancy hormones can make a woman horny. But that's an old wives' tale, isn't it? Though Hell might know what he's talking about, Mo's had three kids.

Are they saying they'd give me the go ahead to fuck her? My dick perks up at the thought.

Then I come back to my senses and snarl, "Fuckin' woman's got to grieve the death of her man. She doesn't just have to wait out his absence, he's never coming back. Last thing she wants is another man pawing at her." It hits me in a flash. I might not mind being a substitute for Skull when I'm taking her to the doctor, but I'll be no man's substitute in bed. When I finally lie with her, it will be because she wants *me* to be there. Not someone else instead. *When?* Christ. The question should be if, if it arises at all. *What the fuck's going on in my head?*

"It was just a thought," says an unrepentant Ink.

Prez unsuccessfully tries to hide his grin before stating, "Moving on to other business…"

CHAPTER EIGHTEEN

Melissa

As much as I didn't want to, I knew living in limbo wasn't doing me, and by association, the baby, any good. I couldn't just go on half-hoping half-worrying, I had to come down on one side of the fence.

If Skull had been alive and he was the man I thought he was, he'd have moved heaven and earth to come back to me. He hadn't, so he has to be dead. I torture myself at the thought of him dying alone and hurting, and hope it was quick. Not knowing how the life of my man ended is difficult to accept, but I need to come to terms that he's gone, and I'll be heading on through life alone.

Though I'd told Pyro outside of the hospital that I knew he was dead, a small kernel of hope remained inside me, until later that same night when it was pronounced that lockdown was over.

There's a general feeling of relief, a relaxation of tension, but to me it seemed like the last nail was being hammered into a coffin. The club had given up on him, and now I must too. I have to be realistic. Any last hopes I've been harbouring of having my man back at my side crumble into dust.

While her mother-in-law had been ecstatic, and has already

left with Hellfire, Violet understands the decision has a different impact on me.

"You should stay here," she encourages.

"I don't know what I want to do, Vi. He's gone, and somehow, I've got to accept it. I just don't know how." I've cried enough tears today, and I don't want to shed more. All of my misery can't be good for the baby. "If I stay here, I'm reminded of him every day. If I go home…" I'll be reminded of him there. He was living with me. His clothes will still be hung in my wardrobe, his manly stuff in the bathroom.

"If I go, Pyro can have his room back."

She dismisses that. "Pyro can move into Skull's now, or you can if you prefer. There's space for you, whichever way you look at it. These past weeks must have shown you how much you're part of the club. We want you here, Mel."

I came to the compound with a biker. What's here for me now he's gone? What does anywhere hold for me?

"I've got to find a way to move on, Vi. I'll think it over tonight, but I believe going back to my own place will be the best thing for me to do." Or maybe I'll sell up and move somewhere new, somewhere that doesn't hold memories. "I've got to make a life for me and the baby."

"It's our baby too," she reminds me. "I don't want to lose touch."

"I'm not cutting the club off, Vi." It would be stupid to do that. I've made so many friends here, and Pyro's been such a great help. "If I stay, I'm not sure I'll do more than just exist, if I force myself out of this bubble, then hopefully I can move on."

"Don't think we're going to abandon you. I'll come and drag your ass back if we don't see you."

"Vi, you've become such a good friend. I want to keep that friendship. I just think I need to find my own space. I'm…" I choke up, "I'm not an old lady, so here I don't have a place. Oh, I know you're going to contradict me, but we've got to face facts."

"He may still come back." Her voice is quiet, but firm and optimistic.

She's probably one of the few holding out hope. Sure, there's a part of me that still does, that can't give up on the man who fathered my child. But unless he's lying in hospital unconscious, he could have gotten a message to me somehow. If there is a valid reason, oh how happy I'd be. But if there's not, I've got to face something that's possibly even harder than concrete evidence, he's dead. That the man I believed in, the man I gave my heart to, was never what I'd thought him to be. That Skull wouldn't have walked away from me without a backward glance. If he came back now with no genuine excuse and wanted to pick up where we left off, I'd be extremely wary about it. It's one thing for a woman to return to a man who's abandoned her, very different if that woman has a child, even one not yet born. I wouldn't subject a baby to a childhood where his or her father couldn't be trusted not to walk out.

It's easier to think of him as dead. Too many questions, and too many directed at myself and how I could have been fooled if he's alive.

Violet's waiting expectantly, so I let her in on my thoughts. "Much as I'm grieving for him, Vi, if he does return, I don't think it's possible to pick up where we left off." I might still love a dead man, but a man who thinks he can take off leaving everyone behind him to worry? That's not the man I knew.

"You're going to decide to leave, aren't you?" Her regret shows on her face.

I can't lie to her. "I think I am."

The next morning, Pyro doesn't like it when I tell him I plan to go home.

"At least you'll be able to sleep in your own bed."

"I'll sleep on your fuckin' sofa," he warns. "I don't like the idea of you being alone."

"Pyro, come, sit." I invite him to park his ass beside me. "We're friends, aren't we?"

"Of course we fuckin' are."

"Then we're going to stay friends. I've… lost my man." It's still so hard to say it. Every time I do, another little piece of my heart breaks, and maybe I'm drawing nearer to accepting it. "I need to come to terms with that, and I won't be able to do that here. Not with every man wearing a cut the same as his, not with people talking the same as he did and not when I'm being referred to as Skull's old lady, or when I know the only reason I'm here is because that's what I am. *Was*," I correct.

"I wear a cut and talk like a fuckin' biker. You gonna shut me out too? Because I fuckin' remind you of him?"

"No, Ro, no. I want to stay friends. If you will, I want you to come to the hospital visits with me. If you will…" I hesitate, wondering if I'm asking too much. "If you'd like to be, I'd like you there at the birth."

Pyro's eyes open the widest I've ever seen. He swallows before he answers, his Adam's apple bobbing in his throat, "You really want that?"

I swallow. "I do." Then hold my breath for the answer. It's a lot to ask of a single man.

But his face breaks into a huge grin. "I'd like that too. Seems I'm already invested in my niece or nephew."

"I'm looking forward to finding out which it is." But only because he'll be at my side sharing the joy with me. On my own, I wouldn't be able to cope so well. I don't know why, but in this short space of time, Pyro's become my rock.

"Me too, Mel. Me too."

"I'd like you to come visit as much as you want. The only difference is I won't be here, sleeping in your bed."

He glances at me quickly, opens his mouth, then looks away. He sighs. "You need help getting anything ready. The nursery painted…"

"I'm not going to ask that much of you."

"You can't really see me waving a paintbrush around, can you?" His eyes open in mock horror. "I was going to say I'd send the prospects around." He winks as I burst out laughing. "I'm going to fuckin' miss you darlin'."

"I'm going to miss you too," I respond, genuinely.

"You planning on leaving straight away?"

I nod. "I'll just call for an Uber…"

"No you fuckin' won't. I'll take you." He glances at me. "You can come on the bike if you're feeling up to it, if not I'll take a car."

"I'm not ill. And I haven't put on weight yet…"

"Mel," he starts in a warning tone, "you could put on a good few pounds and still be fine to ride."

I ignore him. Soon I will be gaining weight and there will come a time when I won't be able to be behind anyone on their motorcycle. But for now, I'm fine. I'm looking forward to riding again.

He takes me home, removes my house keys from my hands and takes his time looking around while I stand rolling my eyes. What does he expect? A rapist hiding under the bed? He checks out the garage, makes sure my car starts, then, comes back inside.

"You sure?" His stare is intense.

"I'm certain. I'll be fine, Ro." Well, I'll try to be. Try to summon up the will to get up every day and carry on with life, even though there's a big part of it missing. I can see by the expression in his face that he understands, without me putting it into words.

After giving me a moment's examination, he sighs. "Okay then. I'll go. But you've got my number in your phone. Anything, Mel, anything. You need a carton of milk or have a fancy for ice cream? You're feeling down and want another body around? Anything, just call me." He pauses for a moment. "Not sure how good I'd be painting your nails but I'm willing to give it a go."

I laugh, and mock punch his arm. "When I can't see my toes, you might need to."

His hand curls behind my neck, and he pulls me in closer, pressing his lips to my forehead for a second.

"Take care of yourself, Mel."

"You too, Ro."

When I hear the sound of his engine fade into the distance, I realise I'm truly alone for the first time since Skull disappeared. I shiver, hugging my arms around me. Glancing around my living room, it strikes me how little of Skull is left behind. Okay, so most of his stuff he'd kept in the club, but apart from the clothes I know are upstairs, there's not much else here. An open Harley magazine, a candy bar wrapper in the wastepaper basket. No photos, no knickknacks.

At least there isn't much to remind me.

I stand, my head tilted, my brow creasing. *Did Skull ever live with me?* There's hardly any evidence that he did. Based on what I see around me, he could have been a figment of my imagination.

I rub my stomach. "I don't even have a photo of your daddy, baby." Skull wasn't into taking selfies, even with me and would always cover his face if I tried to take one of him, in the end I'd given up seeing how much it upset him. I think I'll ask around at the club, someone must have one, even if he's at the edge of a group shot. It pains me to think I could forget what he looked like.

I try to settle back into my old routine. The one I had before Skull. I go to work, do my job as best I can, then come home and force myself to eat a lonely meal for one. I try to convince myself I lived like this for years, it can't be that difficult to slip back into old habits and return to the woman I was before Skull. But it's hard, he changed me in so many ways. He might not have left much of himself behind, but the memories are there, and along with them, expectations. I can't help but look up when I hear a loud engine noise or fool myself I hear his key in the lock. His voice echoes around the house, though I'm only hearing it in my head.

His ghost seems to haunt me, almost to the extent that I change my mind and return to the clubhouse, but my sensible head tells me I've got to face life alone sometime. It must be like an addict coming off the drug of their choice, at first impossible to see how they can make it through, but with the knowledge, in time, there'll be light at the end of the tunnel, and less reliance on the crutch they used in the past.

Of course, Skull had left something behind, something that keeps me determined when I feel like giving up. His baby, now inside me, but part of him too.

So, I stick it out, getting used to the loneliness that had never been labelled that way before Skull, believing that's the best thing to do.

In the evenings I get a call, from Vi or Jay, and even from Pyro too. Steph seems to be on the rotation as well. I smile, thinking they have probably arranged they'll all keep in touch, but won't overwhelm me with more than one call a day.

Tonight, it's Pyro.

"How you doing Mel? You need anything?"

"No, Ro. I'm good." He can't see the tear I've just wiped from my eye.

There's a pause as though he's unused to social calls on the phone. Then, "Will you come to the clubhouse this weekend, Mel?"

"I'm going to Denver..." I'd come to realise it's time I told the truth to my mom and dad.

"Good idea. I'll drive you."

It takes more than a few minutes to convince him I'm perfectly capable of driving myself, and no, I don't need a prospect following me. In the end I promise to text him when I arrive at my parents, when I leave there and, when I get back home.

I set out early on Saturday. On the way I wondered how to approach the two difficult subjects I was going to have to broach. Which should I start with? In the end, it's a simple enquiry about my health which makes one option flow naturally.

Mom and Dad take the news they are going to be grandparents in their stride, with a mixture of congratulations and concern. Mom asks a ton of questions about whether I'm eating well. I'm able to reassure her that I appear to be one of the lucky ones and, knock on wood, haven't experienced morning sickness, or not as yet.

Of course, the conversation comes around to the father.

"Where's Skull, Melissa?" Dad frowns. "Not happy he let you drive here alone. Do I need to get my shotgun out?"

My face falls as my father's joke fails to have the effect he was going for. Then a tear starts to roll down my cheek, fast followed by another. My mom's arms surround me, holding me close, murmuring words of comfort while Dad stands to one side, his face taut and set.

When I can finally speak, I pull away from her and try to explain. "It's not what you think, Mom, Dad... he's dead."

"What the hell? Where? When? How? Oh, baby girl, come here." Quickly I find myself in Mom's arms again, and I sob harder into her chest, just like I had as a child. Only then it was over a broken toy, not a broken life and dreams which have died.

Their questions are so hard to answer.

"You should have told us before," Mom says after I've tried my best. "We'd have come down to Pueblo, been there for you. I hate to think of you going through this alone."

"And he didn't know you were pregnant?" Dad waits for confirmation.

"No. Look, the situation's terrible. It breaks my heart Dad, but the club has looked at this every which way, then the other as well. The only explanation that makes any sense is that somewhere, out there, waiting to be discovered is a body."

I sob again, having had to put it so starkly.

"And they're going on...?"

"His phone can't be reached or traced. Cad thinks it's most

likely damaged." *As is its owner.* "He's not used his bank or credit cards, nor touched his bank account."

Dad's eyes widen, but he doesn't ask how the club knows. "Have you reported him missing to the police?"

"Yes Dad, no sign of him. He's not been arrested or turned up injured or dead."

Mom looks to Dad, then me. She places her hand over my heart. "What do you feel in here, Melissa?"

I draw in a deep breath. My eyes flick to hers. "At first I refused to believe it. But as time goes on, I've accepted he's gone. I have to, or else I can't move on. It's hard, Mom, but I need to be strong for me and the baby. No point hanging onto an impossible dream. I won't be seeing Skull again. I know it."

Dad doesn't seem to know what to say. He paces the room, shaking his head. Finally, he draws to a halt in front of me. "Skull dragged you into that motorcycle club..."

"The club didn't have anything to do with him going missing. And he dragged me, as you put it, into a family who've given me so much support over these past few weeks. They're not criminals, Dad. They're as hurt about Skull being gone as I am. It's been good to grieve together."

"Are you still going to consort with them? Now that he's no longer there?"

I shrug. Pyro, I'm certain, will stay a friend. Vi, Jay and Steph too. As for the rest of the club, whatever they say now, I can't help but think but as time goes on and the memory of Skull begins to fade, any responsibility toward me will disappear along with it. So I'm truthful in my response.

"I've made friends, Dad, good ones. I'll keep those up. But I won't be part of the club any longer."

"I'm just glad someone was there for her, Rufus," Mom chides him, gently. "Would rather it had been us she'd come to, but I can understand. They were the ones who were out searching."

"I'd have spoken to the police..."

"They've done that too, dear. I doubt there's more that anyone could do. Now Melissa needs to think of herself, and that grandchild of ours she's carrying."

Mom turns the conversation back to womanly things with a genuine interest and growing excitement in my news. Dad gives a grim nod, realising continuing talking about Skull won't bring my man home, or provide any more answers than those I've already given.

He leaves the room.

It's a weight off of my mind that they know. I'd hated keeping such a big thing from them. Over the course of the weekend, Mom offered for me to move to Denver and live with them, but I've got my house, job, friends, and, for now, the club back in Pueblo, so I didn't give it any serious consideration. Her offer to come and stay with me after the birth was gratefully appreciated and accepted. What do I know about looking after a baby?

Back home my house is quiet, and my rejection of my parents offer seems perhaps hasty. But telling myself things will get better in time, I resume my routine, determined I can do this by myself.

Not that I'm totally alone. I have become used to the sound of motorcycles along the road outside, sometimes stopping, sometimes driving on.

I begin to settle in my house, the ghost of Skull becoming easier to live with. Though they try to persuade me, I don't visit the compound, fearing it would raise his spectre all over again, when I believe I'm slowly coming to terms with my loss. It still hurts, but sometimes I can get through the day without tears.

When it becomes clear I'm not returning to the club, Pyro begins to visit regularly. To my surprise, the prospects start tidying my neglected yard, and doing handyman jobs around the house. I've not actually got them painting the nursery, it's still too early for that, but they have cleared some of the junk I have stored and moved furniture which would have been too heavy for me.

Violet, Jayden and Steph visit regularly, and even Mo's popped around. I've resumed baking, and now usually have a tub of something or other for them to take back with them. I'm told everyone is grateful.

I go to work, and gradually the topic of Skull going missing thankfully is dropped. I've offers of help from Beth and the others, even Carter offering assistance if I need anything.

I know I'm lucky to have so many people looking out for me.

If I wasn't pregnant, maybe I wouldn't be able to cope as well. I miss Skull with every fibre of my being, and I wish he was still here with me, but he's not. It helps that he left me with a new life growing inside. Something to live for, a new life to love.

I'm reminded every day, from sore breasts to the additional urges to pee, and now, to the growing evidence of a different shape to my stomach.

"You're starting to show," Beth points out one day as we walk to our cars after work.

"I know," I say, proudly, stretching my top over my bump to show it off, when normally I'd hide the size of my stomach.

"When do you find out if it's a boy or a girl?"

"Next week." I grin. I don't know who's more excited, Pyro or me. He's still determined to be with me every step of the way. "Thursday."

"Oh, I won't be here."

I snap my fingers. "Of course, not. You'll be living it up in Vegas. I forgot."

She jumps up and down with excitement. "I can't wait. I've never been and always wanted to."

"Me too," I laugh back, her joy is infectious. "All the sights and sounds of the strip. Not that I'm jealous." I pout.

"Maybe you can get your friend Pyro to take you."

I slap that down immediately. "Pyro's not that kind of friend. He's just looking out for me."

"Hmm. He spends a lot of time with you."

Because he's doing it for his dead brother. Not for me.

Sometimes I regret that. When he places that innocent kiss to my forehead whenever he leaves me, I have to resist raising my head and accidentally letting our mouths meet.

Must be the pregnancy hormones making me horny.

CHAPTER NINETEEN

Pyro

Mel's got this adorable little baby bump going on. I keep sneaking glances when she's not looking. I can't wait until she can feel it move, and perhaps she'll allow me to place my hand on her stomach to experience it. That's my niece or nephew in there, I keep telling her, but really, I'm feeling almost paternal. It might not have been my sperm that created it, my dick might never have experienced the inside of her cunt whether gloved up or bare, but it doesn't stop me feeling I've been with her every step of the way on her pregnancy journey.

Only one thing better would be if I got up the nerve to tell her how I really feel about her.

She's one hundred percent focused on doing everything right for the baby and is not in the market for a man, which is lucky as I won't need to look for places to bury a body. I know I'd kill any fucker who touched her with his hands, let alone put his cock anywhere near her.

There are so many times while I allow myself the only liberty I can take when I wish my lips could feel her mouth, and not just touch the skin of her forehead.

I'd like to think we're good friends now. I can make her smile, laugh, and I am happy she responds to me. Of course, she hasn't forgotten Skull, but the initial pain has lessened considerably.

I don't want to fuck our friendship up. If I press my case and try to get more, I may end up with nothing at all.

She's eighteen weeks now, and today we're going to see the baby. I'm so damn excited I keep dropping my tools and can't keep the grip on the nut I'm turning.

"Yo, Ro."

Now I've an excuse to give up. I stand. "Prez."

"Just wanted to say I hope it all goes well today. Mel's having her ultrasound, isn't she?"

"Yes." I nod. I've been trying to keep my reaction low-key and hide my feelings from my brothers.

"I wish I'd seen Theo, you know? Not met him when he was already seven months." His face falls. "I let Violet down, I would have been there for her if she'd have felt she could come to me."

I don't know what to say, so settle for, "She knows that, Prez."

"I'm pleased, Ro, that you're going to be there for Mel. Fuckin' sorry that Skull can't be."

We both raise our fists to our hearts momentarily. Still no body, but he's dead, we all know it. Respect to our lost brother now always shown whenever his name is mentioned.

"Couldn't leave her to do it alone, Prez. She's club."

"See if you can bring her around after, Ro, she's stayed away too long. I bet a lot of us would like to see the picture of that new Devil she's incubating."

I've already decided to pay out for the best quality one they can offer. "I'll do that." Hopefully I can persuade her to come to the club. Surely Mel will enjoy showing it off? As long as it plays along, we'll know whether it's a boy or a girl as well.

Prez suddenly grins. "I'm jealous as fuck, you know? I'll have to wait until Vi gets pregnant again."

I smirk. "That's up to you, Prez."

As he laughs, I glance up at the clock. "Well I better get going. Don't want to be late."

"That you don't. Get out of here, Ro."

I show him my middle finger as I walk off.

I take a car, Mel's stopped riding on the back of my bike now, not so much because she's too big, but she's terrified she's going to fall off. I suppose our supposition that Skull was killed in a riding accident doesn't give her confidence.

Pulling up outside her house, I toot the horn. The door opens, and she steps out. As normal my gut clenches at just the sight of her, and my cock starts to swell. *Down, fella, down.* I mentally recite all the parts of an engine.

By the time Mel's eased herself in, my chubby has, at last, diminished.

"Ready for this?" I ask as I drive down the road.

"Don't get too excited, Ro. The baby may not cooperate, and we might not be able to see what sex it is."

"Just seeing it will be great. Hey, what's the matter?" My hand closes the gap between us and squeezes hers. "What's up Mel?" *Is she wishing it was Skull sitting beside her?* Be strange if she wasn't, I suppose. But sometimes, like now, I have to force myself not to get jealous of a dead brother.

But she's not thinking about her old man. She's got something else on her mind. "I'm scared they'll find something wrong with the baby, Ro. What if they do? What if its organs are inside out or something? Or it doesn't have a head, or it's not developing properly."

I don't make platitudes and tell her it will be fine. What do I know? Tightening my fingers on hers once again, I just reply, "Then we'll deal, okay? I'm right here beside you. Anything shows up wrong, we'll find out the options and make decisions from there."

Turning my head, I catch her eyes which are open wide. But I do hear her almost whispered reply as I focus my attention back on the road.

"What did I do to deserve a friendship with a man like you, Ro? I honestly don't know how I'd have come this far without you."

I have nothing to answer her with. Instead, I promise, "I'll be with you the rest of the way too. You can't get rid of me now. I'm like some nasty rash you've picked up and can't cure, I'm here to stay."

I turn toward her again, this time, to wink.

As I hoped, she laughs.

But she's tense in the doctor's office. I stay by her side, holding her hand as the nurse puts a clear liquid on her stomach, I go still when they place the wand to her skin. I hold my breath as the doctor moves it around, then feel tears prick in my eyes when I hear a cross between a fast thumping and a whoosh whooshing sound.

"There it is." The doctor turns the screen around. "See? The head, there's one arm, the other's hidden, and there are the legs.

"Is it sucking its thumb?" Mel asks in wonder while I'm too choked up to speak.

"Looks like it, doesn't it?" The doctor proceeds to take measurements and makes satisfactory sounds. "Everything looks to be exactly how we'd want it. And fits nicely with your due date." Then she adds the words I hoped to hear, "Would you like to know what you're having?"

"Yes," we both say together.

"Now this is my best estimate," she warns. "There's still a chance I could be wrong, but from what I can see, I'm fairly confident you're having a boy."

A son. No, a nephew. Fuck, I have to remember that. But I couldn't feel any prouder.

"Pyro, are you crying?" an astonished voice asks.

"Nope," I deny it, brushing my tears away. "Got something in my eye."

"Strangely that happens to a lot of dads," the doctor says drily. "Must be dusty in here."

Mel giggles.

"Can we have a photo, doc?" I cough to clear my throat.

"Of course."

It's not long before I'm holding a colour picture in my hands. I hold it reverently, before passing it and the cardboard envelope over to Mel. Her eyes are glistening, she's completely oblivious to the nurse wiping the gel from her stomach.

"You can get dressed now."

I sit stunned during the rest of the appointment. I'd known Mel was pregnant, sure, but actually seeing the baby? While I know it was still small, not quite six inches long and still with one fuck of a lot of growing to do, I already know I'd give up my life to keep him and his mother safe. *I love him.*

I don't know how, or why, I just do. And however Mel will have me, as a friend if not a lover, I'll be by his side as he grows. I couldn't feel more for that blob on the screen if I was his true father.

"I didn't expect that," I tell her in the car, after we get in but I've yet to start the engine. "I didn't expect he'd be so well formed. He was a recognisable baby."

"Thank God," she says with feeling, and follows her heartfelt statement up with, "I'll tell you what I didn't expect."

"What?"

"You to cry."

"If you say one word of that in the clubhouse…" I growl.

"If I promise I won't, will you take me there now?"

I turn to her completely thunderstruck. She's looking a bit nervous as if I'm going to refuse. For a moment I can't say anything. My arguments to persuade her to filling my head, I find it hard to change direction. I ask to make certain I've under-stood her.

"The compound?"

She gives a small smile. "I thought going back would remind me of Skull, then I thought your brothers would soon forget me. But they haven't, have they? Everyone who's visited has tried to persuade me back. The club's still got prospects doing the odd jobs. Because I hadn't been, I kind of lost the nerve to go. But now? Now with the physical evidence of my baby inside, knowing he's healthy and everything looks alright, I suddenly feel confident. You were right, Ro. This baby's got more than grandparents, he's got you and his other uncles and aunts who deserve to know him."

"Fuckin' got that right, darlin'." The corners of my mouth turn up. "I was actually under orders from the prez to kidnap you if I had to."

"You were?" She sounds surprised Demon would give a damn.

"Too damn right," I confirm. "You're one of ours, Mel. Ain't nothing changed."

She draws in a sharp breath, and I look at her concerned, but it's to find she's smiling.

Inside, I'm delighted it's the first place she wants to go.

As soon as she steps in through the door to the clubhouse, she can be left in no doubt I'd told her no lies.

"Mel! 'Bout fucking time," yells Ink delightedly. His words are echoed from all quarters.

"Alright, alright. She's been fuckin' welcomed. Now what the fuck is she having? Some of us have got money riding on this," Lizard grumbles, while pulling her in for a hug, his actions softening his words.

I glance at her once he lets her go. We hadn't discussed whether she wanted anyone to know. But there's a big wide grin on her face, and she gives me a slow nod.

I've got permission, so I waste no time, opening my mouth to give a hearty shout of, "It's a boy."

Half cheers, half groans, and dollars change hands. Mel's taking it all in good fun and laughing.

"Congratulations, Mel." Demon's stepped up to her, expectantly holding out his hand palm up.

Mel stares down, wondering what he's doing. It's not positioned as though he expects her to shake it. I know exactly what he wants, so I slide the envelope out of my cut and extract the photo.

"Jeez. He *has* got a dick," Demon's says, holding the picture close.

"Let me see..." Beef takes it out of the prez's hands. "That's a dick? Hope that's going to fuckin' grow."

"Beef!" Steph, who's hanging onto his arm snorts, while grinning accurately in Mel's direction. "Of course it will grow. Just like the rest of him. How big is he now, Mel? Describe him to me. What does he look like? Can you see fingers and toes?"

Letting go of Beef, with one hand on Max's harness, she beckons Mel to follow her into the kitchen where the rest of the women are getting dinner prepared.

The fact there will be another baby boy on the compound seems a topic of awe for my brothers. Maybe because in some ways it makes up for the loss of Skull. Something of him that will still remain proving that part of him lives on. As I watch and listen while they pass that photo around, I wonder if at some point in the far future, that baby will become a man taking his seat in church. One never knows.

"Hey, where's that picture? We haven't seen it yet."

Paladin takes it from Mace and passes it to Jay, who spares a quick kiss for her man, then disappears back into the kitchen.

I mingle, get a beer, but it's with the hope Mel's not becoming overwhelmed. I don't want to intrude, so pause to one side of the doorway so I can hear the conversation inside, I lean in to hear better.

"Now you know it's a boy, Mel, any thoughts about naming him?"

"Are you going to name him after Skull? What was his real name?"

"Kris," I hear her reply. "I don't know, I'd rather go for something more modern."

"Archie?"

"That's like the number one name now," Mel laughs. "Something modern and unusual then."

I don't know why I should be relieved she's not inclined to name the baby Kris. Maybe because it would be a permanent reminder that he's not mine.

Of course Jeannie persuades her to stay and eat with us. It's good to see her smiling and joking with the women, while my brothers are pretending not to be interested in the baby talk but are still passing that fucking photo around. I catch more than one sneaking looks from the piece of paper to her stomach as if realising there really is a tiny Devil in there.

Except for Paladin who's not particularly interested, but then he's from Tucson, and it's far from the first sonogram picture he'll have seen.

"Congratulations, Pyro." Wills slaps my back loudly.

In a sudden lull in the conversation, his words ring out and catch everyone's attention. Mel's heard, and cocks her head to one side as if interested to see my response.

Embarrassed, I offer, "Ain't nothing to do with me. I'm not the father."

Mel's face is unreadable, a sadness flickers over it. *Does she regret that I'm not?* Nah, I've just reminded her his real dad isn't here, that's all it can be.

"Hey, let me see." Thunder takes the photo and examines it. "Ugly motherfucker isn't he?"

The women gasp, the men all laugh, but when Thunder winks at Mel, she knows he's joking.

"Better looking than you already, asshole," says Demon.

"That wouldn't be hard," Rusty agrees.

And just like that, *thank fuck*, the attention is off me.

"Ro, come over here."

Wandering back into the bar area, I go to where Pal is chatting with Judge. "Wassup?" I pull up a chair, turn it the wrong way around, and sit on it, folding my arms over the back.

"Judge, here, is thinking about getting a new exhaust. He's looking at this type, have you fitted one like it before?"

I take the parts list he's been examining. "Hmm, have to do a bit of a workaround, but yeah, I can make it work."

Of course, we start getting into details and are joined by Sparky who offers some ideas. It's quite a while later that I look around to see how Mel's doing and notice her yawning.

Excusing myself, I walk across to her. "You look tired. Want to go home?"

She looks up gratefully. "I didn't want to pull you away."

"No worries, darlin'. You need me? Come and get me, okay? Don't want you overdoing it."

"I'm okay, but I've had enough excitement for one day."

"Let's get you home."

We're halfway to her house when a question out of the blue startles me. "What's your real name?"

"Pyro," I tell her, chuckling. "But if you're asking about the name the government uses, I'm Brendan Evans."

"Brendan," she tries it out, then frowns. "Do you think he looks like a Brendan?"

Fuck. She's suggesting she might name the baby after me? I'm so shocked the car swerves. Luckily, I catch it fast and straighten it before she notices. "Looks more like a Blob to me."

"Pyro," she gasps, swatting at my arm.

CHAPTER TWENTY

Melissa

Even though I've been showing his picture around and sharing the news with everyone in the clubhouse, it doesn't really hit me until I get home that in just a few months' time I'll be holding my son in my arms. A boy.

I really didn't mind what sex the baby was going to be, had been more worried that the sonogram would show whether he was healthy or not.

He was perfect to my eyes, and to the doctor's. Though I do have some sympathy with Pyro's comment that he was a blob. I giggle to myself. Sure, he had the undeniable shape of a baby, but still had a lot of growing to do before he becomes fully formed. Running my hands over my stomach, I make a silent promise. I'll do everything I can to protect him until he's viable and can live outside the womb. I'll take the utmost care of myself and him for another five months.

Of course my protection won't end then. Momentarily I'm scared that I'll have something totally dependent on me, not just for his physical needs, but for being brought up in the right way. If he turns out like the amazing man his father is, I'll have done okay.

I pull myself up sharply. Father? His father is dead, but when

I picture a dad for my baby, it's Pyro's face I see, not Skull's. Does that make me a terrible person?

Skull. I miss him every minute of every day. *Don't I?* Of course I do, except, when I'm with Pyro, there's something about him that banishes all thoughts of my lost lover.

Could I see Pyro and me playing happy family? Him moving in, living with me and being Brendan's dad?

Brendan? Have I truly settled on the name? Well I've got months to decide.

Pyro would probably run a mile if I told him, instead of leaving each night, I wanted him to stay.

My phone rings, startling me out of my reverie. It's my mom. Feeling guilty my first thought had been to share my news with my biker family instead of my blood one, I answer.

"Melissa, honey, sorry to call so late, but I wanted to make sure everything was okay? You had the ultrasound today, didn't you?"

Settling back with my phone to my ear, I tell her my news. "Everything's fine, mom. A normal healthy boy."

"Boy?" she squeals. "I'm going to have a grandson?" Then her voice is more muffled as she calls out, "Rufus, it's a *boy.*"

I hear my father's response. "Already gathered that." I can just picture him with a fond smile on his face.

"And you," Mom speaks directly into the phone again. "Everything going well?"

"Yes, I'm good." I realise I am. While the intense, debilitating grief I'd felt at first hasn't gone away, it has faded and become bearable. The effort I was making to stay strong for my child, is habit now and not forced. "The doctor said everything's going as it should. I've gained the right weight."

We discuss the ins and outs of my pregnancy for a little longer, then, when I yawn, we say our goodbyes, with a promise from Mom that they'll come and visit me soon.

It's been a busy day. I go to bed, tired, but happy.

When the weekend comes, Pyro turns up. I tell him exactly

what I want to do. While I'm superstitious enough not to actually start decorating yet, knowing the sex of the baby gives me the impetus to start thinking about themes, and looking at how I could eventually set up his room.

We have a blast. For some reason after visiting a couple of baby stores, we end up in a Harley store where there's a mural on the wall. Pyro points to the huge image of a motorcycle and suggests that should be in my son's room. I only just manage to stop him buying a remote-controlled bike, saying it's far too soon.

"You'll be buying him a tank and toy soldiers next." I roll my eyes as we leave the shop.

His face lights up. "Now there's an idea."

"Well, I'll be buying him a doll house and dolls," I say, drily.

"What the fuck?" Then he chuckles when he sees I'm holding back a grin. "Choices, eh?"

It's actually a serious point. I shrug.

"Hmm. Big responsibility, isn't it? Deciding how to do this right."

My hands find their familiar position, protectively covering this new life in my womb. "I just want him to be happy, Ro. Whatever he turns out to be, however he wants to live his life. No pressure one way or another."

Pyro's large hand easily covers both of mine. "No wonder I love you, Mel." His words slip out and he pulls his hand abruptly away.

It's just something a friend would say, isn't it? I shouldn't read anything into it.

I respond in the same way, "Love you too, Ro. You've been amazing."

He's the first to break the silence that follows. "It's you who's the amazing one. You're going to make an incredible mom."

I wish I had his confidence. I can only try to do my best.

Monday dawns all too soon. I pull on the clothes I wear to work, realising I'm going to have to get maternity clothes soon.

My own, even the ones with elastic waistbands are getting uncomfortable.

Dressed smartly, ready for the office, I go out to my car, then drive the short way to my job. I get a hot chocolate from the machine, eyeing people carrying coffee with envy, exchanging pleasantries with colleagues, and brief discussions about what kind of weekend we've all had.

Everything is exactly the same as a normal start to the week, until I enter my actual place of work.

Beth, Carter, Shayla and Sian have their heads together near Beth's desk. Odd, we don't all work in the same department, and by this time I'd have expected them to be in their own offices.

Ah. The penny drops. Beth came back from Vegas yesterday, I bet she's telling them the fun she had. My suspicions, I reckon, are proved correct as they're all staring intently at her phone. Showing off her pictures, I expect. I'll wait until later to share my news about the baby and show my own treasured photograph.

I make my way across to her desk, still holding my paper cup of hot chocolate. I take a sip as I approach.

"Hey, you had a good time in Vegas, I take it? Did it live up to your dreams?"

As she turns to me, there's a strange look on her face. She looks almost scared.

Carter's reaction is odd. He moves around me and takes the paper cup out of my hand.

Shayla draws up a chair. "Sit, Mel."

My brows knit together. "What is it?"

"Maybe nothing," Beth says fast. "But you know I've been in Vegas the past few days. I could be wrong, but I saw someone I thought I recognised." Her hand is shaking as she passes me her phone.

"I took a few pictures, so you could see from every angle."

I look at the first. It looks familiar, but too far away. Next she's zoomed in. And the next. I go back and look at them again. My vision starts to go blurry, my head feels faint, I drop the phone on her desk and lower my head into my hands. In every picture she's shown me, I'd seen my old man. I'd seen Skull alive and well, and… his arm is around a pretty young woman, she's pushing a stroller and he's carrying bags in his free hand.

"It could be a sister, Mel…"

I shake my head, trying to push through the dizziness and fog which has descended into my brain. It's not the woman that bothers me. It's the fact I've just seen my man. Alive, when I'd given up all hope and thought he was dead.

He's abandoned me.

Perhaps he had crashed, hurt his head, got amnesia… Perhaps the pope doesn't wear a funny hat and bears don't shit in the woods.

I hit the heel of my hand against my forehead. *Of course, a man like Skull wouldn't have stayed with a woman like me.*

"Here, Mel. Take this."

It's only when Beth stuffs a tissue into my hand that I realise I'm crying.

They try to talk to me, but there's only one person I want. Only one man who can help and understand. Another who was left behind, just like me.

I delve into the bag I'm still carrying over my shoulder and take out my phone. It takes a moment for my trembling fingers to unlock it.

The call is answered immediately. "Yo, you got Pyro."

"Pyro? I need you. C-c-can you come get me from work?"

"Darlin', are you sick? Something up with the baby?"

"Please, just come." I do not want to discuss this over the phone.

"On my way, sweetheart."

I place my own phone back where it came from, then reach out my hand. "Let me see again." Heaven help me, but I'm hoping I made a mistake. What does it say about me that I'd rather Skull was dead?

"I'll send them to you, hold on a sec."

She does, my purse vibrates, telling me her messages have arrived.

"I'm... I'm sorry, Mel. I know you're upset. I wasn't sure whether to tell you or not."

"I told her to, Mel. I thought you'd want to know." I manage a small nod toward Carter. He's right.

My phone's in my hand, I'm viewing the pictures again. Carter disappears, then a few minutes later returns, escorting a man into the office. It's Pyro. He got here fast.

Wordlessly I pass my phone over, looking up to see the expression on his face, wanting the identity to be confirmed, or denied as is my preference. As his jaw goes tight, I know there's no doubt. Skull's alive and well, and was enjoying life in Vegas this last weekend.

"Fuckin' hell," Pyro growls. "Get your shit, Mel. You're coming with me." His eyes find Beth's. "You'll cover for her?"

"She's sick and gone home," Beth confirms.

Pyro helps me to my feet, takes the purse from my hands, and without worrying it could be damaging his masculinity, drapes it over his shoulder instead of my own. He places his arm around me.

I need it. I'm wobbling as I walk, the effort to concentrate on putting one foot in front of the other proving almost too much.

"We're going back to the club, Mel," he informs me as he opens the door to the car he's brought.

"I..."

He looks over as I sit in the passenger seat, but I can get no more words out. "It will be alright, Mel," he tries to assure me.

But how? How can this possibly be made right?

All sorts of stupid things cross my mind, the notion somehow floating to the top that my baby really does have a dad now. A man who could have equal parenting rights. A man I want nothing to do with now I know he left me and allowed me to think he was dead.

The implications of Skull being alive is much harder to deal with than grieving about him being out of the land of the living.

When we arrive at the club, I feel numb. Pyro parks, slips on his cut, then helps me out of the car. Again, his supporting arm encourages me to put right foot after left until we're walking inside.

"Prez around?"

"In his office," Beaver responds.

Pyro leads me on through. He knocks on the door, then, once we enter, helps me to sit without waiting for Demon's permission, or caring what we might have interrupted. He takes the chair next to me, after pulling it closer to mine, so he can place his arm around my shoulders.

When he hands me my phone, I put the security code in, then he passes it over the desk.

Demon's face tightens as he repeats the actions I'd first done, swiping from one photo to the next, then going back through the series again.

"When were these taken?" he asks, as if holding out hope they are old ones.

Pyro leaves no room for misunderstanding. "This past weekend."

Demon uses his own phone. "Cad. Get in here now." That's all he says.

The computer guy's there in a moment. Well, his office is only next door. He views the photos much the same as anyone else, using finger and thumb to enlarge the clearest.

"There's no fuckin' doubt," he announces at last.

There's not. There's the giveaway scar running through his left eyebrow that's clear when you zoom in.

"Where did you get these, Mel?" Cad unsurprisingly wants all the information he can get.

Knowing it's hard for me to speak, Pyro replies for me. "Friend from her work was in Vegas this weekend. She took them there."

"How would she know it was Skull?" Again, it's Cad who queries me.

"She, er, she met him a few times," I manage to get out.

"Can you give me her number, Mel?"

I'm sure Beth wouldn't mind under the circumstances. "Yeees," I stammer out. "But I d-d-d-don't think there's anything more she can tell you. She wasn't c-c-c-certain of course, so didn't approach him."

The computer man's eyes flick to Pyro then to Demon. "I'd like to know her impression. Did he look like a resident or a visitor? See this bag he's holding? It's got a grocery store logo on it. Might mean nothing at all, but if it's grocery shit, he could be a local."

"Or self-catering at an Airbnb," Demon suggests.

"I'd still like to talk to her. There's a way people tend to look when they're tourists. Interested, looking around all the time. Locals tend to be more focused. Any clue we might prompt her to remember would help."

"If he's a local, he'd be easier to find?"

The conversation has been going on over my head. Suddenly those words hammer home and I interrupt, "I don't know if I want you to find him." All three men look astonished, so I try to offer an explanation. "I loved him; thought I still did. Mourned him as though he was dead. Spent months trying to cope living with his memory rather than the man himself." That's not news to them. "This," I point to my phone lying forlorn on the desk. "This proves he left me without a second thought. He knew I'd believe the worst, yet still he left. He could have called, told me he wasn't coming back, but he didn't. He left me to think…"

I sob, and this time it's Pyro who hands the tissue to me.

"He left the club too," Demon reminds me through gritted teeth. "Another couple of months we'd have held a wake. Didn't hold it sooner because of you, but that was in my mind. He let us think he was dead too, Mel."

"I want to find him. Make him wish he was fuckin' dead," Pyro snarls.

"I want to kill him myself."

I'm not sure whether Demon is joking.

"I'm pregnant," I say, hurriedly. "That man, in those pictures. That man is this baby's father." My voice drops and becomes a whisper. "What if he wants custody when he finds out? Or at least, to exercise his parental rights?"

Pyro's eyes have gone wide. "Motherfucker walked off and left you, Mel. He didn't know you were pregnant, but there was a chance. Parental fuckin' rights?" He snorts. "Man like that who doesn't want or deserve a baby, shouldn't fuckin' be entitled to anything."

Demon's eyes flare. "I hear what you're saying, Ro, but I hear Mel too. Wasn't too far back Vi was faced with a custody battle with Theo's sperm donor. There's going to be a risk Skull will decide he wants to be a dad in a few years' time, even if he doesn't right now. There's no saying the courts might not find in his favour."

"What are you suggesting we do, Prez?"

"Kill him?" Cad offers almost hopefully.

"Make him realise at the very least that it's not in his best interests to have anything to do with the kid. Before we do anything… drastic, we get him to sign away his parental rights."

Which means I'll have to do the one thing I don't think I'll ever be ready for. "I'll have to face him."

CHAPTER TWENTY-ONE

Pyro

Mel's realisation that she'll have to come face-to-face with the man who'd walked out on her without a backward glance at her most vulnerable time hits her hard.

She'd been holding it together well, but it was just a dam waiting for the right moment to break. One sob comes, followed by another then more. As tears stream down her face, Demon catches my eye and jerks his head.

It's not that the prez can't deal with a crying woman, he and I both know now she needs comfort and support.

I half lead, half carry her up to my room. While I'd like to be ranting, raving, and working out a plan with Prez and Cad, I know they'll think of everything I could probably put in. It's Mel who needs me now, so I'll leave the next steps to them. Sure thing I know is that we will be taking them.

If that means I'll be putting bullets in my gun and going to Vegas armed with a shovel, that's what I'll do. Right at the moment, anything less wouldn't satisfy me.

Always knew that man was an idiot and a fool to walk out on Mel, but I always thought he hadn't returned because he couldn't. Never once dreamed it had been by choice. Who'd leave such an amazing woman as her without a backward glance?

He hurt her once. Now he's gone and fucking hurt her all over again. How much can one woman take?

I'd hoped I'd one day be lying on my bed with her in my arms but had never expected it would be under these circumstances.

She's wailing, and in between her cries, saying over and over again, "I hate him, I hate him, Ro."

I'm pleased as fuck when her tears eventually dry out, worried as hell what all her distress is doing to the baby. *It can't be good for him.*

Still, I rock her gently in my arms, then eventually, in a small voice she asks, "Am I such a terrible woman, Pyro? I should be glad he's alive. Should be happy that my baby will have a man he can call dad. But I can't be."

"It's the shock," I tell her. "You can't expect to think straight or make decisions right now. Your initial reaction might change." I hope to fuck it doesn't. When Skull hears about the baby, if he wants to go back to her, would she let him? *Over my fucking dead body.*

Club won't have him back, that's for certain. He'll be out bad for sure. Never able to ride with the Devils again, nor any of the clubs we have relations with. No excuse on earth would be good enough for Demon to give him another chance. In the unlikely event she ends up forgiving and wanting him to play house with her, it will be without the cut on his back. That's if we leave him breathing.

Time passes, I couldn't say how long, but as the sun moves position and removes its beams from my room, I'd guess it was late afternoon when a knock comes on the door. Mel's fallen into a restless sleep, so I ease away from her gently, and quietly cross the room. Opening the door, I step outside, pulling it closed behind me.

"How is she?" Vi looks cross, and I guess it's on Mel's behalf.

"Shattered. She's sleeping now."

"D wants to see you, Ro. I'll sit with her while you're gone."

I'm torn. While I want to hear any news, I don't want to leave Mel.

Vi raises her chin. "I know something of what she's going through because of all that business with Angel, when he wanted my son."

"She doesn't need to hear that, Vi," I warn.

"I *know* that. But her emotions, those I can understand. Being pregnant too, been there, done that. If she needs you, you're only downstairs."

If anyone has to sit with Mel, the best is probably Vi. Satisfied that she understands Mel shouldn't be upset any more than she already is, I leave her in the hands of the prez's old lady and descend to Demon's office.

It's empty.

"Church!" Karl yells out, pausing his prospect duties cleaning the bar.

Waving my hand as my thanks, I go to our meeting room.

I can hear it before I open the door. Shouts, exclamations, hands slamming onto the wooden table. My entrance causes a brief lull.

"How's she doing, Ro?"

I shake my head. "Fuckin' terrible, Prez." It's the truth.

"Woman does not deserve this!" Beef snarls.

Prez bangs the gavel. "Pyro, sit down. I was waiting for you, and the rest of you fuckers, shut up. We all feel the same, now we've got to decide what to do."

"Fuckin' end his miserable life," Thunder snarls.

"Think that's what we'd all like, Brother. But first we've got to find the motherfucker. Cad, over to you."

Cad looks serious as all eyes turn his way. "We know he was in Vegas on Saturday, that's when the pictures were taken. I've spoken to Beth, Mel's friend. She was helpful and tried to remember everything she could. The photos were taken in a back street off the strip. Mel's friend was staying at one of the cheaper hotels and was going back to it at the time."

"You think he lives there?"

"If he was acting like a tourist on the strip, I'd say no. Can't tell either way, but Beth said he looked like he knew the area from what she could tell—she, herself, was using an app on her phone to find her hotel."

"He's still not using his bank account?"

Cad shakes his head at Ink's question, and resumes, "No, but it could be he's living off this woman he was with, or he's got cash. I've been in touch with Mouse, who's called on Cara's help."

My eyes crease, and so do those of a lot of people.

Cad sees and explains. "Long story how they first met, but the long and short of it is, if Mouse needs to get into databases he can't, Cara helps out."

Beef's nodding. "She helped find info on Steph when we needed her to."

"She's a sheikh's wife and some sort of royalty where she lives, so doesn't often get involved for political reasons. But she sometimes will. Mel's story tugged at her heart, so she's willing to do what she can."

"What's she found out?" Mace prompts, like me more interested in the information than where it came from.

"It's more what she hasn't," Cad resumes. "First, no Kris Cox owns or rents property in Vegas. He has no vehicle registered to him in Nevada."

"So, he's a tourist." I grimace. Fuck knows where his home base could be. And already, by now, the trail might have gone dry.

"Maybe. Her searches on hotels and rental properties haven't pulled up anything as yet. She checked the airlines, and no one of that name has flown in or out of Vegas."

This Cara can certainly get into a database or two. I'm

impressed, though disappointed. "He could have driven in from anywhere."

"He could," Cad agrees.

"If a man doesn't want to be found, he could be using an assumed name," Paladin suggests.

"What I was coming to," says Cad. "Only lead we got is that he was seen in Vegas."

Prez takes over. "This doesn't sound like it will be easy. We could accept he's alive, pass his details to other chapters and friendly clubs, but for now, leave him in the wind. Or we take proactive steps to find him."

"Find him." Hellfire slams his hand on the table. "Man has to get what's coming to him for walking out on the club. Big disrespect right there."

"He'd have gotten a beatdown if he turned in his patch," Bomber observes mildly. "Skull knows what that entails, he'd been through it before. Can't blame a man for not wanting to go through that pain again."

"Because of that," Demon is shaking his head, "if he'd been upfront, come to us and said he'd wanted to leave, we'd have gone easy on him, and possibly not beaten on him at all. Nah, I read it as he didn't give a damn about the club, nor the woman he left, and just walked away."

"Doesn't make sense." Lizard looks confused. "We weren't into anything shady, neither Pal nor Pyro were working him too hard. He didn't give any indication that he was bored, or the life wasn't for him. What if he came off his bike, hit his head too hard, and forgot who he was?"

"Bit of a stretch there, Brother. But you know, that makes about as much sense as anything else." Prez raises his hand to stop anyone else butting in. "But it seems we're not going to rest easy until we find him and get answers." He nods at me. "Cleanest way for Mel too. She doesn't need to have a cloud full of paternity issues hanging over her head." As I raise my chin back, he continues, "Here's what I propose we do. I'll get onto Red and send him the photos Mel's friend took. Get him to get his boys to keep an eye open, maybe do a few sweeps in the area where he was seen."

Murmurs of agreement go around the table. I'm nodding too. Red is the president of the Las Vegas chapter of the Satan's Devils MC. We've got brothers in the locality, so why the fuck not use them?

"I want to go," Judge growls. "Got scores to settle with that man." When eyes go to the bottom of the table, Wills looks eager as well.

"We," Wills points to Judge and himself, "we prospected alongside Skull. That man was so eager to get his patch, can't understand how he could just walk away. Can't believe he thought so little of the club he tried so hard to get into."

"I want to ask him to his fuckin' face," Judge agrees.

"With my fuckin' fist," Wills suggests.

Prez nods. "Makes sense some of us go there. Anyone else want a trip to Vegas?"

"Expenses paid?" Lizard raises his hand.

"You'll stay at the clubhouse if Red's agreeable. And no, Liz, you're not getting extra to lose at the slots."

"Shucks," says Lizard with a shrug. "Just thought Skull might be playing the tables."

"I'll go," says Sparky, our road captain. "These fuckers will need someone to show them the way." Someone throws a piece of wadded up paper at him.

Prez looks around. "Liz, need you here to keep the tattoo parlour going. Rusty, same with you and the bowling alley. Pyro?"

"The shop would do fine without me, but I need to be here for Mel." I'd rather be seeking out Skull to kill him, but don't want to leave her alone.

Prez resumes, "Judge, Wills and Sparky. You can ride down there tomorrow. Assuming Red's cool with the idea."

Wills starts rubbing his hands together and banging one fist into the other palm.

"Whoever," Demon begins with a glare, "finds him, assuming we're successful, whether it's Red's men or you, you're to take him back to the clubhouse. I personally want words with that motherfucker and want him able to form words when I do, you hear me?"

"Can't we get any shots in?" Sparky moans.

"Just be careful," Prez warns. "Leave him able to speak."

"Man was hurt once because of a mistake, Prez," Beef comments. "I can't see there's any acceptable excuse he could offer, but I do agree you need to speak to him first. Before anyone lets their fists fly."

Hellfire coughs then raises his eyebrows, I return my attention to the head of the table. Demon's looking at Beef, considering his words, then nods. "Okay, slight change of plans. Get hold of him but it's hands off until I get there. Then," an evil grin covers his face, "we'll make him hurt so he'll think last time was a picnic."

There are thumps on the table with fists and stomps of feet after that pronouncement.

Mel's awake when I return. She's sitting up, talking to Vi. I'm pleased to see there's a plate of half-eaten food beside her. At least it appears she's had some sustenance.

"Am I interrupting?"

Mel shakes her head. "No, I'm just going around in circles. I think we've covered all the ground at least three times."

"How are you feeling?" Stepping into the room I take in the sight of Mel's sore looking red and puffy eyes, suggesting she's been crying again. If it was down to me, I'd spend my life making sure she never had cause to shed tears.

"I'll be off now. It's nearly Theo's bedtime and I need to take him home," Vi explains. "We'll talk tomorrow."

"Thanks Vi." Mel manages a half-smile for her friend.

She waits until Vi's closed the door behind her, then turns to me. As she takes a shuddering breath, I notice she's smiling no more. "Pyro, can we talk?"

"Of course." As I take Vi's place sitting beside her, I note she hasn't answered my question, but I can work the answer out for myself. *She's hurting.*

"I want to go to Vegas." Her jaw is set.

That wasn't what I'd expected. "Mel, what's Vi been saying?"

Her hands wave dismissively. "Not on Vi. In fact, she tried to dissuade me. But I think it's the best idea. If I can find him, I can confront him."

I rub my hands down my face. "Darlin', there must be a couple of million people living in and around Vegas, and fuck knows how many tourists at any one time. How the fuck do you think you can find him?"

"Beth managed to," she challenges.

"Coincidence Mel. Even she probably wouldn't be able to come across him again." I decide to let her in on some club business. "You know there's a Satan's Devils' Vegas Chapter, don't you? Well, Demon's going to ask the Vegas prez to get his boys keeping an eye out for Skull. They're locals, they're more likely to know where to start looking. Sparky, Judge and Wills are going to go down there as well. If, and it's a big if, if he's still there and wasn't just visiting, they have more chance of finding him."

"When they do," she ignores the if, "I need to speak to him."

I'd been working out ways of her not having to face him. "You don't have to."

"This is something I'll have to do, if only to get the paperwork filled out."

"We can do that through lawyers…"

Her eyebrow rises defiantly. "A lawyer wouldn't spit in his face."

CHAPTER TWENTY-TWO

Melissa

How can love turn to hatred in a blink of an eye?

When Skull disappeared, he'd broken my heart. When I thought he was dead, I felt like a part of myself had died along with him. I knew I'd always love the father of my child, who, I'd convinced myself would have returned if he'd been able to.

When I found out he was alive, I should have been happy. I wasn't. What he'd caused both myself and my unborn child to suffer, hadn't been deserved. He didn't leave in ignorance of how I felt about him, he must have known how much him disappearing would hurt.

Had I really loved him at all? Instead, had I been flattered by the attentions of a younger man? Allowed myself to be taken in by lies and deceit? The man I thought I knew would never have just left me like that. Maybe I'd been in love with the persona he'd portrayed and never knew the real man at all.

I'd felt no relief knowing he was alive.

Even if I allowed Skull to play any part in his life, there was always the possibility he'd turn his back on on my baby too. My baby deserves a dad he can depend on, a reliable man. A man who steps up when he has no need to. A man who provides a shoulder to lean on when it's required. A man who's good company, a man who shares in both the pain and pleasure. A man who cries when he sees his son for the first time on an ultrasound screen.

My son deserves a man like Pyro to be his dad.

Pyro's fingers are drawing circles on my arm, an action meant to be comforting. His closeness makes me blurt out, "I wish you were this baby's father."

He stills.

God, I shouldn't have spoken my thoughts aloud. I wonder how on earth I can take those words back.

"I do too. Kid deserves a man who doesn't stray. You're right, we need to deal with Skull. Get him out of the picture for good. You want to take your own swing at him, reckon you're entitled. Happy to play the role of the kid's dad, darlin'. Think that's what I'm already doing."

I notice he's avoiding the implications of what I'd said. While he may be a dad for the baby, he's not saying anything about being a husband for me. We don't have that kind of relationship. Dads live separate to kids all the time. I can't ruin what we've got by wanting more.

Pyro sighs deeply. "If you really want to go to Vegas, I'll come with you, okay?"

"Am I awful to say I was hoping you would?"

"Nah, Mel. You and me. We're a team."

I think of the practicalities. I need to take time off from my job. Well, I've got some vacation and sick days built up. That will have to do. Thinking about the steps that I'll need to be taking reminds me of something else.

"Ro," I start, hesitantly, "I don't want to be alone tonight. Can I stay here?"

"Sure," he agrees fast. "In here, or Skull's room? I'm happy to use Skull's. I'll understand why you don't want to."

"No, I meant here with you."

He draws in his breath. Then turns on his side to face me, his hand coming up and resting on my face. "Mel, sweetheart. I fuckin' love being your friend. I fuckin' love looking out for you and the kid. I don't' want anything to fuck that up."

Neither do I. I don't want to say anything that would mean I lose his friendship and support. With this man at my side I can take on the world, without him, I don't know what I'd do. *Friends. That's all he wants. It will have to be enough.*

I backtrack. "I didn't mean it how it sounded."

"I know you didn't, darlin'." His eyes stare into mine. "I'm trying so fuckin' hard. But it's not easy being around you. You, me, sleeping together in the same bed? Not fair on me, and not on you."

"Why's it not fair on me, Ro?" I'm confused. "Or for you?"

"Because I could fuck everything up." He rears up, leaving me feeling bereft. He stands and paces. "Friends. I want us to be friends, Mel."

I, too, pull myself up so I'm kneeling. "We *are* friends," I cry out.

"But I want fuckin' more," he suddenly roars. Then comes back over, his palms landing on the bed either side of me. "I'll say this once, then never refer to it again. I fuckin' want you. I want the whole package, sweetheart. I want to have this baby with you, to have you as my wife and the kid as my son. I want everything."

My eyes go wide.

He gives an abrupt nod, stands and takes the few strides that take him to the door. He pauses only to say, "If you need me, I'll be in Skull's room."

"Wait!"

His back turned in my direction, his hand waves by his side. "Nah, Mel. I don't need platitudes. Shouldn't have laid that on you. It's not your problem, okay? It's mine. I just need you to decide whether you still want me in your life when you know how I really feel about you."

"You feel about me the same way I feel about you, Pyro."

As he goes completely still, I move off the bed and slowly cross the room, each pace even like a hunter stalking prey, as if a sudden move may cause him to flee. "I haven't wanted to let you know because I didn't want to scare you away. If friendship was all you could offer, I was going to accept that. But I want you. All of you."

He still doesn't turn. "You've had a shock today, Mel. A shock no woman should have. If you'd been faced with his corpse, it could have had no greater effect on you. You're probably not thinking straight, and I'm not going to take advantage of that."

"I've been feeling this way for a while now. It didn't seem right, so I tried to fight it. I should have been grieving for what I'd lost, not wanting someone else. My feelings for you gradually changed until every time you left, I wanted you to kiss me properly, not just that peck to my forehead. I chickened out, but so often I wanted to raise my lips to yours."

I've reached him now. Putting my hands around his waist, I lean my head against his cut. "Yes, I'm emotional right now. I can't think straight about anything. But this isn't an impulsive reaction tonight. If," I swallow hard, "if you meant what you said, I can conquer anything with you beside me."

He takes a deep breath then shudders. "I want to feel your lips too. Mel, you can stay here tonight. I'll hold you in my arms, though," he gives a snort, "if we're that close I won't be able to hide the effect you have on me. I'm just warning you. No, let me finish. I'll hold you, but nothing more. Don't want to leap into something you might regret. Moving from being friends to being in a relationship will take some adjustment. Something that could be good is worth waiting and working for. We'll take this slow while we've got this shit storm to work through."

He makes sense. Getting physical with another man while

Skull's reared his head is perhaps not the best thing to do. Though I feel no sense of loyalty toward the man who left me thinking he was dead, there hasn't been any sort of closure. Just a gradual acceptance that he was never coming back, and now I don't want him to.

But I've a niggling worry. "What if we can't sort things out? What if we can't find him?"

Now he turns, taking me in his arms, holding me close to him like he has so many times before. "Let's take this one step at a time. We don't find Skull? We decide what we'll do then. Don't think any of us have really got our heads around the fact he's not dead." He places his fingers under my chin. "Give me those lips now, darlin'."

I need no further encouragement.

As our mouths move together I get the impression that the adjustment from friends to lovers isn't going to be hard at all, once we've got everything straight in our heads. There are a few seconds of awkwardness, when he moves one way, me the other, then our bodies work out what to do, and we start learning a dance which I hope will become familiar over time. His taste is perfect, his movements sure and certain, until all too soon he groans into my mouth and pulls away.

The reason is clear as he grits his teeth and reaches down to adjust himself in his jeans. "That's why we've not kissed before woman." He grins self-deprecatingly. "Knew you'd make me as hard as fuckin' steel."

"There is one way to take our minds off everything," I offer, biting my lip suggestively.

"Nope. Told you how this is going to play out." His head tilts to the side. "Don't doubt how much I'd like to fuck, to make love to you. But the timing has got to be right. Don't want you having any doubts. Don't want any guilty thoughts in your head when you meet face-to-face with Skull. Want you to meet him with your conscience clear."

"What if we don't find him, or it takes months?"

He shakes his head. "I might have patience, but not a lot. Not waiting that long, darlin'. I promise you that. Now, before you can tempt me further, what say we show our faces downstairs and see if Prez has gotten the green light from Red."

Now I'm biting my lip for another reason. "They're all going to be looking at me, aren't they, Ro? The woman whose old man has come back from the dead."

"Nah. You've got to remember, that's our brother we're talking about. Sure, he was your old man, but he wore our patch and fuckin' disrespected it. *That's* what they're most worried about."

I suppose he's right.

I'm still anxious as I descend the stairs with him.

When I ascended them earlier I was in a hell of a state. I couldn't help it, even though I knew my distress couldn't be good for the baby. But slowly the shock began to wear off. Now I'm ready to start dealing instead of reacting. As Pyro slips his large hand around mine allowing me to take comfort from his fingers, I acknowledge I'm feeling more positive now I know he's going to be there for me in every way.

My baby will have a father. Getting to know him slowly has shown me I couldn't have chosen better. Along with my disbelief that Skull's alive, and at the slap-in-the-face rejection that came along with that knowledge, I've now got something to look forward to. Starting a new life with Pyro.

It's just going to have to wait until we can put the old one fully behind us.

"Well, lookie here. What have we got?" Beef comes over and slaps Pyro's back. He looks pointedly down at our joined hands. "Bout fuckin' time, Brother."

"Not doing any claimin' as yet," Pyro growls. "But yeah, we're taking steps in the right direction."

Beef moves to stand in front of me. "How you feelin', sweetheart?"

"Betrayed? Yes," I reply, trying to find the truthful answer. "Hurt, definitely. It was just too much, finding out like that."

"I'm sure it was."

"Ro!" Demon's by the bar, beckoning him over.

He exchanges a chin lift with Beef, then after a little tug on my hand that gets me moving, takes me over to join his prez.

Demon glances at me, then gives me a nod. I take it that my attempt at pulling myself together hasn't gone wasted. He tilts his head toward Pyro. "You told her anything?"

"That we're getting Vegas involved, yes."

"Yeah. I've spoken to Red. He, er, well, once he'd let rip, he was more than happy to try to track that fucker down and to put up whoever we send there."

"I didn't doubt he'd help."

"Help? Had to stop him taking a gun to Skull himself," Prez growls.

"They're Satan's Devils, Mel," Pyro explains at my surprised gasp. "Disrespect one of us, everyone from whatever chapter feels the insult."

I start to wonder just exactly how crazy Skull must be to set himself against this group of men. I've already seen they love and protect fiercely, and now see the opposite side of the coin is the strength of their hate, together with their need for retribution. Skull won't escape unscathed.

"Mel wants to go to Vegas," Pyro explains. He raises an eyebrow at Demon.

"Much as I hate to say it, this could be a wild goose chase. He might already be gone."

I narrow my eyes. "Now I know he's alive, I'm not going to give up, Demon. He's alive, I've got proof. I'll go to the cops if I have to, get the courts involved to get child support."

Demon stills. "You'll be inviting him into the life you want to keep him out of. The life I suspect you'll be living with Ro."

I smile as sweetly as I can. "Then I hope the Devils will make sure that Skull won't be able to interfere with Pyro and me. I'm sure you'll be able to find a permanent solution."

Demon splutters, Pyro barks a loud laugh. He puts his arm around me and tugs me to him. "Christ woman, you're fuckin' perfect, aren't you?"

CHAPTER TWENTY-THREE

Pyro

"A word, Ro?"

"I'm going on up. I'm exhausted." Mel puts her hand to her mouth to cover a yawn as she takes the hint Prez wants to talk to me alone.

I nod at her, worried, trying to assess her state of mind. But she seems genuinely tired, and not surprising, given the knocks she's taken today. "I'll be there in a moment."

I motion to Beaver who interprets it correctly, bringing me a beer while I turn to the man who had spoken. "What's up, Prez?"

"You tapped that?" Demon asks, his eyes following Mel as she makes her way across the room.

"Nah. Heading that way, but not yet, no."

"Keep it like that."

As my brow creases, he explains, "A living brother claimed her."

Beer spits out of my mouth. "I'm sorry? What the fuck did you just say?"

"I think I was quite clear. Skull claimed her. You know it's forbidden for anyone to lay their hands on a woman who

195

belongs to another member, particularly in this chapter. Blackie was killed for that very thing." He names his grandfather, killed by Hellfire with the club's blessing. Hellfire was only a prospect at the time, but everyone knew Moira was his. It's never been admitted, but the clues are all there. Moira fell pregnant, and most of us suspect the relationship is not exactly what it's been made out to be for all these years. We all suspect Demon is Hellfire's brother, not his son. But hell, what do those facts matter? Just like the baby Mel's carrying, and Demon's own kid, Theo, it's just genetics. It's the nurture of a strong father figure which counts in every important way that matters.

But I leave history and memories behind and focus on the present. "Skull's not a member. Hasn't been thought of that way for four fucking months."

"Because we thought he was dead. Now he's living."

I stand, my head moving side to side in disbelief. "You cannot be serious. Take a fuckin' vote. Everyone would say aye to pulling his patch before you've gotten the words out of your fuckin' mouth."

"Careful, Ro. You're verging on disrespect yourself."

"Prez…"

"Hear me out. I don't think that man can offer any excuse worth hearing. But what if he did get that hypothetical bump on his head? What if he truly can't remember?"

"That shit doesn't happen."

"Unlikely, I admit, but it is possible. Bomber said he served with a man who forgot who he was after he'd gotten too close to a bomb blast. And Liz remembers meeting someone with temporary amnesia. Got his memory back, but with fuckin' large gaps in it."

I imagined walking up to Skull and watching his face fill with fear when he realises we've found him. Not for one moment had I considered he might look at me blankly as if I was a complete stranger. What are the implications if he did? Would Mel forgive him? Go back to him? Try and help him regain his memory? Jump back into his bed? Christ. It doesn't bear thinking about.

"Chances are fuckin' slim, I'll give you that. But something stopped that man coming back."

"Or, he selfishly left without feeling the need for explanation to Mel or to us." Fuck. I slam my empty beer bottle down on the bar and snarl at Beaver when he runs up with a new one. He moves swiftly away. "I wasn't going to fuck her, Prez, until we'd had a chance to find him. She needs to be able to maintain the high moral ground while he feeds her whatever fucked up line he'll try. But my patience is only going to last so long. If we have to give up the search, want to bring it to the table. Take away his patch, or I turn mine in. If I can't have Mel as a member, only one option."

"Whoa, hold up there, Ro. Don't say things you might regret."

"Won't be no regrets, Prez. I didn't think I'd ever settle down. I was jealous of Skull when he found Mel as he'd discovered a gem, a diamond that I hadn't known existed. But I said nothing, stayed back, would never go near another man's woman. Even when he disappeared I didn't step up. Became a friend because of loyalty to my missing brother. Remained a friend to be true to his memory. Thought that was all I'd ever be to her. Wasn't going to fuck our friendship up, but I have been there looking out for her and the boy. Then Skull turns up." I pause and look directly at him. "Things have been said. I didn't dream she felt the same way about me. Nah, not when she was with Skull, but when he left, she accepted my friendship, and her feelings gradually became deeper. We only admitted it to each other today."

I pause, look around the club, and am certain when I turn back. "Love this club. Love my brothers. Don't want to leave. But this isn't some flash in the pan thing, this is forever. I can't have her and still be a member, then I've no choice. She comes first."

He doesn't give away his reaction immediately, and his eyes

glaze slightly. "Beef was going to give it all up for Steph," he reminds me. "When you find the right woman, the club isn't enough." He stops and takes a breath. "Not going to lose you, Ro. All I'm asking is we do it properly. Don't want anyone saying because Skull didn't turn in his patch, and we didn't vote it off him, that she's still his property. You keep your relationship respectful until we can make it formal, then all's right between us."

"She's still staying in my bed. She needs me, Prez. As a friend at this point, more than a lover."

"I can live with that."

His hand grips my shoulder, squeezes it gently, then he walks off.

Mel looks fuckin' amazing lying in my bed. Only her head is peeking out from under the sheet, her dark hair lying over the pillow. My gut clenches at the sight I'd never hoped to see.

"You got anything on under that sheet?" If she's naked, it will be fucking difficult to keep the promise I'd just made. I'm a man, after all.

Her face goes pink. "I helped myself to one of your tee shirts. I hope you don't mind."

Of course I don't. Though she's darn near turned difficult into fucking impossible. A wave of possessiveness goes through me.

If she left me now and went back to Skull, it wouldn't just hurt. I think it would be a mortal blow.

Moving forward, I stand at the end of the bed. "What would it take, Mel? What would it take for you to go back to Skull?"

She sits up at my question. The sheet falls revealing she's snagged one of my favourite tees, an Iron Maiden one. *Good taste, darlin'.* "What are you talking about, Pyro? There's nothing at all that would persuade me to go back."

"What if he'd lost his memory and had truly forgotten you? What if there's a valid reason for all this?"

She looks down at her hands. "I've been thinking about that. Am I awful to say it wouldn't make a difference? All these months he's been gone, I keep going over and over things that we said, the way he'd walked out and left me at first for just that one night. He blamed me for something that was down to him. I think he expected me to be the adult in the relationship. I was older, and he persuaded me our age difference didn't matter. But looking back, I think it did. In little ways, it's hard to pinpoint."

I'm relieved as fuck that she wouldn't return to him. "Age means nothing. Any man can behave like an ass. Can throw out his toys when the going gets rough. I don't think age had anything to do with it. Don't think he treated you as well as we thought, but who knows what goes on between a man and a woman behind closed doors?"

I take off my cut and remove my boots, she looks on like I'm unwrapping a present. But I leave on my jeans and tee and lie on top of the covers.

"I thought we were going to cuddle?"

"Still can, darlin'. But we'll do it with the comforter between us. I don't need any more temptation. Prez has just reminded me of something." At her questioning look, I continue, "Until we've come to some decisions about Skull, you're still technically his woman, and therefore, off bounds to me." As she bristles, I stop her speaking by resting my fingers gently over her mouth. "Nothing more than we've already agreed. Just given another reason for it."

"So claiming is for life? Why can't I unclaim myself? I don't want anything to do with him."

"No one would have an argument with that, Mel. Just need to do things properly. Doing it right means we need to put the brakes on until we get answers and everyone's satisfied. Skull's not dead, we're all sure of that. Not saying you have to think yourself his woman while he still breathes, nor that any of my brothers would think less of you for taking up with me. But there's a right and wrong way of doing things. I'd rather wait if that's what we need to do. You're worth it, Mel. Fuckin' believe that."

I wonder if she's going to protest further. I'm already thinking of what else I can say to try to make her understand, while not saying out loud that in the eyes of the club, she's still Skull's property, when not for the first time, she surprises me.

"But you're in here with me?" Her brow creases. "Should I leave?"

"Nah. They'll all know we aren't getting up to shit."

"How?"

"Because they'll see I'm walking bowlegged from the hard-on I ain't getting release from, and also, when we do get to fuck, I'm going to make it my mission to make you scream louder than you've ever done before."

"I didn't, I don't…"

I cock my eyebrow. "Walls are thin, darlin'."

Her mouth opens in an O, then, slowly, she starts disappearing under the sheet.

It might have been the ultimate fuck up of a day, but I bellow a laugh, and make that silent promise to her and myself. One day I'm going to make her scream louder than Skull ever did.

Early the next morning I hear three bikes heading out, the roar of their exhaust shattering the peace. Glancing over at my phone I see it's still early, only five-thirty am. I don't blame them getting an early start, they've got a twelve-hour journey ahead of them, and that's if they don't make any stops, which they'll need to, to top off tanks and stomachs.

Quietly sending them good vibes for keeping the shiny side up, I turn on my side and watch my woman sleeping. No, not mine as yet, but hopefully, soon.

Unused to having company in my bed or sleeping with an unresolved rod of iron in my pants, I've had a restless night, but used it to do some thinking. I'll fly Mel across to Vegas. I wouldn't ask a woman unused to riding to make a seven-hundred-mile journey without leading up to it, even if she wasn't pregnant. No, she can travel in relative comfort. Not that flying economy is a luxury, but better than spending hours on the back of my bike.

My woman and child. Christ. How did I get so lucky? Was it only yesterday I awoke, not daring to dream that we'd be making any commitment? That I had any hope of ever moving out of the friendzone. Now all we've got to do is get Skull back firmly in the rearview, then we can start living. For ourselves.

If it comes to it, I've no worries about leaving the club. Would hate it, but I could survive in the civilian world if I have to. I've managed an auto-shop for years, got all the right qualifications. With my army record as well, I shouldn't have trouble finding employment. I'll definitely be able to support my old lady.

Of course, I'd prefer to stay in the club. Get Mel her own property vest. Idly, I wonder why Skull hadn't. He'd had enough time, just hadn't taken that step. I shift, trying to get comfortable when my mind conjures up a vision of her wearing only a leather cut with my name written on it. Of course, there's that old rule that I know Demon wouldn't insist on, that she gets 'Property of Pyro' tattooed on her back. I'd like that. I'll be sneaky about it, get Violet to design something really attractive, have something to show her before I approach it. Thank fuck Skull hadn't done that, and she has nothing that needs to be covered up.

Her missing cut and tattoo. Signs Skull had never been totally serious? If so, it's not just her he had fooled, but all of us.

"Good morning."

I think her face smiling up at me is going to become my new favourite way to wake up.

"Did you sleep well?"

"Surprisingly I did. I think I must have been mentally exhausted. But now he's pressing on my bladder and I need to go pee."

I nod. Watching her move off the bed, my eyes follow her to the bathroom.

When she returns, I look up from my phone and tell her, "We'll fly to Vegas. It's just under a four-hour flight."

"Oh, thank God. I wasn't looking forward to driving it."

"Thought that. When do you want to leave?"

"I've just got to talk to work, make sure they're okay with me taking time off. Then whenever you think."

"Tomorrow's soon enough. Tonight, the brothers will get to the clubhouse and start preparing to go out searching. There won't be any news today. I'll text Sparky later, ask him to ask Red to get a room ready for us."

"Sounds good, Ro."

"You get dressed and ready, then we'll get a bite to eat. I'll take you home so you can get packed and make the arrangements and I'll come pick you up later." I frown slightly, running over what I'll have to put in place to keep the shop going while I'm gone.

"I need to call Beth and tell her I'm okay. She was so guilty that she was the cause of me breaking down yesterday."

"Christ darlin'. Tell her from me, I'm glad she spotted him. Otherwise we could have gotten blindsided when we least expected it. This way, we know what we're dealing with. Sooner or later, we'll catch up with him."

"What will happen if we don't find him? What will it mean to us?" Her anxious face turns toward me. We'd spoken about this before, so now I think she's talking about the revelation I laid on her about her relationship in the eyes of the club.

I shrug. "I'll take it to the table. Hopefully the brothers will vote him out of the club, so we can be together."

She swings around fast. "Surely there's no doubt they'll do that?"

"Club rules are club rules. We don't break them lightly."

Her eyes widen. "So, we might never be allowed to be together?"

"One way or another, we will, and you can take that and bank it. If it means me leaving the club, then I'll do it."

She frowns. "I hope it doesn't come to that."

So do I.

CHAPTER TWENTY-FOUR

Melissa

Having made my calls, including one to a very relieved Beth, and gotten time off work by playing the pregnancy sympathy card with my boss, I pack a small carry-on bag with stuff I'll need in Vegas.

I tidy and clean my house, just to keep busy. I was startled by Pyro's revelation that he'd leave the club to be with me, just that one statement in many ways showing what had been missing with Skull. Real commitment. A sign that he was going to be all in.

Of course, Skull had once mentioned doing the same thing, but I'd known at the time that would never have worked. Pyro, though, he's more mature and while I'd had doubts about Skull being able to live in the citizen world, I don't have the same fears about Pyro, believing I, and the baby, come first with him.

Having done everything I can, I sit on the couch, leaning my head back, thinking. Suddenly I feel a little flutter in my stomach. *Wind?* Hard to tell. But it could be my baby moving.

I sit still, hoping to feel the sensation again, proof that new life is growing within me.

I'm not surprised there's nothing more. It could have been my imagination.

Pyro comes and collects me as promised. We have dinner at the club and a pleasant enough evening where the elephant in the room isn't mentioned. Then, I again sleep in Pyro's arms with the sheet separating us.

It's an early start to get to the airport. Karl drives us to Pueblo Memorial, leaving us at the drop off point, so we don't have to worry about parking.

"Have you spoken to your Mom and Dad about Skull turning up?" Pyro asks, as we line up for check-in.

"No." I shake my head. "Didn't seem to be any point in worrying them."

"Don't keep them out, Mel. You need people in your corner."

I grimace. "I know, but there's a balance between people trying to help, and you trying to stop them from overreacting. If Dad knew, he might be on the next plane to Vegas with a shot-gun." Half of me isn't joking.

Pyro snorts. "Think he'd have to join the line."

I find out something new about Pyro. He hates flying. On take-off he closes his eyes tightly, and holds my hand, only relaxing when the flight attendant starts serving. *If it wasn't for me, he'd be riding, or at least driving.* Another reason to fall in love with him.

"Are we hiring a car?" I ask, once the plane's levelled out and he seems more comfortable.

"No, Red will have someone picking us up."

"Is the Vegas club different to the Colorado one?"

"Yes, and no. Devils are pretty similar. Their compound is an old warehouse, a few miles out of town. Nothing special." He laughs. "Has Jayden told you about the Tucson club?"

"A few times," I smile. "Has it really got a swimming pool?"

"Yes. It was an old vacation resort and looks like one."

"Has Red got an old lady?"

He snorts. "No. Red, er, Red likes the ladies if you get my drift. Can't imagine him ever settling down."

I bump his arm. "I seem to remember you weren't much of one for settling, either."

"Nah, but it takes a very special woman to give up the single life, and I met you first. There's only one of you, darlin'. Red's out of luck."

I smile at the implied compliment. Then continue my inquisition. "And he's called Red, why?"

"I think you'll find out when you see him."

Pyro's just as tense on landing, so our conversation falters. I sit, watching the ground come into sharper focus beneath, but rather than trying to pick out the sights of Vegas, I'm seeing Skull's face in my head.

The man beside me is keeping me sane, though I don't think he knows he's doing it. If I didn't have him, if he wasn't so earnest in how he sees me and what he feels for me, if his declarations didn't drip with sincerity, and had those words not come at exactly the right time, I'd feel completely destroyed. Worthless. Though those feelings are there, lurking, Pyro is helping to keep them at bay.

I find out the reason for Red's handle much sooner than I'd expected. It's the Vegas prez himself who's driven to the airport to collect us. He almost needs no introduction, his cut with the name and Prez patches were redundant in relation to his thick red hair and bushy beard which scream who he is. Though Pyro uses the words while making the introductions, I really didn't need them.

He's tall, about the same height as Pyro, well-built and his tee, struggling to contain his muscles, shows he's ripped.

I nudge Pyro and he bends down so I can whisper into his ear, "If I'd seen him first, you might not have had a chance."

His eyes widen, then he sees me grinning. His hands come to my sides and the bastard tickles me.

"Stop, stop!" I demand, unable to stop giggling.

"Christ. And I was led to expect a demure pregnant woman." Red's eyes sparkle though, and the way he relaxes leads me to suspect that he was worried he'd have a distraught female on his hands.

He might well have had, if I didn't have Pyro to distract me.

Red's eyebrows have risen at my whispered words and Pyro's response. "Anything I should know, brother?"

Pyro looks at me. I mouth, *don't you dare tell him*. He shrugs. "Mel was just saying…" I gasp. "…that she's never been to Vegas."

"Well, then, let me welcome you on behalf of the city."

Pyro sits up front alongside the Vegas prez. I'm happy to sit in the back, and take in the new surroundings, only half-listening to the conversation between the two men. I can't stop myself searching for the man we've come to find, half-hoping, half-dreading that we'll see him. Of course, it isn't that easy, and anyway, Vegas is vast.

"Judge, Wills and Sparky arrive okay?"

I eavesdrop on Pyro and Red's conversation.

"Yeah, they got in last night. Didn't say they had any problems."

"Any sightings yet?"

My ears perk up. "Nah, had all my guys keeping their eyes open. They've got copies of those pictures you sent. So far, they haven't come up with anything. Will help now your men are here as they actually know him."

"I'll go out myself once I've got Mel settled."

"Hey, Pyro. I want to come along."

I don't miss the glance exchanged between the two men.

"Mel," Pyro leans around the head rest, "I'll probably go on a bike if Red's got one to spare. Easiest way to get through the Vegas traffic."

"I can get you a bike easy enough," Red agrees.

"Well, can I have a car then? It makes sense for me to go looking."

Again looks go between them, and Pyro just says, "We'll see," making me bristle and feel like I'm a child.

Though, I think as I sit back grumpily, they may have a point. I can't ride on Pyro's bike, and I've no idea where I'll be going in this unfamiliar city. I'll end up aimlessly driving around. Even if I do see Skull, finding a place to park a car isn't as easy as pulling a bike off to the side. From the way the traffic's already starting to build up around us, I'll need my eyes on the road, not to be scanning the sidewalks on either side. Still, much as it makes sense for me to be the little woman at home waiting for news, I won't be happy doing it.

"Mel?" Pyro calls my name to get my attention. "We find him, we'll bring him back to the compound. You'll have the chance to speak to him face-to-face. You deserve his explanation."

"Same as the club," Red adds. "Fucker walked out, and he better have a fuckin' good reason for that."

Off in the distance, I can see buildings which I suspect are the hotels and casinos around the strip, but Red skirts around the centre, so I don't see them up close. It makes me wish I was here under happier circumstances and could enjoy Vegas with Pyro beside me as my man.

The best I can hope for is that we find the needle in the haystack we're searching for and that Skull has an explanation that we can accept and provides me with closure. Then, that he rescinds any claim to me even if the club allows him to stay as a member, so I can truly be with Pyro instead.

Eventually we draw up at the compound. It's scruffy on the outside, and the inside looks tired, the couches, chairs and tables all having seen better days. Apart from the age of the furniture and the nicotine-stained walls, the clubroom itself isn't too different from that in Pueblo. There's a bar, pool tables and presumably because we're in Vegas, a one-armed bandit with flashing lights.

Music is playing loudly. There are scantily clad women hanging around which doesn't surprise me, and an older woman behind the bar which does. The men's faces might be unfamiliar, but the cuts and general uniform of jeans and tees are the same as in the club I've just left. There at the bar are the three men who rode up yesterday.

I give a little wave of my hand when Judge turns and catches sight of us. Pyro wastes no time leading me over to them, nor in exchanging greetings after the obligatory back slaps and hugs.

"Anything?"

"Nah." Sparky gets right down to business. He pulls a piece of paper toward him. Peering around Pyro I can see it's a printout of a map of the city, part of which is circled in high-lighter pen. "This is the area we're concentrating on. There's a grocery store as we hoped with the same logo that was on the bag Skull was carrying. There's a residential area here." He lays his finger on the map. "Trouble is, if he stocked up on the week-end, he might not be back for a few days, even if he does live somewhere close by."

"You been inside?"

"Yeah. Showed his picture to the cashiers, but it's a twenty-four-hour place with lots of staff on short-hour contracts. Manager chased us out when we asked who was working on Saturday afternoon."

"Got Keys trying to hack into the security cameras in the area to see if he can find any trace of where the fucker might have been headed after he left the store."

"Twister." Pyro turns and exchanges a man hug with the owner of the new voice. Then to me, he explains, "Mel, this is the Vegas equivalent of Mace."

Ah. The enforcer.

Twister gives me a nod, then continues to Pyro, "At least there was a time stamp on the photograph which gives him a place to start."

"I'm Rosa." The woman behind the bar comes over. She doesn't look like a whore and must be in her late forties or early fifties. I wonder which biker she's with, but don't bother to ask her, it wouldn't provide information as I've only met two of the local men so far.

She lifts the bar flap and comes out. "Red asked me to get you a room sorted. Want me to show you up?"

Overhearing, Pyro gives me a nod of encouragement. I don't want to leave him, I'd rather stay here and listen to his conversation instead, but I suspect he knows I'm tired after the flight and even though I'm eager for information, at the moment I need to think of myself, as well as the precious cargo I'm carrying, and rest. That he does understand is clear when he mouths, *I'll fill you in later.*

The flare in my eyes signals that he better. Then I reach down to lift one of the bags Pyro had brought in with him, mine, but a bellow shouted by Twister summons a prospect instead who quickly takes it from me, picking up Pyro's as well.

"Thanks, Owl," Rosa says to the prospect wearing thick-rimmed glasses as he drops the bags outside a door we've approached.

When she opens it, it's clear we've ousted a resident, belongings have been scooped up and piled on the floor. But the bed looks freshly made and comfortable.

"Bathroom's down the hall, I'm afraid."

An inconvenience, but I'm in no position to complain. I'm just grateful to have somewhere to lay my head. I'd prefer to be here in the thick of the action, rather than try to keep track remotely from an anonymous hotel. "Thank you for putting us up. We'll hopefully only be here a couple of days." The sooner they find Skull, sooner we can get back home.

I feel strangely disorientated. Everything's happened so fast it's like the shock of losing Skull all over again.

Rosa's regarding me, her eyes soften. "I hear you're pregnant. How far along are you?"

"Eighteen, well, coming up on nineteen weeks."

"Know what you're having yet, or don't you want to find out?"

Now I smile as I always do when I think of my baby. "I'm having a boy."

The corners of her mouth curve. "That's lovely. I've got twins myself, two boys. They're fourteen now." She grins wider. "You've got the best times ahead, they're adorable when they're babies. Teenagers? Huh, not so much." But the fond look on her face belies the words. "Still, Red and his crew help keep them in line."

"And you're with—?" The question at this point seems polite.

"Oh, I don't have a man now. My ol' man was the president before Red, but lung cancer took him a few years back. They've let me stay on as a sort of mother to the club."

"I'm sorry," I say, uselessly, but my hand goes out and touches her arm. "I thought my man had died, so I know how you're feeling."

She nods. "I hear things from behind the bar. Hear you've found he's alive. God, I'd do anything to have my man back."

Just as I go to correct her, she adds, "But if he'd left like yours did, I reckon I'd want to finish the job myself."

She sounds so fierce, it makes me laugh. "Just how I'm feeling," I confirm.

"I'll leave you now. You can come down when you want, or I'll send your man up with some food. You'll meet Tiff at some point, she's the only other old lady in the club. She's Fox's, our treasurer."

"I think I'll stay here and unpack." I eye the dresser warily, not wanting to open any drawers seeing the state of the rest of the room.

"I wouldn't worry," she chuckles, eyeing the pile on the floor. "Reckon they've already been emptied out for you.

When she leaves, I realise I feel drained. The flight and the stress of walking into a strange club seem to have taken it out of me. I've become used to being around bikers in Pueblo and am comfortable with them. But that's because I've gotten to learn the men under the leather. Here they're strangers, and while I hope they'll show me the same respect, they are a different club and I don't know them.

Though the two I have met, and Rosa, haven't been disrespectful at all.

Summoning the last of my energy, I open the drawers, find two empty, and unpack both bags, then lie on the bed just to rest my eyes.

CHAPTER TWENTY-FIVE

Pyro

I have a couple of beers, meet old friends and make new ones, then pop up to see how Mel is doing, not wanting her to think I've abandoned her. But when I open the door, I see her lying fast asleep on the bed.

Moving inside I notice two empty bags stood in the corner, showing she must have unpacked my stuff as well as hers. I stand for a moment, staring, realising I've never had anyone to do shit like that for me before. I smile.

Though I've tried to be quiet, some sound I made must have disturbed her.

"Ro?"

"Yeah, it's me darlin'. Want to get some more rest?"

"I'm hungry."

I offer to fetch her something, but she's happy enough to go downstairs. The reason why is apparent when she asks, "Has anyone got any more ideas? Have there been any sightings?"

"Nah, we're in the early stages. The four of us from Pueblo are each going out with someone from this club tomorrow. Makes sense. They know the area and likely places, and we can recognise him the best."

I hold her arm gently as we descend the stairs.

"I've been thinking. Won't he hear bikes coming? Won't he hide, suspecting you could have found him?"

Shadow overhears. "Thought about that, doll," he yells over. "But there's always plenty of bikes around Vegas, it won't raise any suspicions."

"Their road captain," I say into her ear.

Coming closer, Shadow continues, informing her, "We're also loaning not only Pyro a bike, but Judge, Wills and Sparky too. That way he won't recognise the bikes he cleaned often enough as a prospect."

"You better not let anything happen to mine," Sparky growls as he comes over. His eyes examine Mel. "You okay? You look tired."

"Just the journey," she explains. "And I'm hungry."

I'm not surprised she looks pale, not with the shit she's working through. "Let's take you to see Rosa. I bet she'll have a plate she can warm for you."

I find the woman I'm after and get Mel fed, then we rehash all the don't knows that are flying around once again and settle on some concrete plans for the morning. Mel's surprisingly quiet, but then, apart from the four of us, she doesn't know anyone here. And the sweet butts are getting into some action, making Mel discreetly turn her head away.

When she complains her head's hurting, I take her upstairs, wait for her outside the bathroom where she has taken her night clothes in with her to get changed, then help her into bed.

"You really okay?" I'm concerned about her.

"Yes, it's just been a tiring day." Her explanation accompanied by a small smile reassure me, but only a little.

I plan to have a word with Rosa, to get her to take Mel under her wing and make her rest while we're out tomorrow. Today seems to have taken it out of her, and all the stress can't be good in her condition. Would do her good just to switch off for a while.

"You staying or going back down?"

"Just need a quick word with the brothers downstairs, then I'll be back, okay?"

"Okay," she replies sleepily.

I place my lips to her forehead. "Night, darlin'."

She's asleep when I return and as far as I can tell, rests soundly all night. She stirs only when I'm getting dressed in the morning.

"Feeling better?"

She shrugs. "I still feel exhausted. I was going to try to get you to take a cage and persuade you to take me with you, but I think rest would be better for me and the baby."

"Won't get any argument from me, darlin'."

"If you find him, you will bring him back here?"

"I will," I promise. "But there aren't any guarantees we're going to find him soon. I don't have high expectations it will be today. May take a while. Try to be patient, okay?" I study her face. Despite the sleep last night, she still looks tired, dark circles around her eyes. Perhaps she shouldn't have come to Vegas, but back in Pueblo she'd only have been worrying all the time. May as well do her stressing out here where I can keep my eye on her. What worries me most is how she'll cope if we don't find him. Too many questions will remain unanswered, and there will always be a worry about his spectre raising its head to cause problems for her and the kid.

But maybe I shouldn't be so concerned how worn out she looks. She's close to five months pregnant and growing that baby, of course she doesn't have the energy she once did.

Her lips press together. I recognise that look of stubbornness, so am unsurprised when she next speaks.

"You may not find him today, may not find him at all. But if the days go on and there's no sign, I want to be involved in the search, Ro. In case I see something you're missing. I need to look for him myself."

She wouldn't have any more, or any less chance than us. She's not likely to enter some of the places we'll be visiting. But I can understand her need not to be kept on the sidelines all the time. It's the kind of woman she is, not content to sit back and rely on other people. She needs this.

"Mel, I'll agree to that." After some rest and when she seems stronger. "But for now, trust me, Sparky, Judge and Wills. We've all got our own reasons to find him." She might not understand it, but to us our motives have just as much validity as hers.

Her lips remain pursed, and she looks like she's biting her tongue. I don't say more, knowing exactly how she's feeling. If I was her, I'd want to be the one searching.

There's a knock at the door, opening it I see Sparky. I raise my chin to let him know I'm coming now. Leaving the door ajar, I go back and give her a PG kiss remembering until we find Skull, she's still a claimed woman and I've got to behave if I want to keep my patch.

Downstairs everyone's ready and waiting, and we waste no time heading out.

I'm with Cobra and Sarge. I follow them along unfamiliar streets, and eventually into the part of town that runs behind the strip. Cobra points out a couple of hotels that Sparky had indicated on the map last night, one of which is the budget place where Beth had stayed.

The plan is that we'll go to the grocery store, then start driving the roads around there. Luckily, it's not as hot as it would be in the middle of summer, but the air is still warm and dry, and it's not long before my head's sweating under the helmet the law requires me to wear in Nevada.

We take a break around lunchtime, entering a bar for a drink and a snack. I order a burger but don't really taste it. I call Mel briefly to check in with her, then it's back to our bikes. Late afternoon and Sarge calls a stop so he can have a quick smoke.

It's while the bikes are parked up that I get a glimpse and turn away fast.

"There, behind us. Dude wearing a black tee, there's a woman with a kid in a stroller with him." I'm not really hopeful as there have been a couple of false sightings before, and I didn't take Skull to be a family man, not wanting a kid with Mel is likely the reason he ran.

"He's looking at the bikes very carefully," Sarge says conversationally in between puffs.

"Certainly looks like him," Cobra confirms, taking a quick glance down at his phone. "He'll know from our cuts that we're Satan's Devils."

Cobra turns back and leans over as if to inspect something on his bike, then crouches down beside it, peering around the engine.

"They've gone into the snack bar over there."

They turn to me for guidance. As he's my man, I'll take the lead. I fire off a quick text to Judge, Wills and Sparky, giving them the name of the eating place.

"Might not be there long, they mainly do carryout."

"We go over," I tell them fast. "You two wait outside, I'll go in."

"Back exit?"

"I'll get Rope to approach from the rear." It's Sarge texting now. Rope and Cuff are with Wills and are apparently the closest.

"Let's do this then." Pocketing the key from my borrowed bike, I start walking across the road.

"I texted Red to send the prospects with the crash truck."

All three of us wear an air of excitement. Our quarry's so close, I can almost taste it. In my mind I've played out this moment a hundred times, each with Skull having a different reaction. Fear, I expect to be the foremost, and anger we've managed to track him down. Sadness that the rest of his life can probably be measured in hours. He'll beg, plead for forgiveness, come up with some bullshit-filled story about why he left. Or, he'll completely blank me if indeed he has lost his memory.

I glance in the window, there's no man resembling Skull at the counter and no woman or child. In fact, there are only a couple of men who certainly aren't him, looking more like construction workers taking a break. Nonetheless, I eye them carefully in the unlikely event he's donned a yellow jacket as a disguise.

"Man and woman with a kid in a stroller," I snap at the man behind the counter.

He looks left and right shiftily, then shakes his head. "Hasn't been a family in here for a while. What do they look like?"

I don't bother to get out the picture. Leaning over the counter, I grab him by his throat, a scuffle behind me shows Sarge and Cobra are keeping the construction workers occupied.

"Just tell them, Albert. Don't want no trouble with the Devils. It's not like it's our business."

Albert nods, as best he can with my hand making him choke. When I release him, he rushes out, "They said there were men following them, and wanted to get the child safe. I let them out the back…"

Before he can finish speaking, I'm already moving past him, pressing down hard on the emergency exit bar sending an alarm sounding into the air. Albert must have disarmed it for Skull.

We're too late, he's gone.

Just at that moment Rope pulls up. "Got a license plate for you." *He has?* "Got here just in time to see your man Skull getting into a car. In such a hurry they left the stroller…" He points outside the door to the yard. Indeed Skull has, there it sits forlorn and abandoned, he'd not bothered to stop to fold it up, leaving it behind so he could make a fast getaway.

But we're still no closer to Skull. Rope had seen him and let him get away? "The license plate all you fuckin' got?" I roar.

"Nah." He sends me a sneering look and pre-empts my next question. "Cuff and Wills are following him."

Thank fuck. I raise my chin, half in apology, half grateful. Should have known these Devils would have my back just as well as the ones back home.

"What now?" Sarge asks, coming out shaking his fist. Obviously keeping the other two men at bay had involved a physical conversation.

There's nothing we can do here. Skull is unlikely to come back, not for an easy-to-replace stroller. "Let's get back to the compound and wait for news." I'm beyond angry, I'd had Skull almost within arm's reach and I let him go.

Back at the clubhouse I'm even more furious when I answer my phone which rings as I'm entering the door and after hearing what Wills has to say.

"Fucker's gone!" I scream at the top of my voice, making Red look up from some paperwork he's checking behind the bar.

"What do you mean, he's gone?" Red snarls. "Wills and Cuff lost him? One of them come off their bike?"

I stare at the device I'm still holding, shaking my head in disbelief. "Nah. Skull had help. Two cars intercepted and prevented them following. It was stop or be run off the road."

"They get ID on the cars?" Red moves out from behind the bar and comes over.

I hadn't thought to ask.

"Trails not dead," Keys shouts from the other side of the room. "I've tracked that licence plate Rope called in."

"Then let's get moving. Text me the address." Red takes his key out of his cut. "Coming, Twister?"

"Try and stop me."

I nod at both the prez and his enforcer, who don't bother with asking. It's obvious I'll be going along. I even grin as we walk to the bikes. Skull thinks he's escaped and got clean away. Well, he's underestimated the Devils.

In the end it's a large group that pile out of the compound, brothers returning from the search fall into line with the crash truck. I'm anticipating the moment we kick his fucking front door in.

Red soon starts waving his arm, and we slow down then pull over. I'm scanning left and right, but I see no sign of Skull around. Not that I really expected to. He must have gotten the scare of his life and has gone to ground.

Red whistles softly, and we gather around him. "Skull ran earlier, he'll run again if he sees or hears us. That's why I brought the crash truck along. Place we're headed to is a couple of roads over," he says, probably for my benefit. "Any sound of bikes and he'll be off."

"He won't get away from me next time," Cuff growls a promise.

Coming to this address Keys had found was the first thing on my mind. Now I wonder who helped him get away earlier. Something doesn't add up. Was it a coincidence that vehicles appeared to stop Wills and Cuff, or had Skull been able to summon help fast? If so, from who?

When Red continues issuing instructions, I shelve those questions for now. Once we get our hands on the man, he'll give us the answers.

"Pyro, Twister and I will take the crash truck and check the address out. Everyone else, be ready to roll if we need you."

"Red?" I suddenly ask, doubt flooding through me. "What are the chances of him coming back? What if he's left town?"

When the Vegas prez's eyes meet mine, I know he's fearing the same thing. "If he were a single man, it's likely. I'm banking that he might not have thought we could run a trace, or not in such a short time. He's got a woman and kid with him, might have been able to leave his shit behind, but if they're his, they'll need stuff for the child. And we all know what women are like."

I hope he's right.

"Let's do this." Red wastes no more time and takes the keys of the crash truck from the prospect's hand.

It's a short drive, and when the address comes into sight, I whistle air out through my teeth. *Is this place Skull's?* It seems unlikely.

"Has to belong to the broad," I tell Red. "There's no way

Skull could afford to shack up in a place like this. He's a mechanic for fuck's sake."

"We'll soon know."

But Red's wrong. There's no car in the driveway. The garage has been left unlocked, when we open it up, there are only a few of the kid's outside toys lying around. Whoever owns the house and car hasn't come home.

"I want to take a look inside," I suggest, approaching the front doorway. Maybe once I'm the other side of the door, I can find a clue.

"Twister?"

"Right here." He's taking something out of his cut. "Let's see what we've got." As he steps toward the front door and starts to examine it, Red and I stand to shield him from anyone who might be watching the house. It's unlikely. It's a long front yard and well sheltered from prying eyes. But it's a respectable neighbourhood, and they might have someone watching out for their neighbours.

There's a click, then the sound of a door being opened. Twister looks up at a device on the wall and holds his breath.

"Thank fuck. They didn't arm it." He's looking at a state-of-the-art alarm. "Serious shit that."

I nod, recognising the system as one top of the line which Cad likes to use when he can, and once again think Skull's broad must have money.

A friend? Sister? What is he to her, or she to him?

"Pyro," Red's stepped past me and is pointing to a photo display along one wall. Pictures of the kid from a newborn baby in the hospital to how she appeared today, about three years old. Three of the pictures show Skull holding the baby.

I notice two things immediately. One is the unmistakable paternal love and pride shining out of his eyes, and the other? That Skull looks nothing like a biker. Clean cut, wearing a button-down shirt in some, and in another, he's wearing a suit.

"What the fuck's going on?" I slam my fist into a wall.

"Something that fuckin' smells," Red replies, rifling through a desk. "What name did you know him by?"

"Kris Cox."

"There are bills here all addressed to a Donavan Jordan. Presumably that's who owns this house if he's paying for the electric. Oh, and there's a letter here addressed to Clare Jordan."

"That sure looks like a father in those pictures," Twister observes. "Christ, could Skull be this Jordan fella, or is that another fake name?"

Fuck only knows. I don't.

I climb the stairs to the second floor. There's a kid's room, toys everywhere. Another room appears to be the master bed. As I open the wardrobe I see clothes I don't recognise or would never have seen Skull wearing. There's nothing here. Wrong house? Nah, those photos, they don't lie. Something connects the people who own this house with Skull. But, what?

"I want to talk to this man Jordan, whether he's Skull or not," Red rasps as he comes into the bedroom. "Something stinks, Pyro."

He doesn't need to tell me.

He continues, "I'll leave a prospect watching the house. Soon as anyone comes home, I want to know."

His enforcer reappears behind him. "Whoever it is, they expected to return today. There're the makings to prepare dinner and food obviously for the little one in the fridge."

CHAPTER TWENTY-SIX

Pyro

M y lips press together as I think. After a second, I turn to the Vegas prez and his enforcer. "They could be taking a long route home making sure they haven't got a tail. That could be why we've beaten them here. You've seen this place, Red. Everything they own is nice shit, expensive too. Not likely to leave that behind. I think they'll be back, and soon. I'm gonna wait here. Give Skull the fuckin' surprise of his life when he turns up." Maybe it will be his last one.

Red considers for little more than a second. "I agree with you. But a few things for you to consider. One, Skull might have nothing to do with this Donavan Jordan—"

I interrupt. "Those pictures, Red, they tell a fuckin' story. Why have family photos if you're not a part of that family?"

"Could be his sister and nephew. He could have been driving her car."

I shake my head. "Nah." I wave my hand around. "No other fuckin' pictures on display. Only ones have got Skull in them."

Red's own lips thin now. "Okay, say it is Skull. Chances are they might not intend to leave permanently, but that doesn't mean he might not have taken off for a few days. You might have a long wait. I'll get Keys looking into this Donavan and Clare Jordan's details, see if there're any parents or other relatives around and where they might hole up. The other thought you need to have, is that he might not be returning alone. I'm unhappy about the two cars that intercepted Cuff and Wills. He might simply be waiting to gather the troops, whoever they are, and return prepared to find us waiting. Best you don't stay alone." He regards me for a moment. "Don't know if your woman would survive if she lost you as well."

Christ. What a thing to think about. Could Mel cope with another loss? I don't want to know the answer, but I'm not going to risk it.

"I'll take Judge," I tell him quickly, having come to respect the man who's been patched in for less than a year. "Sparky too." Not Wills, not because he's not up to the job, he is, but Mel will need at least one face from home around. It's possible Skull won't return for hours, if he's coming back at all. I'm prepared to stay all night, maybe reconsider tomorrow if there's still no sign. Maybe, by then, Keys will have come up with some other leads.

"I'll stay," Twister offers, cracking his hands together. "I don't mind getting my hands on this traitor."

"Agreed," Red concurs again.

"Tell Mel I'm following a lead," I ask him, knowing she'll be expecting me back.

Red grimaces slightly, but she's an old lady, she won't argue with him. We both know all he'll need to say is club business even though, in this case, it's also very much hers. "I'll try to keep her from worrying too much," he responds at last.

We organise getting the bikes of those of us staying onto the crash truck to be taken back to the compound, then we return to the house. Now there are no bikes or truck in the vicinity to give Skull advanced warning, even if he spends time driving around.

A short while after Red leaves, Judge comes in.

"What's the plan, Ro?"

Noticing Twister's also looking at me, I decide fast. "I want to take them by surprise. Sparky and I will hide down here, you and Twister upstairs. I want them inside, door closed, and with their escape routes cut off."

There's a coat closet by the front door which looks just about large enough for me to hide in. With the warmth of the day, they shouldn't have any coats to hang up.

Sparky sees me eyeing it and jerks his head backward. "Soon as we hear movement outside, I'll hide behind the kitchen door."

"Be useful to listen too, rather than taking them on straight away," Twister puts in. "Once they think they're safe, they might relax and give something away. Perhaps about who ran interference for them."

I raise and dip my chin. I've been thinking about that too.

"It was deliberate, not an accident. Not fuckers thinking they'd pitch their cars against bikes." Judge frowns. "I've been talking to Wills. They had blacked-out windows at the rear. He said he and Cuff were having enough difficulty swerving and keeping shiny side up to notice much about them."

"Licence plates?" asks the enforcer.

But Judge shakes his head. "I don't know if Cuff caught sight of them, but Wills didn't."

Unbeknownst to Skull, we're here and waiting at what we presume is his house, or at least, that of the woman who accompanied him today, and who he looks overly friendly with in those photos that keep catching my eye. Who helped him is a mystery he can solve when he returns, or we track down where he's gone.

An hour passes. Two. Darkness descends. Then, at last, when I've about given up for the night, the sound of a car arriving outside reaches my ears. Twister and Judge disappear up the stairs, Sparky into the kitchen, and I ease myself into the coat closet to be out of sight. I crack the door so I can see out, eager to catch sight of my nemesis again.

The door opens. A woman steps inside, then puts her hand up to disarm the alarm and frowns, obviously remembering she hadn't set it. It's the woman who'd been with Skull, the woman in the photographs. But she's alone, without even her child. *Fuck. Don't like the idea of questioning a broad, but if I have to, that's what I'll do.*

Her eyes flick one way then another. *She suspects.* But then, she starts lifting the cushions on the couch, and I realise she's hunting for something.

Her phone rings. She answers, conveniently puts it on speaker, and places it down, then goes on her knees to keep looking for whatever she's come for.

"Clare." Skull's voice comes over clearly even though distant and tinny. He sounds angry. "Come back. It's not safe."

"I'm at the house now. There's no one here, no bikes around, I drove up and down and checked. It's safe."

"Clare…"

"Don, it won't take long to find it. Katy will never sleep unless she has Pooh bear. You know what she's like."

"She'll have to get used to it," the man she referred to as Don, snarls. "I'll buy her a new one."

"She won't want that. She's been crying all evening, she'll make herself ill, Don. It's here somewhere."

"Fucking three-dollar toy…"

"That's she's carried around since she could walk. That's all I want, Don." She stands up and frowns, then walks into the kitchen. *Christ, I hope Sparky's hidden himself.* Making her voice louder, she calls out, "Can you remember where she put it?"

"I don't know where she put it." Don sounds like he's in despair. It's Skull, I'm sure of it, but the timbre of his voice has changed. The man I knew would have thrown a few f-bombs in, but even in his worried state, damn seems the worst he can use. "Clare. These men are dangerous. If they find out who I am."

"Well it's good I came back. We hadn't set the alarm."

"Find the damn bear, set it and get out. Clare, please. I'm worried about you."

So he should be. I grin to myself.

"I'm going upstairs. It must be in her room."

Leaving the phone where it is, she heads for the stairs. Easing myself out, using the stealth skills I learned in the Army, I move without making a sound and place myself behind her, pressing the red key to end the call as I pass by the table where she left it.

Halfway up she pauses and gasps. Then turning, starts running back down, straight into my arms which go around her like a brace.

"Don," she screams. Then again when there's no answer from the phone, "Don!" The device starts ringing again, but I have no intention of answering it.

Twister's eyes meet mine. "Restrain her," I instruct.

As I expected, he's got zip ties in one of his pockets. She struggles and screams. While we know there are no close neighbours, Judge runs back upstairs, and returns fast with a scarf which he uses to gag her.

I place a call of my own, quickly arranging for Red to send a truck for us.

Sparky approaches. "How the fuck didn't she see you?" I hiss.

"Fuckin' civilians," he grins. "I was standing right behind the door."

Unable to communicate with her voice, Clare uses her eyes to plead and beg, but I have no mercy.

"Skull your man?" I ask, knowing I have to, for now, confine myself to questions which can be answered either yes or no.

Her head shakes in confusion.

I look around, find what I'm seeking, then take it back to her. I tap the man in the picture holding the baby. "This is the man you call Don?"

She nods, her eyes wide and scared. I have no mercy.

"This your baby?" I tap the photo again.

Another nod. Her throat works as she swallows.

"His?"

I clench my jaw waiting for her response. If she says yes, it will confirm what I'm already thinking. He was in a relationship with another woman all the time he was cosying up to Mel.

A third nod.

"You married?" asks Twister, almost casually.

Slowly, her head dips and then rises.

If Skull hadn't already signed his death warrant, he certainly has now.

Outside I hear an engine. Judge opens the door and confirms, "It's Crash."

A minute later, the Vegas VP appears in the doorway. "Let's get out of here."

I'm wasting no time. Skull will be going frantic by now. I've ignored it, but that phone has kept ringing. I leave it where it is and follow Twister leading Clare out of the house.

Twister puts her in the middle of the back seat, then sits beside her. Her tied hands twist together in her lap, and as I get in the other door, sandwiching her between us, I can feel her body trembling. Sparky squeezes in beside me.

Judge sits up front with Crash.

None of us speak on the drive back to the compound. That's done on purpose, not knowing what's happening, not witnessing friendly repartee, not even knowing where they are going, those are all things which can soften a captive up and help get them in the mindset for talking.

Red is waiting for us. He cocks his eyebrow at me. When I mouth 'basement', both rise.

I push her down on a chair—gently, I'm thinking she's innocent except for the information she holds—then I remove the makeshift gag from her mouth.

"Where am I?" she asks, her eyes flitting wildly from left to right. "Who are you?" Her panic seems to increase the more she takes in of her surroundings, and I'm not surprised.

I haven't been down here much before, and it's changed since the last time I was here. New equipment for a start which I suspect might have something to do with Rope and Cuff. The spanking bench probably comes in handier for them, than as a torture device, though the women they bring back might see it differently. There's a St Andrews cross, and a wall where whips and crops are hanging.

A variety of restraints, some quite interesting are also on display.

Then, on the other side, there are pincers, hammers, knives and saws. Hmm. Dual purpose for certain. The soundproofing I know has been installed probably works for both.

Red catches my eye and winks.

Clare, though, her eyes go impossibly wide as she views everything around her.

"What the hell is this place?" she cries out. "It looks like a torture chamber."

Red glances around as if he hadn't seen it before, then chuckles. "It does, doesn't it, doll?"

My face stays straight. I nod at Twister who's followed us down.

Red steps in front of her. "It's Clare, isn't it?" When she nods, he points to Twister. "You know what an enforcer is, Clare?"

She swallows rapidly and shakes her head.

"Well, he's the man who gets information by whatever means. I happen to know Twister is very good at his job, no one leaves here alive without telling him what he wants to know. You know how he got his handle?"

Another shake.

"I'll give you a clue. People who don't talk, quickly find out how twisted he is."

"I don't know what you want to know," she cries out. "I don't know who you are or why I'm here. I'm a part-time librarian, a housewife, and a mother. I don't know anything."

"To be honest Clare, you look like a nice lady," Red tells her.

"And we have no beef with you. But we'd like to have a talk with your husband. Now, you can start by giving us his phone number."

Her head moves side to side. She sounded scared for herself previously, now she's gone white, and when she speaks, her voice has gone hoarse. "If I tell you, you'll trick him to come here. You'll hurt him."

I motion to Red, he nods. "Clare," I start, "we want to talk to Skull, *Don* or whatever his name is. We want to ask him some questions, that's all. Have we hurt you?"

"You kidnapped me," she accuses, sulkily.

"Were we rough?"

She eyes her hands still tied. I step up and though she flinches when she sees me produce my knife, she relaxes when she sees all I intend to do is to cut the zip tie off.

"Give us Don's phone number, sweetheart." I soften my voice.

"What will you do if I don't?" Her voice hardens. "You'll hurt me then?" Her eyes flick nervously toward the implements on the wall.

Red puts his hand on my arm, and gently moves me back, standing in front of her himself. "You see Clare, Skull's got some answering to do. To us, and maybe to you, and definitely to a woman upstairs who's five months pregnant."

Her brow creases, her eyes widen, and her cheeks flush.

Red nods. "The father is Skull. Donavan Jordan, as you know him."

She gasps, and her hand covers her mouth. Her head is shaking violently now. "No. You've got the wrong man. Don would never cheat on me. He'd never do that. That's something he'd never do..." Her head bows, then she raises it again. Her voice now cunning. "That woman, she's lying."

I bristle, but Red shoots me a warning look, before turning back to Clare. "Is she? Perhaps your husband should have the chance to defend himself."

"You're wrong," she says strongly.

"Then let's give him a call so he can tell us the truth himself."

Now her eyes become slits as what she's been told starts to sink in.

No longer so certain in her initial denial? Perhaps.

What's she going to do? Some women, if they find their husband's been cheating on them will turn a blind eye, telling themselves he's a man after all. Finding it within themselves to forgive them. Others? Well, they're out for blood. Hard to tell which camp Clare falls into.

I get the impression she might veer toward the latter one when she suddenly rattles off a number, so fast I have to ask her to repeat it, then key it into my phone. Then, as she'd done an hour or so before, put it on speaker.

I'm not surprised when it's immediately answered. "Who's this?"

"Pyro."

"Where's Clare?" I'm not surprised it's the first thing he says. "If you've hurt her…"

"We've got her," I confirm. "Pretty bitch, your wife. Of course, she might not be so pretty much longer."

"You touch one hair on her head…"

"Whether I do or not is up to you, *Don*."

"What do you want me to do?"

"Come to the Vegas Satan's Devils MC compound."

"You'll kill me," he breathes.

Clare gasps.

"We might, we might not. But if you don't come, your wife will suffer. Every minute you're late, we'll treat her like we treated you, remember? I assure you the basement in Vegas is just as well equipped as the one in Pueblo, and Twister is as good an enforcer as Mace." He'll know exactly what I'm referring to.

"Clare's got nothing she can tell you."

"Neither did you." It was the reason he took so much punishment. We were torturing him for information he couldn't give. "Didn't stop us then, won't stop us now." Well, it had. As soon as we knew the truth, we stopped. But it's likely in his panic, all he'll remember is the pain we inflicted first, and imagine it happening to the woman he presumably loves.

He'd told Mel he loved her.

His voice hardens. "I'm warning you, Pyro. You touch her, and it will be the last thing you do. One scratch, one bruise..."

Twister steps up behind Clare and yanks on her hair. It surprises her rather than hurts her, but the scream she lets out is convincing.

"I need a couple of hours." Skull's voice sounds desperate now.

"You've got one." I start to rattle off the address, but he interrupts.

"I know where it is!"

Does he now? Interesting.

I end the phone call, then look at his wife as Twister steps around to her front.

"Sorry about that," he tells her, not sounding apologetic at all.

Her hands are already up, retying her ponytail, proving she hadn't been hurt if worrying her hair is out of place is her main concern. She looks annoyed she's been used.

"You know what your man's been up to?" I ask her. "He must go missing for months, years. You know what he does?"

Before she can answer, Red steps up, and takes me to one side. "Just spoke to Demon. He said he's catching the first flight that he can, but he's okay if we do the questioning. Any vote must wait until he's here."

I nod. That's fine. Suddenly I realise we've got an audience. I had been vaguely aware of the thuds of boots that have been echoing down the stairs but hadn't realised that most of the club have crowded into the basement. I don't give one fuck. Skull had disrespected every member; doesn't matter which chapter he'd joined. At the very least, and if he can come up with a justification for his actions which makes any sense—doubtful, where Mel's concerned—we'll be making sure he leaves the club properly with a beatdown. And if I have my way, any vote will make sure he leaves his life too.

Turning back to Clare, I repeat my last question.

This time, she replies. "It's his job. He doesn't speak to me about it."

Once again, Red's eyes catch mine. He flashes a message at me, and I raise my chin back.

"What's his job?" Red roars, stepping forward fast as though he's lost patience. "Who does he fuckin' work for?"

Stubbornly she shuts her mouth.

Red's unperturbed as he snaps, "He a cop?"

I'm watching her carefully and see the betraying twitch of her face. A confirmation of what I've gradually been coming to suspect. The unmarked cars stopping Wills and Cuff was the first clue, and what we found of Don in that house wasn't the biker we knew.

Well, won't be the first time a cop's disappeared. Only problem is, she would have to go as well, and no Devil likes killing a woman. Though it might be kinder than leaving her wondering, to suffer like Mel, never knowing what happened to her man after he'd said goodbye that last time.

But they've got a kid. Fuck, more complications.

I'm glad Demon's flying in. Right now, I'm representing Colorado, but I can't see further than justice for my woman. My prez though, he'll do right for the club. Maybe Skull will walk out of here alive, but meet me alone, one dark night, when he least expects it, and then I'll make him pay the ultimate price.

Red continues to question her. "He goes away for a long time, Clare. You ever see him in that time?"

He'd been with the Devils eighteen months straight. Except for the month he disappeared fuck knows where. Though now I suspect I know who he ran to.

"When he's on a job, no."

"Except nine, ten months ago?" I ask to confirm it.

Her expressive face answers for her again.

Now it's me pushing Red out of the way. "You know what he got up to?" I don't wait for her to respond or not. I tell her myself. "He became one of us, a member of the Satan's Devils, acted the part well, too. Soon as he was patched in, he went with the whores."

A slight tightening of her face and a shake of her head suggests she'd rather not know. Then she gives me words. "If he'd otherwise have drawn attention to himself, Don would have done what he needed to do."

Why do women come up with excuses?

"Possibly, Clare, though we'd not have thought that suspicious. But, it wasn't just him fuckin' a whore to keep up appearances, it was worse than that, Clare. Much worse. He decided to take a woman as his own. Claimed her, which in our world is as good as marrying her. He lived with her. Slept with her every fuckin' night. Forgot to use a condom, twice. Then he upped and left leaving her pregnant." What Skull had done makes my voice harden.

She's now hanging onto my every word.

"He come home and fuck you? After he'd been with his old lady without a condom?" Her widened eyes suggest yes. "And what about her? What about the woman he said he loved, the woman he'd promised to spend his whole life with? He never came back, left with no warning. She found she was pregnant with no man to tell. You've got a kid, Clare. What if your husband left for a job and never came back? Disappeared off the face of the earth and you never had any answers. Can you imagine that, Clare? Can you imagine the fucking hurt?"

"No." Her hands cover her face, her denial I suspect more that those things had actually occurred than her answering my question.

"Yes," I insist. "She's five months pregnant with your

husband's baby. It's a boy. Your little girl will have a brother."
She won't. I won't let my kid anywhere near hers. But hell, I'll
lay it on as thick as I need to. "What about her, Clare? What
about the innocent woman he used and discarded? What about
her?"

CHAPTER TWENTY-SEVEN

Melissa

So intent on questioning the woman sitting on a chair, the men haven't noticed me. I've got a wall of leather to hide behind as the men crowd around the woman. While I can't see, I can hear every word. *Skull's married? With a child?* I stuff my hand in my mouth to stop a gasp escaping, while every syllable causes a sharp pain as though knives are piercing my heart.

An undercover cop? I was shacked up with a man who presumably wanted to bring the club down. That was the only reason he'd joined it. Everything he'd ever said to me, and to them, must have been a lie.

I can't hold back any longer, and I scream out three words, "What about me?"

The men blocking my view of her, part. No one makes any attempt to prevent me stepping forward, my hands huddled across my stomach as though protecting my baby bump. No one lifts a finger as I walk straight up to the woman in the chair.

"What about me?" I scream again, spittle landing on her face.

She makes the connection easily, her eyes flicking to my face then my stomach. A myriad of expressions appear on her features, anger, disbelief, sadness. It's hard to predict what she's going to say.

Finally, she settles on denial. "I don't believe you. The baby can't be his."

"You don't believe me?" I scoff. "Well, in about four and a half months I'll have proof. Do you know what it's like, Clare, to be in love with a man you then find out doesn't exist? To mourn the death of a man who's still alive? To be carrying the baby who came into being through falsehood and deceit? Can you even begin to imagine it?"

She focuses on my eyes, as though trying to find something she can use to disbelieve me, but I know my expression is telegraphing pain and hurt.

"If what you're saying is true, you're right, I can't begin to imagine it," she says at last. "But if what you say is the truth..." She swallows. "I don't know," her voice drops to a whisper. "It was his job... Maybe he had to..."

"Job?" I rasp back, interrupting. "I was part of his job?"

But it's the explanation I've been wanting, even though never dreaming I was nothing more than someone he was using. Of course he walked away without a backward glance, I never meant anything to him. I look at her, ignoring her tear-streaked face, and analyse what I'm seeing. She's pretty with high cheek-bones, generous lips and her body? Well, she's slim and has certainly regained her pre-pregnancy weight. Unlike me, who, I suspect, will never lose it. Why would he want me, when he had her?

"This hurts me too."

Four words, but spoken with such anguish, through my own distress I suddenly spare some measure of compassion for her. I'm the living, breathing evidence of her husband's betrayal. Could she forgive him? I can't, and if I was in her shoes, couldn't.

"He's married. I feel sorry for you, but he was mine first." Her mouth twists as she thinks of the practicalities. "Of course, if it's a question of support we can discuss..."

"No fuckin' thing to discuss," Pyro roars, then comes to stand

237

behind me, his palms gently resting on my upper arms. "You don't need to be here, Mel."

But I do. I can't take my eyes off the woman Skull clearly prefers to me. He married her, put a ring on her finger, fathered a child with her. No wonder he didn't want one with me.

I glance down to where my hands still protectively rest over my stomach. "This is his fault, he forgot to use a condom." Suddenly it's important she understands. "I'd have never gone with him, would have turned him down when he wanted to date me if I'd known he had a wife and child. I'm not that woman." Pyro's hands tighten slightly as if confirming he knows that. "I would never go with a cheating man."

"Don doesn't cheat." But she has the grace to look sheepish, and her cheeks are glowing red.

I suspect it's dawning on her that she's been played too. Did he promise he'd be faithful? Did he tell her there'd be no one else?

"I don't believe you," she suddenly spits out. "Don's faithful to me. He promised he would be... I don't know why you're saying all this, but it has to be lies."

Whatever justification or defence she was going to offer goes unsaid as she's interrupted by a noise at the door. Bodies part again, this time to let Skull through. Ignoring everyone else, he runs straight to the woman on the chair.

"Clare, oh my God, Clare. What have they done to you?" He's examining her, running his hands over her as if to see whether she's been hurt.

"Red, Crash? A word?"

I ignore whoever it is that's called the prez and VP away. My eyes instead focus on the man I haven't seen for almost four months. I can't look away. It's strange, there are little differences about him. His voice seems deeper, older somehow, and his bearing is different. It had been hard to believe he was even the age that he'd told me, now he seems to have grown into his years. There's a new confidence about him. Even though he's surrounded and in the proverbial lion's den, he's self-confident and poised as if it's the other men who should be the ones unsure.

"Let her go," he states in a voice full of authority. "She's not part of this. She knows nothing."

"Oh, I think we'll be extending our hospitality to Clare a little longer." Pyro steps away from me.

Red reappears. He doesn't bother to lower his voice. "Skull, here, brought company. Cops. They're outside the gates. His insurance policy to make sure he, and she, walk out unscathed."

Pyro gives a bellow of fury. He stomps across the room and smashes his fist into a wall. I suspect he's wishing it was Skull's face instead. He turns, nursing his hand.

"You brought the fuckin' heat?"

Skull jerks his head in a back and upward motion. "They're waiting out front to make sure both of us walk out unhurt." His voice deepens further, he becomes a man more used to giving orders than taking them. "You lay one hand on me, you go to prison for assaulting a cop. I don't walk out of here? They'll take you all down."

Pyro's voice is full of fury. "You were undercover all this time?"

Skull doesn't bother to nod.

"You were trying to dig up dirt on us?"

Again Skull stays quiet and says nothing in response to Pyro's question. But I know Pyro's right. There's only one reason a cop would go undercover and infiltrate a club. *To bring them down.*

Did he find anything? Should I be worried Pyro's going to be arrested? Has Pyro done anything wrong? But four months have passed. Surely, if anything was going to happen, it would have happened by now. *Did he leave as he hadn't found anything?*

Red steps forward and demands, "You working for the cops or the feds?"

Again, Skull stares back impassively.

"Why did you disappear?" I cry out. The tone of my voice gets Red looking at Pyro with narrowed eyes. It's like he's warning him.

This time, Skull does answer. He shrugs and, giving me a look with none of the heated emotion I used to see on his face, replies coldly and succinctly, "Job done."

I stare in disbelief at the man I thought I had loved, feeling only hatred for him now. It's my turn to speak, and no one's going to stop me.

I can't stop my voice shaking, or sounding more like a wail. "What about me, Skull? How could you do that to *me*?"

His lips narrow, but he utters a lame and inadequate apology, "Sorry, Mel."

"You wanted a woman to fuck while you got your information, so you picked on me."

Clare gasps as I put it so bluntly.

"It wasn't like that." Skull looks at his wife and puts his hand on her shoulder.

"If it wasn't like that, if you loved me, then you would have told me about your wife, left her and stayed with me." Not that I'd want him under those circumstances, but it would have showed he cared. Wouldn't have left me feeling so used.

He looks up and gives it to me straight. "Look, I couldn't, Mel. I'm sorry. I love my wife, and could never leave her."

"If you love your wife, why did you betray her with me?" The wheels are turning rapidly inside my brain. What if he had been single? Would it have turned out differently? Would he have told me who he was and have taken me with him?

I'm an honest person, my civilian life more aligned with his real career than his biker persona. If Skull had talked to me, I might not have liked the fact he'd been living a lie, but I wouldn't have been upset to know I was dating a lawman. That he'd run with a one-percenter club was one of the reasons I'd been reluctant to get into a relationship with him in the first place.

But then, after I'd met the club, met Demon, Violet, all the women and men... My eyes flit to Pyro as I wonder, could I really have played an active role in bringing the club down? Seeing all the people I'd come to love and respect hauled off to jail.

But all that assumes Skull had any feelings for me. I have to accept, he has none now, and had none then. *Skull had used me.* I still don't understand the reason.

"Why, Skull? Why did you drag me into whatever you were doing? Why?" I scramble for an answer. "Did you find me so irresistible you had to have me?" *He couldn't have. Else how would he have walked away without a backward glance?* Another look at his wife shows me he had better at home. She's far more the type of person suitable to be seen on his arm.

But he clams up and I get no answer.

I try again, my voice rising. "Do you have any idea of what it was like? I expected you to come home and you didn't. I thought you were *dead.* Have you any idea of the distress you caused? Have you? You made me *love* you. Made me expect you were my future. I didn't even want a relationship, yet you dragged me into it. Were you acting all the time? Was it all an act when we made love? Why, Skull? Why did you just leave?"

Another shrug from the man in front of me. But this time he follows it up with words. "I'm sorry, Mel. I regret the upset that I caused you, but there was no other way than to make a clean break." There's a slight softening of his eyes, but it's gone in a flash, so fast I think I must have imagined it. "My job had ended so I returned to my wife."

He can't even say he was ever attracted to me. Nothing of our time together had been true.

If Pyro hadn't stepped up behind me, I might have fallen to the ground at that point. I'm shaking like a leaf blown by the wind and I need his touch to steady me.

"Mel," Pyro says, his voice thick with worry, "you don't need to talk to this piece of shit anymore. Go upstairs, we'll handle it."

Finding strength from somewhere, I shrug him off me. If I don't get answers now, Skull will just walk away, and I'll never get them.

"Tell me, Skull, Kris, Don or whatever your name is. You said you loved me. Went out of your way to make me believe it. Claimed me in front of the club. You still haven't told me why? There were sweet butts to fuck…"

"You needed an old lady, didn't you, Skull?" Perhaps Red, not involved, is better placed to put things into perspective. "From what I know of Mel, I can see she's ideal material."

My eyes go to Red, then back to Skull. I can hardly breathe. My chest feels like there's a weight on it crushing my ribs. "You needed an old lady? You picked me as you thought I would do? You never actually wanted *me*? You toyed with my emotions as though they were nothing. When you went that morning, Skull, when you never came back, you fucking destroyed me." My voice, shaking, ends on a cry.

He shifts awkwardly. "It was never my intention to hurt you, Mel. I know the way we work doesn't look good to a civilian, but the club had to believe I was dead. I actually totalled my bike in one of the ravines, thought it would be found by now…"

"Fuckin' coward. You didn't tell us you were leavin' as you'd have had a beatdown," Pyro snaps.

I see spots swimming in front of my eyes and realise while his wife knows, it hasn't been mentioned to him as yet. "I'm pregnant." I move my hands, showing the small baby bump to him. "Pregnant. Almost twenty weeks, and it's yours."

That gets him.

Gets him good.

He staggers back as if someone's hit him. Next thing he knows, someone has. Pyro's fist in his stomach has winded him.

"I think your friends in that car would allow me that one," Pyro growls. "When they hear what you fuckin' did."

Gasping, Skull or whoever he is, slowly straightens. "For getting her pregnant I'll give you that, for doing my job? Nah."

Clare's been silent while I've been questioning Skull. I now risk a glance at her, her sharp inhale when her husband was punched had been audible. She looks worried, as if expecting more violence to follow, or, could it be, that's she's becoming disgusted with her pig of a man?

The Devils can't fight this battle. The cops waiting outside mean their hands are tied, or, at least, for now. But I can.

"What's your name?" I ask, advancing menacingly. "What is your real name?"

He snaps his mouth shut.

"Mel?" asks Pyro.

"He's going to fucking go down," I swear at my man. "So, I need his real name to take him."

"Donavan Jordan," Twister speaks for him. "That's the name we found in his house."

"What the fuck are you talking about?" the man we now know is Don snarls at me. "I was doing a job. I didn't do a crime. You don't have a leg to stand on. Look, we'll sort out something about support for the kid. If it's really mine, I'm not going to deny my responsibility. We'll need to talk about custody arrangements."

"You won't be giving her a penny of your filthy money, and you won't be having anything to do with the kid," Pyro growls.

"He won't be seeing him from behind bars," I threaten.

"Whatcha saying, Mel?" Red asks.

"He raped me. He misrepresented himself. If I'd known who he was, what he was doing, I'd never have given my consent. I didn't give my body to a cop, I gave it to the biker he was pretending to be."

Red's eyes gleam, as he turns to Jordan. "You were sanctioned to fuck for information?"

Skull's eyes widen. "What?" For the first time, his voice isn't steady.

But Red's standing there with an eyebrow raised in challenge. When Skull doesn't say more, he continues, "Your superiors know? Or is this something you did on your own? Did you want an old lady to get information, use her in some way to strengthen your acceptance into the club? Or did you just want a handy fuckin' companion?"

"Don?" his wife asks, almost hesitantly, as though she too wants clarification but is afraid of the answer.

Suddenly he rounds on her. "Why, Clare? Why did you have to go back to the house? We'd have gotten away, been set up somewhere new. But you had to get that damn toy."

"Don't put this on me," she spits back. "We're talking about this… woman here who says she's carrying your baby. Is that true, Don? Is it really yours?"

"Get out of here, Mel," Pyro warns again. But I shake my head. I need to be here. I need this confrontation. I need to be able to make sense of what he's done. So much worse than him being dead.

It had all been a lie from the very first moment I set eyes on him. It was never me he wanted. He just picked me like an item he had on a list at a grocery store.

"Your cut's club property." Red approaches him. "I want it back."

But the man I knew as Skull shakes his head. "It's evidence."

"You're building a fuckin' case against us?" Pyro's face is bright red.

There's a commotion in the room above. Shouts of "Put your hands up!" and another yell of, "Jordan, time's up."

Skull jerks his head upward as if acknowledging the faceless voice. Then looks at Clare apologetically and belatedly answers her question with a demand to me, "I want a DNA test, Mel."

I think of all the things he'd said, that was the worst.

I'm not the only one to think it.

"You don't trust her? You have the fuckin' balls to question the woman you raped and impregnated?"

"It wasn't rape. She consented."

"I don't fuckin' think so," puts in Red. Like Pyro, his face seems to be glowing, his freckles more pronounced. "We're going to see you in court, fucker."

"Bikers taking a cop to court?" he scoffs. He turns to look at one of his colleagues, who's bravely descended the stairs. "I've said all I'm going to, now I'm taking my wife and we're both going to walk out of this compound. You're going to do nothing to stop me."

"Not the last you're going to hear about this," Red warns him.

Out of the corner of my eye I see Clare's taken her cue to stand. But she doesn't walk to her man's side, the man I had thought was mine. No, she stands just off to his left as if uncertain quite what to do.

Skull/Kris Cox/Donavan Jordan beckons her to him, but her eyes widen, and her head moves side to side. I have to feel sympathy for her. How many times has her husband gone away for months or years at a time? Has she been able to contact him at all? Surely, she must worry? His life is at risk if his role was ever discovered. Now she'll have to live with the thought he may be being unfaithful too. How can she live with that knowledge?

That Skull could act like a biker and so successfully the Devils never suspected, again shows he's not the man I thought I knew everything about.

Had Clare ever suspected that he'd been unfaithful while he was doing his job? That he might have to be to keep up appearances? Surely, he could have come up with an excuse of why he didn't want to go with a girl?

I wish he had, then I wouldn't be in this position.

From Clare's reluctance to go to him, I think she's realised she has a lot of thinking to do. I suppose you might be able to forgive a man for a one-night stand he couldn't safely get out of, but to father a child with another woman?

Red puts himself between Clare and Skull and addresses himself to her. "You don't have to go with him," he suggests. "We've got no argument with you. If you need help, we can give it to you."

Clare looks astonished. Her eyes widen, and her hand goes to her head.

"She's coming with me," Skull states angrily.

Clare looks from him to Red, then back again, then sighs. She eyes the mob of angry bikers with disdain in her eyes, then again shakes her head and finally steps closer to her man.

I watch them leave, hoping she'll leave his lying sorry ass, but then, who knows what a woman will do? If I have my way, he'll be arrested and charged. He's destroyed my life and for nothing at all. If he'd found anything on the Satan's Devils MC, surely warrants would have been issued already.

When he walks up the stairs and disappears from my sight, it's anti-climatic.

It's only then I'm aware of the tears streaming from my eyes.

"Church in half an hour," Red announces. "Pyro, see to your woman."

Pyro puts his arm around me. I push him away. My skin feels like ants are crawling all over me. *How could I have been taken in by the man who's just walked away from me and his baby without a backward glance?*

It had been clear every word he'd ever said to me had been untrue. *How could I ever trust anyone ever again?*

Even Pyro.

Suddenly I don't want any man to touch me.

"Don't cry, Mel. Darlin', let me comfort you. Babe…"

"No, Pyro. Leave me alone."

"Mel, please. Let me hold you."

"No!" Again I push him away. How could I believe even him? Skull, *Donavan Jordan*, had targeted me and seduced me, led me to believe it was me he wanted, me he had claimed. In

246

the biker world that was as good as being married. Me. A thirty-four-year-old overweight woman. I'd been right all along; no man wants *me*.

"Mel."

"No. I want to be alone." I turn abruptly. I don't want to see, talk to anyone. I can feel the pitying glances from the men still milling around burning into me.

"Mel, sweetheart." It's Sparky. "Mel…" but his voice trails off as though there's nothing he can say.

They're probably wondering why I believed how a man like Jordan, or any man come to that, could want me.

"Mel, I love you." Pyro's words are spoken loudly.

I swing around. "Do you?" I scream, my vehemence making him stagger a step back. "Do you? How can I believe a word that you or anyone says? How can I ever trust anyone again?"

"Mel, you've had a shock." Red shoos Pyro away. "Pyro, she wants some space. Come Mel." Now it's the Vegas prez trying to put his arm around me, but I shrug him away too.

I walk up into the clubhouse and quickly take the stairs to the room that's been made available to Pyro and me. I slam the door shut behind me.

I draw in air, then sob it out. Then do it again. Huge racking sobs start going through me, my body violently shaking as each escapes. If I thought thinking Skull was dead had upset me, it's nothing to how I feel today. I've been torn apart. Everything I ever believed in taken away: my confidence, my ability to read people, my trust, my love which, at the end of the day, counted for nothing.

I can hardly breathe between my cries.

Who am I? A stupid woman who trusted a man.

Never again.

Never again will I give my heart to a man who has such power to hurt me.

"Darlin'…"

"Get out!" I scream at Pyro. "Get out! Get out! Get out!"

He's suddenly pushed aside from the doorway.

"Leave her be," Rosa says as she enters the room. "Mel, hon, oh, Mel."

Her arms I can tolerate as they come around me.

CHAPTER TWENTY-EIGHT

Pyro

C op or not I should have killed him. May have meant I'd gone to prison for life, or, in Nevada, face the death penalty. But it would have been worth it to wipe that smarmy look off his face and stop those words coming out of his mouth that had so hurt the woman I love.

The woman who's now pushed me away.

I want nothing more than to be the one comforting her.

As I stand, banished from the room from which I can still hear her distraught sobbing, Red approaches me.

His hand lands on my shoulder. "I have no words, Brother. I just don't know what to say. What that motherfucker has done to that woman? He betrayed her trust in the worst possible way. She's going to need a lot of help and support to recover."

"She needs him dead."

"She needs more than that, Pyro. Killing him is our way, a man's way. She was out of control, in a situation she gave no consent to. Thought he'd chosen her as a life partner, she found out she was being used." He tugs at his ginger beard. "Christ, we've all been taken for fools. May have happened in Colorado, but he pretended to be a true Devil, the betrayal touches us too. Yeah, I feel you. Think there's a line forming of people who want to eradicate him, but that won't help your woman in there. Closure is what she needs, and a dead body won't provide that."

A loud wail sounds from the room I'd so recently been thrown out of. I squeeze my eyes shut and tighten my hands into fists to stop myself opening the door that separates me from the woman I love. "I need to see her. Help her…"

Red's eyes soften. "Know you do, Pyro. Know you'd give your fuckin' life to make things right for her. I know this is fuckin' hard for you to accept, but it's not you she wants right now."

She's made that clear. "I thought it would be me she turned to."

"Think, Pyro, think. She was with a man who claimed her, and told her he loved her. Now she knows that was all a game, and she got played."

His words filter through my brain, and I hate the implication. "She doesn't trust me." That's what hurts. Gets me in the gut as though I'd been sucker punched. At the bottom of it is the question, how can she have faith in any man ever again?

"She doesn't trust herself right now, that's the root of it." His eyes go to the closed door, and like mine had seconds ago, close briefly as though he can feel the pain of her anguish. "Her judgment of character will be what is bothering her. Can she ever choose wisely in the future?"

I thought she had chosen, chosen me. "What do I do, Red?" My fist hits the wall, then hits it again. Why did the fucker have to reappear from the grave?

"Prove yourself to her. Take it slowly. Show her you do really love her."

I think back to how Skull had acted. "Skull did that, though. Fuck it, Red. We all thought he loved her."

"She's a loveable woman, Pyro. You're a lucky man."

I would be. If I still had her.

"This can't be good for her or the baby." I smash the wall again. "Christ, I could barely keep my hands off him, Red."

He takes out his phone and looks at it. "I called church. Brothers will be coming in now. Demon's just landed; he'll be in on it too. Pyro, let's sit and thrash this out around the table. You can't do anything for now but give her what she wants. Space."

"I've given her everything I can, Red. Support when Skull went missing. I've been with her every step of the way during this pregnancy. That baby she's carrying? It's more mine than Skull's. I've proved over and over again my feelings for her. I don't know what more I can do. Fuckin' hurts she's pushing me away."

Again, his hand lands on my shoulder, patting it twice before he lifts it away. "And she'll see that when she's thinking straight. Give her space. She's not alone, Rosa's with her. Another woman is what she needs right now."

I bow my head, putting my hands either side of my face. Taking a few deep breaths to steady myself.

"Got to update Demon," Red reminds me. "Got to bring him in on this. We need to think what that fucker found out, and whether it was enough to bring down the club."

Red is right. I can't do anything about my woman right now, and my club needs me. With one final look at the door that had been closed in my face, I follow Red down the stairs and into the meeting room of the Las Vegas club.

The space around the table is cramped, six new chairs brought in. Sparky catches my eye. When I shake my head, he presses his lips together. Demon's already seated in a space next to Red, and Beef is squashed in beside Crash. Both my prez and VP raise their chins toward me, but Red doesn't give them a chance to speak.

"Let's get this started." Red bangs the gavel. "Gonna bring Demon and Beef up to speed." He turns to the man on his right. "Had your man, had to let him go."

That flare lights Demon's eyes more than once as Red lays out the events of today concisely, being interrupted only by quick fired questions, snorts of derision and expressions of hatred together with promises of a painful death.

With the update completed, Demon's gaze settles on me. "Skull indicate whether he left 'cause the case was closed, or because he had enough information to take us down?"

"Considered that, Prez." I notice all the Vegas members are listening avidly. As Red had said, we're all Devils. Feds get a RICO indictment against one of our chapters, the others probably wouldn't escape unscathed, or not without eyes being firmly placed on them. "The only thing I can think of is when we took out Taser. But Runt was locked in his room at the time with a prospect on him. He didn't know what went down and left immediately after."

"Always wondered why he came back," Demon says.

"Well, now we've got our answer." Beef provides his analysis, "He got patched in, which had been what he was after. Earned himself a seat at the table."

"The Silvestri—"

"You didn't kill Angel, Prez. He was already ninety-nine percent dead when old-man Silvestri brought him in," I reassure him, having already revisited the events in my head. "He was beyond salvageable at that point. Sure, if you could have revived him you would have, if only to have struck the killing blow yourself. But fact is, Angel didn't die by your hand. Skull did help bury him, along with Liz and myself. But we were burying a dead man on the instruction of his closest relative."

"I agree with Pyro. I was there, remember? The Silvestri destroyed much of your clubhouse. You were simply standing your ground defending your home, any men killed were either them or you. Even if he wanted to build a case, there was no evidence to be found. The boss, Lucio took his men, both bodies and the living." Red pauses as if he too is reliving that day. One of the Devils had lost his life defending our club, and he hadn't even been from our chapter. The Utah crew had ridden home without one of their own.

"Skull left your club, what, four, five months ago?" Red continues in a reasonable tone. "RICO concerns organised crime. If you'd planned murder they might have been able to build a case against you, but the Silvestri came to you, and you were acting in self-defence. The Silvestri were the ones who planned the attack, they would probably have more to worry about than yourselves. I think the feds would have raided you by now if they had anything that would stick."

"That's my immediate thinking, Red," Demon replies. "I'm hoping he found nothing to go on, so that's why they pulled him out. Fuck knows what he's doing now, but maybe they had bigger fish to fry." I catch sight of Judge nodding. "I will warn the Silvestri, as you say, they were the ones who brought the battle to us, and Skull knows the ringleader is dead—as Pyro said, he helped clean up and buried him. I'll also speak to Drummer and warn him. He needs to know as he's the mother chapter prez." Demon purses his lips as though he's not relishing that conversation.

But Beef reassures him, "I know Drum, Prez. Look, in hindsight we always knew what happened with Skull raised questions. But I've seen him in the club, and his behaviour wasn't suspicious. Any questions I may have had were allayed, and yeah I admit, I had watched him. He played his part too well. This isn't on you, Demon, or on Hell who patched him in, or anyone else in the club. He fooled us all. Drummer will see that."

"No one could see this coming, Prez," I back up the VP. I know Demon well. He'll be second guessing himself that we had trouble within the club and he didn't know it.

"Didn't know him," Red puts in, "but I know you, Demon. Hellfire patched Skull in, which needed a unanimous vote. Seems the facts speak for themselves. Won't be the first time a cop has infiltrated a club and won't be the last either. We deal with the outcome, can't revisit what went prior except where there are lessons to be learned."

Demon acknowledges what we've said but gives no indication whether he's accepted the absolution or not. Instead he turns back to me. "How's Mel coping?"

"Terrible," I say without hesitation. "She's completely broken up. Would have been better to have the confirmation he was dead."

"She need Vi here? I can fly her down."

I consider his suggestion for a moment. "Nah. Not right now, Prez. Let me see if I can handle her first." And fuck I'm hoping she'll start letting me in. Couldn't stand to lose her. Just one more crime to lay at Skull's feet.

"Red?" Red raises his chin toward Demon. "Your town, your mess to clean up if we confront Skull again."

He means move it to the physical level. I want nothing more than to get my hands on the man who's hurt my woman so badly, and hopefully in a dark alley. If I do, he won't be walking away alive. But as Demon has suggested, me satisfying my lust for revenge would bring blowback on the Vegas club. Cops will be watching the Devils carefully, and particularly if Skull gets so much as a scratch. While I don't like it, Demon's right to take any decision out of my impulsive hands and give it to Red instead.

"That's what we're about to thrash out, Demon."

Demon nods, and sits back, folding his arms across his chest, giving Red the floor.

The Vegas prez looks around the table. "To sum up, we found the fucker Colorado wanted found. Most of you were outside heard him admit he infiltrated the club as a plant."

"Agree with what I heard," Crash, the Vegas VP offers. "He's found nothing, Colorado got away clean. Like us, they don't run drugs or guns or take part in organised crime."

"He could have been put in there to get dirt on other clubs," Sparky suggests. "We cross paths with the Wretched Soulz from time to time."

The Wretched Soulz are the dominant club across a lot of the states. Yeah, they're into shit we wouldn't touch, but they don't normally involve us in any of their business, though they do have closer links with the Tucson chapter. But if that's what Skull was hoping to find information on, he'd wasted eighteen months of his time working out of the Pueblo club.

"Why did he take an old lady?" Indian throws a look of sympathy my way.

I frown as I remember. "He encouraged Mel to get close to Vi, get her to talk about the club. When she reported back she'd learned only the rules and regulations, he wasn't happy."

It's Red who takes over from me and expands my answer to their sergeant-at-arms, named because he rides an Indian instead of a Harley. He glances at Demon then suggests, "I surmise he wasn't getting anything from discussions around the table. Maybe he thought there were things as a new patch he was being excluded from. Things which may have been discussed with a prez's old lady."

Demon snorts, and a ripple of chuckles go around. Shows how desperate Skull was becoming if he thought for a moment club business was shared as pillow talk.

"He was playing the long game." Again, my brow furrows as I think back. "He brought Mel to the club before he went about claiming her. Wanted to make sure she was a good fit, he said, and that she could accept the club. Didn't seem unreasonable at the time."

"He'd have ditched her if there was going to be any problem with her, if she didn't get on with the club, or them with her," Titch, an older member with grey hair puts in. "Gave him a chance to see whether he'd found someone suitable. Your woman," he raises his chin to me, "she must have proved herself."

It might have been better if she hadn't, given the way things had gone down.

"What no one's brought up, is are we going to let him get away with it?" a biker called Hammer asks.

Red glances at Demon, then Beef, then looks my way and

raises his eyebrow. I toss him a glare, but I can see why he's silently asking me. I, in turn, look at my prez and VP. Demon raises his hand slightly as if inviting my views.

"If he'd have been any other man, I'd have taken him out, killed him and buried him in the desert. But, he's a cop." As I say it, I realise that the situation would never have occurred if he'd been anything else. "And him being a cop, you can be damn certain, if he even gets a bloody nose, fingers will point directly our way. And that, as Demon said, would leave you in a mess, Red."

Red nods. "My thinking exactly. I do worry about why he was in Vegas, but maybe it's his home base. He was here with his wife after all. Now his cover's been blown…"

"I'll circulate his photo to all clubs and associations I can think of," Keys puts in, earning himself a nod. "Put it on the dark web."

"He might never be able to work undercover again." Red gives an evil smirk. "And there might be someone just grateful to know who and where he is."

"He won't be here long," I suggest. "He was going to up and leave everything. Whether it's cops or feds they'll know it's too risky for him to stay close now. They'll set him up somewhere else, maybe with a new identity. We were just fuckin' lucky his wife wanted that toy for the kid."

"Yeah, what's with that?" asks Titch. "Surely they could buy another?"

There have been no babies in the Las Vegas club for years. I, at least, have experience of Theo.

Demon for one understands as he enlightens the childless members, "My kid won't go to bed without his blankie. Screams the fuckin' place down without it. Yeah, kids can latch on to something. Skull's wife probably thought the risk was worth taking."

Thank fuck she did.

Crash is nodding. "But now, I think it's safe to assume they're in the wind. Key's is doing the right thing, he might pop up somewhere."

"Hopefully dead," Rope offers.

I slowly nod my head. Yeah. I'd like that. While I want to be the one to see him take his last breath, knowing he's six foot under would give me some satisfaction.

"He's mighty young for an undercover cop," Judge puts in. "He told us he was twenty-three when he started as a hangaround and twenty-five when he met Mel."

I bristle and prepare to defend my woman should Judge mention the age difference.

Red shakes his head. "Some men don't look their age. I would have taken him to be older, just from the way he carried himself. But he picked an age that he thought would make him acceptable to the club. Young enough so he doesn't have to explain a long history, old enough to have some experience of life."

"We think he's going to run. Shouldn't we have followed him?" This from Twister.

"No." Red's reply is short and sweet.

"So, you're proposing he gets away scot-free?" Crash's eyes are wide.

Now Red shakes his head. "No, Mel came up with the right idea."

I was wondering whether Red was going to address her suggestion. The more we've agreed that our hands are tied, the more I've been thinking of doing things her way. Though it wouldn't provide me with the same satisfaction, locking him up and throwing away the key could be a good solution. Once he's in prison, well, we've got friends who'd be delighted to have something to relieve their boredom.

Red continues, "She wants to take him on legally, and I reckon she's got a good case."

Murmurs and growls of discontent go around the table. Words like *bikers and cops don't mix* can be heard.

Red's unperturbed. "Look at it this way. He used sex and a woman who'd have been unwilling if she knew what she'd been getting into. Can't believe that was sanctioned. Even cops working undercover are bound by rules. I'm hoping we can get him where it will hurt and not in a physical way. At the least get him disgraced and cost him his job."

"For fuck's sake," I start with a menacing growl. I was going to say that was far away from what he deserves.

But Twister gets in before I can complete that thought. "I like the way you think, Prez."

Twister does? I don't. "I want him to hurt," I yell. "Lose his fuckin' job? He needs to go to prison and we'll take it from there. He should lose his life."

Twister leans down the table and looks directly at me. "Oh, he will. We'll just have to wait until he's no longer a cop."

"Could take years, Prez," Crash warns.

"Yeah. We'll need legal advice. But I say that's what Pyro's woman needs to do." Again, Red's eyes are full of sympathy as they meet mine. "Say you take him out, Pyro. Go to her tell her he's dead. She's got questions with no answers going around her head, no closure, and she'll have done nothing to right her pain. I might only have known her a short time, but she's an intelligent woman, and as I told you earlier, women don't think like us. She needs to be involved, needs her own retribution, something that allows her to take back control. Don't like the idea of putting a gun in her hand, women tend to be better with words. Which means she sits in the driver's seat on this."

Demon says firmly, "I know Mel, and I think Red's correct."

That pulls me up. They had read Mel right. She might want him dead but wouldn't want it to be by her hand. Taking control and bringing a case against him like she had suggested, well, that does, as Red said, put her firmly with her hand on the wheel.

Would it help her get her head on straight?

"One more thing, Brother." Demon's dark eyes find mine.

"Skull didn't deserve the patch that he wore. He wasn't even the man he said. Under those circumstances, he can't claim a woman, or keep her claimed. You're free to do whatever you want in the eyes of the club. I know what all the brothers will say, don't need to take a vote on this."

Hands bang the table in support of my prez's words. Men here might be a different chapter, but we all wear the same patch.

I raise my chin in acknowledgement of what I'd love to have heard even a few hours before. Right now, there's a woman upstairs who may never want to be claimed by a biker again.

CHAPTER TWENTY-NINE

Melissa

I might be a grown woman in my thirties, but right now I need my mom. Rosa's doing her best, but I'm longing for my parents, for the only two people in my life that accept me for what I am, and who I have absolutely no doubt, love me.

"You going to give your man a chance?"

"How can I?" I turn my face toward Rosa, wiping away another tear. "I trusted Skull. Oh, I didn't at first, thought he was too young, that someone like him wouldn't be attracted to someone like me. I was right, wasn't I? Should have run a mile then. But I believed him, believed all the lies that came out of his mouth."

"What do you mean, someone like you?" she says, sharply.

"I'm thirty-four years old. And I think I'd be described as the homely type. Not biker chick material. I'm curvy..."

"Mel, hon. Lots of men *like* curvy. Have you seen Angel?"

I shake my head, not knowing who she's talking about.

"She's one of our club girls. She's curvy, and much in demand. When visiting members come to the club, it's often her they head straight for."

"Bet she's young."

Rosa shrugs. "I'm forty-eight," she offers. "I met my man at twenty-eight. Didn't put him off none. You're thirty-four which isn't over the hill. And, under those tears, you've got a really pretty face."

"Didn't make Skull stick around though, did it?" I should start calling him by his real name, but Donavon, or even Don, doesn't seem right, even in my head. "I work for the local government, Rosa. I could have been a cop's wife. But he never gave me the chance. If he thought half of what he'd led me to believe, he would've never just walked out."

"He already had a wife, Mel, so that wasn't an option. He was in a tight spot, albeit one of his own making." Rosa plays devil's advocate. "He obviously wanted to keep his career choice away from the club. If he'd told you, you might have told them. He couldn't take the chance."

I can't contradict her. I've gotten close to the club. I couldn't risk Vi's man being sent down without warning them. Skull admitting he was undercover would have had to have led to an explanation that he wasn't free to pursue a relationship with me. Yeah, my loyalties may very well have switched to my new friends, instead of the man I professed to love.

"They'd have been out for his blood." Rosa continues, "He probably wouldn't have made it out alive. This betrayal is too great."

"But he's protected…"

"He is now, but then? If he'd told you, he'd have never gotten out of town."

Stubbornly I tell her, "But he could have contacted me and explained after he left…" I remember the despair I'd felt when day after day passed and I'd heard no word.

"Same thing. There was a risk you'd tell the club, and they'd never have given up searching for him."

I still can't get my head around how he walked away earlier without even a backward glance. "Rosa… he was so cold. Even when I told him about the baby. He," again the sobs rise, "he, he asked me to do a DNA test."

"You probably shocked him." She snorts. "That's probably the last thing he wanted to hear in front of his wife. Fuck, that has probably destroyed their relationship."

"You sound like you're on his side, Rosa."

"The only side I'm on is yours. Look. What he's done is despicable. Looking at the cold hard facts I'm not surprised you're feeling as bad as you are. I'm trying to help you. Right now, you're looking at black and white." As she says the colours, she holds out one hand then the other palm facing up. "Somewhere there's the truth, and it probably sits more to one side than the other."

I shake my head. "The truth is, he lied to me then deserted me. Can't get any plainer than that."

She purses her lips, and a moment passes before she speaks again. "Yeah, try as I might, I can't find a way to soften that blow."

"He raped me, Rosa. I'd never have consented had I known I was being used. He violated me. Took my trust and gave it back to me in tatters. He broke my heart when I thought he was dead, then, when I found he was alive, I had to mourn all over again, this time because he'd knowingly left me. Now?" I put my fist to my mouth. *How the hell do I go on?*

She tilts her head to one side while she examines me. "What's Pyro like?"

Shaking my head, I tell her, "I don't know. I thought I knew him, but I didn't know Skull, did I?" I pull up my knees, link my arms around them, and start rocking back and forth.

"Pyro's been with the club a long time," she tells me. "I've met him a few times before, when he's come here with the club. He's a good man, Mel. What you see with him is what you get."

Stubbornly I again shake my head. "How would I know? I'm the dumb ass who believes anything anyone tells them."

"Do you think Demon is stupid? Or Red?"

"Demon patched Skull in."

"Yes, that's true." Her brow creases. "Or was it when Hellfire was still prez? Anyway, to the best of my recollection, I think Pyro's been in the club going on ten years. If he had any failings, I think they'd know. Skull, though, he'd only worn his patch a few months. Talk to Pyro. You need someone on your side, hon."

"I need my mom and dad," I suddenly cry out, feeling like a little kid all over again.

Rosa's arm reaches around my back, and her fingers press in. "That's probably a good idea, hon."

"I need to book a flight. I'll go back to Pueblo as soon as I can." In fact, I might go straight to Denver. What would it be like going back to the club? Will they view me as part of Skull's deceit? *Would they think I knew all along?* I had been pressing Vi for info. *How would they treat me?* Without Skull, without Pyro, I could never return.

Her shoulders rise and fall. "Club will sort that for you, hon. Right now, you shouldn't be travelling alone. You're upset, and, well..."

I'm carrying a baby inside me. It has only been a week, yet it seems so long ago that Pyro and I were so happy to see our son on the screen. To know he was alive and healthy. I'd even thought I'd felt him moving, though I've not had that feeling again and had probably been mistaken.

My baby doesn't deserve to have a sperm donor like Skull.

"Hon, I need to get downstairs and see about getting dinner going. You going to be okay on your own? I can get Tiffany to come up and keep you company if you want."

But I don't want anyone else to know how foolish I've been. Oh, I know she'll already have heard, the rumour mill will be going full force. Everyone must be talking about what went on in that basement. Rosa's been good and kind, and hasn't let her pity or criticism show. But I know what everyone must be thinking, why hadn't I suspected Skull wasn't what he seemed?

"I'll be fine." Belatedly I dismiss her offer of company. "I'm worn out. I'd like to be alone."

"Hon, yes, you must be exhausted. You get some rest. I'll come up and see you later."

I give a final small nod. She goes.

Rest? My body is tired, my mind though, it won't stop racing. There's a loop in my head replaying every moment from the time I first saw Skull, to that fateful morning he'd left. Little things come back to me, like how he'd wanted me to get close to Vi. I shudder, he was making me spy for him, and I hadn't had the slightest suspicion. I feel dirty that he ever laid his hands on me.

So dirty, filthy.

I get to my feet, grab some clean clothes and a towel, and go to one of the communal bathrooms. I lock the door, turn the water hot, then get in and start scrubbing. I raise the temperature and clean myself all over, then again and again, trying to rub the memory of his touch from my skin, but it's not working. The water grows cooler then goes cold, but still I haven't removed all his filth, so I wash myself again.

Suddenly the door I know I locked is opened.

Pyro's standing there. He moves forward, his arm snaking around me to turn off the water, then picks up the towel and holds it out.

"Is she okay?" a masculine voice I don't recognise calls.

"She will be," Pyro replies with certainty. "Come on, darlin'."

I'm standing naked, the cold water having caused goose-bumps to rise all over my skin. I'm shivering, and I hadn't realised I'd become so cold. I let him place the towel around my shoulders unable to even feel embarrassed that this is the first time he's seen me without clothes.

"I can't get clean," I tell him, through chattering teeth. "I could have betrayed the club without knowing or meaning to. I've got filth all over me and I can't wash it off."

"You're clean," he replies tersely, even as he's lifting me in his arms. Before going out through the door he glances down to make sure I'm covered, moving a corner of the towel to conceal an inch of bared skin. "It's him who's covered in shit, not you. I won't have you taking any of this on yourself. If we didn't suspect him, Mel, how could we expect you to?"

We're back in the room, and he places me carefully on the bed and then closes the door. He comes over, lying down behind me, and pulling me to him.

"That's what people will be thinking. What did I know? Was I in it with him? Was I trying to get info on the club? Was I betraying you? I lived with him, how could I not know?"

"No one will be thinking anything of the sort," he states, firmly. "Prospects do their time for a reason, to earn our trust. Skull was clearly in it for the long haul. He knew he'd have to start at the bottom and make his way up. He took all the shit, and a severe beating. We didn't see anything to make us suspicious. We trusted him. The whole club trusted him, Mel. If all of us couldn't see what was in front of our noses, why the fuck would we expect you to?"

"Then you must have doubts about me. Maybe I've been fooling you as well."

"Might as well have doubts about Judge and Wills. They've only patched in recently. Christ, Mel, we'd tie ourselves up in knots if we let one bad apple influence our thoughts about everyone else. Truth be told, there were always some questions about the prospect we'd known as Runt. Not everyone took to him. But he took a beating and came back, was patched in and took the name Skull. That's when we stopped asking questions. He had us fooled, Mel. In hindsight, we'll rethink shit and see there were signs we didn't think to note. But you? Nah. I've been with you every step of the way since Skull disappeared, and every reaction you've had has been genuine." He pauses, then resumes, "Might as well take the blame on ourselves. You saw Skull had the trust of the club, so didn't look further than the surface he showed to you. Yeah, if we had no doubts, why should his old lady?"

Had their faith in him coloured my views? I hadn't looked deeper as I hadn't expected there'd be anything to find.

I bark a mirthless laugh. Me, a woman who'd snagged herself a younger, and very fit man.

"Mel?"

"I've been so foolish, Ro. I believed what I wanted to. I gave Skull what he wanted dressed up in a bow."

"Can't argue, Mel. Skull chose you for a reason, but part of it must have been he wanted you in bed. Any man would. If you weren't claimed, I'd be fighting off a number of my brothers. You're a fuckin' attractive woman, Mel, and that's something you mustn't forget."

Forget? I don't remember knowing it in the first place. But all I say is, "I'm not claimed." *Surely the club won't still expect me to be tied to a traitor?* I want no one to ever refer to me as Skull's old lady again.

He turns me to face him, and his hand brushes the wet hair back from my face. "Mel, I'm an open book. You're one hundred percent genuine. And I'm going to work to prove to you that so am I. This might not be what you want to hear right now, but Skull's out of the picture and I'm free to claim you."

If I'm no longer tied to Skull, I'm free to be with Pyro. But I can't. *I don't want to be claimed by anyone, do I?* Not now, not knowing what happened before.

But he hasn't finished. "I love you, Mel. Love you and already love that baby that's mine in all the ways that count. I want to claim you, if you want to be claimed. I know I can say it until I'm blue in the face, but you can trust me. I will never knowingly hurt you. Won't say I'll never make a mistake, but it won't be with any intention."

Skull told me he loved me. He lied.

Christ, right at this moment I need to believe Pyro's declaration is true, that his words are ones I can take at face value. To be truly loved, for me, and not what I could do. Try as I might, I can't see Pyro has any ulterior motive.

He gives me time, and my mind loops back again. Not to Skull, I'm trying to put him out of my head, but to all the times Pyro has been there for me. From the moment Skull disappeared, Pyro's been my rock and has been proving himself without saying the words. With Skull it was what he said, which were all lies. Pyro? Maybe his actions speak louder.

"Can I ask you something?"

"Anything. I'll answer unless it's something about the club I can't tell you. Not because I don't trust you..."

"Plausible deniability," I say back, remembering what Vi had explained.

"Exactly. What do you want to know?"

"Who are you, Pyro? I don't even know how old you are, what you did before you joined the club."

"I'm thirty-seven. Hopefully not too old for you."

Huh. Is that a dig at me having had a boy toy before? "Well I'm not going for a younger man again."

"We've been talking about Skull, Mel. Not sure he's as young as he says." He sees the expression of disbelief on my face. "Yeah, well, to get where he has and do the job that he does, he must be older. Must have been part of his ploy, thought we'd not suspect a younger man of being what he was, an undercover cop."

Another lie he'd told me. When will it stop?

"Anyway, getting back to me. I went into the Army straight from high school. Became a munitions expert. I used to blow shit up."

"That's why you're called Pyro?"

"Yeah. I can start fires and I can put them out." He winks.

"Did you do any tours?"

His arms tighten slightly around me, and his face grows tense. "Too many. I don't usually talk about it. But if you want to know..."

I place my fingers over his lips. "I don't."

He breathes out and relaxes. "When I got out, I wasn't sure

what to do. Served with a guy who rode with a motorcycle club, and he'd shared some of the details with me about the camaraderie and the family. The idea stuck with me. When I got home, I was, I don't know, lonely? I no longer had a team around me. I'd toyed with the idea of buying a motorcycle, had learned to ride one in the Army, but hadn't seriously thought about joining a club. I went to the Harley store in Pueblo. There was a guy there wearing a Satan's Devils' cut, he was picking up something for his bike. He looked about my age. We got chatting, he was giving me advice about various models. His name was Demon, and he was the VP. He invited me along to one of their parties, and, well, the rest is history."

"Have you ever been married? Sired any kids?"

"You're looking for skeletons where none exist. My dad died when I was a kid, my mom moved out of state to be with family when I joined up, and we sort of drifted apart. She's married again now, and I don't get on with her husband. He doesn't approve of MCs."

"Siblings?"

"Nah. Oh, they were planned, but a drunk driver took my dad out when I was two, so it never happened. So, only a mom who I don't see, no ex-wife or ex ol' lady, and definitely no kids. Won't lie, there's been a few ladies over the years, but nothing serious, and no one to think they have a claim on me."

Suddenly I realise how patient he's being. "Thank you."

"No worries, darlin'. I know why you pushed me away. I don't blame you. Now, do you want me to get you something to eat?"

I couldn't force anything down. I'm feeling nauseous after this dreadful day. "I just want to sleep."

"Then, sleep darlin'. I'll be here with you."

CHAPTER THIRTY

Pyro

M el had been in that shower for ages, long enough for a prospect to come find me when the sound of water kept running and didn't turn off. I'd asked Twister to use his lock picking skills then he'd stood back, and I'd stepped inside.

She looked broken.

I can't get clean.

I'd had to swallow hard to suppress the fury I'd felt that she was the one left feeling dirty and violated, and not the man who'd walked away from her. She shouldn't be feeling like that. She's the innocent victim.

It had been my first sight of her gorgeous body with those generous curves that were hidden under her clothes, but my cock didn't even twitch. I just wanted to stop her tears, and, when I saw her shivering, lend my own body heat to her.

Somehow I knew she wasn't going to send me away, especially when we started talking. If she'd have asked me for proof of my service, I'd have given it to her. Got Red to vouch for the length of time I'd been with the Devils and dug up my birth certificate to prove my age. Fuck, after what Skull did to her, how does she know who to trust?

People say actions speak louder than words, but Skull was

such a good fucking actor, he'd had us all fooled. He'd lived and breathed his cover. If we couldn't tell he was rotten, fuck knows, she couldn't have known.

I'm a bit worried she hasn't eaten tonight, but the day's taken it out of her. She's pregnant and has been through the emotional wringer. If she can rest, get her brain to switch off, that will do her the most good.

My stomach growls, reminding me I've not eaten either. When it growls again so loudly I'm worried it will disturb her, I gently ease myself away from her sleeping form. She rolls over and settles again. *It's safe to leave her.* I won't be far.

I go downstairs. "Prospect?" Meat immediately comes over.

"Go stand outside Mel's door. If she wakes…"

"I'll come get you."

I nod.

"Pyro? How's Mel?"

"Calmer, and asleep," I tell Sparky.

"All this can't be good for her or the baby. You taking her back to Pueblo?"

"Yeah. I wanted to have a word with Demon. See what he wants us to do." I glance around the room.

"Prez and Beef have already gone back." Sparky realises I hadn't known. As I raise my eyebrows he continues, "Yeah, this will have shaken the club hard. He thought he needed to be there."

Of course. I can just imagine all the questions flying around in Pueblo, not least the concern the feds might come knocking at the door. I rake my hands through my hair.

"Have you been able to speak to her, about doing this legal?"

"Not yet. But I think Red's right. This can be her revenge. She needs it, Sparky. Right now, she's spiralling out of control. But," I warn him, "I'm putting the idea of killing Skull on hold, not putting it off indefinitely." My eyes flare.

"I hear you, Ro, I hear you."

"Now I need a beer and some food."

When he nods, I make my way past him and go into the kitchen. Rosa's cleaning up. When she offers to get me something to eat, I tell her gently I'm more than capable of cooking myself some bacon and eggs. While I do just that, she busies herself making a sandwich then wrapping it in Saran Wrap for Mel, she tells me, in case she wakes and is hungry later.

"You know, she wants her parents," Rosa confides, when I thank her for staying with Mel earlier.

I didn't, but I nod. It's not hard to understand why. "I'll take her to see them when we get back to Pueblo."

Rosa sighs as she puts the last of the things she's been working with away. "Well I'm off to bed."

I notice she looks tired herself. "It's been a long day."

She gives a feminine snort. "Getting my two horrors, Tristan and Tom off their X-Box and into bed wasn't fun tonight. Teenage boys, who'd have them?"

Me, I hope. Well, one at least in a few years' time. Maybe it's best not to be warned in advance. Though I do lean over and joke with her, "It'll be you worrying about them bringing girls home next."

"Don't tell me that." She laughs as she leaves me alone.

I reckon she'll be fine. She might not have a man, but she's got a club full of members who'll keep her boys on the straight and narrow, or not, as the case may be.

Mel's still asleep when I get back to the room. Having dismissed Meat who was still standing guard outside her door, I undress as quietly as I can, making sure my boots don't thump on the floor. Leaving on my jeans, I lie down on the bed beside her.

As I close my eyes, all I can see is that motherfucker telling her to get a DNA test, his malicious words and dismissal of her winding me up. I don't think I've heard anything so spiteful in my life. Finally, fuck knows when, my mind eventually switches off, and I fall asleep.

It's still dark when I awake to find her moving beside me.

"You okay?"

"I need to pee," she explains.

"Put the light on. I'm awake now."

She leans over and switches on the lamp on the table next to her side casting a dim illumination across the room. She swings her legs off the bed, then walks across the room and disappears into the hallway.

The clubhouse is deathly quiet, all I can hear is the hum of the air conditioning. It's that time of the night between the late-nighters having at last taken to their beds, and the early risers not yet stirring.

My door opens again. One look at Mel's face, and I know there's something wrong. Immediately I'm out of bed and moving toward her.

"Darlin'?"

"I'm bleeding."

Oh fuck. No.

"Much?" I try to keep panic out of my voice.

She nods. "Too much, Pyro." Her voice is shaking. "Pyro…"

"Get dressed, darlin'. I'll wake someone and take you to the emergency room." I'm already pulling on my boots as I'm speaking.

I realise I have fuck all idea whose room the door that I'm banging on belongs to.

"What the fuck?" Crash pulls it open.

"It's Mel. It's the baby. She's bleeding."

"Give me two minutes to throw some clothes on. I'll meet you downstairs."

"Pyro?" Mel's right behind me. "Pyro, I…"

"We'll get you checked out. It's probably nothing." I try to reassure her, while deep down inside I have the dreadful feeling that something is very wrong. Even I know bleeding is not a good sign in a pregnant woman.

She clutches my hand as Crash drives. When we arrive the emergency room isn't crowded, and they prioritise her, rushing her into a room to be examined. She still hangs onto me, her fingers tightly wrapped around mine, even though the nurse wants to throw me out.

"It's my baby," I tell her with a growl.

It's eerily similar to that visit to the doctor's office just a week ago, when Mel undergoes another ultrasound examination. But this time, there's a significant difference. Last week we heard the reassuring, exciting sound, of a heart beating. This time, there's nothing.

The technician moves the probe, this way and that, but nothing changes.

"Is the machine fuckin' working?" I snarl.

"Wait here." She disappears.

"Pyro, I'm scared. There's something wrong, isn't there?"

There is, but I try and reassure her. "Something's up with their fuckin' machine," I tell her, not believing it for a second.

The technician's back, with someone else with her. A man in a white coat. He too examines Mel. Her face is strained, and she looks so pale. I will myself to smile at her. "He's probably sleeping," I tell her. But even I know hearts don't sleep. They keep beating.

They do another ultrasound, this time with a probe that's inserted into her vagina, but their faces don't change. No smiles of relief, no words to tell her everything's going to be fine.

Finally, they clean the gel off her stomach, the doctor stands by looking so fucking serious.

"Just tell me doctor," she cries out, my gut twisting at the anguish in her voice.

"I'm very sorry Ms Martins."

"No," Mel gasps. "No. No. No."

"Mel," I grasp her hand tighter, but I can't find anything to say. *I'm sorry* is totally inadequate.

"No!" She's almost screaming now. "There's a mistake. There has to be."

I pull my distraught woman to me, holding her tight in my

arms. Looking up at the doctor over her shoulder I ask, already knowing there's nothing he can say that I want to hear, "What do we do now?"

"I'll give your wife a sedative."

"No," Mel wails. "It might hurt the baby."

But nothing can hurt him now.

It can hurt her, though. When I'm old and grey I know I'll never forget that night. Never forget when Mel at last comes to terms with the fact her baby has died inside her. What we hadn't realised immediately, was the fact it had to come out, and how. She wasn't even given the luxury of having time to come to get used to it.

Because Mel was experiencing heavy bleeding, they decided they needed to do an immediate dilatation and curettage. Mel screamed when she realised they were going to take her baby from her. I talked to her, trying to calm her. They gave us space until she was numb with grief, accepting all hope was gone.

Then they took her away.

Fuck, there's no more baby. No more expecting that in just over four months we'd visit the hospital looking forward to bringing a healthy baby home with us.

I thought I knew how a broken heart felt from what Mel had already been through. I hadn't had a clue. To see her wheeled away to deal with a baby that wouldn't take a first breath was devastating.

By then the waiting room was filled with Devils, strangely quiet and hushed, reverent in their silence.

I go and update Red.

"Skull's a dead man walking," Red growls, but quietly considering there are medical staff around.

As far as I can tell, almost all the Vegas club are here. It's a sign Devils pile in to give support, even when there's nothing anyone can say or do to make the situation better. Nods and chin lifts offered with scowls from all around confirm no one has any doubt that Mel losing the baby has been down to Skull suddenly reappearing in her life.

When was the damage done? When she'd first found out? I shake my head to rid myself of those thoughts. They don't matter. They can't bring back her—*our*—baby. *How is she going to get through this?*

What can I do?

"We'll bury the baby in our plot," Red suddenly says. "Know it's not much, but both you and Mel might like to know he's among brothers."

I hadn't thought about what would happen to his tiny body. I know I don't want him disposed like waste. He might not have taken breath, but to me he was already living, and much more so to Mel. To bury him properly... I think that would be something to help start the grieving process. I tell Red so and thank him sincerely.

"Pyro..." Suddenly Red's hand is pressing into my shoulder. "We're here for you. For you both."

I raise my chin to him. Mel's lost our baby and she's my focus now. Red's acknowledging that this is also a loss for me.

Hushed conversations are interrupted as suddenly an older couple appear. They barge in, then come to an abrupt halt. The woman's voice stopping in mid flow, "Where's my daught—"

Red steps forward. "Mr and Mrs Martins?"

It's Mel's mom and dad. Red must have called them. While I've never met them before, I feel a wave of relief. I'd do anything for Mel, want to be there for her, but I'm lost as to how to make this right. Someone to share the burden is welcomed.

I step forward. "I'm Pyro, Mel's man." From their reaction, she's told them about me. I go on to explain what's happened as briefly as I can. Her mom's eyes fill with tears, though those of her dad's harden.

It's him who goes to speak but is interrupted.

"Family of Melissa Martins?"

Fuck me, but a dozen bikers all stand. But it's me and her

mom and dad who step forward. "You can go and see her now. We'll keep her in for observation for a few hours, then, she can go home.

Mel's groggy, but awake and looks completely lost, a shadow of her usual self. I stand back as her mom goes to her, holding her tight. Now there are tears again, this time from both women.

The doctor comes in briefly to check on her, as he goes out, I mention the plans for burial, and he agrees to prepare the paperwork to release the remains of the foetus to me.

I've watched men die, lost brothers and have attended too many funerals before now, but I don't think anything has ever affected me so badly. I'm firmly convinced, if Skull hadn't reappeared, that baby would still be breathing. It's only my need to stay strong for Mel that keeps me drawing in air.

I nearly forget to ask but remember just before the doctor leaves. "Oh, Doc?" I ask, quickly. "Can you do a DNA test on him?"

"Of course," his eyes narrow. "But it's a bit late to be worried about paternity. That woman there has enough to deal with."

He thinks I'm going to use it to prove she's been unfaithful?

"Not what you think, Doc. We know who the father is. Just want to have something to prove it."

His brow furrows as he tries to make sense of my request, but it seems it's easier for him to just acquiesce. "I'll make the arrangements."

I thank him, then walk back to Mel. She's still clutching to her mother.

"Can I have a word with you?" It's her dad, and he looks grim. "I need to know why my daughter lost her baby. Is it because of her association with your club? Has anyone hurt her?"

He's in his late fifties, but right now, he looks like he'd personally take on whoever harmed his only child. I have no regrets as I hand him his target.

"Skull. We found him. He's an undercover cop," I sum up

quickly. "Mel's relationship with him had all been a lie. He's already married with a wife and kid."

His eyes go wide, and twin red spots appear on his cheeks as he indicates I should follow him out of the room. I don't want to leave her, not for a moment, but there are things he, as a parent, should know.

We make use of the two chairs in the corridor. He's sharp, I soon discover as I go over what's happened during the past few days.

"My daughter's in there, broken," he starts when I've completed my sorry tale, his eyes watery with distress.

I can only make a promise. "I don't know how, but I swear I'm going to put her back together."

His lips thin as he realises I'll be attempting the impossible. "How, Pyro? How?"

I tell him. "I love her, sir. I lost the baby too, it was mine more than Skull's. I..." I gulp, "I heard his heart beating, saw him on that screen. He was mine."

Reaching out his hand, he pats my leg. I try to push my own emotion down. "We're a biker club, we've got our methods of retribution..."

"Don't tell me more," he warns.

"There's nothing more to tell. Before she lost the baby, before she had that to add to her misery, we had decided to put the fight into her hands rather than the club acting on her behalf. Give her something to focus on. Let her take back the control he took from her." I now have my doubts, and whether she'll ever be in the right mindset. "She wanted to report him and what he'd done. Take him to whatever court she could. It seems a good case for misrepresentation and his successful attempt to involve an innocent citizen in what he must have thought was a criminal underworld."

Once again, his lips thin, and he tilts his head. "You're right," he says after a moment's thought. "And now more than ever, she'll need something to focus on." He goes still, the wheels turning in his head as he considers, then, a grin just as evil as I've seen from any of my brothers spreads over his face when he informs me, "It's a good thing I'm a lawyer."

It's my turn to widen my eyes. "Is this where I give you a dollar?"

The grin disappears and is replaced by a sad smile. "If you want, but on behalf of my daughter."

CHAPTER THIRTY-ONE

Melissa

There are times when a woman needs her mom, whatever age she is. Especially with things only another woman can understand, even if they haven't been there themselves.

I know there's a chance any pregnancy might not go to term, it's the fear of any woman carrying a baby. A fear my mother would have had at the back of her mind when I was inside her. That the worst didn't happen to her doesn't affect her ability to comprehend exactly how I'm feeling.

Grief, first and foremost. Sorrow I won't get to know my son or hold him in my arms. Misery that my body's now empty. The difficulty of coming to terms with my loss, wondering how or if I'll ever be able to accept it.

Guilt, that it was my fault. Was it that too hot shower followed by the cold? Maybe that I'd travelled when pregnant? Or, was it that my reaction to Skull turning up had been over-dramatic?

Anger. Rage. That Skull caused me to miscarry his baby.

When Pyro and my dad had disappeared, the doctor had returned, but provided no answers to my questions. It might be my first miscarriage, but certainly not his. It can happen with no reason, he told me. If I miscarry again, maybe then they'll look for a cause.

"Sometimes it just happens," Mom tells me reasonably after he's gone.

But I'm in no state of mind to believe that. There is a reason. If Skull hadn't reappeared, I'd still be carrying my baby.

I swing between despair and rage as I wait to be discharged. Pyro's being as supportive as he can, but I can see he's trying hard not to say the wrong thing, opening his mouth as though wanting to speak, then second guessing himself and shutting it again. In my more rationale moments I know he'll be hurting too, he's lost a son the same as I have. Yet, I can't help being self-ish, wanting all the misery myself and not being able to share his.

He's been talking in whispers with my dad. Under other circumstances I'd be pleased at how they're getting along, now I'm suspicious as to what they're so animatedly discussing.

I veer between wanting Pyro close at hand and wanting nothing to do with him. My head's muddling everything up. If I'd never been drawn into the club, I wouldn't have stayed with Skull. But how can I hate people for being nice and accepting me? Everything in my head is fucked up.

Mom's patient, but my swiftly changing moods are trying her parenting skills. If she tries platitudes I end up frustrated, if she encourages my anger, I swiftly change it to guilt, and if she tries to tell me I'm not responsible for killing my baby, I tell her all the reasons why I am.

I'm a complete mess.

Two days back at the club and I'm feeling no easier. Even though I'm not really ill, I've spent most of the time up in the room we'd been allocated when we first arrived in Vegas. I wish I wasn't in an alien place, would much rather be in my own home, but due to the bleeding that's still continuing, Pyro and my parents don't want me to fly.

"Hey, Mel." Pyro stands, hesitantly in the doorway.

Well, he's just heard me dismissing my mom and not very pleasantly, I've no doubt his cautious approach is him questioning my mood right now.

I sigh. "It's okay, come in." What's unfair is that Pyro and I had been so close to cementing our relationship until Skull stepped in and blew that away.

What's he going to say now? I'm fed up with people asking me how I'm feeling, as I don't know. I could tell them the truth, then only a moment later, find out that had been a lie, as I'm now feeling something else.

But he surprises me. He stands just inside the door, not coming right in. "Mel, will you come with me?"

"Where?"

He shakes his head. "Trust me, okay?"

Go with him? I notice my parents are standing behind him. Dad looks serious, mom's expression holds a mixture of grief and oddly, anticipation. She's also nodding encouragingly.

Downstairs, it gets even stranger. Leather clad men are milling around, on seeing me, they fall silent, then start walking out the front door.

"What's going on?" I ask, looking around. Then my eyes fall on a tiny coffin, resting on a black cloth on a table.

I gasp, my hands covering my face. Feeling guilty I hadn't asked what had happened to the baby. I'd just assumed the hospital would deal with whatever was left and hadn't wanted to know the details. When I'd left I'd been too befuddled with the residue of the anaesthesia, when I'd thought about it, I'd been too scared to ask.

"Is that...?" I ask to be certain.

"Pyro arranged it," said my mom.

It's Pyro who steps forward and carries him, so lovingly and carefully as though he was a living child. I follow him out and watch as he places the wooden box containing my son into the back of an SUV, then sit in the rear seat with my mom, while Dad and Pyro are in the front.

It looks like every biker from the club is following behind. I don't know where, I don't ask why. My mind focused on the loss. My hands rest on my stomach. That's where my son should be, that's where he belongs. I should be able to feel him moving… But he's not there. He's gone, and his remains are in that box.

We go to a graveyard on the edge of the desert, grass beneath our feet kept watered and green. Escorted by bikers wearing their Satan's Devils cuts, I follow Pyro to one part of the burial ground where all the gravestones have one thing in common—the Satan's Devils name etched into the granite.

A small hole has been dug, just the right size for the tiny coffin Pyro is holding.

Red steps up, as Pyro carefully lays it down. "We'll never know if Baby Martins would have become a Devil, but he was conceived in the club, and is one of our own. Here he'll lie, knowing he has brothers watching out for him. Even though he never knew life, in death he will never be alone."

I feel choked up. Tears blind my vision.

"Sleep, baby boy." Pyro's voice is deep.

"Sleep in peace, child," says my dad, though Mom is openly weeping against his shoulder.

Someone hands me a rose. When I step forward to place it in the grave, a shadow briefly passes over the coffin, looking up I see a kestrel flying. Symbolic, as if my child had grown wings and flown.

I'm incapable of speech, so I think the words instead. *Bye baby. I love you so much.*

Then I'm crying, hard, wracking sobs shaking my body. Pyro's arms hold me tightly as he rocks me, his tears mingling with my own.

I hadn't realised I needed to say goodbye. There's no doubt it had helped. No contrary view that the support of these men who can be gruff and rough helped me get through those first dark days.

After the funeral, I had no longer kept to my room. No longer felt awkward when a man simply patted my shoulder as he passed me. No longer had the need to hide when I heard snippets of conversation, as their feelings only mirror my own. There's only one outcome I can focus on. The reason I lost my baby has to be resolved. Skull has to be taken down.

But he can't be killed. Even if I wish he'd remained, at least in my head, no longer breathing. I can't risk the safety or freedom of the man I love or these men I call friends.

"Mel?"

I raise my head as Dad and Pyro walk over.

"Skull needs to feel our revenge. Are you strong enough to do it?"

They pull up chairs and sit down. My eyes narrow. But they soon elaborate on their plan.

Dad puts it into words. "Skull started a relationship with you under false pretences. Those false pretences included making you a spy to get information on the club which he otherwise might not get. He got you pregnant..."

"There's no proof," I interject, my mouth twisting as I remember he'd tried to deny it.

"We'll get proof." Pyro shifts uncomfortably. "You'll be sent the copy of the baby's DNA test."

I just stare at him, shaking my head.

"I'm sorry, Mel. I asked the doctor to do it."

He had? I have only two words for him. "Thank you." It will be something concrete that Skull won't be able to deny. "How do we get Skull's?"

"There's probably something left in his room," Pyro suggests.

"Or we demand that he provides a swab," Dad suggests. "What he put you through Mel, was psychological torture. There's no way of proving that led to you losing the baby, but your suffering when he left, then when he turned up again, should be enough."

"He raped me. I didn't give my consent."

Dad shakes his head. "I don't think we'll get him on a rape charge, though we can try. He didn't force you into bed, even though he misrepresented who he was."

"Will he go to jail?" I ask hopefully. That's the outcome I want—to know he's suffering every day for the wrong that he did.

"I can't promise you that, Mel. There are so many factors. But we'll take it as far as we can."

"We don't know where he is."

Pyro raises an eyebrow toward my father.

Who responds, "We know his real name, and his employers will certainly be able to find him. He'll be working for the cops or feds."

"I'll have to face him." My tone gives away neither one thing nor another.

Dad grins. "You're my daughter. As soon as Pyro suggested we give you the lead in getting retribution, I knew this was what you needed, and that you are fully capable of following it through."

"You'll be my lawyer?"

"I'm an attorney in the state of Colorado where the crime occurred. So yes, I'll represent you."

As I realise I'll be expected to tell my lawyer everything, I press my lips together and shift a little awkwardly. Seems I don't need to explain.

"Strange as it may seem, I do know how babies are made." He smiles.

I glance down at my hands. In some ways getting revenge, making Skull face up to his crimes sounds good, in others, well, it won't give me my baby back. Though knowing he hasn't walked away unscathed would be some comfort.

Pyro seems to read my mind. "Be interesting to know whether Clare's still with him. Might be he's lost his own family."

Is it wrong of me to hope that's what happened? To know

that Skull will lose his own child and know one-hundredth of the pain I'm feeling is welcomed.

"You don't have to decide or start anything now." Pyro leans over and covers my wringing hands, stilling them.

Dad looks from him to me, then stands and leaves us alone.

"It's just so hard, Ro. I, I…"

"Come with me, come outside." His arm comes around me to support me as we go out into the rapidly setting sun of the Vegas evening. He leads me over to a bench and sits down, patting the wooden seat beside him. "Can I just hold you, Mel?"

"I'm not being fair to you," I start.

"Life's not fair." He stares up at the stars just starting to show. "Fair is none of this happening. Fair is for us to have recognised Skull for what he was long before he was patched in. Fair is you never meeting the man." He pauses. "But if things were fair, I wouldn't have met you."

"You'd have been saved a lot of pain then."

"No, Mel. This rough patch, I know neither of us can see a way through, but we'll get there, I promise you."

"Maybe you should find someone else." *Someone who's not broken.*

"I'm not going anywhere, sweetheart. I promise you, good or bad, we're in this together."

His pained expression makes me remember the different one he wore just two-and-a-half weeks ago, the joy on his face when we heard the baby's heartbeat for the first time and saw the picture on the screen. His pride when showing the photo of *his* son around. He lost his baby too.

For the first time, guiltily I allow him to share my loss. "Are you hurting, Ro?"

His hand grips mine. "More than I can fuckin' put into words."

He's a man, so he doesn't let it show.

"We should grieve together." That's what we haven't been

doing. I've been selfish, just thinking of me, and not about what he lost too.

"That's what I want, Mel. To help you through this, as you'll help me. We both need to heal, and for that, we need to go home. When the doctor clears you to fly, we'll go back to Pueblo."

I'm pretty sure I'll get the okay from the doctor on my next check-up. The bleeding, that final physical reminder of everything I've been through, has, at last, stopped. "Can we visit the grave again, before we go?"

"Of course we fuckin' can. I'd like to as well." Pyro gives a small smile. "Seeing him there, among brothers, seems right. Comforting, somehow. We can come back to Vegas whenever we want or need to."

He's right. It's weird but buried where he is makes me feel I'm not leaving my son alone, or unprotected. There's a peace, a comfort in having a place where my baby lies. I don't know what strings Red pulled, or whether he just did it not caring about rules, but it was the right thing to do.

We sit, letting the night descend around us, no need for more words. I'm happy he knows there isn't anything more to say. Not right now.

The next day my parents are getting ready to leave.

"Come back to Denver, Melissa." My mom's concerned eyes meet mine.

"No, Mom. I've got my job, my friends, and… Pyro." I look at them. My parents dropped everything to come be with me and ended up in the midst of a biker club and seem to have taken it all in their stride. While they've stayed at a hotel, they've been here every day. I do wonder what they really think about my continued association with the club, which is why I hesitated before saying Pyro's name.

"Skull dragged you into this world," my dad starts, his face serious. "This club isn't to blame for anything that happened to you, unless there were illegal activities for Skull to find out."

I stop him. "We assume he found nothing…"

"I agree," he replies fast. "I've had conversations with Pyro, got to know Red and Crash a bit too. I put my judgement on the back burner and listened to what they had to say. I'm an attorney, Melissa. To you I'm your dad, and I've not brought my work home, but I've seen, and heard, a thing or two. The Satan's Devils may live by their own rules, but if they step over the lines, I guess it's with good reason." He glances at my mom. "I like the way this club supports you—not every MC treats its women in such good ways. What I have to admit worries me is that your mom and I, well, we accepted Skull, though we didn't much like that he was a biker. He seemed a good man for you. I still can't get my head around how he had us all fooled. I'm concerned about it happening again."

"It won't." It's all become clear in my mind. "Skull was an anomaly. There's no reason to suspect Pyro isn't exactly what he seems."

Suddenly the arms of the man we're discussing come around me, pulling me back against his firm chest. "I've nothing to hide. Get someone to investigate me."

Dad looks at him with respect. "You understand it will be for our peace of mind?"

"Long as you know the club won't share much. But I've managed the auto-shop for years, and my service is a matter of record."

Dad reaches out his hand, Pyro takes and shakes it. Saying, as he does, "I'll bring Mel up to Denver as soon as she's ready."

"I'll start finding out what needs to be done," Dad agrees. "And how to best put the case together."

Then Mom's hugging me, and I'm hanging onto her, a hairbreadth away from changing my mind and going home with them after all. The main thing that stops me is somehow sharing Pyro's pain lessens mine.

All too soon they have to leave, and a prospect drives them away in the club's SUV.

CHAPTER THIRTY-TWO

Pyro

"Good to have you back, Brother."

"Fuckin' good to be here." I nod at Demon sat at the top of the table, then return chin lifts with each of my brothers in turn.

"Don't know what to say to you." Beef shakes his head, large sorrowful eyes meeting mine.

But they don't need to put it into words. I hold up my hand. Over the past couple of weeks, I've heard enough platitudes to last me a lifetime. "Mel and I know you've got our backs, that's enough."

"Is it though?" Hellfire spits out from the opposite end to his son. "I take as much responsibility as anyone else for not seeing what was wrong with Skull. I was the one who patched him in."

"Whoa, hold up there, Hell," Demon begins, "it was a club vote. If everyone hadn't said 'aye', he wouldn't have gotten his patch." His eyes scan each one of us. "There are no fingers to be pointed. We all had concerns that he came back after that beating he took, but our only thought was that he might want revenge. Even the vague suspicions we might have had weren't close to the mark. The question is, how the fuck could he have fooled us like that?"

Lizard holds up his hand. "I saw something on TV once. These cops who go undercover have to *become* the person they're pretending to be. Living a lie becomes living the truth. If he'd been part of an MC before, he'd have known exactly what behaviour we'd expect."

I nod. I'm wondering whether Keys will get anything back about that. He's promised to keep in touch should we get proof this wasn't the first time he'd been undercover in a similar role. Of course, he's liaising with Cad and their counterparts in other chapters. If there's something to be found, one of them will find it.

"He played his part well," confirms Ink. "Not a model prospect by a long shot, but we'd have been more suspicious of him if he was. I, personally, don't think he'd been with another club. Didn't come over that way. I think they put in a fresh face new to this particular type of job. Any prior knowledge or experience of a club would have made us look more closely at him." He pauses, then continues, "Fuckin' good at undercover operations though. I never suspected a thing."

"Does it matter?" I ask them. "What we've got to deal with is now and not then."

Prez interrupts, "It's relevant if there were things we should have spotted and missed. Don't want to be in this position again. Cad, have you completed those second background checks on Beaver and Karl?"

"Yeah, Prez. Turned nothing up. Been talking to Mouse, Keys and Hard Token about putting in a process to vet prospects and hangarounds better, sharing info between chapters. Trouble is, we're dealing with the cops. They can concoct and support any background process so it would stand scrutiny."

"So, we remain at risk?" Prez pinches the bridge of his nose. "Better keep our businesses clean then."

"Stop prospects burying bodies?"

"Fuck no," groans Thunder. "I don't want to go back to the heavy work."

"We're small fry." Beef's brow has deep lines etched on it. "Even if we were into illegal shit in a big way, taking down the Satan's Devils MC isn't going to make big headlines."

"What are you thinking, Beef?"

"Prez, I've just been mulling over the conversation we've already had. That the Wretched Soulz might have been his target, or maybe even the Mafia by way of the Silvestris."

"Got any further than what we already discussed?"

"Not really," Beef sighs. "But it could have been what he hoped to find out. Talk about our associates that wasn't discussed openly at church. We know there's no one else here, but what about the Wretched Soulz? Could he have been part of a larger operation?"

"Fuck." Prez's quiet for a moment. "I've already told them about Skull, but not to look inside their own houses. Guess I'm going to have to have another chat."

"RIP cool?" Hellfire asks.

Demon shrugs. "Hard to read him. Making the admission we'd patched in an undercover cop wasn't easy. He was taking it back to the table. Guess I'll get an update when I next speak to him."

He lowers his head into his hands after speaking and takes a deep breath. Fuck, I don't envy him having those conversations. I'd heard the one with Drummer hadn't been as bad as he'd feared and focused more on future prevention. But as for RIP? This is the second time in a year we've gone up against the Wretched Soulz, when normally we co-exist without often crossing paths. But an MC can't afford to upset the dominant. There's a chance it could risk losing our charter if they think we've been careless. A few glances are being exchanged around the table. The Soulz approve our rules and regs including the vetting of prospects. Could they blame us for letting Skull in? That Demon's thinking along the same lines is confirmed when he next opens his mouth.

"I promised to give Drummer the head's up if anything

further goes south. Let's hope it doesn't. Getting back to what we can deal with. Skull." Prez brings the meeting back on track. "What's the plan?" He looks at me.

"Plan is when Mel's feeling mentally stronger, she'll bring a case against him. Her dad's doing the groundwork now. Trouble is, once he submits the disposition, it's pretty clear they'll want to interrogate her."

"She ever going to be strong enough for that?"

"You fuckin' bet," I growl. "My old lady's got inner strength. Just got to give it some time to come back."

"How is she doing, Ro?" Hellfire's voice oozes sympathy.

"She has good days and bad days."

Ink's eyes half close. "She going to come back around?"

The old ladies have been visiting her, but she's not yet been to the club. "I hope so." It's the best I can offer for now. "Vi's helping, Demon. I think in her downtimes Mel's worried that you might think she was a spy."

"Never," he growls. "She was innocent. But note that, Pyro. The fact she feels awkward now, all part of the case against the motherfucker."

"Can't see how he can keep his job," Mace observes. "I hope once he's not wearing a badge, you'll take the restraints off us."

I nod, though it's Demon's call. I've had more than one conversation with the enforcer about finding Skull and showing him extreme prejudice.

Mace shakes his head. "Could save a fuck ton of money if we find him and take him out without the legal shit."

"He's disappeared, Mace," I remind him. "Only way to dig him up is to get him to appear in court, and any damage to him then would shine a light straight on us. And anyway, we're not spending money. Mel's attorney is providing his services for free."

"Which means she's got the best."

Her dad certainly has a vested interest in getting justice for his daughter.

"Keep us posted, okay? Updates every church." Again, Demon pinches the bridge of his nose. "I'm actually siding with Mace. If Skull turns up prior to going to court, if it's safe, we'll revisit a permanent solution then. No guarantee the cops won't close ranks and he'll get away and walk free."

"But only if we can guarantee Satan's Devil's come away clean," our VP warns. "Skull's damaged the club enough, don't want to add seeing men behind bars for the crime he's done."

Everyone nods in agreement. But I reckon, like me, they're already making plans.

Although Skull had been the main topic, Prez moves on to the normal business of the club. I contribute where necessary, finding a comfort in returning to the men I've ridden beside for so long. I smile when, as I expect, Liz says something inappropriate, in return receiving glares from the top of the table. Cad stays serious, offering good observations. Thunder is all for action, and Mace thoughtful. I know and can predict how most people around this table will react in any given situation.

Brothers in Vegas were Devils and had done what they could to make me feel welcome and one of them. But it's this crew I'm pleased to return to, and this chair my rightful place.

At last Demon closes the meeting. I immediately stand, taking my bike key out of my cut.

"You sticking around for a beer, Ro?"

"Nah, Sparky. I've got to get back to Mel."

I waste no time making the short journey between the club and where she lives. I let myself into her house with the key she'd given to me, growing tense at the sound of weeping. I follow it into the living room. She's sitting on the couch, an open book beside her. Hurrying across, I move the volume to one side, quickly glancing down to see what it is, and pull her into my arms.

It's the fucking baby book Vi had given her. *Why is she torturing herself?*

I simply hold her until her tears begin to dry up. It's only when she's grown calmer that she tells me what in particular has got her so upset.

"I was reading about miscarriage, Ro. Trying to work out why it happened."

"Oh darlin'."

"I wouldn't want it to happen again, so I was trying to see what caused it."

"We know why," I tell her, forcibly. "We know who's fuckin' fault it was. And if the doctors couldn't give you answers, Mel, you're not going to find one from reading a fuckin' book."

"I want to move." Her sudden change of subject takes me a moment to catch up. "I've been looking at places…"

"I'm more than happy to look for a new place with you. It's something we should be doing together."

I hate the thought she's thinking of herself and a lonely future. "I want you darlin', that's not changed. I know we haven't discussed me claimin' you further, but there's nothing I want more."

"I'm not ready for sex."

"Not what I'm pushing for Mel. It will happen when it happens, you've got to get fit and clear your head. The right time will come along, no need to hurry it."

She sits and turns so she's facing me. Looks down at her hands, then up into my face. "I think I want children, Ro."

That's an easy statement to respond to. "So do I. Sweetheart, I didn't give a damn who fathered that baby we lost. He was already mine. Can we replace him? Nah, never. He'll always be a part of our lives even though he was never born. Can we have another little person? Yeah, we can."

"What if I miscarry again?"

I take a breath, trying to choose my words carefully. I should have realised that was the root of her problem. On top of the grief of what's she's lost, she's worried she'll never carry a baby to term. "Unlikely. I'm convinced it was circumstances, and nothing wrong with you. But if you do, we'll deal, okay? It's up to you whether you want to take the risk again."

"What if I don't?" she asks, contradicting her earlier statement. "You've just said you want a family…"

"I want you, Mel. If you don't want to put yourself through that again, then maybe we can adopt."

She's quiet, thoughtful. "I'd like to try to give you a child."

"You will," I say confidently.

"Soon?"

If you fall off a horse you're supposed to get back on it again. Does the same apply to being pregnant? I run the idea through my head. The answer's not hard to find, I'd spent the last few months preparing to be a dad. "When the doctor gives you the all clear and we finally go to bed, I won't use condoms if that's what you want." And fuck, I'll have to hope I'm not firing blanks. Always did everything I could to prevent getting a woman pregnant before, never thought until now that there's a possibility I can't.

"Oh, Pyro," she sighs, and gives me a small smile. "I don't know what I've done to deserve a man like you. You've stuck by me, and it's been nothing but hell, but you've been there, every step of the way." I go to speak but she stops me, saying the words I haven't heard since Skull raised his ugly head. "I love you, Pyro."

"Darlin'," I begin, then grin. "Can't say what you did to deserve me, but it must have been fuckin' bad. But nothing's changed the way that I feel, I love you too."

I'd love to show her how much, but for now, I'll make do with just holding her instead.

That we'd reached the stage where grief has lessened to the point where we're once again in a place to say and hear our mutual declarations of what we feel for each other, seemed to have been a turning point. Sure, she still has bouts of misery, times when the tears would begin to fall, but they become less often. She starts talking of a future again, rather than analysing the past.

The first weekend she ventures to the clubhouse, Mel breaks down when she sees Vi cuddling Theo and is consoled by the understanding of her friend. Within moments there's a group hug going on when they're joined by Jay and Steph. All four women weeping together, as sorrow is shared.

It's also there, in the clubroom, that for the first time since the miscarriage, I hear her laugh.

She's cleared to return to work. Whether that has helped put her on more solid ground, I'm not sure. Maybe having a routine once again balances her out, I couldn't know. But when I walk in one day, I hear her on the phone.

"I'll ask Pyro to bring me up Friday evening. That way we can get a start on Saturday morning." She catches sight of me and smiles. "Yeah, looking forward to it, Mom. See you soon. Love you."

She looks at me, her lips curving upward once again, her cheeks a little pink.

"I take it we're going to Denver."

"Do you mind?"

"Mel, I'm over the fuckin' moon if you think you feel strong enough to get this shit started."

She stands, walking over to me with her hands outstretched. It's natural to take hold of them and pull her into my arms. When I lean down to place my lips to her forehead, she's staring up, her eyes hooded, her lips slightly parted.

Taking a chance, I lower my mouth to hers.

She opens for me.

It's not a kiss full of unbridled passion, but it's the first we've shared in weeks. I enjoy the moment, sweeping my tongue into her mouth, melding my lips to hers. I don't push it, and don't indicate I want more. After a moment I pull back.

"Now that was a nice welcome home."

"I'm sorry," she starts, but I stop her.

"Darlin', it will happen when you're ready. I'm not pushing you now."

Little steps.

We might not yet be at the place where we can make love, but we're basically living together. It wasn't even a conscious decision. Since we've come back from Vegas, I've stayed in her house, she didn't invite and I didn't ask her. Was going to object if she had any other ideas, I couldn't stand going one night without holding her, without hanging on to the person who represents everything good in my life.

I'm conscious that while she has a permanent place in my arms, we haven't ever been intimate. Am I feeling the pressure of what will be our first time? Like fuck I am. My cock wants me to press her, my head tells me to hold back, convinced that things will happen in their own good time. Nothing forced can ever be right.

But damn, all this waiting. Being so close to her, my cock's had to get extremely friendly with my hand.

It's Thursday evening, the last night before we head up to Denver tomorrow after work. I'm sitting with a tablet on my lap looking at parts for a Harley a customer has asked me to customize. He's given me his budget which isn't a lot, so I'm trying to work out something within it that he might like. She's sitting next to me reading one of those books she loves.

Casting a glance sideways, I see her cheeks flushing. I nudge her arm. "Good part?"

"What?" she jumps guiltily, as if she'd forgotten I was there.

I chuckle. "Darlin', I reckon you've just got to a dirty bit."

I think if it had been a paperback she'd have snapped it shut. "I don't know what you mean," she says primly, closing its cover and putting her e-reader down by her side. "What are you doing?"

"Uh uh. Someone's changing the subject."

"No, I was getting bored reading."

I laugh louder. "If the way you're blushing is you getting bored, I'm looking forward to seeing you excited."

She wriggles a bit closer, her eyes finding mine. "Well, you did promise to make me scream."

"And scream louder." But I don't make a comparison or say his name.

"Could be time you showed me, Ro," she suggests, a little mischievously, with a twinkle in her eye.

"Yeah?" My tablet's placed down in under a second and I'm on the floor on my knees in front of her, running my hands up her thighs. "I must remember to thank that author."

"Ro!" she exclaims, but grins.

"Hmm." Leaning forward, I take her lips, pressing my mouth down hard. As she opens and my tongue sweeps inside, I leave her in no doubt how much I want her. My cock's gone from zero to full mast in seconds. *This is our first time,* I remember. Huh. I start to feel nervous now.

But all I can do is show her my kind of loving and hope that it works. My hands are actually shaking as I ask, "Can I take off your shirt?"

She's anxious as well, I can see it in her face.

"Seen you naked before Darlin', then wasn't the time, but nothing I saw put me off in the slightest."

My reminder of that day in the shower makes her face fall, but then the realisation that I'm still here together with my reassurance, makes her brave. Sitting forward she pulls off her tee in the way women do, crossing her arms over, grabbing hold of the hem and slipping it off over her head.

Her bra is functional, and I make a note to buy her some expensive satin and lace, she deserves to feel as pretty as I think she is. But plain though it might be, just the sight is enough to arouse me further, and I can't wait to loosen my jeans.

I try to stop my hands trembling but can't as I reach for the front clasp of her bra, a questioning look in my eyes. A brief second of hesitation, which I think is more down to her being uncertain of my reaction, rather than her having second thoughts now, and then she gives a sharp nod of capitulation.

I fumble but manage to get the fastening undone, then reveal perfection to my eyes. Generous tits that are certainly more than a handful even for my big hands. Brownish areole surrounding already erect nipples.

"Fuck, Mel, you're perfect. Did I tell you I was a tits man?"

I don't waste a second before leaning forward, taking one into my mouth and sucking on it, then doing the same to the other. Her breasts cushion my face, I could suffocate here and die a happy man.

I plump, knead, suck and nibble, cataloguing all her sounds, what she likes, what doesn't affect her, mapping out her pleasure as I take mine.

"Fucking gorgeous, Mel. Want to see more darlin'." At last I pull away, I get to my feet, my hands inviting her to stand with me, and then go to the button of the skirt. "You know I find your work clothes sexy, but I'd prefer to see what's under it now."

That little flicker of hesitation again, then she nudges me to give her some space and undoes the button that I hadn't pushed through the hole properly, then slides the zip down. The skirt pools at her feet.

"Panties too." The request comes out hoarsely.

Inelegantly she slips them off, then kicks them away. She tries to cover her tummy, but I take hold of her hands and pull them apart. It's not flat, it's curvy, and as for her thighs, I gently move her around so I can see the back as well as the front, then have to tell her, "Christ, Mel, did I tell you I was an ass and thighs man?"

She giggles. "I thought you liked tits best."

"With you, seems I like everything." And oh, the possibilities.

Unable to resist, I slide my finger down her neatly trimmed pubic hair and through her labia. "Hmm, must have been a good book, you're soaking." Licking her cream off my finger, I glance down to see her pupils are dilated.

I move her around, with my hand on her shoulder I encourage her to sit down.

"I want to see you." Her face looks up at me expectantly.

"I've got a problem here. You've got me rock hard already, you touching me, even having your eyes on me, might finish this before we begin."

"I forgot you were an old man."

"Old?" I growl while thinking how happy I am that she feels confident enough to joke around. "Remember that when you can't walk in the morning."

"Promises... Oh."

Instead of undressing I've sunk back down to my knees and in a fluid movement belying my years, my mouth zooms in on her sensitive part.

It takes me a moment to find the spots which set her alight but finding them I'm merciless while she thrashes and squirms, and yeah, I have her screaming and it's pretty loud. Then I do it all over again. Me? I'm having the time of my life. Don't think I've ever tasted anything so sweet before.

"I want you!" she yells out after the third time. "I need you Pyro."

I hate to disappoint anyone, and I'm not going to make her ask twice. Not this first time, anyway. In a flash I have my boots off and my jeans undone, and out of all my clothes in record time. Her eyes show she likes what I'm revealing, but there's a slight flicker of concern when she sees I'm a big man.

"You'll get used to me," I tell her confidently, positioning her as I want her, one of her wonderful curvy thighs over mine leaving her wide open to me. A bit awkward making sure we don't crash from the couch to the floor, but I can make it work.

She feels like heaven, I think as I push inside, taking my time so she's able to adjust to my size. *I feel like this is where I'm meant to be.*

Then I freeze. "Darlin', I'm bare."

"I don't mind."

"Is that just arousal talking, or are you serious?" I haven't moved since I remembered. "I've a condom in my wallet, just got carried away."

"I'm okay with it if you are."

My cock seems to get harder at the thought of coming inside her. "You sure it's not too soon?"

"It isn't. Medically there's nothing to hold me back. If it happens, I'd like your baby Pyro. But if you're…"

"There's nothing I want more, sweetheart."

If she wants a kid of mine, if she wants my sperm to bear fruit within her… to see her grow with my baby inside… I can't think of anything better. I just need to slow myself down or I'll be shooting my load well before time.

I push in deeper, then retreat, then do it again. A few more repeats and I'm fully in. I pause, breathing deeply.

"You can move."

I huff a laugh. My pause isn't for her, it's for me. "Give me a moment, babe, or I'm not going to last."

She's so damn responsive as I suck on her nipples while thrusting inside her, encouraging noises leaving her mouth. When her muscles start to tighten, she moves her hand down. Lightly I brush it away and take over for her, stimulating her clit at the same time as I'm making sure the head of my cock hits her G-spot every damn time.

Her orgasmic cry takes me over, and there's nothing I can do to stop it. My spine tingles in anticipation as my balls draw up to my body, then I'm coming, bare, inside a woman for the very first time in my life.

When I regain my breath, I lean my forehead down to hers. "Jesus, Mel. Do you think we've made a baby?" My voice sounds like I feel, full of awe, hope and wonder.

"I don't know," she replies. "I think we might need more practice."

CHAPTER THIRTY-THREE

Melissa

I'd researched and asked the doctors. Despite rumours and myths to the contrary, there was no reason to wait. Once I'd stopped bleeding, it would be safe to try to fall pregnant again.

I wasn't totally sure Pyro would feel the same way as me, but I've an empty space inside me that I'd like to have filled. This time with a man who wants a baby with me.

Pyro had been right, he had made me scream, and very loudly. He's the biggest man I've ever been with, and the sex was amazing. It wasn't just physical, we seemed to connect on every level, making it easy for us to throw in some teasing.

But Skull had taken me bare and had then regretted it.

I wake the next morning, as he'd promised I would, feeling stiff and sore but in the best of ways. I'll just have to make an effort to move normally to throw Beth off the scent. Though I don't know why I'm worried, she'd have probably assumed Pyro and I were having sex anyway, as he's moved into my house.

The physical discomfort doesn't worry me, but my mind flicks back to the arguments I'd had with Skull, those two times he'd forgotten a condom, but certainly hadn't stopped to have a discussion about whether he should wear one or not.

"Mornin', darlin'." Pyro's all-seeing eyes stare into mine, and he starts frowning. "What's up?"

"We might be pregnant," I tell him, my teeth worrying my lip.

His expression sharpens. "You got regrets?"

"No, but…"

"If you're worried about me, I haven't got buyer's remorse. You should know me by now, I don't go into anything without thinking about it. You're mine, I'm yours, and if there's a baby growing inside you, then it's ours and I'll be more than happy about it. Hey, what you shaking your head for?"

"I was just thinking you couldn't get any more perfect. You always know just the right thing to say."

"Only say it as I see it." He throws off the covers and gets out of bed, reaching up over his head and stretching, his large cock bobs as though saying good morning. My tongue comes out to moisten my lips. He notices, then groans. "You and I have got to get to work."

He's right. We have, and I am a bit sore.

He turns and looks at me seriously. "Take your e-reader to work today. Read some more of that book during your lunch hour. Might get you in the mood for another round tonight." He winks.

"We're going to my parents later," I remind him.

He rolls back his head. "Shit, well you're going to need to be quiet then."

I throw a pillow at him. "I am not having sex in my parents' house."

He comes back to the bed and starts crawling up it, stopping when his hands are either side of my head and he's staring down into my eyes. "What about making love, then?"

I shake my head.

"Damn."

He continues to stare for a moment, then lowers his hips, letting me feel his rock-hard erection. "You move the sheet and open your legs and I think you'll find I'm just in the right position."

"I've got to get to work," I squeak.

"Uh, come on."

"You're insatiable," I reply, giggling as I do exactly what he suggests.

In the end, I am late, but only by a couple of minutes. I caught up time by washing and drying my hair in the quickest time ever.

"You look better. You've got more colour in your face."

I acknowledge Beth's comment while she gets us both a coffee from the machine. Something I thought I'd have to wait another few months for. Beth continually does little things for me, blaming herself for me losing the baby. She thinks if she hadn't told me about seeing Skull, I wouldn't have miscarried.

I've tried to explain I assign no blame to her, but she's convinced it was somehow her fault.

Perhaps it would help to let her in on my secret. I lean in and whisper so only she can hear, "Pyro and I are trying for a baby. No one else knows, so keep it to yourself."

"You are?" Her delight is palpable. Then her face falls. "But isn't it too soon?"

"Physically, no, emotionally it's down to the couple. This is my chance to do it right."

"With the right man."

I nod. "Exactly."

It won't replace the baby I've lost and who I'll always mourn, but hopefully my son will have a brother or sister even though they'll never meet in this world.

"So," Beth catches up with me during the lunch break, when I'm not reading the book Pyro suggested, "you going to Denver to get the ball rolling this weekend?"

I'd told her what I was going to be doing and working with my dad to bring Skull down.

I nod around a mouthful of sandwich. "Yes. I think I'm in a

better place now. A couple of weeks back I wouldn't have been able to stand up to being questioned."

The normally gentle woman's face hardens. "I hope you bring him down. He should go to prison for what he's done to you."

As the break time is over, we part and go back to our respective desks, me thinking on the way, a prison cell is just where I'd like Skull to be.

The day passes like any other, boring and uneventful. The hours ticking by slower than normal as I'm looking forward to seeing my parents again, and this time having Pyro beside me. They'd only seen him when I was at my lowest point, and while I know they admire how he'd supported me; it will be good for them to get to know him as he really is.

We take the car, I haven't been on the back of Pyro's bike for ages and would have enjoyed having my arms around him, but the weather's not looking particularly good for riding this weekend. The two-hour journey passes fast as we fill the time with talk about our week at work. While neither of us feel we need to comment on how we've moved our relationship up a notch, there are touches, gestures, and heated looks which say more than a hundred words ever could.

Arriving we find Mom's got a pot roast ready. I'd texted her to let her know what time we were getting there, and she's timed it so we just have a moment to take our bags into our rooms. Mom and Dad live in a three-bedroom house, and they've given us separate sleeping arrangements.

I'll miss sleeping without Pyro's arms holding me and am a bit nervous about what he's going to say.

"Their house, their rules, darlin'." As usual, he takes it in his stride.

Back in the dining area, Mom's got the table set and food is ready to be served. For a moment it's all about getting the delicious smelling food plated up, then a few minutes to enjoy it.

When the worst of his appetite is assuaged, Dad pauses with his fork halfway to his mouth. "Checked you out, Pyro."

"Yeah?" Pyro seems completely unconcerned. While he'd told Dad he could, I'm peeved on his behalf.

But Dad gets in before I can protest.

"You were a decorated soldier." He sounds impressed.

As I turn to Pyro with a look of pride, he shakes his head. "Along with a lot of others."

"Said you'd rescued members of your platoon putting yourself in danger."

Pyro just shrugs. "This beef is excellent, Mrs Martins. Cooked just how I like it."

Dad catches my eye and nods. He likes a man who doesn't boast, and respects one who's served his country.

"Going to go into a few things later." Dad refers to our forthcoming discussion about Skull. "But there's something both your mother and I want to know about." He looks at me, then back to Pyro. "And that's whether your club is into anything illegal. You know I talked about it with Red when I was in Vegas, but I need to know whether he was giving me bullshit. That will affect how I approach the case."

"You asked Skull that," I remind him.

"Skull would have said anything as we now know. I want to hear it from a man who I think will give me the truth."

Pyro's plate is now clean. He shakes his head when Mom offers him more, then turns and fixes his eyes on my dad. "Club used to run guns. Dealt in drugs. The strip club we own, well, it was a cover for prostitution." He sees my expression and adds, hurriedly, "Long before I patched in, Mel. Club started way back in the eighties. Of course, we weren't Satan's Devils then."

"Has all that stopped?" Dad sounds like he's conducting an interrogation.

"As I said, before my time. When Hellfire, that's our current president's dad, took the top seat, he cleaned up the club and aligned us with the Devils. We had to obey their rules and regulations."

"Why do you call yourself one-percenters?" Mom asks, her brow furrowed. "If you don't do anything illegal?"

"We don't deal in drugs or guns anymore and our strip club is clean. We run other businesses too and earn our money legit. But we steer clear of citizen laws as much as we can. At the end of the day we protect our club and way of life by whatever means."

When he finishes speaking, Pyro's lips press together, and his jaw is set. I hope Dad doesn't press him, because from his expression he's said about all he's going to say.

"If you and my daughter get together—"

"We *are* together," Pyro interrupts.

Dad continues as if he hadn't spoken. "I want to know if you'll protect Mel, keep her safe and keep her away from anything your club might get into while you're protecting it, as you say. I want your assurance she won't be involved with anything that's against the law."

"You have my word, sir," Pyro replies respectfully. "I, and my brothers, will protect Mel with our lives."

It must be the way Pyro's said it, but all of a sudden my mom starts fanning herself, saying, "Oh my. Where can I get me one of these bikers?"

Dad frowns at her, then barks out a laugh. "I think you might be a tad past it, dear."

The glare she gives him is so fierce it's hard not to giggle.

As if realising he's stepped onto shaky ground, Dad makes an abrupt change of subject. "If everyone's finished eating, why don't we go into my study, and start looking at this case."

Mom waves off my offer of help and starts clearing up the plates. "Just remember, this isn't a case, Rufus. This is our daughter's life."

As if knowing I need support, Pyro takes hold of my hand, bringing it to his lips and kissing it gently, before leading me in the direction my father has taken. Out of the corner of my eye I see my mother pretend to swoon.

I look around with interest when I reach Dad's den. While they've always lived in Denver, they moved to this house a few years back, and I've never had cause to spend time in my father's domain. While he has an office in the city, it's clear he does a lot of work at home. The walls are lined with shelves holding serious looking tomes, and there's a high-backed comfortable leather chair behind a desk.

A tower PC and monitor give it a twenty-first century vibe, while the rest of the room could be something out of a Dicken's novel. It suits him, and I like it.

In preparation for tonight, he's brought two spare dining room chairs in, and now he waves Pyro and me toward them.

"Whisky?" he offers.

Pyro readily accepts. When a quick memory of last night resurfaces, I decline, requesting just water. Two shots are quickly poured and distributed, and a glass passed to me.

"Tonight," Dad starts, his face growing serious as he slips into attorney mode, "I want to get some of the details so I know where to start and who I'm going to be taking on."

"What do you mean, who?"

"Cops can place officers undercover, or it could be the feds. Do you know which it is?"

Pyro nods. "We touched on this in church." As my father raises a disbelieving eyebrow, Pyro snorts. "Sorry, nothing religious. It's the name for our meetings."

Dad grins. "Yeah, my office has 'morning prayers'." It's obviously another metaphor for briefings.

"Skull didn't admit to who his employer was, but you're right, it's either cops or feds. The Colorado Chapter of the Satan's Devils hasn't been on anyone's hit list, or not that we know. Our mother chapter in Tucson has even worked with the cops and helped them once or twice. We think whoever planted

Skull might have been looking to our associations, rather than the club itself."

"Associations with…?"

"There's the local mafia, the Silvestri family. While we don't work with them, we have to co-exist. Then there's the dominant club, that's the Wretched Soulz."

"You have many dealings with them?"

"Only when we have to. But any club must keep on their right side."

Dad drums his fingers on the table. "So, you think the feds are looking at a RICO indictment against an MC, either yours— which is unlikely—or the Wretched Soulz who they've been trying to take down for years?"

Pyro raises and dips his head. "They've had some successes in the past."

"They have," Dad agrees with Pyro. He types something on his screen. "Then if we think the feds are more likely, I'll find out who's the SAC, the Special Agent in Charge," he qualifies at the bemused look in my eyes. "What I need from you and Pyro are all the details so I know what we're putting forward. Pyro, let's start with you at the very beginning. Knowing the background before Melissa came on the scene would help. When and how did Skull first approach the Satan's Devils?"

"It must be getting on two and a half years ago now," Pyro starts, blinking slowly as though wading through memories. "Cad would probably be able to supply the exact dates. You know, this shit's been going around and around my head, but for the life of me, I can't remember anything suspicious. He came around the club as a hangaround for a few weeks. We had an opening for a prospect, he jumped at the chance."

"Jumped?" Dad's eyes light up. "Overeager?"

But Pyro gives a negative shake. "Nah. Many men like our lifestyle, especially when they've been hanging around and have come to our parties, where, er, anything goes. They get a taste of the reward which might be at the end of their prospecting days.

Like myself, many are attracted to the idea of being part of a brotherhood, a team. We test those who express an interest, make sure they know the hard work they'll have to expect. Of course, some don't make the grade as they don't understand the concept of putting their backs into everything and anything asked. So, yeah, I've seen prospects come on board all excited to have a stab at being part of the club, and Skull was no different."

"He made the grade," Dad ponders. "He work extra hard to make it?"

Pyro huffs a laugh. "Skull shouldn't be underestimated. If he was perfect, then that might have raised more than one eyebrow. He did enough to get by, no more, no less. And like a lot of prospects knew the places to hide and the excuses to get out of some of the shittiest jobs."

Dad nods, taking it all in.

"You beat him..." I say, hoping to speed this up.

Dad's eyes open wide.

Pyro shakes his head at me. "That came later, and yeah, I'll go into that too. But I'm answering your dad's question." I pretend to zip my lips, making Pyro smile. Then he turns back to my father. "We don't take people on lightly. When someone comes into the club, they are stepping into our lives, into our family. Lots of people want to join, not everyone makes it. They go through a probationary period until we know they're a good fit, can be trusted, and are going to be loyal."

"To sum up, he passed your test, and you trusted him. Would he have known any information about the club prior to that point?"

"No," Pyro responds. "Well, not in detail. Prospects don't come to church and aren't given the same information as patched members. With time, they may learn more of the type of shit they need to keep to themselves, but not enough to bring us down. By the point we ask them to bury a body, we're usually pretty certain they can be trusted. Or, the hole they just dug will be for themselves."

As Dad laughs, I cast a sideways glance at Pyro, wondering whether he's serious or joking.

"What's your process? How do you test a man?"

"Push him to his limits. See what he's capable of doing. Prospects can do anything from serving behind a bar to cleaning shit from the toilet. If they are asked to clean a member's bike with their toothbrush, if they want the patch badly enough, they'll do it with a smile."

CHAPTER THIRTY-FOUR

Pyro

I may have mentioned burying a body but luckily both Mel and her dad thought I was joking. Though another look at Mel's face suggests she's not quite as certain as Rufus. Whether I was serious or not is something she'll never know. That would come firmly under the heading of club business.

"Skull, or the man we now know as Donavon Jordan, passed all this with flying colours?" her dad asks.

"Yes." I grimace. "Of course, he wasn't Skull then, but as a hangaround he used the name Kris Cox. When he started to prospect, we called him Runt." I break off, shaking my head. "How the fuck does he keep track of all his names?" It's a rhetorical question, no one answers, which prompts me to resume. "Well, he looked like a skinny kid, and among our other prospects, resembled the reject of the litter. Of course, that he accepted the handle without complaint was all part of the process, as you called it."

"Mel said you beat him? Part of the test?" Rufus' expression has hardened.

"No, but in his case, it was the turning point." I sit forward and clasp my hands between my legs, staring at Mel's father intensely. "We had a situation, someone was fuckin' with the club."

"How?"

I shrug. "A dead body was left in the dumpster behind our strip club. Turned out to be a dead tramp who died of natural causes, but it got the cops' eyes on us. Then there were parts going missing from the auto-shop, even a drive-by shooting at the compound, though no serious injuries thank fuck. Things were escalating, and we had to bring it to a stop. Everything pointed to it being Skull, or Runt as he was then, who was behind it. We, er, tried to get him to admit it."

"By using your fists?

By using torture.

"Pyro, if I'm going to represent Mel in court, I need to know everything. If I don't, and information's thrown at me I'm not aware of, our whole case could come undone. You tell me it all, and I'll decide how I use the information but only as far as the case goes. You're protected by attorney/client privilege. If I don't need to use it, the information stays here in this room." He stares at me for a moment, then adds, "Skull, Runt, or whatever you want to call him, you can be sure he won't keep quiet about it if turns out to be relevant."

He's got a point. I swallow hard a couple of times. "It wasn't a proud moment for the club, but the trouble was escalating. We tried to persuade him to tell us, but he wouldn't. Didn't know at the time it was because he couldn't, nothing was down to him, even though it appeared to be."

"Appeared to be?" Rufus parrots.

"Skull was in the right places at the right times. He was the common denominator. All the evidence pointed his way."

Again, Rufus' face hardens. "Am I right to suggest you used torture to get him to admit it?"

I nod. "I wasn't personally involved, but yeah. He was hurt, not too badly, as another member found out the truth and Skull's... interrogation... was immediately halted, but psychologically? Must have been a point when he thought he wasn't going to walk free."

He casts an eye toward his daughter. "This trouble with the club. It stopped?"

I raise and lower my head again. "The member who was actually behind it isn't with us any longer and won't be causing trouble again." Not going to admit he's buried six feet under out in the desert. Rufus might want full disclosure, but I'll say nothing that might bring harm on my club.

For a few seconds, Rufus stares at me intently, as if trying to read whether his daughter will be in any danger if she continues her association with the club. I gaze back just as earnestly. It's him who breaks first, accepting I've been honest in what I've said. "What happened with Skull?"

"He left the club. We thought it would be permanent. We'd destroyed his trust in us."

"But he must have come back?"

"He did." I frown, remembering it. "He told us that he wanted to be part of the loyal brotherhood we'd shown ourselves to be. He'd been impressed by how we banded together to protect what was ours. He said he understood why we'd made him hurt, that if the positions were reversed, he'd have no reservations in doing the same. Brotherhood, to him, was everything. He became a full member, and that's when he got a new name. Runt became Skull, because he had a hard head."

"And you trusted him because of what he said. Probably some guilt involved due to the way you treated him." Rufus frowns. "Good way for an undercover man to get on the inside."

"We remained unsure for a while," I said, thinking back. "It wasn't expected, we thought he might be out for revenge. He was watched, but never put a foot out of line. As the months passed, particularly when he claimed Mel as his ol' lady, we relaxed. He became as trusted as any member. But," I raise my hand to show I'm not finished, "when he went missing, we considered all options. Of course, thoughts circled back to what had happened before, and wondered whether he'd bided his time waiting for vengeance. We couldn't understand how or why he disappeared off the face of the earth, and one consideration was whether he was setting something up."

"That's why you called us all in on lockdown?" Mel asks, and I have to remember this is new to her. "You said it was because he could have been taken by an unknown enemy of the club."

"That was a possibility too, Mel, but unlikely. We don't have enemies, so yeah, we suspected Skull instead." I inwardly shudder at the memory of me checking over what we thought might have been bombs.

"So," Rufus starts to sum up, "you never fully trusted him, but there was nothing to suggest why. You put the doubts on the back burner, and nevertheless, you gave him his patch."

"Some of the distrust may be me looking in hindsight," I admit, then remember what had come up at one of our churches. "Wraith, the VP of the mother chapter in Tucson warned Demon to watch him, but as Skull settled in as a member he said and did all the right things."

"What did Wraith pick up on that you didn't?"

I shrug. "I can't answer that. I know Demon kept a close eye on him after Wraith raised his concerns, but he was the model member." I raise my eyes toward Rufus. "We never fuckin' suspected anything close to the truth."

Rufus nods. "Did Skull know there was an undercurrent of distrust?"

"We didn't discuss it in front of him. I can't tell you whether he picked anything up."

"Okay. Moving on. When did he approach you, Melissa?"

I raise my hand. "Mel doesn't know the implications of the timeline. I'll say this first. It wasn't long after he patched in that he said he had a woman he'd like to bring around the club. See if she liked us, and if we were going to accept her."

"That the usual way you do things?"

"Not normally, but then, Colorado doesn't have many old ladies. Pal arrived with his woman, Jay, Buzz has been married to Sindy for years, same with Bomber and Hellfire with their old ladies. But going by the other clubs, when members find a woman they like, they're prepared to walk through hell and high water for them, even offering to give up their patch if the club doesn't vote them in."

"So what Skull was proposing was different?"

"He was a new member, fresh to the table. Didn't think too much of it at the time. But if Mel hadn't liked his new brothers, or we didn't take to her, it might have made him reconsider getting deeper into a relationship with her. In a way it seemed sensible to check her out, and for her to see if she liked the life-style." I glance her way, but she doesn't seem hurt, just interested.

In fact, she speaks up for herself. "That's the way he sold it to me too. Though, to me, he said he'd leave the club if I didn't like it." She pouts, then adds, "Which was just another one of his lies."

"Yes," Rufus surmises, sparing a glance of sympathy toward his daughter. "If Melissa hadn't worked out, his intention was probably that he'd move on to another woman who was more suitable."

I glance at Mel quickly. Her father's gotten to the heart of it. Her face has gone tight, but I think she's already accepted she was the means to Skull finding out more about the club.

"Looking back," he addresses his daughter, "does this fit the facts as you saw them then?"

Mel takes over. "Yes." I reach for her hand, it trembles. "He targeted me as he thought I was someone who'd fit. I was not a person anyone would be suspicious of meeting. It was an odd coupling, as he was so much younger."

"Appeared to be," I put in tersely.

"Well," she shrugs, "his appearance worked. What woman wouldn't be flattered that a younger man wanted her?"

"Any man in his right fuckin' mind would want you, Mel," I growl, vowing I'll spend the rest of my days making her believe it.

I notice a hard look has crossed her dad's face as he realises how little self-confidence she has, and how much Skull weakened even that.

"He inveigled himself into your life. You brought him to meet us."

Mel nods. "He led me to believe it was serious."

"Your mom and I thought it was."

Rufus hasn't seen serious yet. Just wait until I can demonstrate how much I feel for his daughter. Now, though, is not the right time.

"Tell me about getting pregnant."

I can see Mel's shifting a little awkwardly in her seat, uncomfortable addressing the topic in front of Rufus, so I wink at her. "Well, you see a man has…"

"Pyro!" she gasps.

Her dad chuckles. "I don't need that level of detail. Though I do need to ask some personal stuff. Who was responsible for contraception?"

Mel's now bright red. I send her a chin lift of encouragement, while wishing I didn't have to listen to this. But if it gets to a court, she's going to need to become immune to discussing the private details of her life.

"He was," she says, after taking a deep breath. "He used condoms. One night he didn't, and we got away with it. The next time, well, you know the rest."

"Was there any discussion about using them or not? Did he give you the choice?"

Mel shakes her head. "It was, er, in the throes of passion shall we say? He forgot, and I, well, I didn't notice."

"Tell your dad what happened the next time," I prompt. "Skull's reaction when he realised."

"It was when Beef got patched over. We'd both had a few

drinks at the party which followed, well him a lot more than me. When he realised what he'd done, he became angry when I refused to consider the morning-after pill." She wipes her eye which is clearly watering. "He said something about bad timing and walked out. Stayed away all night but came back the next morning and said he'd come to his senses. Then not quite two weeks after that, he was gone."

Now it's Rufus' face that's gone red. "He was *angry?*" He leans forward. "Did he hurt you, Melissa?"

"Only with words," she says fast. "He was more annoyed with himself than me."

"Hold on." I motion to them both to give me a moment. "He mentioned 'bad timing'? Did he explain that at all?"

She shakes her head.

Rufus sits back. "Could be he already knew his assignment was ending. This is a man who in his real life already has a woman and child. Of course, he didn't want to take risks with you. Yet, down to his own stupidity, he did." He pauses and breathes deeply trying to get himself under control. I realise then how hard this will be as a father representing his daughter, and how difficult it must be to separate his professional interest from the personal one.

"He didn't need Mel just for sex," I explain. "He could, and before he got with Mel, did, get that easily from the club girls."

Rufus looks at me sharply. "You have women hanging around your club?"

I come clean. "We have five sweet butts, club whores." At his thinly veiled expression of disgust, I explain, "Whether or not we're into legal or illegal shit, we like to keep club business close. By having women who depend on the club, we can keep it in the family, if you like. They are there for the benefit of the members and for what they get out of it. And before you ask, they're there voluntarily and free to leave at any time."

"And what exactly do they get out of it?"

"Board, lodging, pocket money, and bikers who give them a

good time. If they didn't enjoy what they do, they wouldn't stay."

He seems slightly appeased.

"You said Skull went with these women?"

"Yes, when he was first patched in. Though not from the time he met Mel." I've confirmed that. I asked them. "He wouldn't have been thought any the worse of if he had an old lady and used the whores too. Not that anyone in our club does that, but in others? Well, it's considered part of the lifestyle. But the fact is, Skull did not."

"He was, however, stepping out on his wife."

My shoulders rise and fall. "What we saw was a man who committed to his ol' lady once he found her."

I notice Mel's still holding the water she'd been given an hour or so ago and hasn't touched it. Leaning forward, I take the glass out of her hands and place it on the desk in front of us. "You okay, darlin'?"

She gives a small rise and dip of her head. I send a pointed glare toward her father.

He takes the hint. "Let me get a few more details, then the two of you can get some rest. Just talk me through what happened when Skull disappeared."

"Mel was a mess," I speak for her. It's hard for me not to choke up as I take my mind back to those initial days. "We didn't know whether he was dead or alive, whether he left voluntarily or had been taken. Club took the decision to go on lockdown, that means bringing everyone in who might be a target so we can protect them, family as well as club members. When nothing happened, it seemed the most likely scenario was that he'd had an accident, and we just hadn't found him."

"You reported him missing?"

"To the cops, yes. Mel found out she was pregnant. Skull had known it was a possibility, but he never checked." At this point I'm speaking through gritted teeth. "I stepped up, at first because he was my brother, and then, well, I've always held Mel in the highest respect. My feelings grew and changed as we spent more time together."

Rufus looks from me to Mel, then back to me again. "Your relationship..." he starts, pauses, then continues, after coughing to clear his throat, "you became close... physically?"

"No," I say fast. "Not that I didn't want to, can't deny that. But Mel was grieving, she needed time to come to terms with her man's disappearance. We moved slowly, until the point came when both of us were ready to take the next step. But events interfered with that. Mel and I became..." I'm equally at a loss as to how to admit to him I've fucked his daughter, "close, only very recently."

His eyes widen a little as though he hadn't expected that. "Because, four and a half months later, Skull turned up?"

I raise my chin in confirmation.

Rufus copies the gesture back. "Tell me how you found him."

Mel takes over the story. "If my friend from work, Beth, hadn't seen him and taken his photo, we might never have known. But she went to Vegas for the weekend and stumbled across him. Pyro and I, along with other members of his club went to see if we could track him down, and we did. That's when we found out he was nothing I'd believed him to be, and then I lost..." She starts crying.

I get out of my chair, pull her up and hold her tightly.

"That's all for tonight," I tell her dad, gruffly, then, even if it is rude, I lead her out of the room without saying anything else to him.

"I don't give a fuck," I start, as I take her into the room she's been allocated, "if your parents want to keep us apart. I'm not leaving you. This evening's been fuckin' hard on you."

"And on you too, Pyro. But we do have to dig it all up. If I'm taking him on, my dad's interrogation will be nothing in comparison to a defence lawyer."

That she's right doesn't mean I have to like it.

"You didn't want whisky. Is that in case?"

She gives a tiny nod. "If we're not going to do anything to prevent it, I want to do this right. From the very start."

"You did nothing wrong before," I tell her, willing her to believe it, not wanting her to carry around any guilt. "If the stress contributed to or brought on the miscarriage, then that's all on Skull, nothing on you."

"But my reaction…"

"Was the same as any normal person's, Mel."

"I just want to be careful, you know?"

I do. I help her undress. Then, in deference to being in her parents' home and not in my assigned room, I leave on my jeans and, like I have so many times before, do nothing more than lie on the bed and wrap her in my arms.

CHAPTER THIRTY-FIVE

Melissa

"Sleep well?"

As Mom gives a pointed look to Pyro he replies without missing a beat. "Like a f… baby."

I hold my breath wondering if she's going to say anything, reminding myself I'm in my thirties and shouldn't be scared of my mom knowing what I get up to with my man.

But when she winks at me before turning back to getting breakfast going, I know we probably did exactly what she expected and ended up sharing the same bed.

Biting back my desire to defend myself and tell her we didn't get up to anything, I ask instead, "Where's Dad?"

"In his office. He's been there since early this morning. He wants to see you both when you're fed."

Well, that's the reason we've come here. We eat, then waste no time going to the room where Dad's holed up. There are papers all over the desk which last night was tidy.

"Ah, come in, sit," he says distractedly after only a brief glance up. "I've been doing some research. This is where I've got with my thinking." He removes his glasses, polishes them, then replaces them on his nose. "First, Skull was at the MC as an undercover cop, more likely a federal agent, placed there to unearth criminal activity. By drawing Mel into it, by making her part of the club, he was knowingly involving her in any illegal activity that may have been committed."

"But there was nothing…"

"Pyro, it's not what he found, but what he expected to, or could have, found." Dad gives him a hard stare which makes him shut up.

"Now, he offered an inducement to Melissa."

"What inducement?" It's my turn to interrupt.

"The inducement of having a relationship which you were led to believe was serious and long-term. Would you have gone with him otherwise?"

"No," I say, indignantly. "I wasn't, and have never been, someone who'd want a fling. Any relationship would need to have at least the potential of being permanent."

"Exactly. Secondly, the FBI's own guidelines for their agents say that no undercover activity involving an inducement to an individual to engage in crime shall be authorised unless the subject is engaging, has engaged or is likely to engage in illegal activity."

Pyro raises his eyes at me.

"Of course," Dad continues, "their guidelines also say that it is okay if the person is predisposed to engage in the contemplated illegal conduct, which could be their out."

"Because she's remained with the club." Pyro's quicker than me.

"Yes. Though we will counter that she discovered, as presumably Skull did himself, that the club is not involved in illegal activity. At the time Skull, presumably, believed that it was. Of course, there are exceptions. An innocent can be dragged in if it's necessary to protect life or prevent other serious harm."

"That's not the case."

"No, I don't see how that argument could be offered up. Oh, they might try, but I think we'll be able to refute it. They'd need to offer proof, but I doubt they could find any."

"So that's the legal ground? What about what happened to me?" It's all well and good talking about whether I was potentially being dragged into a life of crime when other things are more important instead. "What about how it affected me mentally? I lost my baby."

"Hush." Pyro's reached for my hand and is now squeezing it. "I don't think your dad has finished."

Dad's eyes view me with a parent's concern. "That, obviously, sweetheart, is the crux of the case. But first I have to use the lawyer speak to show Skull was acting wrongly. It's the personal hurt and distress to you which was the damage caused. Now we look at how to measure it." He pauses, again, and looks at some notes on his desk. "First, if Skull was doing this with the blessing of his handler, then I don't doubt there will be written reports about you. The first thing I'll do is demand we get copies of them. That will show how far the invasion of privacy went."

"And if he didn't involve his superiors?"

"The rest of our case stands and perhaps is strengthened. Secondly, there was the psychological torture when Skull disappeared. You had no clue he was still alive and went through the process of grieving."

"Can we go back a step, Dad? Wasn't it rape? The man I lived with was not who I thought he was."

"No, beating a dead horse there. Obtaining sexual consent due to having a false identity is not a crime. And feds specifically give immunity from prosecution for their undercover agents for using a false identity. I think we'd waste time and would lose that point." At my look of disbelief, he continues, "There's precedent where cases of misrepresentation haven't even reached the court. Think of the can of worms it would open, a man, or a woman, who portrayed himself as single, but was married— well, if there was a conviction of rape in those cases the prisons would soon be overfilled."

"Skull was married."

"Yes. But if that was the sole complaint, would you be reporting him for rape?"

I'd want to slap his face, scream, rant and rage, and accuse him of acting without my consent. Dad's right. I would not. "So, what do we go on?" I'm not happy I can't throw that charge at Skull, but Dad knows his stuff, and I'll have to concede on that point.

"That he used you, an innocent civilian, for a purpose you were not aware of. That he left without a backward glance shows while he tricked you into what you thought was a permanent relationship, he had no such feelings for you. That he took responsibility for protecting you from pregnancy, that he failed in that and again, didn't check to find out whether or not there were ramifications. There were, and then you lost the baby, possibly due to the stress. I know there's no medical evidence to support that, but also none against it. If it goes in front of a jury, that's something that could sway them."

"I've got the DNA results back," Pyro informs him. "I found Skull's old toothbrush in the box of his belongings that someone packed up. I've sent both results to an expert Demon's used in the past."

Of course, we've no doubt Skull's the father, but the court may have.

"So, we can prove whatever he says, it was his baby."

Was. I blink rapidly to fight back the tears. My son's true father might have been a bastard, but Pyro would have raised my son well and showed him the rights and wrongs of the world, which don't include being a cheating liar.

I feel my hand being squeezed. Pyro showing his support yet again.

Dad drums his fingers on the desk. "The initial step is to file a claim with the FBI. They will either agree or dismiss it."

"If they don't agree we've got a case?"

"Then you can file a lawsuit against the agency and raise a

civil suit against them in the United States District Court. Of course, they may not respond, in which case we can go straight to court. We might want to consider a Federal Tort Claim. Section 28 applies as you were injured by the wrongful or negligent act of a federal employee while he was carrying out his official duties."

"Injured?" I query.

"In this case, mentally. We have to show that, of course. There's no doubt Skull misused you and went against the FBI rules when he blatantly tried to corrupt you and involve you in, what he believed at the time, was an MC conducting illegal activities."

Pyro's eyes narrow. "I'll need to take this back to the club, sounds like it's going to involve us."

Dad purses his lips. "I'll need a statement, of course, that your club does not run illegal activities. The feds have ninety days from obtaining evidence to make charges against you. That time's long past, so it's safe to assume Skull has nothing. If they try to dispute that, we'll point to Skull being pulled out of his assignment presumably with no results. Now that might seem contradictory, but at the time, there must have been justification for placing him in your club for such a long time."

"Desperation," Pyro suggests. "They love bringing what they see as outlaw motorcycle *gangs* down." I notice he almost spits out the penultimate word of his sentence.

"Indeed. At the time, Skull was trying to infiltrate what the feds saw was an OMG. A good reminder of their terminology, Pyro. We can emphasise you're a riding *club*."

I've just remembered something. "The club worked with the United States Marshals and helped bring a real gang down, when Steph was being kept alive to give evidence against the Warped Jokers. Surely that places them in good standing?"

My dad nods. "Anything like that helps. As does what you said earlier, the Tucson chapter having good relationships with the cops."

Pyro chuckles. "I wouldn't say good relationships, but yeah, they helped the cops and feds a couple of times."

Dad takes off his glasses, and this time, lays them down. "I'll start preparing the paperwork. This has to be done right, Melissa, so it will take time. I've got to prepare you. Probably the best you can hope to get out of it is monetary compensation. Whether they keep Skull on, or dismiss him, will be down to their internal processes. You need to think about how much you want. Cases which ask for one million or less are normally settled quite quickly. We can go for more if you want."

"That won't hurt Skull," I say bluntly, "and money won't return my lost baby to me." I wanted to see him locked up. It appears Dad's warning me that's unlikely to happen.

My father looks thoughtful. "Let me get it all down on paper and we'll see where we can go from there. Once I've got all the facts straight and have completed more research, we can discuss whether Skull did anything against the law. At the moment, I can see he went against FBI guidelines, so believe all we can do is present that case to them." He sighs. "I know what you're thinking, Melissa, and I'd love to be able to lock Skull up behind bars, but we're going to have a hard enough time getting any reparation as it is."

Beside me, I see Pyro tense. Then he turns to me and asks, "You sure you want to do this, Mel?"

It doesn't take me a second to reply, "I'm certain. Fighting is what I need to do. I can't give up now. I need to know that what he did was wrong. If at the end of the day, the government pays for his crime, at least it's an admission that what he did wasn't right. And if I can do something to prevent the same thing happening to anyone else, that's what I need to do."

Dad stays buried in his office while Pyro and I catch up with Mom. Later that afternoon we're back in the car and returning to Pueblo. As Pyro drives I lean my head back and think over the last twenty-four hours. It hadn't been easy at all, reliving everything, dredging it back up had been distressing. But the result is

I'm feeling a little easier. *I'm doing something.* It might not end up with Skull in prison or even losing his job, but some recognition of the wrong that had been done to me would go a long way. I won't let him get away unscathed, surely he'll get a reprimand at the very least?

Am I a cruel person to want to know what's happening between him and his wife? How she would be able to forgive him is beyond me. She might have been able to turn a blind eye that if it was to keep him alive, he had to go with a club girl to prove he fitted in. But to start a relationship and father a baby? Surely she could never accept that.

I hope she's making him suffer.

It's what he deserves.

Nothing will restore the baby which died inside me. But part of my fight is for him and the life he never knew. Although there's no scientific link between the miscarriage and what Skull had done to me, no one will ever convince me that it wasn't my distress at his behaviour and how I allowed it to affect me that caused my baby's heart to stop beating.

What if I'm pregnant again even now?

Nothing could replace the child I lost, but another might fill this emptiness inside me. Pyro's indicated nothing other than that's what he wants too. I can't wait to see his face light up when he sees the sonogram, this time, knowing he'll have fathered a daughter or son.

For the first time in weeks, I'm returning home with hope, not total despair. Allowing into my mind optimism that a future with a good man will be mine, a family, if we're lucky, and on top of that, revenge on the man who hurt me so badly.

Who couldn't agree, when all the facts are known? I'd been used, abused, and discarded. I deserve justice, both for myself and my never-to-be-born child.

CHAPTER THIRTY-SIX

Melissa

The wheels of justice grind slowly.

A month has passed. The files have been prepared and submitted, but Dad's had no news. Pyro's moved in with me, claimed me officially, and I'm now in possession of a leather vest all of my own, with a Property of Pyro patch on the back. I know most people wouldn't understand, but it makes me feel loved and protected, this visible symbol that he's my man.

I don't even object to the idea of getting a tattoo, not after seeing the beautiful designs Vi does, but as there's a tiny risk to a pregnant woman, Pyro's declared we'll put it off. Despite Lizard's assurances that he makes hygiene his top priority at the tattoo parlour, and little chance of infection, it will have to wait.

I'm not actually pregnant as yet, but it's far too soon to be worried, and I have to admit I enjoy the trying.

Am I getting over Skull? No, I never will completely. Pyro is a wonderful man, always taking time to reassure me, but sometimes doubts creep into my mind. I was claimed once before, didn't stop me from being abandoned.

I tell myself Skull had his own reasons for leaving, that they were nothing to do with me. Thing is though, I know what it's like to have a man walk out and disappear. In the depths of the night, and sometimes during the day, I worry it might happen again. Then have to take a moment to calm down and remind myself, Pyro and Skull are two completely different men.

When doubts creep in I hate Skull more than ever. Memories of what happened and fear that history will repeat itself is what prevents me fully trusting in my good luck now. Pyro's arranged for me to have counselling, and I've been diagnosed as suffering PTSD. What the counsellor had said made sense, my expectations have been reshaped by my experiences. In simple terms, I'm now always waiting for the other shoe to drop.

Pyro's not in the club when I arrive, I tell myself it's because he's at work. A little voice inside worries, *he might have left without a trace.*

My relief when he turns up makes me angry. I might have the right to doubt myself, but never this man who's done nothing other than show how much he loves me and how reliable he is.

Damn Skull to hell.

"Hey, beautiful."

"Hey back at you, Ro." I turn to greet the man who reminds me every day how I appear in his eyes. It's the gleam of appreciation that has convinced me that what I am, he likes.

"You been catching up with the girls?"

"And Max." I've been at the club all evening. I'd popped in to drop off a dessert I've made and a fresh batch of muffins and had been dragged into conversation and stayed.

"We're going to have a fuckin' dog one of these days, I can tell," he smiles.

A puppy, yes. I'd love that. One a bit smaller than Steph's guide dog though, and I doubt we'd have it so well trained. Both Pyro and I would be inclined to spoil it.

"Uh oh, watch out." Pyro pulls me in front of him as though I'm a shield as Bitch walks past, her back arched and tail held high.

Laughing I swing around. "I'll never get over how that darn cat has all you big men so scared."

"I've got scars from that darn cat, I'll have you know," he replies. "Hey, Beef. Bitch got you yet?"

The VP grimaces and rolls up his sleeve. "Tried to move her so Steph could sit down."

The red lines on his arm look angry and sore. I grin, wondering not for the first time how soft these men are to tolerate a cat who hates the male sex. As she's put Max in his place more than once, I suspect it's not just human males she hates. If they're asked though, they say they give her room and board as she's a good mouser. I think it's more than that. I think it's because like many of them, she's a misfit with an attitude and nowhere else to go.

"Have a good day at work?" Pyro asks, leading me across to the bar to get a drink.

I make a so-so motion with my hand. "It was a workday, like any other." Work was okay, it was my co-workers that were the bother, or one in particular. Having seen how much Pyro cares for me and how he's not afraid of public demonstrations to prove it, Beth keeps trying to get herself an invite to the compound. I've a sneaking suspicion she'd like a biker of her own. After what happened to me, I'm not sure I should drag anyone else into this world, however wonderful I've personally found it. Now that I've got Pyro, that is.

"Do you want to eat here tonight, or go home?"

"Seeing as I brought dessert," I smile, "here, I think."

I'm back to cooking, and the club appreciates it. So much I'm tempted to ask whether it's me they like or what I bring for them to eat. Ink was opening my car door as soon as I pulled up earlier, but instead of greeting me, he immediately looked over into the back seat.

"Mel, if you keep bringing this shit around, I'll have a club of members too fat to do their work." Demon approaches, speaking around a mouthful of muffin.

"Led by an overweight prez," Violet chuckles as she comes

out from behind him, her hand patting what looks to me like a rock-hard muscular stomach.

I'm just sitting down at the table to join Pyro and his brothers to eat, when my phone rings. Taking it out and looking at it, I see it's my dad.

"Dad, I'm…"

"Melissa, I need to tell you something."

Instead of putting him off as I intended, I'm all ears. "Has something happened?"

"Got a response. The SAC wants you to come into his office. The FBI want to talk to you."

I frown, and look around, noticing my side of the conversation is being listened to. "Is that a good or bad sign?"

"Means things are progressing. They want to see you next week. You'll need to come to Denver. I've cleared my calendar."

"I'll be there. I can't talk now, Dad. Just about to have dinner."

We say our goodbyes, and then I end the call.

Pyro's looking at me with his eyebrow raised.

"The FBI want to talk to me at their offices. Dad doesn't know if it's a good sign or bad."

"Good," pronounces Thunder who's sitting opposite me. "It means they're not dismissing it out of hand."

There is a general murmur of agreement from all around.

"I agree," says my man from my side. "But doesn't mean they're not looking to find a reason to discredit Mel."

I straighten my back. "I've just got to tell the truth and be convincing." That shouldn't be hard. It was Skull who had to fabricate everything, unlike myself.

"Hmm, about that truth," Lizard starts.

Mace throws a screwed-up piece of kitchen towel at him. "She's not going to be telling them about the size of your dick."

I fall for it. "I don't know how big his dick is," I say, primly.

"It's…"

"She's got to tell the truth, brother," Mace reminds him. "Very small was what you were trying to say."

"Whether it's small, big or fuckin' medium," Pyro remarks, deceptively calmly, "my ol' lady doesn't fuckin' want to know. And you, Mace, can take over for me while I'm gone. I'm going to Denver with Mel."

"Got a particular job on?" asks Judge.

I tune out as they talk about an engine being rebuilt.

Mechanically I eat the food that Vi and Steph had cooked up, musing how a blind person has become so confident in a kitchen she's had to learn. I'm constantly admiring the way she compensates for her loss of sight by using her other senses, which includes her sharp tongue when she finds someone's put a tin back in the wrong place. They don't tend to repeat their mistake, but I think that's partly to do with Beef backing her up.

I shake my head, not fancying the tiramisu that took hours in the making, but once it's plated up, enjoy seeing the expressions of delight as loaded forks enter other mouths instead.

All this I take in while my mind's whirring. *I'm being given a chance to tell my side of the story.*

Pyro nudges me. "Ready to go home?"

"I'm already nervous," I tell him, as we walk through my front door. We haven't yet found a house we both like, but I find it hard to think about moving with everything else on my mind.

"Sure you are. That's natural. But you've just got to tell them what went down. Facts will speak for themselves."

"I wish you could be with me."

"You'll have your dad. And in this case, he'll know what to say better than I would."

"So, I just tell the truth, huh? About Liz's dick?" I wink.

He launches himself forward, tilting my chin until I'm forced to look into his eyes. "That's the last time that word linked to the name of one of my brothers comes out of your mouth, Mel."

"Or what?" I taunt him.

"Or I find ways of punishing you."

"Yeah?"

"Yeah. On your knees, doll."

Now his hands are on my shoulders pushing me downward. If this is his version of a penalty, I may have to think up some other names to use.

"Hmm," I say as I start unbuckling his belt. "Do you think Beef's dick is as big as everything else about him?"

"I'll give you a big dick, woman," he growls. "Now get it in your mouth and stop talking."

But I can hear the amusement in his tone.

Before Pyro, I couldn't understand why any woman would want *that* in her mouth. But with him, I wanted to try everything. That he loved it, I knew from the first time he'd hesitantly suggested it, after he'd spent a while eating me out.

Hiding my reluctance, I try it.

It gives me power. Oh, he might fist his hand in my hair, but I'm the one using my tongue to pleasure him. Pyro's a man who lets you know exactly what he's feeling, with grunts, groans, and words of encouragement. It's those that drive me on.

"Darlin', pull away now. Want to come inside you."

Quick as a flash he's pulled me up and is pushing me in the direction of the couch. He leans me over the back cushions, then works my work skirt that I'm still wearing up over my hips.

"Fuckin' love you in skirts," he comments, as he proceeds to yank my underwear down. In doing so, he's folded himself, so it's him on his knees now.

And now it's his tongue pleasuring me, his fingers working in tandem as he expertly brings me to the edge and soon I'm tensing and crying out.

He kicks my legs open further, then with one hand on my back, pushes me down over the back of the couch, then positions himself and enters me from behind.

I'm not particularly interested in who's got the biggest, longest or thickest cock in the club, though I bet Pyro would qualify on all counts. It's what he can do with it that matters. He pushes in hard making me gasp, then starts that rotation of his hips which makes his dick rub over exactly the right spot. Sometimes I can now come from that alone, sometimes I need extra stimulation, but I wait for Pyro to provide it. He knows exactly what I want.

He rubs at my clit just the way I like it and I lose it as an orgasm floods through me.

While I'm still shuddering, I feel him swell, and then that amazing feeling of him coming inside me, I swear I sense him filling me up.

He leans his weight over me, not pressing down, just letting me know he's there while our lungs heave in unison. Then, I feel him slip out.

He lifts me as if I weigh nothing, carries me to the front of the couch then sits me down. Instead of cuddling, he's lifting my legs in the air and holding them up.

"What are you doing?" My lips curve and I'm laughing.

"Making sure my cum doesn't run out." He looks down at where my pussy is wide open to him. "In fact, you could do with a plug."

I don't have to ask what he means, when he pulls me in closer and I feel his cock, rock hard once more, entering me. Another position, it's different, he gets in deeper. Again, I gasp and writhe, as he wrenches another orgasm out of me before chasing his own for himself.

I love every position we make love in, but this is one of the best as it allows me to watch his face contort, his eyes dilate, then the way his head goes back as he lets out a deep groan of satisfaction.

My man has stamina. I'm not complaining.

This time Pyro gently puts down my legs when he pulls out and reaches for one of the boxes of tissues we've strategically placed all around the house. Every room, every surface has a memory of him now.

Then we're cuddling, me held tight to his chest.

"Fuckin' love you, Mel."

"Love you too, Pyro."

He's thoughtful for a moment. "Do you want me to get tested?"

"What?"

"To see if there's anything wrong." He points to his cock.

"No, Ro. It can take time. Just because I fell fast last time, doesn't mean I'll fall fast again. It's too early to worry. Anyway," I nudge him gently with my fist, "I'm enjoying the practice."

"Can't deny I'm finding it no chore, darlin'."

"I'm glad to hear it. Now about your brothers' dicks…"

This time he stops me with his mouth on mine, but I can feel his body shaking with laughter.

CHAPTER THIRTY-SEVEN

Pyro

I love seeing Mel on the road to recovery. She's come through so fucking much and is starting to emerge the other side. Sure, she has moments which are darker, you don't get abandoned and then find the man you thought was dead come back to life without it leaving some scar.

I can see the effect each morning when I leave for work. There's a nervousness there, a clinginess before letting me go.

Today is no different. I tell her my normal form of goodbye, "Got my phone with me, darlin'. I'm only a call away. You know the number of the shop too. You get worried? Just call."

She shrugs it off, trying to act as though she's not scared I'll be leaving and never return. "I trust you, Ro."

"I know you do. Fuck the FBI wanting to drag everything back up." I sweep back my hair, wishing going to this meeting was something I could do instead. There's no doubt it's making her anxiety worse. I thank fuck she agreed to see the counsellor I'd arranged. Sometimes I wonder whether it's her state of mind that's affecting her, stopping her falling pregnant again.

It's another thing I hate about Skull. He got her pregnant, something I've so far failed to do.

"Go on, Ro. You'll be late. I'm leaving just after you." She makes a shooing gesture with her hands.

"I love you." I say it as forcefully as I can. "I'll see you later, okay?"

But as I walk out to my bike, I pause a moment. *Skull might have used those very same words.*

All of a sudden, I know just what to do. If my plan doesn't work, nothing will.

"What we got on today, Judge?" I ask, tossing my bike key into the pocket of my cut as I arrive at the shop.

"Two services, one new exhaust." He waves to the cars which citizens must have brought and left. "One has a problem with the gearbox." He then indicates the bikes, the first in line I recognise. "Thunder wants new tires back and front and wants an oil change at the same time."

I grin, relishing my position which means I can allocate jobs. "You start on the cars with Wills, I'll do Thunder's bike." I much prefer to work on two wheels, rather than four.

"Morning."

There's a voice I didn't expect. The prez doesn't normally come to the shop this early in the day.

"What's up, Demon?"

He jerks his head toward the office, his intention is clear, so I lead the way. As we pass it, I indicate the vending machine. "Want a coffee?"

I understand his grimace and the shake of his head. It was put in mainly for waiting customers to use. It's drinkable, just. Does the job if all I want is to wet my throat.

"What can I do for you?" As he props himself against the wall, I perch on the desk.

He frowns, and I begin to suspect I'm not going to like what he has to say. "Red's been in contact. Up to you and your woman to say yes or no, but he wants some of your time."

Okay. So far, nothing to worry about. "For what?"

Demon's arms are folded across his chest. He takes a breath. "He wants you to take Mel to Vegas to speak to Clare Jordan."

I'm immediately shaking my head. "No fuckin' way, Prez. Has he lost his motherfuckin' mind? Mel's just moving on. Going to speak to the FBI is going to be hard enough, seeing that woman bragging she's got the man isn't going to do shit to help her."

"From what Red's said, she's cut him loose," Prez responds in a mild voice. "Fuckin' hard on Mel, I agree. If I thought this was just to rub shit in her face, I'd refuse to have her anywhere near Vegas, but I get the view Clare's kicked Skull out on his ass. She's looking for closure too, and it might just aid Mel as well."

"That motherfucker." I slam my fist onto the desk, wishing it was Skull's face instead.

"There are two women involved, Ro. Might just help them both to talk through their issues together."

I gaze unseeingly at the floor, unsure what to do for a moment or two. Then I look back up as he starts speaking again. "Vi never knew why she was raped, that there was a reason behind it. When she found out, I think it helped. Sure, she learned shit about her parents that she'd never dreamed of, but truth has a way of coming out. Better if you're armed with it, than left in the dark."

"You think Clare's got something Mel needs to know before she's faced with the feds?"

"Could be, Ro. That's my thinking."

Christ. I think of last night, how we were joking and fooling around. If it were up to me, I'd wrap Mel in a protective bubble and keep her there. But it's not my decision, this battle she's taking on, is hers. I'm just behind and beside her all the way.

"I'll speak to her, Demon," I tell him at last. "See what she says. If this is something she thinks she can do, I'll take her to Vegas. But I'm not just laying it on her, I'll give her the choice."

"Fair enough," Demon replies. "Red's managed to get seats

reserved on this evening's flight. Let me know soon if you're able to go."

He leaves, and I place a call to Mel, explaining what Red wants her to do. It's not the first time she surprises me.

"Red offered Clare help, didn't he, Ro?"

He had. I confirm it.

"I trust Red's judgement. If he thinks this is something I should do, if it's to help me and her, I'll do it. I feel sorry for her, Pyro. She's lost a man too."

"Have I told you how much I love you, darlin'?"

She laughs, quietly as she's at work. "A time or two." Then whispers into the phone, "And I love you."

The day passes both slowly and too fast. I try to throw myself into work to occupy my time, but equally, don't want the moment of confrontation to come too fast. *What's Mel going to do?* From what I remember, Clare's tall, willowy and blond, the complete opposite to Mel who, while she finds it hard to believe, is exactly the type of woman who rocks my world. What she doesn't need is to be faced with the woman Skull preferred. A woman with whom Skull actually wanted children.

But now, he's lost her as well. Do I take pleasure in that? Fuck yeah. I hope their separation has hit the fucker hard.

Mel's waiting when I collect her from the house, both of us having gotten off work early to catch the Friday evening flight. She didn't say much before getting behind me on the bike, but her face showed her concern.

When she gets off the bike at the airport, I give her one last chance.

"You don't need to do this. Not quite how I planned to spend this weekend."

She takes a deep breath, then says, "I do, Ro. I need to."

By the time we arrive at the Vegas clubhouse, it's getting on midnight. After a full day at work followed by the flight, I know Mel will be tired, so we greet friends and then make our way up to the room we've again been assigned. Mel pauses at the doorway, her face pained. Then she grimaces and steps inside.

I hate that she's remembering what happened last time we were here.

In the morning, after Rosa has ensured we're fed, Meat says we've been summoned to Red's office. Inside, Red's seated behind his desk, and in front of him, on one of the three chairs he's had brought in, is Skull's wife, Clare, holding a cup of coffee in her hands.

She looks up when we enter, but no one speaks until we've taken our seats. I make sure to position myself between the two women. If this turns out to be unpleasant, I want to be a buffer between Mel and her.

"Mel," Red kicks it off, his eyes examining her searchingly. "Thanks for coming. You too, Pyro."

I raise my chin and notice Mel responds with a small nod.

Clare looks to Red as though seeking permission, then sits forward on her chair, placing her now empty cup on the desk. "Melissa, I'm so sorry. When I heard…"

Mel shrugs, but doesn't say a word.

"I met Don when I was still at school. We were childhood sweethearts if you like, even made Prom King and Queen. Most likely to get married, and we did." She frowns. "We've been, were, together seventeen years."

Mel pulls herself straight, her eyes creased. "How old is he?"

"Thirty-one. Though he could pass for a lot younger, and, indeed has. That's part of the reason why he was asked to go undercover in the first place."

Taking Mel's hand in mine, I tighten my fingers around it. There'd never been a need for her to worry about what she'd thought was a large difference in age. But what's one more crime laid at his door?

Clare resumes, "He was a cop, did some work with the feds, and was recruited from there. He's worked undercover on and off. The longest before this time was a year. The feds must have thought this was a serious enough job to let him stay under for such a long time."

Red interrupts and explains, "Undercover assignments normally last no longer than six months. They need reapproval after that time, and then again after each half year passes." He looks at the woman sitting beside him, his eyes softening slightly. It was very different to how he'd viewed her when I last saw her in the club. "I've explained to Clare about prospects needing to serve their time. Skull, Donavan, would have known it was going to be a long commitment, that he probably wouldn't find anything until he was patched."

"And not even then," I break in. "He found nothing, which must be why he was pulled out."

Clare nods. "That's what I suspected. I didn't know what he was doing, he kept his work secret. I didn't mind, me not knowing kept him safe. I couldn't say anything out of turn, even if I wanted to. Six months passed, I expected him back, but no. His assignment was continuing. Then another five, and he'd returned for a month. I must admit I was scared for him to return to whatever he was doing after that, but he told me it was safer than ever."

Bastard. Because by returning he'd allayed our suspicions. My eyes meet Red's, his face is grim.

Something clicks. "He wore his patch for six months after that."

Red raises an eyebrow at me. "Sounds to me like he wasn't given approval to extend his time. Seems a mighty coincidence and could explain why he was recalled."

Mel breathes out audibly. "You think he applied for another extension and was refused?"

"Could be," Red shrugs. "Or maybe he made the request himself as he realised he was wasting his time."

Bad timing. I remember the words Mel had said he'd used. The bastard had known his time was up. Whether at his request or someone else's, he knew he was going to leave.

Mel digests her own thoughts for a moment, then turns back to Clare. "Did you have any contact with him while he was undercover?"

She shakes her head. "No. I knew what to expect. It was too dangerous for him to expose himself, but his handler would get the odd message to me. I never had any idea what he was doing. But, one thing I never suspected was that he'd be unfaithful."

"He hadn't all that time," Red reassures her. "Prospects get mighty friendly with their hands."

"Unless he went with a woman outside of the club," I say, with a frown. "But I'm unable to say whether he did or did not."

Clare makes a gesture that conveys she'd believe almost anything of him now.

"After… after everything was exposed, Don tried to reassure me that we'd be okay. He told me agents sometimes suffer from Dissociative Identity Disorder when they're under for such a long time. That's when they become the person they're trying to be. He said he'd only ever ask for short-term assignments again."

I huff a short laugh. Bastard's defence is that he believed himself to be a biker? Well I'm a true one, and I'd be fucking faithful to Mel while I knew I had her waiting at home. I certainly wouldn't go out of my way to start a relationship.

"If it's a recognised condition, did he receive counselling?" Red asks.

"No. He didn't want to have it on his record that something was wrong. Because of your complaint, Mel, he didn't want to lose his job. But, he had changed." She bites her lip. "I don't know, he was angry, angry at you, me and Cordelia, that's our daughter. And while he was angry, instead of trying to pacify him, all I could think about was the injury done to me, and to you, Melissa. He'd gone from your bed to mine without a thought. He'd been careless enough to get you pregnant, and, when he heard about your miscarriage, he was pleased. A problem had been solved."

Mel tenses. "I expected that."

"He'd been gone almost eighteen months straight, with just those few weeks in between when he was hurt. I had to survive on my own, and I found that I could. What I found harder to accept, was him back in my life, knowing what I did." She leans forward again, staring intently at Mel. "I can't thank you enough. If I hadn't been confronted with you and Don, I'd never have known what had happened. I'd have been left in ignorance."

"Wouldn't that have been better?" asks Mel. "You might still be married."

She nods. "Yes, but to who?" She shudders. "He cheated once, he'd do it again, I'm sure. He wasn't the man I thought he was. It was better to know."

"Skull hit her," Red puts in, clearly wanting to speed things up. "She came to the club for help. Skull wouldn't take no for an answer from her, but he's had to take it from us." Again his eyes soften as he looks at her, and she responds with a small smile. It makes me wonder just how personally involved Red is. But he quickly knocks that on the head. "Rosa's taken Clare under her wing, and Cordelia, *Delly*," he grins, "has been accepted by the club."

"You living here?" I ask.

Clare shakes her head. "Not now, but I did, for a bit." Again, she addresses herself to Mel. "Red said you were going to be talking to the feds. Don had told them how you discovered who he was. He must have told them kidnapping was involved. They questioned me, I said it was nothing of the sort. That I was invited to the Vegas compound and went of my own accord." Now she glances to Red. "I didn't want to get anyone into trouble, not people who were doing what they could to right a wrong."

She pauses to take a breath, but no one interrupts, seeing there's more she wants to say. "Melissa, I don't know how you coped. I don't know how you've come through. I've, er, I've been trying to put myself in your place. A man just walking out? Then finding out he was alive and not dead? That anything he ever said had been a lie? That…"

Don't put it into words, I silently beg, seeing how still Mel's gone by my side.

"Clare wanted to pay her respects, Mel," Red says, ensuring she doesn't complete her list. "I took her and we put flowers on his grave."

Mel stands, her hands covering her face, then she pushes past and I'm fast following her out the door. In the hallway outside I pull her into my arms, and she sobs. When her tears start to slow, she stammers out, "She's a stronger person than I. To do that, Ro? To visit a grave of her husband's child? A child that wasn't hers?"

"She wanted closure too, Mel." Red appears in the doorway. "I held her myself when she saw the headstone and she cried. It's the visible sign of Skull's crime against her, against you and against the club." His eyes come to mine, a question I interpret as, *Is she alright?*

Mel's next words give him the answer. "I can't go back in, Ro."

"You don't have to, Mel," I reassure her.

She turns in my arms and looks at the Vegas prez. "Can you thank her for coming to tell me her side of the story? We were both duped, weren't we?"

"I'll thank her. Oh, and Ro. One other thing you should know. Skull's undercover again."

"Where?" I clip out.

But Red simply shrugs. That we don't know and may never discover.

CHAPTER THIRTY-EIGHT

Melissa

P yro had been concerned after I again gave into my sorrow when speaking to Clare, but it had been that touching action she'd taken that had gotten to me. That she, faced with her own hurt, had addressed mine as well, just showed her humanity. Once I'd processed her words, I'd realised there were two women in this, both hurt, and for the same reason. It just added to my determination to get justice.

I walk into the offices of the Federal Bureau of Investigation with my head held high, and my attorney, my father, beside me.

"Thank you for coming to see us Ms Martins. Mr Martins, you're here in your capacity as your daughter's attorney?"

"I am," Dad replies. "Though on this occasion she's foremost my client."

"I'm Agent Forsyth, and my colleague is Agent Booth. This is an exploratory meeting to enable us to get a better under-standing of your complaint. We will record it…"

"I'd like a copy of the tape."

"Of course, Mr Martins."

Forsyth looks down at a copy of the paperwork my father had sent him. I know it by heart, having read and re-read it, to make sure I don't trip myself up.

"You made some serious allegations against Agent Jordan. Ms Martins, would you like to tell us what the basis of these allegations are?"

My father sits forward. "The basis of our complaint is that a federal agent failed to protect a civilian from harm. That in order to obtain information, he dragged an innocent person into what he considered at the time, to be the underworld of crime. As a result of ensuing events Ms Martins is suffering PTSD."

Agent Forsyth looks slightly bored as he turns back to me. "I know the bones of the facts are contained in the report, but to make the situation clearer, Ms Martins, if you would, can you take us through how you met Agent Jordan, and how he allegedly drew you into this life of crime?"

I take a breath and look at my father, he gives me a nod and a quick smile of encouragement.

"I was out for a drink with friends from work. Skull, that's the name Agent Jordan was using," I pause, but there's no acknowledgement at all, "well, uninvited he came and joined our group at the table. I didn't think he was interested in me at the time, but my friends thought he was, and invited him to a party on the Sunday. I hadn't expected he'd turn up."

"You knew the man who became known to you as Skull was a biker at that point."

"Yes, he was wearing his cut."

"And that was exciting? A walk on the wild side? What did you do to encourage him?"

I bristle. "I did nothing to encourage him. Quite the opposite in fact. I tried to put him off, but he was insistent. The fact he was a biker initially made me cautious. His approach struck me as strange."

"Why strange?"

Now I shrug. "I'm older. I thought he was only about twenty, then he told me he was twenty-five. But still it seemed odd. I'm hardly what you'd think of as a biker chick."

"Nevertheless, you entered into a relationship with him. Did the biker lifestyle appeal to you?" Booth interjects.

"Not at all," I tell him, truthfully. "That was part of what put me off. You hear so many things about biker clubs. Men passing women around, stuff like that. Leaving aside their reputation for illegal activities. No, a biker for a boyfriend was the last thing I wanted."

"And you told him that?"

"I probably didn't use the exact words, but yes, that was the impression I gave him."

"I'll ask again," says Booth. "Why did you agree to become his," he consults his notes, "old lady."

"I didn't. Not at first. But he was persistent and encouraged me to go on a date with him, and then another and more after that. You could say he wore me down, and it became easier to say yes to exploring a relationship."

"Are you sure it was that way around?" Forsyth resumes. "Are you certain you weren't pursuing him?"

"I've enough witnesses who'll say exactly which way around it was."

"Bikers?" snaps Booth.

My dad growls quietly, and cuts in, "I've a list of names prepared for you. These people all work for the local government office in Pueblo. Ms Martins hadn't met any other bikers at that point."

The two agents exchange a look with each other.

I decide to stand up for myself. "The probable situation as I now know it, is for some reason, Skull needed a woman to infiltrate the club and get information which the other old ladies, particularly Violet Black, wife of David, the president, might have. On our first date, Skull went out of his way to tell me specifically the club wasn't into illegal activities. This must have been contrary to what he believed at the time, otherwise he wouldn't have been placed there." Booth goes to speak, but I don't give him the chance. "The fact is that I, as an upstanding citizen, wouldn't have gone anywhere near the club had I known he'd had suspicions about them. He deceived me and entrapped me with false information."

"That's what you say now." Booth seizes his chance. "But I offer a contrary view. You went in with your eyes open as you wanted excitement in your otherwise quite boring life."

"Objection," my dad throws in as though we were in a court room. "Can we please stick with the facts? You are in no position to say what Ms Martins state of mind was, nor whether she considered her life satisfactory or not. The case is she did not rush into a relationship with a biker, as will be confirmed by numerous witnesses. Agent Jordan pressured her until she accepted. They had several dates before he took her near the club. I have a list of places and dates and times they took place. There's nothing to suggest this is the behaviour of a woman who wanted to join a biker club."

The agents put their heads together and speak in hushed tones, Booth pointing to parts of a document in front of him.

"These dates…"

"I have a list of them," Dad puts in, sliding over a piece of paper. "There will be receipts I'm sure, unless Agent Jordan didn't expense them."

"Agent Jordan claims you were enthusiastic about getting to know about the club. That bikes had always intrigued you, and that you hinted their illegal activities excited you."

"Look at me," I cry out. "Do I look like a woman who'd ever think she'd be comfortable riding a bike?"

"How did you get to Denver?" Booth asks.

"I drove, in my car," I reply honestly. With the forecast of snow Pyro didn't want to risk either of us on his motorcycle.

"But it's true you regularly ride on your boyfriend's bike?"

I'm getting annoyed. "I do now, but back then I thought my weight would unbalance it. It was riding with Skull that showed me I could enjoy it. When he first picked me up and expected me to ride I was horrified."

"So you say now," Forsyth mumbles.

Dad gives me a little shake of my head. *Don't get emotional,* he'd told me. *They'll try to trip you up.*

Now it's my father who steps in. "Getting back to the illegal activities you mentioned. Are you saying Skull briefed Ms Martins on things that he suspected were going on in the club? If he'd found no evidence before he met her, any information in that vein would have been false, and another example of how he set out to entrap her. I don't need to have the relationship I do with Ms Martins to know any such discussion would have sent her running. Again, I refer you to my list of witnesses who can all attest to her character. Ms Martins hasn't had so much as a speeding ticket in her life."

I want to high five my dad but restrain myself.

Dad's got the bit between his teeth. "Agent Jordan took Ms Martins to the club under false pretences, that is undeniable. Then he commenced a sexual relationship with her where he undertook responsibility for contraception, a responsibility he neglected on two occasions, the second resulting in a pregnancy, unwanted by him, but wanted by Ms Martins who'd been led to believe, by the fact he publicly claimed her, that he was in a long-term and permanent relationship with her."

As Dad lays it on the line, both agents make a move forward, but he doesn't let them speak.

"Agent Jordan disappeared. Ms Martins had to assume, as the months passed, that as the man she knew had given her every expectation he'd return to her that day, that he was lying dead. She was pregnant and alone, suffering devastating grief."

"She went back to the outlaw motorcycle gang. Not the action of an upright citizen."

"She went back to the motorcycle riding club," Dad corrects, "who might call themselves outlaw for historical reasons, but the fact is, nowadays they engage in no criminal activities. They regard themselves as a family. Skull, or Agent Jordan as we now know, was accepted as one of their members. They were grieving too, so it was natural they took Ms Martins in, so they could grieve together. They are good men and women who stood up to offer support to who they saw as one of their own. Ms Martins wasn't a girl who'd walked in off the street, she was a claimed woman of one of their members and had been treated as family. I think that's the actions of any woman who found herself in such dire circumstances, seeking support from those around her. Seeking out the company of people who were also trying to make sense out of the bizarre and distressing situation she'd found herself in. They were seeking their brother, her man. They were in the best position to help her."

"What methods were they using to try to find him?"

"They reported him missing to the cops." I shut any idea they were doing anything illegal down. If they were, I didn't know about it. "If the cops knew he was alive and well and working for the FBI, they never fed that information back to us. They never said a word to ease my grieving." I add fast, "I didn't know he was married, nor that when he'd left me, he'd returned to his wife and child."

Saying it aloud makes me start shaking. Dad sees, twists the cap off a bottle of water, fills a glass, and passes it across.

"When I found that out… If I'd known," I try again, "I wouldn't have gone anywhere near him. It's one matter to represent himself with a different identity, quite another to hide that his lies about commitment were just that, lies. He wasn't free to make any promises."

Booth and Forsyth exchange a look between them.

Forsyth is the one to speak. "When undercover, our agents have to become the person they're representing. If it had been expected…"

"Skull didn't have to fuck anyone or could have gone with a club girl if he couldn't keep it in his pants, or had a relationship and never taken a woman to the club. The club rules do not demand a member fucks, and the brothers don't question whether a man wants to remain celibate."

"You're being very blunt," Booth notes scathingly. "Is your language because you spend time with bikers?"

"My language is because I thought Skull and I had made love. That our baby came to be as a result of an expression of the emotion we both shared. But to him, it was just fucking. I was used, in circumstances where I wouldn't have given my consent had I known who he truly was, and certainly if I'd known he had a wife waiting on him." I pause then cry out, "Have you any idea what that feels like? I'm no cheater, would never have dreamed of going with a man who was already taken. But he made me into the other woman."

"You sure the baby was his?"

As I gasp in air, the expected question strangely taking me by surprise, Dad passes another piece of paper across. "We used DNA from his toothbrush, but you can redo the test if you want. A DNA sample is also in storage at the hospital where the child was... delivered."

"When I found out he wasn't dead, but alive and living with his family, I miscarried." I tell them what they'll already know, bluntly. Then again, without giving them a chance to speak or voice their own objection, "Oh, I know mental distress can't be proven as the cause of the miscarriage, but the timing fits. I found Skull, found out the truth, and... my baby stopped breathing."

My head falls into my palms. Then, when I raise it and reach for some more water, I spill it as my hands are violently shaking.

"Do you need a moment?" Booth asks, for the first time his eyes lose a little of their hardness.

Dad's brow is creased, and while it might not be the professional front he wanted to present, he reaches over and lays his hand on top of mine. "You okay?"

I take a deep breath and work on calming myself down. "I'd prefer to get this over with."

"I take it you've seen Ms Martins is suffering from Post-Traumatic Stress Disorder?" Dad asks to buy me some time. "There's a report there from the psychologist who's been treating her. There obviously is no evidence that the stress from Skull's disappearance then reappearance caused her to miscarry. But it had such an effect that she's still continuing to suffer the loss of self-esteem and self-confidence, with the result she has heightened anxiety. Those are the facts. What seems irrefutable to any reasonable person is that such distress could have contributed, if not caused, her miscarriage. The effects of the psychological torture imposed on Ms Martins will probably remain with her for life." He pauses before delivering the punch line. "The psychologist's report is evidence Agent Jordan failed to protect a civilian from harm. In fact, he inflicted it."

The agents also take the opportunity to drink some water.

"You have one of the bikers living in your house, Ms Martins," Forsyth observes, breaking the silence that had fallen.

"How… how do you know that?"

He just raises an eyebrow. *Stupid. He's the FBI.* They must have had someone checking me out.

I glance at Dad, he raises his chin, then lowers it again.

"When Skull disappeared, I was distraught. I'd never felt that kind of hurt before. All the brothers stepped up, but Pyro, well, he was like my rock. He was there when I discovered I was pregnant. From that point on, he did what he could to make my life easier." I swallow, trying to put it into words. "At first it was a duty to the brother who had disappeared. That's what these bikers do, make sure family is cared for. Being together so much, our relationship changed."

"I'd like to point out, Ms Martins was essentially a single woman at that point. Her man had gone, and as time passed, he was unlikely to return."

"So, you started a physical relationship with this… Pyro?"

I shake my head at Forsyth and deny it. "No. Although my feelings changed toward Pyro, I was still carrying the baby of another man. Our relationship didn't develop that way until after I'd found out the truth about Skull, and after I'd recovered from the miscarriage. I did not hop from one man's bed to another."

Booth leans forward. "Part of your case is that Agent Jordan drew you, an *innocent* woman, into a life of crime. Seems like you didn't need a lot of encouragement, and after you entered it, you stayed."

"Objection." Dad raises his hand. "Skull assumed it was a *life of crime* as you call it. What Ms Martins discovered was something entirely different. She found a club based around the concept of family. That's why she stayed, and why Agent Jordan left. He left because he found the premise he'd been working on was false. He clearly found no evidence of wrongdoing."

"And how do you come to that conclusion?" Booth won't give up.

"Because there have been no charges." Dad shifts impatiently as though he shouldn't need to teach them their jobs. "It's well over ninety days since the investigation was brought to its abrupt end. As you are aware, any charges must be brought within that time, unless you're going to insist the investigation is ongoing. In any event, our argument stands. Agent Jordan recruited Ms Martins as he thought she would lead him to what he believed was the truth, and therefore inducted her into the criminal world, or that's how he saw it at the time."

Forsyth isn't giving ground and he proves it when he takes over again. His voice is stern. "And we refute that. Kidnapping is a crime. The Satan's Devils have a chapter in Vegas do they not?"

What? Oh, shit.

I hope I'm hiding my reaction as he continues. "Agent Jordan has told us his wife was kidnapped," he looks down at his notes, "by members of the Las Vegas club and also four members of the Pueblo chapter."

But Dad's there. "I am unaware of any kidnapping. The man who impregnated Ms Martins and so callously left her had just been found. Of course, she wanted answers. Clare Jordan was invited back to the compound, and Agent Jordan invited to join her. Not a hair on either of their heads was harmed."

"That's not how Agent Jordan relates it. No invitation was extended, force was involved."

"Have you asked Mrs Jordan for her interpretation of the events?"

As Dad asks the question, I hold my breath for the answer, hoping Clare's stayed true to her word.

There's silence for a moment, then Forsyth admits, "Mrs Jordan confirms your story, saying she wanted answers herself, but Agent Jordan remains adamant on the point."

"I suggest Agent Jordan has a vested interest in making the club look bad," Dad, who I've brought up to speed with our visit to Vegas, suggests. "You've more witnesses to say otherwise."

"Are they still together?" I ask. Pyro had suggested we don't let on I've seen her, and it seems a question they'd expect me to ask.

"I don't think that's any of your business."

"So there's nothing to back up this story of kidnapping," Dad states. "Unless you have evidence, it's the word of your man against a number of others, including, it would seem, his wife."

They don't like it, but don't contradict him. After a moment the two heads bow together. Then Forsyth looks up. "Please wait here."

They leave the room.

"How do you think it's going?" I ask, my eyes watching the closed door.

"You're telling the truth, Melissa. That's all we can do."

I notice my father staring at something, then his eyes go to the recording device which hadn't been turned off. *They're watching and listening.*

Taking his cue, I say nothing more. The clock ticks loudly and counts off the minutes. I know exactly nine of them have passed before the two agents return.

They don't bother taking their seats.

"Thank you very much for coming in, Ms Martins, Mr Martins. We will consider what you have told us today and give you our written response as soon as we can."

"Just before we leave," Dad doesn't yet stand, "I have requested all documentation and any photographic evidence you might have which refers to or shows Ms Martins. I trust that will be delivered to my office without delay."

Again, they exchange looks. I'd say they look uneasy. After a few seconds have passed, Forsyth nods his head. "Of course, Mr Martins."

They're obviously waiting to escort us out of the building.

Pyro's out front. "How did it go?" His anxious eyes flick from me to Dad.

I make a seesawing gesture with my hand. "Hard to tell."

CHAPTER THIRTY-NINE

Pyro

Mel looks like she's been put through the wringer. I've been questioned by the cops before—what biker hasn't? —so I know how challenging that can be. The police get you going around in circles and try to trip you up and make you contradict yourself.

"Let's get you home."

"We'll meet you there," I tell her father.

We've arranged to stay with her parents overnight and head back in the morning. I think both Rufus and I knew exactly how hard this would be for her. We knew she would be dredging everything up in front of people who don't want to believe her.

"Do you want to talk about it?" I ask, as I drive behind Rufus' car.

"They tried to make something of the fact you and I have a relationship." Her voice is quiet. "They kept calling your club a gang."

"Because that's how they think of us, darlin'. It isn't right, but there you go. That's what we're always up against. In their world they consider us the same as any criminal gang."

"That's not fair."

I smile at her objection. "It is what it is, darlin'."

Flicking the indicator, I make a right turn, then pull the car up behind Rufus' on the driveway. Before I've turned the engine off, her mom has opened the front door and is looking out anxiously. I notice her face relaxes slightly when Mel steps out of the car. I think she might have suspected she'd be in tears, and to be honest, that wouldn't have surprised me either. She's just had everything bad that's happened to her exposed and dissected, and I'd be astonished if the feds hadn't tried to discredit her.

But I'm not going to interrogate her, she's had enough of that for one day. Instead, I'll talk to her dad.

As Mel disappears into the house with her mom, I turn to Rufus. But he anticipates my question without me having to put it into words.

"We'll talk in my study."

I trail behind him, unsurprised his first action is to pour two whiskeys. He downs half of his in one go.

Then raises his eyebrow when he sees me watching. "I know I've heard it all before, but hearing it again today? Fucking hard."

It's the first time I've heard him swear.

"Mel cope okay?"

"Solid as a rock. They couldn't shake her."

I sit down and take a sip of my own drink. "How do you read it?"

His shoulders rise and fall. "They're trying to wriggle out of it, of course. Will try to protect one of their own. They did bring up the kidnapping."

I sit forward sharply. "What did they say?"

"That Skull's wife wasn't confirming his story. It's Skull's word against everyone else."

Good on Red for keeping tabs on her and offering his support. Both women had been used by the same man. Though she'd been scared at the time, if Clare hadn't been brought to the Vegas compound and seen Mel, and witnessed her husband's reaction, she'd never have known about his deceit. He'd have continued going undercover for months or years at a time and could have been with any number of women while she sat at home waiting.

We discuss what the FBI agents had said and Rufus' impressions for a while, then our conversation peters out.

"Well, let's go and join the women."

"Sir, could I ask you something?" I've been waiting for the right moment. I'm not totally sure this is it, but I'll take my chance. For some reason, I feel strangely nervous. At Rufus' nod, I swallow. "I'd like your permission to ask your daughter to marry me."

I hold my breath. Of course, if he says no, she's a grown woman and can make up her own mind. I don't really need his go ahead, but after the way Skull treated her, I want to do everything right. And that means trying to get her family on board with our relationship.

I've shocked Rufus. For a moment his face is unreadable, and it dawns on me, having a biker in the family might not be what he wants or hoped for his daughter. As I watch him, trying to gauge his reaction, his lips suddenly curve.

He holds out his hand, I take it. Instead of shaking it as I expect, he lays his other on top. "Pyro, I couldn't have chosen a better man for my daughter. You've stood by her through thick and thin. I know you'll never do anything to hurt her." His eyes appear to water. "Even now, you're doing things right. You have my blessing, and I know I speak for Angela too."

I feel choked up myself.

Now we do shake hands, and, as neither of us are capable of speaking, we leave his study.

Mel and her mom are in the kitchen, sorting out food. Mel's chuckling, and I'm pleased to see she's coping after the interrogation she went through today. Suddenly the ring I have ready is burning a hole in my pocket. My plan had been to take her out to a swanky place and do everything properly, but nothing seems more right than sharing this moment with the other people who love her.

There, in the kitchen, in the space between the sink and the cooker, I lower myself onto one knee in front of her and take her hand.

As she looks down, her brow furrowed in confusion, I take a deep breath and ask, "Melissa Martins, will you do me the honour of becoming my wife?"

My other hand holds tight to the ring box in my pocket.

Mel stares down.

"For goodness' sake, Melissa. Put the poor man out of his misery." Rufus chuckles, making her start as if she hadn't realised she was supposed to reply.

"Yes." The word sounds shaky. She says it again, her voice getting firmer with each repetition, "Yes. Yes. Yes. Yes."

I stand and slip the top of the box open, showing her the diamond ring inside. Big enough to impress, not too big to be ostentatious. "Will this do?"

She's still as a statue as I slip the ring on her finger. Fuck me, I estimated well, it's a perfect fit. The moment almost as good as when I gave my property patch to her.

Then she's in my arms, and our mouths meet in a passionate display that's probably not appropriate in front of her parents.

Beside us her mom squeals and claps her hands. "Oh my! We've got a wedding to plan!"

I hadn't thought as far as that. But now she's said it, and the glow in Mel's face as she turns to show the ring to her mother let me know that this is a good way of moving on from everything that's happened.

The shit's not over, I know that. But we can concentrate more on our future, and less on our past.

As Mel and her mom start talking a mile a minute, already discussing things like dresses, bridesmaids and cakes, Rufus' hand rests on my shoulder.

As he leans in, he says quietly, "They needed this."

"We all did," I correct.

The next day we return to Pueblo. The main topic of conversation, particularly among the women, changes from Skull's betrayal to planning a wedding.

Days pass, then turn into weeks. Mel and I settle into a routine that's comfortable for us both. We find a four-bedroom house we both fall in love with and start the process of making it ours.

Having been determined to find the source of a rattle in a relatively new engine, I'd been delayed at work. When I come home, it's to find Mel sitting in the dark.

I switch on the light, quickly noticing her face is streaked with tears. "Darlin'?"

She wastes no time in telling me, "The FBI have dismissed my complaint. Oh, they wrapped it up in legalese, but the essence of it is, they can find no evidence of wrongdoing on their agent's behalf."

I close my eyes. It's exactly what I had feared, that they'd circle the wagons to protect their own. "What happens now?" I know Rufus won't let it drop.

"He's submitting a claim under the Federal Tort Claims Act."

This I know, as we've already discussed, could result in her being awarded punitive damages, but won't have any effect on what happens to Skull. It seems he's going to escape without any disciplinary action.

"There's more," she continues. "With the letter, Dad received a file full of documents and photos. Skull was writing up every conversation I'd reported to him. Even Theo's fucking teething problems. He documented everything—except for the fact several of those conversations were after sex." She sneers as she says the last. "There were also photos of me with you, me with Vi, me with Demon... at the barbeque, or just in the club. He must have been taking photos all the time, and nobody noticed."

We're always on our phones, it's just the way of the world nowadays. I can't remember if Skull had his out more often than anyone else, but if he had, we probably wouldn't have thought much about it.

"Dad said it was an invasion of my personal privacy. *I* wasn't the one being investigated. My God, Ro. Did he expect me to incriminate myself, pick up a gun and shoot someone?"

"I've no fuckin' idea." I realise I'm too far away from her. Crossing the room, I sit beside her and pull her into my arms. "Skull was getting desperate. He'd gotten no results. He was probably taking tons of images hoping to pour over them and find something he could use. Same with the documents."

"Dad has asked for nine hundred and ninety-nine thousand dollars, Ro. He said if it's under a million cases can get settled reasonably fast. My baby's life is worth one dollar under a million."

I hold her tighter. "It's not just for him, Mel, it's for everything you suffered, from the moment Skull walked out your door."

"Even now they could dismiss that case too. What are the chances of anyone believing me when the FBI has closed ranks?" She pulls away from me, stands and starts pacing. "I can't believe they had the balls to write he'd done nothing wrong. For all he suspected, he could have been putting me in danger. That bastard gets away with no stain on his character, and I have to live with the knowledge the FBI think I'm…"

"Living with a criminal and associating with an outlaw motorcycle gang. Join the club, sweetheart." I stand, trapping her in my arms once again. "You're marrying a biker. You wear my property patch. There will always be people who look at us that way, but we don't give a fuck. We don't give a damn for citizen laws. You know what's at the bottom of why we're hated so much?"

She gives a small shake of her head.

"We've got something everyone wants. Family, people who have our back, brothers who protect what's theirs, as well as what belongs to their brothers. We're a tribe, hon, and you've joined it."

Her head tilts to the side and she presses her lips together.

"If you don't like it, there's still time to run." I wink, showing I don't believe she'll take that option. "The people who really matter, your friends, your parents, they don't give a damn. Who gives a fuck about anyone else?"

Her hands come up to rest on my shoulders. "You're right, Ro. This isn't always going to be easy. But I've never been happier than when I've been with you." She pauses, then grins. "I don't give a fuck what anyone else thinks."

Later, as we're lying in bed after I've given my woman the loving she deserves, she turns to face me.

"I don't care about the money, Ro. If I'm awarded it, it's the principle that counts."

She'll get no argument from me about that. I just hope she'll win, it will be the vindication she needs. Skull, she can leave to me.

"What you thinking, darlin'?"

"If, and it's a big if, I get the compensation, would you mind if I gave it away?"

We don't need money. Even if I didn't have wages coming in from the club, we'd make do. What makes her happy is all that counts. "Your money, you do what you want with it. Out of interest, who would you give it to?"

"A charity that researches the reasons for miscarriage and into how they might be able to prevent them."

I grip her hand hard. "Can't think of one offhand, but we'll find someone to give it to who'll use it for the right purpose. And I agree, it's the right thing to do.

If she wins, that is. If she doesn't? Well, I'll make sure she gets justice in any event.

CHAPTER FORTY

Melissa

"Oh my. You look beautiful, Melissa."

"Mom," I warn, "if you cry, I'll cry, and that will ruin my makeup."

She sniffs loudly and turns away for a second, dabbing at her face. "I'm not crying, just got some dust in my eye."

"Huh. I may be blind, but even I can see through that. Max, come here. Mel doesn't want you slobbering all over her dress."

Wondering how Steph knows what her dog was about to do, I can only giggle.

As if I'd asked, she answers, "He always makes a beeline for you, Mel. And don't think I don't know it's because you're always giving him a cookie."

"Not all of it," I protest. "Just a few crumbs." I mean, how can anyone resist when those soulful brown eyes are turned on them?

"Your mom's right. You look perfect. That dress really suits you."

I turn to thank Vi, then glance at Jayden and Steph, all wearing dresses in midnight blue, the same colour and material, but the style to suit their personal shapes. Jay's is short, showing off her shapely young legs. Standing slightly to one side, part of, but also I know feeling a little bit lost, is Beth, similarly dressed in blue. I give her a warm smile, remembering her delight when I'd asked her to stand up with me today, though I suspect some of her pleasure was that at last I was letting her have a glimpse at life inside the club.

"You all look…" I struggle to find the right word. There's only one which will do. "Gorgeous. And just look at Theo!"

Theo is dressed in a miniature tux. Toddling now, he's wriggled out of Vi's arms, and is making a beeline for the dog. "No, Theo!" His mother stops him before he gets to his target, swinging him up into her arms. "No dog hairs, not today. Not when you're looking so fine."

"Sorry, not sorry," mumbles Steph, making us laugh.

"If it's not him, it's cat hairs from Bitch," Vi gloomily says.

It's winter, and while I'd have loved a wedding held in the yard at the compound, it's far too cold. Mom was delighted when I'd agreed to hold it in a posh hotel instead.

Neither Pyro nor myself are religious, and my parents aren't particularly either, so we'll be married here as well. As I watch the snow falling outside the window, I'm pleased we don't need to bother with cars, or being transported from place to place.

"You got stepladders we can use?"

The odd question gets me turning to see Vi and Jay staring up at Beth. Unfazed, she tells them, "Nah, I'll kneel down instead."

"Bit of a risky position to be on your knees around bikers," Steph warns.

Just like that, they've made me giggle again. Beth, at over six feet tall, towers above me and them. As Vi steps closer and seems to measure herself and pretend to estimate the difference, I know her gentle teasing is breaking the ice. Beth must have been unnerved to walk into this group of strangers.

"You know we might be able to find you a man your size," Jay offers, thoughtfully. "Most of the club are tall."

"I've noticed," Beth responds, a gleam coming into her eyes.

I shake my head and hope trouble's not on its way. The men Jay's talking about are confirmed bachelors.

While the others joke on, I feel glad I have my family around me, both my mom and my adopted sisters from the club, as well as my work friend. I'd be feeling even more nervous without them. The butterflies having a ball in my stomach don't seem quite so bad with them around.

Why I'm so full of nerves, I've no idea. Do I think Pyro won't be waiting for me? We may have joked about him running a mile before it gets to the time for him to say, 'I do', but surely, I don't believe that would really happen. If there was ever a man more dependable, I've yet to meet him. I try to shake off the sudden bout of anxiety, knowing my fears are all part of Skull's legacy.

One thing I know is I'm not making a mistake marrying a man the world views with suspicion. It's the way the authorities view me too. Whether I marry Pyro or not, what happened with Skull has tainted me forever.

"You ready?" a deep voice sounds from the doorway. It's Dad.

"She is." Mom gives me a peck on the cheek, then hurries away to take her place in the hall downstairs. One by one, Vi, with Theo holding tight to her hand, Jay, Steph, led by the faithful Max and lastly, Beth, step up, kiss me too, then follow her out.

Dad stands for a moment. "I'm so proud." His voice croaks.

"I'm only getting married, Dad."

His head shakes. "No, it's more than that. I'm so proud of how strong you are, the way you survived, and the way you've put your finger up at the world and held your head high. Pyro's just been introducing me to his friends, brothers as he calls them. And you know what, Mel? The way they speak about you? So respectful. No, they're proud of you too."

I hadn't cried before, I feel like doing so now.

He holds out his arm. "Come on. Let's go make sure Pyro can't run away."

I laugh, like I'm meant to.

My nerves rise again. I'm not one that likes being the centre of attention, always prefer to remain at the back. Now all eyes are on me as I make my entrance. Everyone's here from the club —except for the prospects Karl and Beaver. I even invited the club girls, having at the back of my mind the thought that it's to show them Pyro's definitely off the market, though he's never shown any intention to stray. Breezy gives me a little finger wave as I pass by, indicating the gesture has been appreciated. Moira, Jeannie and Sindy are sitting alongside their men, all giving me huge smiles.

My other work colleagues are here too. I spy Holly and Macey, next to them sits Shayla, and Carter and Brice are just behind them.

I start in surprise as I see Red, Crash and Twister from Vegas. Red and Crash are next to Demon, and Twister is sitting with Mace. As I pass the enforcers, Twister growls, "Just here to make sure you don't back out."

As my eyes widen at his words, Mace adds in a loud stage whisper, "Don't worry, Mel, I'm keeping an eye on Pyro. If he makes a move to the door, I've got plans." He taps his nose.

It's while I'm trying hard to suppress my laughter that I at last turn my attention to the man waiting for me to make my way to him. Both he and his best man, Beef, are wearing tuxedos. I've already promised they can exchange their jackets for cuts after the photos. Pyro hadn't been able to decide who of his brothers should stand up beside him, so in the end they drew straws. Beef won, or lost, as the others joked with him.

But the VP was a good choice. He glances back over his shoulder, then nudges my man. Pyro's eyes gleam in appreciation and can't remove his gaze as I finish my journey to him. When I reach him, Pyro takes my hand, squeezing it so tightly, his expression so full of love, my heart feels like bursting with overflowing joy.

The ceremony itself passes in a blur. I stammer out the vows I committed to memory, and Pyro speaks from the heart. We exchange rings, then sign our names on the marriage certificate. Then it's done.

Dad's hired a professional photographer, and it takes an age as we pose for a hundred different shots, but I don't care, this is a day that I'll always want to remember. Most of the photos have me cracking up with laughter, as Beef, Demon and Pal lift their women into the air trying to make them the same height as Beth. Then Beth folds to her knees for the bridesmaid's group shots, and, as Jay had predicted, gets several inappropriate offers which she dismisses good-naturedly.

Tables are laid out with cloths matching my colour scheme in the dining room. Speeches are said. Pyro pretending to slide under the table when Demon lists what he's done for the club with obvious embellishments, which have everyone rolling with laughter.

It's a great afternoon, and everyone around me seems to be having fun, just as I wanted. It's our special day, and everyone we care about is here to share it.

When the formal activities are completed, Pyro and I have our first dance together. Once that's finished, I lead him off the floor, picking up my purse on the way.

"Where we going?"

"Just come with me, Ro."

"Fuck, Mel. This is the Ladies' bathroom." He looks around as if there's a firing squad waiting to kill him for simply having stepped into the female domain. There's no one else in here, so I reckon he's safe.

Instead of answering him with words, I take the pregnancy test out of my purse. I don't need to say anything. Immediately Pyro stops worrying about anyone coming in, in fact, I think he stops breathing as I enter a stall. Moments later I come out.

"What's it say?"

"Got to give it a minute," I remind him. And, as I'd done so many months before, I put it into his hands.

I could be pregnant, or the nerves of the upcoming wedding might have muddled up nature. Pyro stands, his eyes fixed on mine. I know he wants this to be positive, as much as I do.

I don't look away from his face as he glances down. Then he throws back his head and draws in a deep breath.

"Fuck," he growls.

My face falls.

"Best fuckin' wedding present in the world."

Wait. What?

"Ro?"

Before he can answer the door opens behind him.

"Get out," he roars, without turning around to check who it is. The unknown person must have decided their need wasn't urgent as the door immediately closes again.

"Ro?"

His hands tremble when he hands me the stick so I can see for myself. There's a plus sign. I'm having Ro's baby.

He picks me up, spins me around, then quickly puts me back down. "Sorry, I shouldn't have…"

"I'm not made of glass, Ro." I grin, wondering just how protective he'll be now I'm pregnant again. "And let's keep the news to ourselves, for now."

But Pyro's looking at me intently as he seriously says, "No, Mel. I want everyone to know. If heaven forbid, anything is going to go wrong, I don't want to suffer in silence or hide the pain." His hand cups my face. "Everyone out there, sweetheart, well, this will make their fuckin' day too."

Put like that, how can I refuse?

We exit the bathroom, finding a line waiting outside. Beth's crossed her legs and is bouncing with her hand between her thighs. It's so exaggerated, so I know she's putting it on. But I don't have a chance to say anything, as Pyro grabs my hand and takes me back into the ballroom.

He motions to the DJ who cuts the music mid-song, then bangs a spoon against a glass. When everyone is looking our way, he, to my embarrassment, holds the stick I've just peed on high in the air and yells, "My wife's fuckin' pregnant."

The room erupts.

As if he hadn't made it clear the first time, Pyro shouts again, "Mel's havin' my baby!"

My parents are the first to come up to us. Mom has tears in her eyes, and I know she's remembering what happened before. Dad congratulates Pyro, then has to move off as everyone comes over to give us their best wishes. When I'm hugged for the tenth time Pyro starts warning them off, pulling me to one side protectively.

"It's early days," I repeat over and over again. But no one seems to care about that.

When my friends and the Tucson club have had their say, Red approaches. "Really good fuckin' news, Mel." He leans in and kisses my cheek, then shakes Pyro's hand. "If anyone deserves to be happy, you two do." I expect him to walk away, but he hasn't finished. "Clare's staying close to the Vegas club, thought you should know."

"She okay?" I ask, genuinely wanting to know.

Red's brow creases. "She's strong, became independent when he was gone such a long time. She's well able to cope on her own. Problem is, the bastard isn't taking it well, and is trying for custody of the kid. Threatening her to get her to go back to him. She's worried about him planting evidence to say she's an unfit mother. Seems none of us knew what a motherfucker he really was, not even the woman who's been by his side for seventeen years."

"Asshole," Pyro snarls, then raises his jaw toward Red, who jerks his chin in return.

"Hey, girl." Beth's pulling my arm, dragging me away from the two men.

They both wave me off, Ro's eyes following me as I'm pulled across the room.

Giggling as I have to run to keep up with her long strides, I ask, "What, Beth?"

"Him, there. What's his name?"

I look around. There are three Devils propping up the bar. "Which one?"

"The one with no ink."

Lizard's there with full sleeves on both arms, Mace standing alongside, is also heavily tattooed. There can only be one man who fits the bill. "Ink."

"That's what I said," she says indignantly. "The one with no ink."

"Ink," I say again, feeling my lips curve.

"Jeez. Have pregnancy hormones already gotten to you? What's the man in the middle's name?"

"Ink," I laugh. "That's his name."

"Ink? But he's got no tattoos." She stares over my head as if to check.

"I rather think that's the point," I tell her drily.

But she's already lost interest in his name. "Can you introduce me?"

This is what I feared might happen. "Are you sure you can handle a biker?"

"If you can, I can," she winks, "and will you look at that." I turn to see Ink, who'd been leaning against the bar, is now standing straight. Beth fans herself. "I do believe he might actually be taller than me."

Well, she's a grown woman, I sigh to myself. She can make up her own mind. For an answer I grab hold of her hand, and much in the same way as she'd done to me, drag her across the room.

"Hey, Mel," Liz calls out as we approach, "are you going to introduce us?" His eyes roam over Beth appreciatively, taking more than a moment to reach from her head to her toes. With her height, there's a long way to go.

I admit I've probably been around bikers too long as I never used to be this direct. "Sorry, Liz, it's not you she's interested in."

Mace raises an expectant eyebrow.

"Or you." I chuckle when he exaggeratingly puts his hand over his heart.

"Yeah, Ink. It's you. Ink this is Beth, Beth this is Ink. The rest is up to you."

Beth gasps, but now it's me winking at her before I leave and go to find my own man, my husband and father of my child.

CHAPTER FORTY-ONE

Pyro

I've been a married man for four months. Four months, which have brought me nothing but joy. A couple of weeks back Mel had her scan and we saw our daughter for the very first time.

I've watched over her as though she's made of china, trying not to let anything upset her. Reassuring her how glad and fucking happy I am that she's mine whenever she gets that lost look in her eyes, a look I'm overjoyed to be seeing less often as time passes.

We'd had good news a couple of weeks back. Her claim had been settled in full. The judge had reviewed the evidence and determined she had been dragged into something by an agent who hadn't paid sufficient attention to her safety. If, as was expected at the time, she was walking into a dangerous club, he'd put an innocent civilian at risk. Her good character, as vouched for by so many people, had shown she'd had no previous criminal leanings. He awarded the amount that had been asked, and I'd applauded as she'd made an anonymous donation to a charity that Cad had investigated and said was trustworthy.

Now I'm free to concentrate on our life, my wife and child. A daughter. A little girl. I'll still mourn the son I never saw born, but hell, I'm going to be a dad. I can't fucking wait.

I watch Mel sleeping, there's a small smile on her face as though she's having a good dream. I hate to wake her, but I promised that I would.

"Mel, Mel, darlin'?"

"Huh?" She rolls over.

I grin and roll her back. "Mel, darlin'. Just saying goodbye like I promised to do."

"You will come back?"

One time another man told her goodbye and never returned. "You can bet you're fuckin' life on it. I'll be back later today. If I'm delayed, it will be tomorrow at the latest, okay? You stay here at the club. Vi's going to talk baby shit with you."

"Demon and Vi are pregnant too."

"Yeah, how about that? They kept that quiet for a while." They'd announced it last night. Vi's three months along now, so our babies will only be a couple of months apart.

Mel's more awake now. "Jay's over the moon. She's already offering to babysit. Hmm," her hand is exploring, "someone's woken up horny."

I'm as hard as a fucking rock, but that's normal around her. "Shit, Mel. I've got to get going. But hold that thought, I'll be back as soon as I can."

She gives me one more rub to torture me. I put my hand over hers and lift it away. "I'm sorry I've got to go, but there's this special part..."

"I know, I understand, Ro. It's just..." Her face falls and she bites her lip.

"I'm coming back," I tell her again, "and soon. I'll pay you back for making me spend the whole fuckin' day sporting a hard-on. You just think how you're going to deal with that when I get home."

Having made my threat and suggestively waggled my eyebrows to make her giggle, I kiss her, then pull down the sheet, putting my lips to her stomach where my daughter is nestled inside. "See you soon, baby girl. Be good for your mom."

Mel chuckles. "Right now, she can't be anything else. It's when she gets bigger that she'll give me grief."

Neither of us can wait until she starts to move.

"Don't lift anything heavy, don't…"

"I know, I know," she sighs, and grumbles. "I've got another four months of you nagging me to be careful, haven't I?"

"It gets worse. You wait, Mel," I threaten. "I'll…"

She gasps, puts her hand to her stomach.

"What is it?" I'm leaning over her, my face taut with concern.

"She moved. I swear. She moved."

I place my hand where she's just had hers. For a second nothing happens then… I feel a faint fluttering under my palm. "Is that her?"

"Yeah. I think it is."

My fucking God. I've just felt my baby move. All of a sudden it makes what I've got to do more imperative. But I'm reluctant to leave now, when my daughter's just nudged my hand.

A hoarse whisper sounds from outside my door. "You in there, Ro?"

"Go on," she says. "We'll be here when you get back."

"I *am* coming back to you." I hold her gaze with mine.

"I know you are."

I stand, look at her one last time, then sliding my gun into my cut and taking my wallet and keys off the stand, exit the room.

Mace is standing outside. "Ready?"

"Let's do this."

"Archer's expecting us," Mace tells me as we descend the stairs, keeping our voices down. It's four am and most of the brothers are sleeping. "Got everything you need?"

"Yeah, I gave it to Karl to stow on the bike." He won't get patched in if he's fucked this up, so I've got every confidence he'll have followed my instructions with the utmost care.

"Best get moving then. Got a long ride ahead of us, Brother." He slaps me on the back, and I follow him out front.

The prospect is waiting by the bikes, his mouth open wide in a yawn. "Want me to come along?"

"Nah." This is one trip we don't want to draw attention to ourselves. Mace and I have already left our cuts behind. I'm a mechanic, unless we're unlucky enough to get a puncture, there's not much I can't fix by the side of the road. I can't carry much else in my own saddlebags, but Mace has got the toolkit I wanted to bring in his.

The bikes start with a roar, but if we've woken anyone up, the brothers will understand. What we're heading out to do has been carefully planned in church.

It ends today.

After three hours of riding we stop to top off our tanks, then waste no time getting back on the road. It takes two more tank fills before we reach our destination, a shady bar on the edge of town.

A man comes out as he hears the Harleys.

"Archer?" I approach him, holding out my hand.

"Yeah. Pyro?"

"That's me. This here is Mace."

Archer kicks out at a stone on the ground. "Fuck this," he growls, wiping his hand over his face. "You fuckin' sure?"

I can understand how he's feeling. "No doubt."

"I've kept it quiet, only my VP knows. And of course Huff, who picked it up on the dark web."

"It's the best way," I tell him. "Fucker will be on his guard the whole time, anyone looking at him sideways will make him run and go to ground." Not only that, if they don't know, they can be completely truthful when the inevitable questions are asked.

He's shaking his head, then looks up over toward the distant hills, but I don't believe he's taking in the view. "We've got a shipment coming in next week. If," he slams his fist into his hand, "if Huff hadn't found the info your crew's been posting around, we'd have all gone down." His eyes come back to me. "Owe you, brother."

"Nah. Got personal reasons for doing this. You don't owe me fuck all. It's my thanks you'll get when the job's done."

"You gonna stay? Meet the club?"

"No," Mace puts in fast. "Trust you, trust your men. But the fewer people who see our faces around, the better."

"Gotcha there." He looks from me to Mace. "Which one of you is the explosives expert?"

"That will be me, and I've got it prepared." I walk back to my bike. The small amount of C4 and remote-controlled detonator is well disguised. "Put it under the seat, it's magnetic." I show him where I mean by demonstrating on my bike.

"Collateral damage?"

"Explosion won't be big enough, as long as no one's riding up close. I'll be watching, and I'll pick my time."

"Got an errand he can run. I'll send him out on his own. My VP will make sure he doesn't get a chance to check his bike before he leaves." He waits a moment, weighing the equipment of death in his hand. Then jerks his head to the building behind him. "Doesn't look like much, but the food's more than edible. You wait here, and I'll tell you when it's in place. Shouldn't be more than an hour or so."

We take his advice. He's right, the food's good. But we eat more to pass the time than to satisfy any appetite. My current hunger is not for food.

At last I get a call with instructions. I follow them. Archer has picked a good spot, somewhere for us to hide, with good visibility of anyone coming along the road. It's an isolated and dangerous spot, the road twisting and mountainous with steep drop-offs.

"He's coming," says Mace into my ear.

I heard the engine too. The bike comes into sight. Using the binoculars I brought along, I check it is indeed my target, then I choose my moment and press the innocuous looking button on the remote I'm holding.

The bike bursts into a ball of flame.

Archer really has chosen well. In his final split second the rider's veered to the right, and the bike's flown over the guardrail and disappeared below.

I even totalled my bike in a ravine. Thought you'd have found it by now.

Not then, we hadn't. But you certainly have now Skull, or whatever name you're going by at the moment.

"Agent Jordan has been retired." Mace slaps my back. "Permanently."

It's only on the ride back that I let myself feel the relief that at last Mel has gotten the justice she deserves. The citizen law might not have done its job, but the Devils got revenge in the end. I grin, confident that Cad's made sure a certain security tape in an auto parts shop in San Francisco, on the other side of the country, has a picture of myself clearly picking up the part that I needed.

We ride through the night, both of us eager to get home. It's the early hours of the morning when I at last walk in.

Karl, again yawning, takes a package from under the bar and hands it to me.

In the bedroom, I put the custom-made part on the dresser, then look at my sleeping wife.

I'd walk through hell and high water for her and my kid.

Another black mark on my soul? Worth it for her.

"Pyro?"

"Yeah, I'm back."

"Did you do what you needed to?"

"Yeah, darlin', I did."

Quickly divesting myself of my clothes, I climb in beside her, pulling her back against me.

"Sleep babe," I tell her, unnecessarily. She'd relaxed immediately with my body surrounding hers. A gentle snuffle and the sound of her deep breathing tells me she's already drifted off.

Twenty-four hours apart was too long, and I'm content simply to hold my wife and unborn child in my arms. Having spent most of yesterday riding, I follow her into the land of dreams soon after, secure in the knowledge that from now on our nightmare has gone.

INK'S DEVIL

SATAN'S DEVILS MC COLORADO CHAPTER #5

Ink

The tall girl intrigued me, I'd never been with anyone who could match my height. At first it was going to be a one night stand to enjoy a new experience. But that wasn't enough and I shouldn't have, but I went back.

It's not forever, I'm not that kind of man.

She's a citizen and not someone to be pulled into our underworld.

Except, I didn't pull her in, she was already there.

She should be in jail, not me.

Beth

I go for what I want, and I wanted Ink. I knew it was only going to be a one-off, but he came back for a repeat. I couldn't let myself fall for him, so decided to enjoy it while it lasted.

My life was normal, uncomplicated, until my estranged brother dumped me in a mess. A fiasco which ended up with Ink taking the rap.

He wouldn't be in jail if he didn't care.

But whether he does or not doesn't matter if he's going to be there for the best part of his life.

READING ORDER

Turning Wheels
Drummer's Beat
Slick Running
Targeting Dart
Heart Broken
Peg's Stand
Rock Bottom
Joker's Fool
Mouse Trapped

Paladin's Hell (Colorado Chapter #1)

Blade's Edge

Demon's Angel (Colorado Chapter #2)
Devil's Due (Colorado Chapter #3)

Truck Stopped

Devil's Dilemma (Colorado Chapter #4)
Coming Soon

Ink's Devil (Colorado Chapter #5)

Note 1:

Each book can be read as a standalone, but to get the best reading experience for the Satan's Devils, read the books in the order above.

Note 2:
While the Blood Brothers series is completely separate to the Satan's Devils series, there is some crossover. Turning Wheels continues the story of a minor character who appears in Second Changes, and some characters appear in both series.

OTHER WORKS BY MANDA MELLETT

Demon's Angel (#2) Demon and Violet

Devil's Due (#3)

ACKNOWLEDGMENTS

Often an idea for a book is sparked by current events, or a new story I've read, and this is certainly true for Devil's Dilemma.

A few months ago I read something on the news about undercover cops who formed relationships with women in the group they were infiltrating in the UK, and the hurt and pain these women went through after the men upped and left without a word. I immediately knew I needed to use the basis of this story, and knew who was going to be my own undercover cop in the scenario.

I did have issues transporting the ideas into the US, and got embroiled in many legal and procedural aspects which are obviously very different from those in the UK. Despite my copious research (the FBI Guidelines for Undercover Officers is not fun bedtime reading!), this was the fastest book ever to come out of my head and go onto the page. It just seemed like Mel and Pyro wanted their story to be shared.

I know from my beta readers that the twists and turns in this book came as a surprise to them, and I hope there will be no spoilers to ruin the surprise for new readers, but hey, it will happen.

As well as this story flowing so well, my wonderful team of

beta readers, editor, proofreader, formatter and cover designer also responded fast, and with amazing comments. I am therefore able to bring you this book a month early, following fast on the heels of Truck Stopped.

I'm very pleased with how this book has turned out, and believe it deserves a good cover. I'm beyond honoured to have two fellow authors as models, the wonderful Colbie Kay together with KB Bennett. Thank you to Randy Ris Sewell of RLS Images Photography for answering my plea for a suitable cover photo and to quickly respond with such a great image. I hope you like it as much as I do. A massive thank you, as always, to Lia Rees, my cover designer, who worked on the cover and brought Mel and Pyro to life.

Usually I keep my ideas close to my chest when writing, but this time I let my editor know the general plot a couple of books back. She immediately wanted me to move this one up the agenda as she wanted to see how this one played out. I think her encouragement inspired me to get it written so quickly. Thank you Maggie Kern for your ideas and input, and fast turnaround of the drafts. You know I love you, woman.

Beta readers. Again, thank you to the usual culprits, Tami (my location advisor), Danena, Sheri, Terra, Zoe, Nicole, Alex and last but not least, my husband Steve. This book was unusual as, instead of waiting until they reached the end, I think most of you messaged me at some point expressing your surprise at the plot turns. I believe I had most of you fooled as to what was going on. That was my aim, and my delight when I knew I had achieved it. I really can't thank you enough.

As I indicated, all my ducks fell into line to bring forward the publication date, and that includes Melanie Darrow who turned the proofreading around in record time. It does help this is the third time we've worked together, so she's getting to know my style, and vice versa.

Tracy Wood, my PA. What can I say? An amazing woman who keeps my social media going and produces the graphics I'm unable to do myself. Hey, I'm good with words not pictures. Thank you, Tracy. Long may we work together.

I have left the most important to last, all you readers who take a chance on buying my books, and then telling me how much you enjoy reading them. My whole day can be boosted by one message, one comment or one review. You may have no idea how much it spurs me to write more.

The best way of telling me is to leave a review on whatever platform you read on, or anywhere you can review. I read and appreciate every review good or bad. Reviews help authors make sales, sales allow authors to pay editors, models and photographers, cover designers etc, and put food on the table.

What's next? Well, another Devil of course, and I think you can guess who. Beth was pretty intent on targeting Ink at Mel's wedding. Did she end up getting her man? Ink's Devil will be along soon.

STAY IN TOUCH

Email: manda@mandamellet.com

Website: www.mandamellet.com

Sign up for my newsletter to hear about new releases in the Satan's Devils and Blood Brothers series.

Facebook reader group: https://www.facebook.com/groups/mandasbadboys/

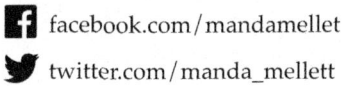

facebook.com/mandamellet

twitter.com/manda_mellett

ABOUT THE AUTHOR

Manda's life's always seemed a bit weird, starting with a childhood that even today she's still trying to make sense of, then losing her parents in the late teens. Going from the tragic to the bizarre, who else could be unlucky enough to have had two car accidents, neither her fault, one involving a nun, and another involving a police woman?

There isn't enough space to list everything that's happened to Manda, or what she's learned from it. But by using the rich fabric of her personal life, psychology degree, varied work experiences, and amazing characters she's met, Manda is able to populate her books with believable in-depth characters and enjoys pitting them against situations which challenge them. Her books are full of suspense, twists and turns and the unexpected.

Manda lives in the beautiful countryside of Essex in the UK, the area's claim to fame being the Wilkin's Jam Factory at nearby Tiptree. She can usually find jars of jam which remind her of home wherever she goes. As well as writing books and reading, Manda loves walking her dogs and keeping fit. She lives with her husband of over 30 years, who, along with her son, is her greatest fan and supporter.

Manda is thankful that one of the more unusual, and at the time unpleasant, turns her life took, now enables her to spend her time writing. Confirming, in her view, every cloud has a silver lining.

Photo by Carmel Jane Photography

Printed in Great Britain
by Amazon